HOME
SWEET
HOME

Ruth Irons grew up in South Wales before studying music at Exeter University, and then musical theatre at the Royal Central School of Speech and Drama. She worked as an actor, musician and music teacher for many years before turning to writing as a creative outlet, completing courses with Curtis Brown Creative and the Writers Bureau. This is her second novel. Her first, *The Perfect Guest*, was published in June 2024.

Ruth lives in Kingston upon Thames with her husband and two daughters.

HOME SWEET HOME

RUTH IRONS

ZAFFRE

First published in the UK in 2025 by
ZAFFRE
An imprint of Bonnier Books UK
5th Floor, HYLO, 105 Bunhill Row,
London, EC1Y 8LZ
Owned by Bonnier Books
Sveavägen 56, Stockholm, Sweden

A CIP catalogue record for this book is
available from the British Library.

ISBN: 978-1-78530-755-3

Also available as an ebook and an audiobook

1 3 5 7 9 10 8 6 4 2

Typeset by IDSUK (Data Connection) Ltd
Printed and bound in Great Britain by Clays Ltd, Elcograf S.p.A.

MIX
Paper | Supporting
responsible forestry
FSC
www.fsc.org   FSC® C018072

The authorised representative in the EEA is Bonnier Books
UK (Ireland) Limited.
Registered office address: Floor 3, Block 3, Miesian Plaza,
Dublin 2, D02 Y754, Ireland
compliance@bonnierbooks.ie
www.bonnierbooks.co.uk

For my parents, Thirza and Rick

'I have always depended on the kindness of strangers'

Tennessee Williams, *A Streetcar Named Desire*

Chapter One

I noticed her as soon as she walked into the pub that night. There wasn't anything particularly stand-out about her, but she had a certain presence – a way of moving through a space that drew the eye. A sharp pinch of January air swept through the door with her, carrying the faint traces of a floral perfume. She wore a cropped leather jacket and an oversized woollen scarf in forest green. A paisley maxi skirt flicked up at the heels of her brown leather boots. Her arms were crossed over her front in a self-conscious pose that seemed at odds with the way she strode.

'Jules?'

Scott's voice drew my gaze back to his face. 'Sorry, what?'

'The lodger thing. I just wondered if you'd thought any more about it?'

I sighed. I had thought more about it but I wasn't sure Scott wanted to hear what I had to say.

'Come on,' he said, his playful mock frown creasing his forehead. 'Hit me with it. I'm a big boy, I can take it.'

I smiled. Even the serious conversations in our lives were never immune to Scott's sense of humour. Perhaps that meant we sometimes ended up laughing when we should have been tackling grown-up issues, but I wasn't complaining.

'OK, since you've laid your cards on the table, I'm going to be brutally honest.'

He closed his eyes as if bracing himself.

'I'm not entirely convinced by the lodger idea—' I held my hand up to stop him interrupting. 'It's just . . . I know the house is big for the two of us, and I know we could do with the financial help, but . . . I'm a bit worried about opening up our home to a complete stranger.'

'OK, OK,' he said with a placatory nod. 'I completely hear where you're coming from, but – and you know it pains me to say this – we might have to be sensible here.'

I took a breath and blew the air out slowly. When *Scott* was suggesting sensible behaviour, you knew things were serious. And maybe he was right. The fact neither of us had particularly well-paid jobs meant a three-bedroom house in Kingston upon Thames took its toll on our finances.

'And it wouldn't be forever. Just until we pay off most of the loan.' He shrugged and I saw a familiar twinkle in his eyes. 'And maybe save up a bit for when we start trying for a baby—' now it was Scott's turn to hold up his hand to stop me interrupting '—which may or may not be soon, you know, whenever, I don't mind, I'm relaxed about it.' He raised a hopeful eyebrow as he took a swig of his pint and I couldn't help laughing.

'You are such a softie, honestly. I think you're the broodiest man in the history of would-be fathers.'

'Guilty as charged, and completely unashamed,' he said, placing his pint back down and smiling at me.

'OK, *maybe* I can see where you're coming from with the whole lodger thing—'

'Amazing!'

'*But* . . . I'm the one who works from home every day, so if we did decide to go ahead with it, we'd have to be super selective. You know, get someone who's busy in the day and isn't in my space the whole time.'

'Absolutely! Oh my God, of course.' He was nodding with unbridled enthusiasm. 'We'd hold proper interviews, get references, DBS checks, primary-school behaviour reports—'

'You're a nutcase.'

'You married me.'

'Well, I guess I'm a nutcase too then.'

He grinned, clearly feeling this was progress in his mission to get me on board, and thus decided to end this evening's coercion here rather than push his luck.

He downed the remains of his drink and stood up. 'I'm going to get another pint. Red wine again for you?'

I looked at the crackling log-burner next to our table, then leaned back against the ancient, peeling leather of the sofa. 'Actually, I think I'll have a Baileys,' I said in a conspiratorial whisper.

His eyes glittered and he gave me a cheeky grin. 'Cosy. Like it. Think I'll have one of those too.' He nodded his approval, reaching into his back pocket for his wallet.

I watched him approach the bar and stand next to the woman in the floaty paisley skirt, who was leaning over to give her order to the barman. As she stood back, I noticed she was almost the same height as Scott. He wasn't exactly a giant, but at five eleven he was a good six inches taller than me. She flicked a smile at him while they waited for their drinks, and Scott nodded, his eyes creasing and narrowing in the smile he reserved for greeting strangers.

He carried our drinks back to the low table, the ice clinking against the cut-glass tumblers. The woman at the bar slid her purse back into her handbag, throwing a 'thank you' to the barman. Her golden hair fell forwards in waves as she rummaged in her bag.

'Cheers!' said Scott, and we clinked glasses.

I sipped the creamy liquid, feeling the soft burn of it down my throat. The Wych Elm was one of our favourite haunts. Cosy and welcoming, it was close to the station but tucked away down a residential street. We'd stumbled upon it when we first moved here a year ago, and now a couple of Friday-night drinks had become a bit of a routine.

The log-burner was throwing out some serious heat, and one side of my face tingled with the warmth it cast. I turned away, my gaze alighting again on the woman, who was now standing in the open space in the middle of the pub. I couldn't take my eyes off her. Because now her bag-rummaging had become more urgent, her movements jerky and deliberate. Her pretty face was set in a scowl and she was mouthing something to herself. Something that contained the word *fuck*.

I glanced at Scott to see if he'd noticed, but he was scrolling on his phone. The woman was looking around the pub now, as if expecting someone to come and help with whatever her bag-related emergency was. Two young blokes by the door, probably in their twenties, were eyeing her up. But the way their eyes swept over her it seemed they were more in observation mode, rather than poised to spring up and offer help.

Now she was pacing left and right, as if she didn't know what to do with herself. She swept a hand through her hair, shook her head, looked up to the ceiling and this time, audibly, said, 'Please, no.'

Something squirmed inside me. I couldn't ignore her distress any more, so I set my drink down, stood up and walked towards her.

'Hey – are you OK?'

She looked at me, eyes widening. 'Oh my God, I'm such an *idiot*!'

'What's happened?'

She reached out a hand and squeezed my arm, a strangely intimate gesture. I took it to be a thank you for coming to her assistance. 'I've just been to see a friend's new flat on the South Bank – and I've gone and left my bloody keys there. My housemate's away on tour and I have no way of getting into my sodding flat. Shit! This is the worst bloody thing that could happen . . .' Her voice trailed off as she went back to rummaging violently in her oversized leather bag. 'My other friend was supposed to meet me here, but she's just stood me up, so basically I'm completely screwed.' She stopped her rummaging and stared at me with a defeated expression.

'Umm . . . could your friend – the one on the South Bank – meet you halfway to give you the keys back?'

She turned to me and blinked twice. 'I suppose I could ask him, yes. Good idea.' She looked to be about our age, mid-thirties, with pale blue eyes, like the shallows on a sunny beach, a thin nose and pale eyelashes, delicate features in a narrow face. There was a certain vulnerability about her that belied her self-assured mannerisms and the way she spoke.

'What's up?' Scott's cheery voice interjected. He'd come to stand next to us.

We filled him in on the situation, speaking in almost perfectly alternate sentences, like children reading in a school assembly. I was aware that we sounded bizarrely rehearsed.

'Well, call your mate now, and let's see if he's up for bringing the keys halfway. What would that be – Wimbledon?'

Scott was in problem-solving mode, a role he relished. And he was good at it. Always looking out for the best way to proceed, the most logical conclusion to draw.

'Of course.' The woman brought out her phone. 'You're right, that's what I'll do.'

She tapped at the screen and held the phone to her ear. Scott and I looked at each other, and a strange awkwardness settled on me. The three of us were standing in a huddle in the centre of the pub, Scott and I watching a complete stranger make a pleading phone call to her friend. I thought the two of us should go and sit down, but when I imagined it, I realised that would feel even odder, like we'd abandoned her to her problems and didn't want to engage any more. So we just stood there, watching her brow crease as the seconds ticked by. She began chewing her bottom lip, then whispering, 'Come on, Matt, come on. Pick up.'

Eventually she brought the phone down and stared hopelessly at the screen. 'He's not picking up. Fuck!'

'He might do in a minute . . .' My voice lacked conviction. It's a funny thing, but even at this point I think I realised he wouldn't answer. There was a sort of acceptance within me that we would be finding some other solution to this woman's problem. I don't know, perhaps I'm projecting backwards and thought no such thing. All I can say for certain is that an unease had settled in the pit of my stomach. An unease to which Scott was clearly oblivious.

'Could your other friend help you out?' I asked. 'The one who stood you up?'

She gave a frustrated sigh. 'No, unfortunately she's from out of town and was only on a flying visit. Missed her train connection, so God knows where she is now.'

'Look, come and sit with us and try Matt again in a few minutes, yeah?' Scott's voice was casual and friendly.

'That's so kind of you.' She cast a tentative smile at me, as if seeking reassurance.

'Of course, come and join us. No point in you standing in the middle of the pub on your own.'

Her face suddenly broke into a dazzling beam, her eyes wide and glittering. I half expected her to say something like *I thought you'd never ask!*

In what seemed like one deft movement, she whirled towards the bar, her skirt swishing around her shins as she scooped up the glass of white wine she'd ordered before discovering her house keys were missing. The three of us sat down on the worn leather sofas, the woman next to me, and Scott opposite.

She put her wine down on the table and set her palms on her knees. 'I'm so sorry, I've been in such a flap I've

7

not introduced myself. My name's Orla.' She pressed one hand to her chest as she said this, and I heard a very slight pushing down on the 'r' sound.

'I'm Jules, and this is my husband Scott. Orla . . . is that Irish?'

'It is!'

'Are you from Ireland? You don't have much of an accent,' I said.

She gave a girlish laugh and tucked her hair behind one ear. 'That's what drama school does to you! You spend so much time analysing your voice and your tone, as well playing different parts of course – and that's before you even consider what a melting pot places like that are. I think all of us on that course came away with some sort of generic south-of-England accent.' She wrinkled her nose and took a sip of her wine.

'And is that what you do now?' Scott said, shuffling forwards on his seat, suddenly fascinated. 'Are you an actor?'

'Yes. Which is nowhere near as glamorous as it sounds, believe me.' She took another sip. Her phone was resting in her lap and I saw the screen light up. Her eyes flicked down, but she ignored it. It went dark again. 'What do you guys do?'

'Well, I work in HR for the council – it's Jules who has the interesting job!' This was a typical Scott response. He was always glossing over his own job in favour of hearing me talk about mine.

'Oh?' Orla swivelled towards me, her eyes wide with expectation. Or did I detect the hint of a challenge there? A trace of *come on then, impress me.*

8

'Scott always bigs me up like this, but like you say about acting, my job sounds a lot more glamorous than it is.' I was downplaying. I adored my job. 'I'm actually a children's book illustrator.'

'Oh my God!' She clutched her hand to her chest again. 'That sounds amazing! Wow, how did you get into that? I mean . . . obviously by being bloody good at drawing, right?'

I laughed. 'Well, I suppose so. Yes, it's kind of that simple. I always loved drawing, and used to draw characters from the chapter books I read – you know, as I imagined them in my head. Then I went to Goldsmiths to study children's book illustration and that's where I met Scott.'

'And do you work for specific authors all the time, or . . . how does it work?' Orla had shifted closer to me and was studying my face as if hanging on my every word. It was flattering.

'Um . . . I have two or three authors I always illustrate for, but generally I'm freelance so I never know what's coming up next or how busy I'll be. Much like acting, I imagine.'

'Absolutely.' She nodded. 'Everyone always says to me, "How do you cope, not knowing when you're going to get paid, or how much money you're going to make, or how available you're going to be?" and you know what I tell them? I cope because I absolutely bloody love it.' She flashed me a bright smile. 'And I can tell you feel exactly the same way.'

I raised my glass in salute. 'I wouldn't change it for the world.'

Something thawed inside me then. She got it. Very few people understood the life of a freelancer, especially one that didn't earn very much money. They didn't understand that doing something you love every day was so much more valuable than a predictable routine, or earning shedloads of money. Then I felt the familiar pang, and my internal monologue gave its usual refrain: *That's easy for you to say – you have a partner with a sensible job, and a mortgage-free house. You're not exactly suffering for your art.*

'Anyway.' I suddenly wanted to change the subject. 'What type of acting do you do?'

'Well, whatever I can get really.'

'Will we have seen you in anything?' Scott asked.

I rolled my eyes. 'Does everyone ask you that?'

'Yes they do, actually, and I always give the same response – not unless you have a particular penchant for badly paid, poorly attended fringe theatre.' She gave a self-deprecating wince and Scott and I laughed. 'Although,' she continued, 'if you were into Irish TV in the early 2000s you might have spotted me in *Kilcroom High*.'

This sounded like a throwaway comment, but I noticed her eyes dart quickly between us, and I knew she was waiting for a reaction. Because everyone of our generation had heard of *Kilcroom High*, even if you didn't watch it. I took the bait.

'You were in *Kilcroom High*? I used to love that show!'

'Oh, that's great to hear!'

'Wow!' Scott looked like an excited puppy. 'Even *I've* heard of that, and I was barely interested in anything that wasn't *Star Wars* from the age of about ten. Wasn't that the show set on the beach, like a sort of Irish *Home and Away*?'

Orla laughed. 'That's the one. *Home and Away* crossed with *The Famous Five*. I wasn't one of the big stars of the show, but I appeared in one season.'

Scott had grabbed up his phone and was googling. 'Yes, here you are!' He turned his phone to show us and I leaned forwards to take it from him. Sure enough, there was a barely teenage Orla, same honey-coloured hair, posing with a group of about six other similar-aged children on a beach. She was leaning an elbow on the shoulder of the boy next to her, and was dressed in wide-legged jeans and a red crop top which showed her bare, narrow waist. She wore a choker around her slender neck. They were all sitting or standing on rocks, the sky cornflower blue and a shaggy dog at their feet.

Scott took his phone back, tapped the screen and read. '*Orla Sullivan joins the cast of* Kilcroom High *in a captivating performance as Alice's younger cousin, Riley.*'

'I think I even remember watching some of your episodes now I see that photo . . .' The red crop top and the dog had stirred something in my brain. 'Wasn't there one where you had to rescue the dog from a cave or something?'

'Yes! That's right, good memory!' Orla's face was alight, her eyes twinkling. 'Monty got caught in the pirate's cave and the water was coming in—'

'—and you ran and got a rope and some dog food from somewhere . . . Oh! The old guy who manned the car park!'

11

'Old Henry! Ha ha, yes, that's it. That was one of my first episodes, actually. It was meant to be the middle of summer but we filmed it in October and it was bloody freezing in that cave.'

Orla downed the dregs of her wine and picked up her phone. 'Right, I should try Matt again, see if I can get my keys back.'

Something deflated inside me then. For all my initial uneasiness, I felt I'd mellowed over the course of our conversation. I wanted to talk to Orla for longer. I wanted to tell her more about my illustrating, to watch her fascinated face as she listened. I wanted to hear more stories about filming *Kilcroom High*, and learn about the fringe theatre she did.

I watched her tapping her phone and holding it to her ear for the second time. Her face was set once more in that serious frown, and when she caught my eye she waved her crossed fingers at me as if to say *wish me luck*. The bell rang for last orders.

Eventually she opened her mouth and I thought her friend must have answered. But no.

'Hi Matt, it's Orla. I've been a complete tit and left my keys at your place. Anyway, give me a call when you get this so we can hatch a plan about me getting them back. Sorry to be a pain.' She hung up and then started typing. 'I should probably text him too just in case he doesn't bother listening to the message. To be honest, he's a bit of a party animal so he's probably in a noisy club right now and the last thing he'll be doing is looking at his phone.'

Scott and I glanced at each other as if to say, *what do we do now?*

Orla threw her phone into her bag and sat up straight. 'Right, well, thank you both so much for lending me your ear and for the lovely chat! Sorry to gatecrash your romantic evening.'

'You haven't gatecrashed at all,' Scott said. 'It's been great meeting you.'

'But . . . what are you going to do? I mean, do you have another friend you can stay with?' I asked.

'Or a way of breaking into your flat?'

'Scott, she's not going to do that!'

Orla laughed. 'Actually, some of the places I've lived that would have been easy enough, but unfortunately this flat is pretty secure, plus our landlord's a nightmare, so I wouldn't risk damaging anything and losing our deposit.'

She stood up and rummaged one last time in her bag, as if hoping the keys would magically appear.

'But what are you actually going to do?' Scott said.

'Um . . . I'll probably head into town and book into the Premier Inn or something. Bang goes this week's rehearsal pay!' She gave a tight laugh then, as if she was trying to make light of the situation, but not finding it funny.

Scott and I flashed each other a look, and I knew we were both thinking the same thing. I gave the tiniest twist of my mouth, wondering what my next question would be, but Scott seemed to take this gesture as giving him the go-ahead.

'I mean . . . it's not ideal, you spending your week's pay on a hotel, is it?' he said. 'Why don't you crash at ours? It's only round the corner. Then you can get your keys from Matt tomorrow.'

I felt something slipping away from me.

Orla's mouth opened slightly, her gaze darting from me to Scott and back. She licked her lips and I noticed her delicate chin wobble. 'Guys, that's honestly above and beyond . . .'

'Don't be silly. We've got a comfy spare room and we're going home now anyway.' Scott gave a nonchalant shrug. 'And I know we've only just met, but I'm not getting serial-killer vibes from you, so . . .'

Orla hooted with laughter at that, wiping under one eye with the back of her index finger. 'You know, maybe if I gave off serial-killer vibes I'd be getting more interesting roles at the minute! No, but seriously, are you guys sure?'

I wasn't sure, but what could I say?

'Absolutely,' we chimed in unison.

So then it was settled. We stood, put on our coats and made our way out of the pub in our newly formed triangular friendship. It was such a small act of kindness, I told myself. And it had seemed that way at the time. So inconsequential.

Chapter Two

'Oh my God, look at this place!' Orla said as we approached the front door. 'It's humongous!'

I felt a familiar twist of guilt that sometimes accompanied showing people the house. We really had lucked out. It was far from palatial, but it was certainly above what most people in their early thirties could afford. The neatly paved driveway was home to our little red Fiat 500, but there was room for at least one other car in the space. The house itself was semi-detached, with a wide bay window, redbrick lower half, and mock Tudor-style beams with white render above. Scott's aunt had kept it well, and in the year we'd been here we'd even managed to keep the plants that bordered the driveway alive.

Seymour Avenue was a wide road, the houses set back from the kerb by a strip of grass, then a pavement. They all had large front areas, some used for parking and others as gardens. Gnarled, old trees were dotted along the road, their giant roots cracking pavement slabs in places.

We entered the house and I flicked on the lights, dropping my keys on the side table. 'We're actually really lucky . . . Scott's aunt left us the place.'

Orla nodded, looking around at the pale blue walls, the crisp white paintwork, the caramel oak flooring. 'It's beautiful.'

Scott always tells me we don't owe anyone an explanation as to how we've come to live in a place like this. 'You don't need to apologise for having a nice house, Jules.' And I knew he was right, but knowing we could never have afforded it on our salaries, I somehow felt compelled to explain. Yes, we still had a loan that needed to be paid off (which we'd taken out to cover inheritance tax), but that was much less than a mortgage on this place would have been. Not declaring the truth about the house somehow felt like cheating. Especially when speaking to an underpaid actor who was sharing a rented flat.

'Nightcap?' Scott said, rubbing his hands together.

'Sure!' said Orla, and we followed Scott through to the kitchen.

Settled around the breakfast bar, nursing the last of a bottle of Limoncello I found at the back of a cupboard, we fell into comfortable conversation.

Orla told us about the play she was currently rehearsing, which was opening on Monday at a pub theatre called the Black Lion in Southwark. It was a modern retelling of the story of Persephone and Hades, set in an office block in New York. Orla was playing Demeter, reinvented as the CEO of the company. Her face was serious as she explained all this, which made us crease up with laughter when she ended her spiel with, 'It's really the biggest pile of shite you've ever seen.'

'And *can* we see it?' asked Scott with his excited puppy-dog face.

I expected her to recoil at this idea if she found the project as embarrassing as she'd just implied, but her eyes lit up. 'Yes! Come along, it'll be great craic. Just make sure you drink enough at the bar downstairs first so you're happy to endure two hours of abysmal American accents and overused strobe lighting.'

I noticed more traces of an Irish accent seeping into her voice the more she relaxed, her 't's softening and her 'r's becoming more pronounced.

Eventually, we'd finished the Limoncello, and it seemed the evening had run out of steam.

Orla raised her arms above her head and stretched, before letting them fall to her sides. 'What a beautiful evening, thank you so much, guys. Considering I've been rendered homeless for the night, I'm in unexpectedly high spirits.'

'Well, don't speak too soon,' said Scott. 'We haven't shown you the dungeon you're sleeping in yet.'

Orla laughed. 'I'll take a dungeon, no problem. I'm so exhausted, honestly, I could sleep anywhere right now.'

We showed her up to the spare room in the attic. This was the largest bedroom, but had been the most tired-looking when we'd moved in. We'd moved our own stuff into the first-floor bedroom at the front of the house while we decorated the attic, and then we'd started having this discussion about the lodger, so hadn't moved back in yet.

It really was the perfect room to rent out. It was large, with two oak beams spanning the ceiling space. The walls sloped down to eaves storage on both sides, and a tall window with a Juliet balcony overlooked the back garden. A two-seater sofa sat against one wall, facing a wall-mounted TV, and there was a tiny boxed-in bathroom. The bed was a king-size and the mattress had taken me, Scott and our friend Nick the best part of two hours to manoeuvre up from the ground floor.

'Oh my God, it's just stunning,' Orla said, throwing her handbag onto the bed before collapsing onto it herself in a starfish pose. 'I'm going to be right at home here.'

Scott was up at stupid o'clock the following morning for his habitual Saturday morning run in Richmond Park. As always, he'd thrown me a 'fancy joining me?' as he pulled his T-shirt over his head, prompting me to issue my usual response of groaning and pulling the duvet over my head.

By nine thirty I was sitting at the breakfast bar, sipping my first coffee of the day. My fingers played with the torn edge of the envelope Scott had left on the table. I'd only briefly glanced at the glaring red repayment amount, before shoving the letter back in, my mind replaying the conversation we'd had in bed last night.

'It kind of seems like fate has dealt us a helping hand here,' he'd whispered as we lay in the dark.

'Fate? Since when did you believe in that bloody nonsense?'

'Since tonight when the Good Lord sent us an Irish angel to rent our spare room—'

I'd whacked him with my hot water bottle then, trying to stifle a laugh. 'Oh my God, you meet an attractive blonde in the pub and suddenly you're religious?'

'The Lord works in mysterious ways, Jules . . .'

I laughed. '*You* work in mysterious ways, you absolute nutcase.'

'No, but in all seriousness, don't you think it could be a good idea just to think about it? I mean, you were saying you would be wary of a stranger . . . well, we've just spent a great evening with Orla and we definitely know we'd get on with her. Plus, you wanted someone who'd be out a lot – and this is perfect! She's an actor, doing shows right left and centre, back-to-back rehearsals during the week, then performances in the evening—'

'But she's already got somewhere to live.'

'Yeah, a crappy flat in town with a landlord who's a "nightmare" apparently. Don't you think it's worth at least asking?'

And that's the question I'd been mulling over as I drifted off to sleep, and it was the same question I was mulling over now as I played with the envelope. It had been lovely hearing the optimism in Scott's voice last night as he talked about Orla being the answer to our financial conundrum. When his aunt had left us this place, we hadn't realised quite how much the house would cost. Scott's initial elation had turned to despair. This was a house he remembered from his childhood. It was special. And with him having no close family left, I knew he really didn't want to lose it. Of course it made financial sense to sell up and move to a smaller two-bed further out – but if we did, I wasn't sure we'd ever manage to work our way back up to the type of house we had now. And Scott would have lost that link to his family.

'Morning!'

I felt myself flinch. 'Oh, hi. Morning.'

'I'm so sorry, I made you jump! Did you forget I was here?'

'No, not at all, I was just . . . how did you sleep?'

'Like a baby, seriously that bed is *so* comfortable. I don't know how to thank you both for coming to my rescue last night. You absolutely didn't have to do that, and I'm so grateful.'

'Honestly, it was nothing.'

'Your home is insanely beautiful, and you're both gorgeous – I had such a fun evening.'

'We did too. Would you like some coffee?'

'That's very kind, but no I won't, actually. I've got to leave in ten for rehearsals, so I'll grab one at the station.'

'You're rehearsing on a Saturday?'

'Yep, we're opening on Monday, so rehearsal schedule is pretty brutal at the moment. Technical rehearsals all today, then dress tomorrow and Monday. I'm in town practically all weekend so plenty of time to get my keys back from Matt too.'

'Did he get back to you?'

'Yep, he found them on his kitchen counter when he got in at about three a.m.' She rolled her eyes. 'Honestly, I'm such an idiot. I should never have taken them out of my bag, but he gave me this super cute double-mask theatre keyring and I made a big show of putting it on my keys and saying how much I loved it, and then I just forgot to put them back in my bag.'

'Easily done.' I gave her a smile and experienced a pulse of adrenaline that made my fingers clammy on the envelope. Maybe this was the right moment to ask her. I mean, Scott was right – she did seem perfect. And how likely was it that someone this fun, easy to get on with, and with such a well-fitting work schedule would pop up again? If we were going to interview people for the room, then last night had been a pretty thorough interview, and even if Orla didn't realise it, she'd passed with flying colours.

I decided to make tentative steps. 'So, what's your flat like then? Do you like living there?'

She wrinkled her nose and set her handbag down on the counter. 'It's OK. I mean, it's not ideal, but it's close to the station. My flatmate's also an actor, and she seems to get back-to-back UK tours, so she's hardly ever there . . . so I get the place to myself.' She shrugged.

'You said your landlord was a nightmare . . .'

'Oh God, yeah he is. Very pernickety about stuff, and he likes to do spot checks on the place, which I'm pretty sure isn't legal—'

'It's not.'

'Yeah, well, he doesn't seem bothered about that. And obviously it's hideously overpriced, but that's renting in London, I guess.'

I took a deep breath. 'You know, Scott and I were considering renting out the top room.' I gauged her reaction carefully. Her eyebrows lifted ever so slightly. 'So if you're hating it at your flat then . . . I mean, I know it's further away from the station, but . . .'

'Oh my God.' She clutched her hand to her chest in a mannerism I'd noticed several times now. 'Are you serious?'

'Of course. I wouldn't offer if I wasn't.'

'But . . . don't you have to check with Scott first?'

'It was his idea, actually.'

'You guys are just insane . . . it's like you're my guardian angels or something!'

I laughed, thinking about Scott calling her an 'Irish angel' last night. *I guess we're all angels.* 'Not at all. We're looking for someone and it's obviously better if it's someone we've met and get along with. To be honest, I was dreading doing some kind of formal interview process. So it's serendipitous really. I mean, if you want to?'

She grinned. 'Are you asking me if I want to leave my mouldy, overpriced flat with an absentee housemate and a creepy landlord to come and live in a five-star, newly renovated penthouse with two really amazing people? Ummmm . . . let me just think about that for a moment.' She screwed up her face and rested her index finger on her chin and I couldn't help laughing. She really was a lot of fun.

We swapped numbers and email addresses, and I said I'd speak to Scott later and finalise the rent amount. She said she'd speak to her housemate and her landlord to see how quickly she could leave the flat. But she didn't foresee a problem – her friend had been wanting to live with her boyfriend for ages, so she'd probably ask him to move in and take over her contract.

'This has been the best result of someone losing their keys in the history of key-losing.' She beamed at me, then checked her watch. 'I'd love to stay for a celebratory coffee but I have to catch my train. I'm just going to pop to the loo . . .' She pointed towards the front door.

'Yep, it's the door on the right in the hallway.'

'Grand,' she said, practically hopping with delight towards the toilet.

I smiled and took a sip of my coffee. Scott would be over the moon I'd bitten the bullet and gone ahead with this. I was excited about surprising him with the news when he got back from his run.

As I lowered my cup, my gaze snagged on Orla's handbag. It was large and floppy, made of worn leather, and in its crumpled form on the counter I could see the red corner of her phone case peeping out, next to a packet of tissues. Something made of pink glitter stuck out behind the packet, glinting in the January sun that streaked across the breakfast bar.

I don't know why I did it, but I reached out my hand and pinched the object between my thumb and forefinger, pulling it gently. It was a small plastic star with glittery liquid inside, and was attached to a short silver chain. I tugged further and a cluster of keys jangled towards me. I felt a surge of heat through my body. *Don't be ridiculous, Jules, these can't be the keys. She'd have easily found these in her bag. This must be a set of keys for something else.* But as they dangled from the glittery star between my fingers, I spotted it: the keyring she'd said Matt had given her, the gold faces of the tragedy and comedy masks, frowning and grinning at me.

Chapter Three

Scott got back about ten minutes later. I was still sitting at the breakfast bar, staring at the cold dregs of my coffee. 'How was your run?'

'It's beautiful out there. Bloody freezing, but gorgeous and sunny. I saw deer!'

I gave a soft laugh. We moved here a year ago, and every time we went to Richmond Park we saw deer, but still couldn't get over the sight of them roaming the ragged grasses just metres away from where we walked. We still exclaimed 'deer!' in excited whispers whenever we spotted one.

Scott crossed to the tap and ran himself a pint of water, gulping it down and wiping his chin. 'Has Orla gone?'

'Yeah, she just left.'

'And have you thought any more about what we talked about last night?'

This moment wasn't how I'd imagined it playing out only minutes before. I'd thought I'd throw my arms around Scott's sweaty neck and announce, *Guess what? I asked Orla if she wanted to be our lodger and she said yes!* and then Scott's eyes would widen and he'd say, *That's brilliant, Jules! I thought it would take me at least another week to persuade you!*

24

But now my feelings of elation had been tainted. I had the same news to share, but I had something else too, and I didn't even know if I wanted to say it . . . how it would sound out loud, and what the implications were.

'OK, so there is news on that front.'

'Right, tell me the news,' he deadpanned with a serious frown I assumed was meant to mirror my own expression.

'Well – I asked her to move in, and she was thrilled and said yes, basically.'

'What? Oh my God, Jules, I did not expect you to say that! Wow, check you out being all impulsive!' He grinned at me and I felt a surge of trepidation. 'So what's wrong then?'

I sighed. 'I don't know why I did this, but when she went to the loo she left her handbag on the counter, just here . . .' I tapped my finger on the wooden surface.

'OK,' he said slowly.

'The bag had sort of flopped open, and there was this little keyring thing lying there, so I pulled it out and . . . and it was a set of keys.'

Scott pulled his chin in and gave a puzzled frown. 'But that doesn't mean it was *the* set of keys, does it? I mean, she might have house keys, car keys, work keys?'

'She told me that her friend Matt, the one whose house she'd left the keys at, had just given her a theatre mask keyring – and it was on there, plain as day.'

'Oh my God,' he said, his expression incredulous. I felt a swell of relief. Scott was as confused and concerned as I was. But my relief was short-lived. 'She's going to feel like such an idiot!'

'What do you mean?'

'Well, when she rummages in her bag again and real-ises she had the keys all along!'

I'd missed out a crucial piece of the story. 'She also told me that Matt had called her back and that he'd found the keys at his flat on the kitchen table. She said she was going there later today to collect them.'

He paused. 'OK, now that *is* a bit weird. Although, I suppose the two sets of keys theory is still in play? I mean, she's an actress, so it's feasible she's in posses-sion of more than one theatre mask keyring . . . maybe she collects them or something? Maybe that's why Matt bought her one?'

I nodded slowly. 'Maybe.'

'Anyway, it's not a big deal, is it? The main thing is that we have a lodger, it's someone we like, and we can start paying back the loan and saving up some money.'

He beamed at me and I wondered how he was so eas-ily capable of brushing this under the carpet. He'd always been a glass-half-full sort of person. That was one of the things I'd fallen in love with. This, however, seemed almost like wilful ignorance. But then, what did I think had happened? What was my suspicion? That Orla had, for some bizarre reason, pretended she'd lost her keys? Why? It didn't make sense. Which made me realise I was probably being ridiculous. Like Scott said, the ones I'd seen in her handbag must be a different set of keys.

Orla called me later that evening, fizzing with excitement as she told me she'd sorted everything out. Her landlord had agreed to transfer her rental contract over to her

26

housemate's boyfriend, who would be moving in at the end of the following week when the housemate returned from her theatre tour. Scott and I opened a bottle of prosecco and toasted our new lodger.

At midday the following Friday I watched a minivan pull up in front of the house, the taxi company's contact details emblazoned across its grey metal doors. I imagined a surly driver emerging, begrudgingly helping Orla to heave all her worldly belongings from the back of the vehicle, tutting at the extra effort this particular job had entailed. But as I opened the front door and emerged, blinking into the winter sun, I heard laughter, and watched them both lugging a cardboard box from the boot.

'You're just an absolute superstar, thank you so much!' Orla gushed, the driver's plump face reddening as they set it down.

'Jules!' She bounded over to me, enveloping me in a vice-like hug and planting a kiss on each of my cheeks.

'Hey, it's good to see you!' I said. 'You fitted all your things in one van?'

'Well, I'm a bit of a nomad so I don't have a great deal.'

'Do you want help up to your room with these, love?' said the driver, fixing Orla with an earnest stare as he gestured towards the cardboard boxes.

'Ah, you're an absolute gem, but no, don't worry. If we could just unload everything then I can lug it up there. You've already gone above and beyond,' she said, sweeping back to the van and squeezing his upper arm as she brushed past. He trailed after her like a puppy, and

I smiled to myself. Here was a woman who knew how to use her charms.

When the driver had left, giving two happy beeps of his horn as he disappeared down Seymour Avenue, Orla and I set about carrying her stuff upstairs. And there really wasn't much. I didn't know a great deal about Orla at this point, but by casting a cursory glance over her belongings, I could deduce one thing about her – she wasn't materialistic. There were a few battered old duffel bags, two weathered cardboard boxes and a padded guitar case, the stitching coming loose on the front pocket. She informed me she played 'rather poorly'. Upstairs, I asked if she wanted help unpacking but she said no, not to trouble myself, I'd already been *such* a help. So I retreated to my studio.

The box room was only small, but it had everything I needed. My large, height-adjustable drafting table was laid out in front of the diamond-shaped leaded windows that overlooked the front drive. On a side desk sat my iMac and scanner. One wall was taken up with shelves upon which I kept books of all shapes and sizes, some of which I'd illustrated, others that I used for inspiration or reference. There were also two trailing pot plants, a poseable wooden mannequin I'd had since sixth form, and several chunky scented candles my best friend Maggie had given me over the years.

I took out my fineliner pens and tried to focus on outlining my watercolour of a small, blonde girl and a shaggy brown dog in a hot-air balloon. I could hear Orla moving around in the room above, and I imagined her setting up the space as she wanted it. I was tempted to take a cup of tea up, so I could have a nose around and see what she'd done to the room, what sort of possessions she had on display. I felt I wanted to get a better handle on what she was *like*. Then I reminded myself that she was a lodger, not a housemate. This was not going to be like university where you knocked on each other's doors holding a bottle of wine and two mugs, or sat on each other's beds talking about the latest boy drama. She wanted to be left to her own devices as much as I did. I decided I shouldn't set a precedent where we were too involved with each other on a day-to-day basis.

It was just as I picked up a thicker pen that there was a knock on the door.

'Hello?'

'Hi, Jules, can I come in?'

'Of course.'

She'd changed; her long legs were now clad in skinny jeans and her cropped leather jacket worn over a baggy red jumper.

'Wow, is this where you work?' she said, her gaze sweeping over the bookshelves and framed sketches and paintings on the walls.

'Yep, this is my makeshift studio.'

'Did you paint these?' She gestured to the pictures on the wall.

'Some of them. These ones here . . . and that one. Most of them are by other illustrators I love, though. Just a bit of inspiration, you know.'

'You're so bloody talented,' she said, gawping at a print of the cover of *Forgetful Freddy Frog*, the first picture book I ever illustrated.

I felt myself preen with the compliment and for a moment was reminded of the taxi driver, basking in the warmth of Orla's praise. She approached my desk. Looking down at my coloured and partially outlined picture, she shook her head. 'That's so beautiful. Wow, you're so lucky to have such a talent and to be able to do it for a living.'

I swivelled towards her in my chair. 'I'm sure you could say the same thing – you're making a living from your talent.'

She gave a monosyllabic laugh and leaned back against the bookcase, hooking her thumbs into the pockets of her jeans. 'Wait until you've seen the play to decide whether I'm talented or not.'

'Well, I'm sure lots of girls auditioned for that *Kilcroom High* role – and it was you who got it. That's got to be talent, right?'

'Well . . . I hope so.' She stood up straight then. 'Which reminds me, I'd better get going. A few of us are having dinner in a pub before the show tonight.'

'Oh God, I'm so sorry I haven't even asked about opening week. How's it going?'

'OK, not too bad. A few minor slip-ups . . . there was a lighting issue on the second night, which was unfortunately when the *Time Out* reviewer was in, but apart from that, it's ticking along.'

'We can't wait to see it! Did you manage to reserve us tickets for tomorrow?'

'Yes! Absolutely – best seats in the house.' She gave a wink before adding, 'All the seats are the same,' in a stage whisper. She walked towards the door. 'So I'll be home super late tonight, and then I'm heading in early tomorrow cos the director wants to "tweak" a few things before the matinee . . . so if I don't see you, I'll catch you in the pub after the show?'

'Great, see you then. Got your house keys?'

'*Definitely!*' she said, tapping her handbag before winking again and shutting the door behind her.

This was perfect, I thought. She was off doing her own thing. She had her own set of friends and a busy schedule, just like Scott had said. I felt a swell of satisfaction. We'd made the right decision.

Scott and I so rarely went to the theatre, it felt like such a treat. We wound our way through the back streets of Southwark, following the blue dot on my phone, until we reached the Black Lion. The only giveaway the venue was anything other than an old pub was a glass display case attached to the wall outside, which held a poster for the show. People clustered around patio heaters on the pavement, cigarette smoke curling around them. Scott held the door open for me and we entered the hubbub of the place, weaving our way to the bar.

The pub was high-ceilinged, the walls adorned with black-and-white photographs in gilt frames, depicting Southwark in Victorian times, interspersed with posters from past performances. The clientèle was a mishmash of local old men who huddled round circular tables at the periphery of the room, and theatregoers who milled about, clutching programmes and tickets. We ordered drinks then made our way round to a small booth where Orla had instructed us to pick up our tickets. They were handed to us in a white envelope with our surname, 'Burton', written on the front.

I felt a tingle of anticipation as we all made our way up the dark staircase and into the theatre space. It was much smaller than I'd expected. The seating was raked, and we filed in, taking our places in the fourth row and wedging our coats around our feet. The air was stale and hot, and peering towards the doorway I wondered how many more people they could fit in.

Eventually, a woman with a grey bob shut the door and gave a signal to someone sitting behind us. A hush descended as the lights dimmed and a silver glow shimmered on the blackness of the stage. A chorus of other-worldly voices began singing from somewhere as, slowly, cloaked shapes shuffled onto the stage from the wings, forming a tableau.

Then the lights snapped on.

Orla marched onto the stage, pencil skirt stretched over her thighs, black stiletto heels clicking on the floor. Her blonde hair was swept up in a neat chignon, and she clasped a clipboard in one hand, a pen in the other. She immediately began barking orders at a short, rotund man in what, to my ears, sounded like a perfect American accent. I glanced at Scott and he turned to me, mouthing the word 'wow!' and grinning before turning back towards the stage.

I could feel myself smiling every time Orla appeared. She was so unlike her real-life character, I just couldn't get over the transformation. Everything, from how she looked to the way she moved to how she sounded, was completely different. It was ridiculous, but I felt a sort of

pride as I watched her perform. I had a strange compulsion to turn to the person next to me and say, *We know
her – that's Orla.*

During the interval we jostled back down to the
bar. We sipped our drinks and talked about Orla and
(in hushed tones, in case any friends or family of other
cast members were within earshot) how she was the best
thing in the play. And it was true.

The second half was overlong, and I could sense the
audience becoming restless around me. I hadn't been able
to completely understand the structure of the play, and
found the frequent interjections from the dark, hooded
chorus rather jarring and detrimental to the plot. But
what did I know? As we waited in the pub afterwards
for Orla to emerge, we chatted about what we'd say
to her, and how we'd have to make sure we were only
complimentary about all aspects of the show.

At last she appeared through the doorway that led
from the staircase, her hair still in a chignon but now with
golden tendrils framing her face. I ran a hand through my
own dull brown, shoulder-length hair, briefly wondering
what it would do if I tried to coerce it into a similar style.
Orla wore her big red jumper, her leather jacket slung
over one arm. The little round man from the play was trying to say something to her as she jostled through the pub
and she leaned down towards him, a patient smile on her
lips as she nodded in agreement, before her eyes locked on
to mine. Her face broke into a wide grin and she bobbed
up and down as she tried to get through to us.

I watched her approach, noticing heads turning
towards her as she made her progress across the pub.

Arms shot out to squeeze hers, and she turned to say 'thank you' to the audience members who threw compliments her way.

She wrapped her arms around both of us simultaneously and squeezed hard. 'Thank you *so* much for coming! It's so good of you.'

'Our pleasure,' I said. 'It was amazing, honestly.'

'Jesus, you're brilliant!' effused Scott. 'That accent . . . wow, I would never have guessed you weren't American if I didn't know you.'

'You guys are *too* kind.'

Scott bought us more drinks and Orla introduced us to some of the cast.

I watched her recounting funny stories about things that had happened in rehearsal and mistakes they'd had to deal with during the first week, and I noted how the faces of the cast turned towards her like flowers towards the sun. She was one of the tallest cast members, and this, combined with her exuberant movements and her glittering laughter, made her a presence that was hard to ignore.

At one point, just as I was finishing my glass of wine, she leaned into me and said, 'Don't be tricked into buying drinks for actors, they'll never buy you one back,' before winking and disappearing to the bar, returning with drinks only for the three of us.

The evening drifted on and gradually the crowd thinned and cast members slunk off. Scott and I hugged and air-kissed people whose names we hadn't grasped but who, in the last couple of hours, had felt like friends. It was as we settled in a quiet corner, just the three of us, that Orla sprang up. She tapped at the pockets of her jeans, then grabbed up her jacket, grasping at the fabric. 'Shit!'

'What? What's wrong?' I said.

'I've left my bloody phone up there!' She cast her eyes wildly round the pub and I had a flashback to the first night we'd met her, when she'd forgotten her keys. 'God, I'm such an idiot.'

She marched over to the bar and I watched her lean over towards the barman. He shook his head and shrugged, then pointed towards the booth where we'd collected our tickets. A woman was there, counting cash, and Orla renewed her pleas to her, the woman's face creasing into a sympathetic grimace as she shook her head. A man at a nearby table stood up and went to Orla's side. He wore all black and had a utility belt slung around his waist. I wondered if he was a member of the stage crew. He beckoned another man over from the opposite side of the pub and that man took out his mobile, tapping at the screen.

Orla glanced over at us and raised her crossed fingers like she had done in the pub that time as she tried to call Matt. I watched her turn back to the man on the phone, who was speaking to someone. The woman from the booth interjected with something the man then relayed to whoever he was speaking to, and the other man said something to Orla, to which she smiled and nodded. The barman came out and crossed over to the group too, joining the huddle of problem-solvers as they all explained and pointed and bustled about trying to help Orla, who stood in the midst of the group, eyes wide with the same sort of helpless charm I remembered from when she'd lost her keys.

'I'll go and see what's happening,' Scott said, standing up.

I gave a snort, nodding my head towards the group. 'Are you worried she hasn't got enough people working on it?' My voice came out derisory in a way I hadn't intended it to. I sounded petulant, when all Scott had wanted to do was go and check Orla was OK.

His face flashed with a wounded expression, but he rallied with his usual humour. 'Well, I thought they might need my superior problem-solving skills.'

I smiled, trying to soften the edges of whatever I'd just felt. Just then the pub door opened and a pink-haired woman in a puffy jacket came in brandishing a huge bunch of keys, to cheers from Orla and her protectors. I couldn't hear what Orla was saying but she appeared to be gushing at the woman, squeezing her arm and thanking her profusely as the woman unlocked the door to the staircase and they both disappeared.

Scott lowered himself back down into his seat. 'Drama over, I guess.'

The woman appeared a few minutes later, followed by a beaming Orla, holding her phone aloft like a trophy to more cheers, some from random strangers who I'm sure didn't even know what had happened. Orla grinned at her saviours, clutching her hand to her chest and thanking everyone as if she'd just won an Oscar. She made her way back over to our table.

'Oh my God, Celine the stage manager is an absolute *lifesaver*! And thank God she was having a pint in the pub round the corner and hadn't gone home with the keys or I'd have been screwed. Crikey, how many key-related dramas does a girl need?'

Scott and I laughed, but I felt something stir inside. Something uncomfortable I couldn't place. Scott caught my eye and smiled, but it was a genuine, easy smile, and I knew he didn't feel the same way I did. Looking back, this was probably the first moment I felt this emotional fork in the road. Scott and I were usually so in tune when it came to our reactions to people; this was the first time I felt we might not be on the same page when it came to Orla. It was only slight at this stage, but I watched him grinning at her, hanging on every animated word that came from her mouth, then I looked at her myself, then back at Scott, and something small and tight inside told me that although we were looking at the same person, we were each seeing someone different.

My father always said I had a talent for reading people. And as soon as I met Scott and Jules I had them down: he was the empath, and she the cynic. Call it a sixth sense, or whatever. You see, Scott is one of those people who's a natural nurturer. He needs someone to look after, someone to care for.

Jules . . . not so much.

It was obvious the night we met that she was more wary than him about asking me to sit down and have a drink with them. And it was Scott's suggestion I crashed at theirs for the night. Where I got generosity from him, there was reservation from her. It was only subtle . . . I don't think most people would have even noticed, but like I say, I'm intuitive about these things. It's like a little tingle I get. I can only imagine how much convincing it took for Jules to ask me to move in with them. But, as she told me herself, it is Scott's family house, so perhaps she defers these decisions to him?

It's OK. I'm pretty sure I can work on her. Because that's my other talent – making people feel good about themselves. Winning them over. Bringing out their compassionate side. I knew as soon as I met Jules that I'd need to thaw a bit of the frostiness I can feel in her, just under the surface. I don't mind; I like a challenge.

Although I'll have to go easy – I know I'm an extrovert, guilty as charged! I'll have to rein it in a bit with Jules. Don't want her feeling like she's opened up her home to an overexcited actor who's going to be in her face all the time! No, it'll be fine. I can work my magic without being too outrageous.

And it'll be worth it. Because I've got a good feeling about this place, and these people. And I need to make sure Jules doesn't mess it up for me. I need her to realise that asking me to live here was a good decision. That I'm the perfect lodger.

Chapter Four

In the days following Orla's play, I tried to understand my uneasiness that night. In the end, I could only attribute it to anxiety about Orla's scattiness. We'd seen her lose her keys and her phone in the space of just over a week – and we'd invited her to live in our house. I suppose I was worried we had someone on our hands who would leave taps running, or get locked out when we were away, or forget to pay her rent and prompt awkward conversations. But as the next few weeks slipped by, there were no such events. Orla had no more daytime rehearsals, so she'd usually stay in bed late, then slip out about midday to go into town and meet friends or go shopping before her evening performance. There were days in a row when we didn't see her, and our evenings always belonged to just us. Scott frequently commented on how well things were working out and I had to agree with him. Things were settled and calm.

That was until one day in early March.

The chill of winter was dissolving into milder, wetter days. But every so often there was a bright blue day, with a high, clear sky and a tinge of warmth to the sun's rays. It was on a Sunday morning just like this that Orla appeared in our kitchen at about ten o'clock.

'Gosh, it's so beautiful out there! I don't know what I'm going to do today, but it's going to be outside.'

I smiled at her over my coffee mug. 'That's a good plan. We've not had many days like this so far this year.'

Scott was buttering his toast and he looked up and squinted out of the window towards the back garden. 'We could all go for a walk in Richmond Park?' He smiled at me, questioningly. 'Bet we see deer,' he added with a wink.

I felt a pang of irritation, not having envisaged the three of us doing something together. Sunday was usually a time Scott and I spent together, the two of us, or occasionally with Maggie and Nick. And I wasn't keen on the idea of spending the day with our lodger. I know we'd been to see her show, but that was simply to be supportive. This felt different.

'That's a fab idea!' said Orla. And that was that.

Within an hour we were all traipsing out of the house and towards the park. Orla spoke in her usual animated way about the show, and audiences, and favourable (and not so favourable) reviews, and cast gossip, including who was supposedly shagging who, and who hated who. It was a world away from my work, alone in my solitary bedroom studio, only interacting with others via email, with sometimes the odd meeting in central London.

'So what's the plan after this week then, when the show's over?' Scott asked as we walked through the arched metal gates into Richmond Park.

'Good question,' Orla said. 'Well, my agent's managed to get me a couple of auditions for the end of this week, so hopefully something comes of those. They're both plays, one central and one in Shoreditch, I think.'

We walked along the periphery of the park, the gravel path crunching under our feet, and the distant cries of playing children drifting across on the breeze. Dogs barked and crashed through bracken.

'Deer!' said Scott, nudging me playfully and nodding towards a cluster of red deer who were grazing under an oak tree.

'Just incredible, isn't it?' said Orla, turning towards the creatures. But as she turned, her step faltered, her hands moving outwards suddenly as if to balance herself.

'Whoa, watch yourself. You OK?' said Scott.

She stood up straight and squeezed her eyes shut, taking a big breath in.

'Orla?' I said, resting my hand on her arm. 'What's wrong? Do you need to sit down?'

'I . . . I don't know . . . I just sort of had a head rush.' She flapped her hands towards her face and took another deep breath.

I noticed a wooden bench a few metres away. 'Come on, sit down,' I said, guiding her to the seat by her elbow. I delved into my bag and produced a plastic water bottle, which I pressed into her hand. Her fingers trembled as she took a sip.

'Has this happened before?' said Scott.

She shook her head. 'Not . . . not for a while.'

'Have you eaten anything today?'

'No – that's probably it, isn't it? Stupid, really, coming on a long walk without having breakfast first.' She gave a soft laugh, but it was unconvincing.

We sat for a few minutes, Orla taking small sips of the water, and me rubbing her back gently, just for something to do. Some way of comforting her. A woman with a dog stopped to ask if we were OK, Orla offering her a weak smile and reassuring her she was fine, just 'a bit light-headed'.

When she was feeling strong enough to stand, we decided to make our way to Pembroke House. This pretty, Georgian building is a popular wedding venue, but also a cafe and gardens. Here, we found a seat inside by large French windows, and Scott went up to the counter.

'The sugar will be good for you,' he said, setting a hot chocolate with marshmallows and a slice of lemon drizzle in front of Orla.

She picked at the cake, her long fingers breaking off the smallest morsels before popping them into her mouth. It was disconcerting, having her present but quiet. Occasionally she'd scrunch up her eyes and put her hand to her chest, or her head, and Scott and I would cast worried glances at each other. At one point, a man with a green apron emerged, unbidden, from behind the till and set a glass bottle of mineral water and a tumbler of ice in front of Orla. She smiled and thanked him.

When we'd finished, I went outside and called us an Uber. We were halfway to Richmond on foot, but I didn't trust that Orla would make it back the way we'd come, or on to Richmond so we could get a bus back. She protested, saying she didn't want us 'going to any trouble', but Scott and I were firm in our decision. The last thing we wanted was for her to pass out on the walk home.

But at home there wasn't much improvement. 'I think I'll go up and have a lie down,' she said, rubbing her forehead. 'Thanks, guys.'

'Can we get you anything? Do you need painkillers or a cup of tea?' I asked.

'No, honestly, I'm fine,' she said, her voice drained of its usual colour. I was reminded of a child seeking confirmation from a parent that they would be able to stay home from school.

We listened to her footsteps padding up the stairs, then we settled opposite each other at the kitchen island.

'That was weird,' said Scott.

I shrugged. 'Everyone feels a bit light-headed sometimes.'

'Yeah, but it did last quite a while. And also . . .'

'Also what?'

'Well, she didn't seem that surprised? I mean . . . if I was feeling that dizzy for that long I'd be like "Oh my God, this is so strange, what's wrong with me?"'

I nodded slowly. I hadn't really considered that, but now Scott said it, I realised he was right. There was a sort of resigned weariness to Orla's episode. Like she was used to feeling that way.

'When you asked her if it had happened before she said, "not for a while". Maybe we need to find out if she has a condition we should know about,' I said. 'I mean, if she's got something, then we need to know. She is living with us, and all her family are back in Ireland.'

'Yeah, you're right. You'll ask her?' He looked at me with hopeful eyes, the silent implication that it was better if I, a woman, broached the subject rather than him.

'Yes. I'll ask her.'

It was five o'clock when I knocked on Orla's door, mug of tea in hand.

'Come in,' came the weak voice from inside.

I opened the door a crack at first, wondering if she'd be half asleep in darkness. But the room was bright, the blinds of the Velux windows open and a sharp breeze sweeping in through the wide French windows. Orla lay semi-supine on the small sofa, flicking through a magazine, and she twisted up to sitting as I came in and placed the tea on the coffee table.

'Oh, thank you so much, just what I need.' She smiled up at me. Her hair was falling in messy straggles and her face was pale.

I cast my gaze around the room, which I hadn't seen since she moved in several weeks ago. It was messier than I'd been expecting. There were coffee rings on the low table and several dog-eared paperbacks scattered across the floor. Socks lay on the carpet at the foot of the bed, and the bed itself hadn't been made, the duvet bunched up in the middle of the mattress. A thin white bookshelf we'd picked up at Ikea was set against one wall, more books stacked haphazardly on its shelves along with a couple of dirty mugs. A used towel had been dropped outside the bathroom, and next to it a crumpled chocolate bar wrapper.

Orla sipped her tea with her eyes closed.

'How are you feeling?' I said.

She cradled the mug in her hands. 'Much better. I'm sorry for scaring you guys.' She winced apologetically.

'You don't have anything to apologise for. We were just worried. I mean . . . we *are* worried. You said this has happened before?'

She sighed and her eyes flicked up to the ceiling as if she was trying to recall details. 'I think the last time was about a month ago maybe . . .'

'OK, that's quite recent.'

She nodded. 'And the other times I can't really remember the details—'

'The other times? You mean there have been several?'

She looked at me sheepishly and bit her bottom lip. 'I mean . . . not *that* many. You know, a few.' She wrinkled her nose and gave a quick shake of her head as if to convince me of the insignificance of these episodes.

'Orla, I know it's none of my business, but perhaps you should go to the doctor about it?'

'Oh, God, no there's no need for that!' She flapped her hand at me.

'But it might be anaemia or something. You know, something easily sorted out with a couple of iron supplements.' I didn't really know anything about anaemia, but I thought I sounded vaguely convincing.

Orla looked as if she was considering what I'd said. 'I mean . . . yeah, maybe.'

'Look . . .' I sat on the tiny sofa next to her. 'Your family are all back in Ireland and you're living here with us. We need to look out for you.'

She squeezed her eyes shut briefly before opening them and fixing me with an earnest stare. 'God, you're right.' She gave a deep sigh. 'I'm being selfish. This isn't just about me, of course. I guess I'm used to making my own way, being independent, you know? And now I'm living here with you, and you're both so supportive and kind . . . of course I need to think about you too. You don't want to be worrying I've passed out in my bedroom, or wondering why I haven't come home.'

'That's exactly it,' I said, nodding emphatically. I felt a surge of relief. She understood.

'OK, I'll make a GP appointment for next week. Happy?'

I smiled. 'Happy.'

Chapter Five

I spotted Maggie as soon as I pushed open the door of the Grey Horse. She was settled in a corner, two margaritas already lined up in front of her, chuckling to herself at something on her phone screen. She wore a chunky yellow jumper and her cropped black hair was perfectly tousled with an artful white-blonde streak emerging from her hairline. She was effortlessly cool, and she always made me reassess my choice of clothes whenever we met. I cast my eyes down and looked at my mud-streaked boots, faded jeggings and fake Barbour jacket, wondering why I'd thought this was appropriate attire for hanging out with my eternally fashionable best friend.

Our eyes met and she side-stepped around the table to hug me. 'Ah, it's been too long!' she said, her fresh, citrus perfume washing over me.

'I know, it feels like forever since we've done this! How have you been?'

'Oh, you know, can't complain. Well . . . I *could* complain, because Nick has gone and got himself a brand-new Vespa costing five grand when we're supposed to be saving up for a deposit on a house, but anyway, that's perhaps for when we're a few margaritas in . . .'

'Oh shit, so he's properly in the doghouse then?'

'Yep,' Maggie said, and we clinked glasses. 'He's really looking forward to seeing you both next weekend by the way. Sends his love.'

'Ah, that's great you can still make it. Although I always feel a bit silly doing a birthday thing, you know, as an adult.'

'Well, that's exactly why Scott and I have to take the reins and make sure you celebrate these things properly. And it's not exactly a huge party, is it? It's just inviting another couple over for dinner and drinks.'

'I know.' I nodded, not wanting to seem ungrateful. 'I really appreciate it. And I also appreciate having you to myself now, so we can chat properly without the menfolk around!'

'Amen to that!' she said, and we clinked glasses again.

The first drinks didn't touch the sides, and I was up at the bar before long ordering us another round. I told Maggie about Orla and the strange way we'd met, but how relieved we were at having found someone to rent out the upstairs room. I also explained about *Kilcroom High*, then told her about Orla's play. I was about to tell Maggie about Orla losing her phone that night, and about the dizzy spell in Richmond Park, but I realised I didn't quite know how to frame either of those things. What was I saying? That she was forgetful? That would explain her losing things, but not the dizzy spell. That she'd suffered a run of bad luck? It was hardly that. Everyone lost their keys and phone sometimes. As I shaped these mini-anecdotes in my mind, I realised they sounded boring and irrelevant, so I didn't share them. Instead I asked Maggie about her work.

'You won't believe it . . .' She eyed me with a mischievous grin. 'But I got that promotion!'

'What?' I half-shrieked, causing a couple at the next table to glance over at us, but I didn't care. 'You *got* it? I'm sorry, we've been here for almost an hour and talked about your fiancé's new Vespa and my new lodger, but you didn't think to tell me that you got the new *job* of your dreams?'

She beamed at me and did a little bounce in her seat like an excited child.

'Oh my God, this is unbelievable, Maggie, you absolute superstar. So what's the role exactly?'

She gave a theatrical cough and placed a palm against her chest. 'Communications Director at Kind UK, "one of the south-east's most dynamic charities to emerge post-pandemic, and one with a growing presence across the UK" . . . according to the *Independent*.'

'OK, *this* is a cause for celebration!' I stood up and crossed to the bar, ordering a bottle of prosecco and making sure they put it in a big silver bucket with shedloads of ice, for extra effect.

I overfilled our glasses, watching the cloudy foam spill onto the sticky table and we giggled and licked it from our fingers, already quite tipsy from the margaritas.

I raised my glass, made a toast, and we laughed and talked and drank until the words and the bubbles blurred the evening into night.

It was 1 a.m. when I put my key in the lock and stepped into our hallway. We usually left a couple of downstairs lights on when one of us was going to be home late, so I wasn't surprised to see the glow from the kitchen. I *was* surprised, however, to hear the laughter. I set my keys down on the side table and shrugged off my jacket, the floor seeming to tilt slightly as I reached up to the coat hook. After taking a moment to steady myself against the wall, I made my way into the kitchen.

Scott and Orla were sitting at the circular dining table in front of the patio doors. Scott had his feet up on the chair next to him and was casually leaning back with his hands clasped behind his head. Orla was opposite, one leg drawn up as she sat, hugging it and resting her chin on her knee. Half a bottle of red wine and two glasses were on the table between them.

They looked up simultaneously.

'Jules!' Orla said, her face a picture of delight.

'Hey, love,' said Scott, reaching out an arm towards me. I went to stand next to him and he slid his arm around my waist, tilting his head up towards me as I bent to kiss him. 'How was your evening? How's Maggie?'

'She's great, yeah.' I nodded, glancing towards Orla and feeling a strange tightness inside me. I didn't want to share any more details. 'We had a lovely time. Probably a bit too much to drink.'

'Well, cheers to that,' said Orla, raising her wine glass and taking a sip. 'It is Friday, after all.'

'So, how has your evening been?' I asked. 'Both of you?'

'Well,' Scott said. 'I ate a pizza and watched a documentary about penguins, so it didn't get off to the most raucous start. But then Orla got back from her show and we decided to open a bottle—'

'Or two!' She giggled, and I found my gaze flicking towards the kitchen counter where an empty bottle of Shiraz stood.

My smile, like my insides, hardened.

'Let me get you a glass!' she chimed, leaping up.

'No, seriously, I've had enough to drink.' I crossed to a cupboard and brought out a pint glass, filling it from the tap and gulping down the cold water. Orla sat back down.

'I think I'm going to go up,' I said.

'OK, love. I'll be up in a minute.'

I nodded and walked towards the door. 'Night, Orla.'

'Goodnight, Jules!'

As I turned up the stairs I heard their voices resume, and caught a glimpse of Orla reaching forwards to refill Scott's glass.

It was another hour before Scott came to bed. I'd been lying in the darkness with the room spinning, feeling simultaneously exhausted and wired. I hadn't been able to drift off, listening to their muffled voices from downstairs and the occasional burst of laughter. Wondering what they were talking about.

'Oh no, you're still awake,' Scott said as he climbed into bed. 'We didn't keep you up, did we?'

'No,' I murmured sleepily, hoping not to be dragged into a conversation.

'It's Orla's last night of her show tomorrow,' he whispered, slipping his arms around me and kissing my cheek.

I felt my mood sink even further. I pictured her at home every evening. Coming downstairs to open a bottle of wine and sit and talk to us. 'So what's her plan then?'

'Well, she had a couple of auditions this week, so hopefully something will come of that. And she's joined a temping agency, so she's got daytime work as of Monday.'

'OK, that's good,' I said, feeling relieved she'd been organised enough to sort that out, and also that she'd be out during the day.

'Are you OK, Jules?'

'Yeah, I'm fine.'

He held me closer. 'You still like Orla, don't you?'

'Of course. What's not to like?'

'OK. It's just, if you don't like her then it's kind of my fault we're stuck with her, cos the whole lodger thing was my idea—'

I conceded a quiet laugh. 'I still like her. She's a lot of fun. And anyway, we're not stuck with her, are we? She won't be here forever. And if things don't work out she can always find somewhere else to live.' I felt the reassuring weight of Scott's arm on the side of my waist. 'She said herself she's a bit of a nomad. Perhaps she won't want to stick around for ages anyway.' I listened to Scott's soft breathing, wondering if he was asleep. Wondering if I was saying these words to him, or to myself.

Chapter Six

The following week was busy with work. I had a tight deadline for some preliminary sketches, and a publisher had come back with some revisions I needed to make on another book. The hot-air balloon story was complete, but my scanner wasn't big enough to work with double-page spreads, so I had to make my usual trip into town to the specialist, who then emailed me the digital copies back for editing. All these tasks were time-consuming and needed slotting together alongside other projects so my time wasn't wasted.

Because my work was freelance and project-based, it meant I never had a steady stream of work to occupy me. There could be weeks when I hardly had anything to do and I'd be able to make a trip into town for more art supplies or fit in a swim. Then other weeks, three deadlines would loom at the same time and I'd be run off my feet. But I loved the unpredictability and found I did some of my best work when under this sort of pressure. And this week was definitely one of those pressurised weeks. I often found myself working through lunch without noticing, and in the evening only stopping when a soft knock on the door from Scott coaxed me downstairs for something to eat.

Orla was enjoying the sociability of her new temping job at a hotel in town, and although she now finished work at five thirty, we hardly saw her in the evenings. Scott and I would eat at about seven thirty, and by the time Orla appeared an hour later, we were usually watching TV in the living room with mugs of tea and a bag of Maltesers between us. Orla would cook some pasta or a ready meal and take it up to her room.

She always left the kitchen exactly as she'd found it – everything washed and dried up and replaced in drawers and cupboards, the counters wiped down and the cloth hanging over the tap. Whenever I noticed this, it made me think of the dishevelled state of her bedroom and brought about a pang of affection. If it was in her nature to be untidy, she must be trying extra hard to keep our shared living space so pristine. She was really trying to be a good lodger.

Saturday was my birthday, which also happened to mark the end of my crazy week. All my sketches, revisions and digital scans were in, and my original copies had been couriered to the publisher. And it felt *so* good to start the weekend knowing it was all done.

I was woken up by Scott bringing in a tray upon which he'd set a mug of tea, a plate of toast and peanut butter, a bowl of blackberries and cream (I'd always preferred blackberries to strawberries), and a miniature red rose in a tiny green vase. The rose was made of faded red plastic and had been a joke Valentine's gift a few years ago. I didn't know where Scott kept it, but it always made me laugh when it popped up on any occasion he was expected to make an effort for me.

I propped myself up on the pillows and gave him a sleepy smile. 'Thank you, sweetheart. Aren't you just adorable?'

'Well, yes, actually.' He leaned in and kissed me tenderly.

'Aren't you going on your run this morning?'

'Nope, not today. It's not every day my wife has a birthday on an actual Saturday, so I'm going to use the time to spoil her rotten, and also get some bits together for when Maggie and Nick come over later for the thing that most definitely *isn't* a birthday party especially for you.'

'OK, I'll allow it to be called a birthday *dinner* . . .'

'Right, gotcha. Birthday *dinner*, but definitely not a *party*.'

'Is it going to be a bit awkward with Orla around? We haven't invited her . . .'

'She's our lodger, Jules. I don't think she'd be expecting to be invited to your birthday bash when it only involves us and another couple.'

'I know, it's just . . .' I sighed. 'I feel like the lines are a bit blurred. We met her in the pub, and we've been to see her play. You had drinks with her the other night. Maybe we've been too friendly—'

Scott leaned over and kissed my forehead. 'You're overthinking this. She won't be expecting an invite, and if she gets home late and we're still having a few drinks then she can come and join us if she wants.'

'What do you mean "gets home late"?'

'From her shift at the hotel.' Scott looked at me and I stared blankly back. 'She's on the late shift on Saturdays – four to ten. I thought I told you that?'

I felt relief surge through me. 'No, I thought she was only working weekdays. OK, that makes things less awkward. She'll be out.'

Scott nodded and gave me his amused smile. 'Yes, she'll be out until late so we don't have to lock her in her room so she can't socialise with us.'

'That's not what I meant . . . I just didn't want her feeling awkward if we were all downstairs and she hadn't . . . anyway, it doesn't matter.'

I ate my breakfast and watched Scott bustling about the bedroom getting dressed, feeling a delicious mixture of laziness mixed with anticipation at seeing Maggie and Nick later. I had a luxuriously long shower, then Scott drove us into town. He said he had a few things to get and I wanted a quiet stroll around so we went our separate ways and agreed to meet back at the house later. Maggie and Nick were coming over at about five, and although the idea of the evening being all about me made me slightly uncomfortable, I wanted to treat myself to something new to wear to mark the occasion.

I tried on a couple of dresses in Jigsaw. They were too long, and I found myself imagining what Orla would look like in them. My shorter, softer frame was not, I was sure, the intended model for these delicate, bias-cut creations. Orla, with her tall, willowy figure, would float beautifully in them. I pulled my stomach in and mussed up my shoulder-length hair, trying to look nonchalant and sophisticated. But no, I was not pulling it off. And anyway, they were too expensive.

I headed to Mango in the shopping centre instead, where big red signs declared 'Mid-Season Sale!' This is more promising, I thought. Here I found a long-sleeved shirt in cobalt blue, and a pair of black jeans. Peering at myself in the fitting-room mirror I felt more like myself. This was definitely more my vibe.

Buying both seemed a bit much, and I already had several pairs of jeans, so I just bought the shirt, then headed to the local indie bookshop, Parade's End Books. Every year, on my birthday, my aunt Celia sent me a crisp £10 note in a cheesy, flowery card, which always contained a pre-written poem about what a special niece I was. The type of card and the amount of cash had remained constants since I was about ten, and it was so sweet.

Celia was my mum's only sister, and every year the arrival of this card made me promise myself I'd be a better niece and go and visit her in Chichester. After all, it wasn't that far away. So now I gave myself my habitual yearly talking-to, promising I'd not only write to her, but make a plan to go and visit. She was my only remaining link to Mum, and I owed it to her (and Mum) to be the niece her birthday cards seemed to think I was. I always spent Celia's £10 on a book, so in Parade's End, I picked up the latest Lisa Jewell I'd been waiting to come out in paperback.

Scott had told me to take my time – I knew he was food shopping and doing some prep – so I stopped for a coffee and croissant at Boho Cafe on the way home. I sipped my coffee and read the first chapter of my book. The cafe was quiet, soft jazz floating from speakers above. As I finished my drink and my chapter, I began feeling restless. I thought about Scott and all the trouble he was going to for my birthday, and I felt a pang of guilt that I was just sitting here luxuriating. So I headed to Sainsbury's to pick up a bottle of pink prosecco on the way home. I loved that Scott wanted to make a fuss of me, and I felt I'd perhaps protested a bit too much when he'd suggested birthday celebrations. So now I decided to go home, pop the prosecco in the fridge, put on my new shirt and some make-up, and make an effort to act every bit the Birthday Girl.

I heard voices as soon as I pushed the front door open, then the unmistakable sound of Maggie's giggle from the kitchen. She must have arrived early. I dropped my shopping bags at the foot of the stairs, stopping to retrieve the bottle of prosecco, before heading towards the kitchen. Sure enough, Maggie was perched on a bar stool at the kitchen island, and opposite her wasn't Scott, but Orla. Two heads turned towards me as I walked in.

'Jules! Happy birthday!' chirped Orla, sweeping towards me and clasping me in her arms, planting two kisses on my cheeks.

Maggie slid off her stool and wrapped her arms around me. 'Happy birthday, my lovely. You're back early. Scott thought you'd be treating yourself to a mammoth shopping spree complete with facial, massage and manicure.'

'Oh, that sounds perfect!' said Orla, grinning at me.

I looked at her sincere expression and realised she hadn't caught the sarcasm that laced Maggie's voice. But then, why would she? She didn't know Maggie, and clearly she didn't know me either.

I laughed. 'Well, you know how extravagant I can be when it comes to my birthday.' I raised a mocking eyebrow at Maggie and waved the bottle in the air.

'Wow, a whole bottle of prosecco! You're really treating yourself this year. Don't tell me you've bought that *and* the obligatory book as well?'

'Not only those . . . but a new shirt too!'

Maggie clutched her chest in feigned shock, and my gaze flicked towards Orla's still-beaming face as our banter washed over her.

I crossed to the fridge and wedged the bottle on its side next to a bag of salad then turned back to them. 'I can see I don't need to introduce you to each other. When did you arrive, Maggie?'

'Oh, only about half an hour ago. I was going to help Scott but he dashed off because he forgot balsamic vinegar or something. Nick'll be here in about an hour. Hope you don't mind us showing up earlier than planned?'

'No, of course not – the earlier the better.' My eyes alighted on a circular tin peeping from behind the bread bin: Maggie had brought over a homemade birthday cake. I felt a swell of gratitude towards my friend. 'Shall we get the party started?' I said, swiping a bottle of tequila from the drinks cupboard and holding it aloft.

Maggie blew out her cheeks and checked her watch. 'Three p.m. – be rude not to.'

'What about you, Orla?' I said. 'Time for a cheeky margarita before you head off to work?'

'Absolutely!' she said, her smile lighting up her face as if she was genuinely delighted to be included. 'I mean, I'm not driving . . . I can be a bit pissed on reception, right?'

I laughed. 'Having worked in hospitality at uni, I can confidently say being a bit pissed only ever improved my customer service skills.'

Orla and Maggie laughed and I felt the party spirit sluice through me. I set the three glasses side by side and mixed the ingredients in the silver tumbler Maggie had bought me for my birthday last year. As I placed the final segment of lime on the third drink, Orla pulled her phone out of the back pocket of her jeans. I hadn't heard it ring, but she stared at the screen and said, 'Oh shit, sorry. It's the agency calling.'

I handed a drink to Maggie and we *cheers*ed as Orla strode out of the room into the hallway. 'Hi,' we heard her say. 'Everything OK? . . . yeah at four o'clock, I'm about to . . . oh, OK . . .'

I felt awkward listening to Orla's phone conversation, so tapped into Spotify on my phone and began playing a Santana album through the Bluetooth speaker. 'To match our drink vibe,' I said, raising my glass towards Maggie.

'*Salud!*' she said.

It was a few minutes later that Orla appeared, her posture somewhat deflated. She rolled her eyes at us as she slid back onto the bar stool and I killed the music. 'What's wrong?'

'Bloody agency double-booked me for today. And apparently the other guy got in there first, so the hotel don't need me.'

'Oh no, that's rubbish,' said Maggie. 'Does that mean you won't get paid?'

'Yep. Those are the terms I'm afraid.'

I felt a twinge of annoyance at the injustice of this. 'That's so unfair when it's their fault. They should shoulder that cost when they've promised you work.'

Orla sighed. 'That's a nice idea, but I don't think those sorts of rights are afforded to the lowly temp.'

I didn't know what to say. 'I'm sorry, Orla.' I slid her drink across the island towards her and she picked it up with a sad smile. I'd not seen her look dejected before, like all the energy had been sucked out of her.

'Anyway,' she said, looking up and, I could tell, trying to brighten her demeanour. 'It's your birthday, which is no time to be glum. So cheers! And happy birthday to Jules!'

We all clinked glasses and sipped, then fell into conversation about Orla's work and the auditions she'd just done. As my margarita waned and Maggie slid hers across the table for a top-up, I realised I didn't know what Orla was going to do now work had cancelled. Would she stay here with us all afternoon? If I were her, I was sure I'd feel like a bit of a third wheel and make my excuses. But as I watched her chatting to Maggie, tipping her glass back then pushing it across the table for a refill, I realised she wasn't going to make her excuses.

She wasn't going anywhere.

Chapter Seven

I'd imagined getting home and perhaps taking time to straighten my hair, and carefully apply make-up before choosing the best earrings and maybe a necklace to go with my new shirt. Spritzing myself with my favourite perfume before descending the stairs and making drinks for Scott and me as he cooked and we chatted while waiting for Maggie and Nick to arrive. But Scott was still at the shop, and Maggie was downstairs alone with Orla, and for some reason that had triggered a quiver of anxiety inside me. I couldn't relax and take my time getting ready while experiencing this urgent need to be back down there with them. So I quickly ran upstairs, pulled my new shirt over my head, tugged the price tag off, then slicked on some cherry lipgloss before running back down and rejoining them.

It was only a few minutes before I heard the front door. 'Look who I found wandering Richmond Road unsupervised!' announced Nick as he and Scott appeared in the kitchen doorway. He walked towards me with a broad grin and outstretched arms. 'Just returning him to his rightful owner! Happy birthday, Jules.'

He squeezed me into a bear hug and I rose onto tip-toes, as was always my impulse when hugging someone of Nick's stature.

'Lovely to see you, Nick. Thanks for coming.'

'God, you know me – I never willingly miss out on birthday shenanigans!'

We introduced Nick to Orla who kissed him on both cheeks, much to Nick's amusement. He made a joke about actor-types and Orla howled with laughter. I felt a surge of relief – Nick was big and loud and could be relentless with his teasing and banter. But it seemed Orla had tuned in to him.

I explained about Orla's work cancelling on her as Scott rummaged about in carrier bags and set out his ingredients and utensils. I looked pointedly at him as I added, 'So that's why she's here and not at the hotel.' But Scott seemed only to home in on the fact she'd been let down and now wouldn't be paid for the afternoon, which he and Nick agreed was absolutely scandalous. There seemed to be no more to say about that then. No one asked Orla if she had any plans for the rest of the day.

When Maggie set the table, she laid five sets of knives and forks, five water tumblers and five wine glasses. There was never a moment's question as to whether or not Orla would be joining us.

I felt a tension in my jaw as I poured chilled Muscadet into the wine glasses and lit a cluster of ivory tea lights on the dining table. I don't know why, but I couldn't shake my annoyance. Orla and Maggie dragged themselves from the bar stools and made their way to the table, barely breaking eye contact as they chatted animatedly. They sat next to each other, Nick and Scott on either side, and me opposite them on the circular table.

Scott had made a starter of bruschetta with feta cheese and roasted vegetables. The feta was creamy and the vegetables glistening and warm. He wasn't keen on feta, but he knew it was a favourite of mine and I slid my hand over his and gave it a squeeze, mouthing 'thank you', which prompted a proud smile from him. Everyone was complimentary, and even more so about the chicken and Parmesan risotto he produced for the main course.

Conversation bubbled along, but was led primarily by Nick and Orla, who were the loudest personalities around the table. Orla had tapped into Nick's sense of humour and was ribbing him mercilessly. This was refreshing to see. Nick was always the joker: most people laughed along with him but couldn't match his banter. Orla more than matched it. Although it got to the point where I felt the need to try and prevent the entire night from becoming the Nick and Orla show. 'Isn't it amazing about Maggie's job?' I said to Scott.

'Bloody amazing! Nick was telling me about it when we were walking back,' Scott enthused. 'Tell us more, I mean – are you still based in Richmond or do you have to travel?'

Maggie took a deep breath and I smiled across the table at my friend, relishing the joy she was experiencing at speaking about her job, her passion. Her eyes sparkled and she gestured with her wine glass, the golden liquid sloshing about inside with her tipsy movements. I looked across at Orla, wondering if she felt left out, not knowing about Maggie or her promotion. But I watched her expression and had to hand it to her – she looked as engaged and thrilled as the rest of us.

'So yeah, that's really the crux of it.' Maggie gave a self-deprecating shrug, her face still beaming.

Orla leaned forwards then, placing her palms on the table. 'Errr, I think you'll find you've left out one of the coolest parts.'

I felt a jolt of puzzlement, waiting for Orla to continue.

Maggie threw her head back and laughed, extending her hand to give Orla's arm an affectionate squeeze. 'I knew you'd bring this bit up.'

My puzzlement was joined by a twist of childish jealousy. *I knew you'd bring this bit up.* As if they were old friends. The laughter, the arm squeeze.

Orla grinned at Maggie before turning to Scott and me. 'She gets a vehicle provided for her! And not just any vehicle . . . the cutest little minivan you've ever seen, in that gorgeous purple colour the Kind UK logo is in.'

I felt my smile harden on my lips. In the brief time I'd been out of the room, Orla had clearly extracted all the information about Maggie's promotion – she even knew what vehicle she'd be driving and what the Kind UK logo looked like.

'Wow, that sounds great.' My voice was tight but I couldn't help it. I wondered if they'd noticed, but Orla and Maggie were too busy hunching over Maggie's phone screen, Orla pointing and saying, 'Yes, show them that one!'

Maggie turned her phone to show us the gleaming purple Toyota minivan, the doors emblazoned with the curved, lilac-coloured ribbon logo of Kind UK that looked like two people hugging.

'It might seem like a grand gesture,' said Maggie, 'but it's really so they can rope me in to transporting equipment, posters, merchandise and other members of staff to all our events.'

'Well, I think it's a thing of beauty,' said Orla. 'And I'm only a little bit pissed off you didn't get the promotion a few weeks earlier so you could have helped me move in.'

Everyone laughed and the rigid smile stamped itself back onto my face. *Loosen up, Jules. She's just being friendly. Isn't it a good thing she gets on with your friends?*

'Anyway,' said Maggie, pushing her phone back into her pocket. 'Tonight isn't supposed to be about me. It's about Jules's birthday! Sooooo . . .' She stood up and crossed to the kitchen, calling 'Kill the lights, please!' to which Orla leapt up and flicked the row of switches by the door.

There was a moment of silence then as the predictable, stumbling beginnings of 'Happy Birthday' rang out. The glowing cake made its way towards me, Maggie's beaming face illuminated above it as she trod gingerly from the kitchen, trying not to extinguish the candles.

I smiled and blew the candles out, and Nick instigated three cheers, which everyone joined in on with gusto. The cake was a glossy chocolate fudge, which Maggie knew was my favourite. She'd written my name on the top in swirly white lettering, a row of candles arched over the top.

'I thought I'd stop at ten candles,' she said.

'Very wise.' I nodded. 'Thank you so much, you lovely person.'

'You're welcome,' she said, winking before turning to retrieve a stack of dessert bowls, a knife and a small jug.

'God, Mags, you even remembered the cream!'

'Well, I wasn't going to go to the trouble of making your absolute favourite cake in the world and then spoiling it by not providing double cream, was I? What is it you said the last time we ate at the pub? *No one can possibly prefer chocolate fudge cake without cream. It's a scientific impossibility.*'

'Well, it's true!' I laughed.

I carved up the cake and we sat, shovelling in goopy mouthfuls, making appreciative noises. When we'd finished, Maggie produced a package wrapped in shiny gold paper, tied with a blue ribbon.

'Maggie, you made the cake, you honestly didn't need to—'

'OK, stop,' she said holding up her hand. 'It's your birthday . . . accept the bloody present!'

I sighed. 'Thank you.'

I pushed my chocolate-smeared bowl to one side and opened the present on the table. Inside was a rolled-up canvas tote bag that had my name printed in red letters on the side, then underneath 'loves wild swimming'. There were little printed pictures of woolly hats, ducks, goggles and fish. Inside the tote was a pair of woolly socks and a glittery, aquamarine thermal flask.

'Ah, this is so perfect!' I said, throwing my arms around Maggie and kissing her cheek before getting up to hug Nick. 'Thank you both so much.' I stroked the stripy woollen socks, feeling the softness beneath my fingers. Maggie knew how much wild swimming meant to me. A younger me would have turned her nose up at it, but since Mum died it had become a sort of therapy for me. I'd tried it once on a whim and had found the complete obliteration of every thought in my head from the shock of the cold water to be the closest thing to respite from my grief that I had ever experienced. I tried to go as often as I could, and when I was too busy and didn't make it for a while, I felt dark thoughts and sad memories clouding back into my mind like a storm on the horizon. That's when I knew I had to get back into the water.

'Sorry, it's yet another wild-swimming-themed pressie,' said Maggie, grinning apologetically.

'Please don't apologise! It's a theme I love,' I said. 'As you can see from the fact that gorgeous poster you got me for Christmas is hanging in pride of place at the top of the stairs.'

The poster was a beautiful, oversized watercolour of a woman from behind, walking into the sea. The words read: 'Into the water I go, to lose my mind and find my soul.' You could get similar prints from lots of online shops, but Maggie had commissioned a friend of hers to paint this one, and I adored it.

'Is that a hint?' said Scott, a mischievous smile playing at his lips.

'I don't know what you mean?' I said with a mock frown.

He turned to Maggie. 'Jules wants another screw fixing in the wall because the painting's so heavy.'

'Excuse me!' I slapped him playfully. 'Since when do I wait for my husband to do such jobs? I'm quite capable of drilling a hole and fixing a screw myself, thank you very much.'

'Don't burst his bubble, Jules,' Nick said. Then in a stage whisper, 'He's trying to look all manly in front of the guests.'

We all laughed, Scott the loudest.

'I'm so sorry, Jules.' Orla's voice broke through our laughter. Perhaps she didn't appreciate not being included in the banter. 'I didn't know it was your birthday, so I didn't have chance to get you anything.' She looked uncharacteristically serious.

'Oh my God, Orla, you weren't expected to get me a present, for goodness' sake! Until a few hours ago you thought you were going to be at work. Don't give it a second thought.'

In truth, I was thankful that Orla hadn't got me a present. I'd been concerned before about the blurred lines between Orla the lodger and Orla the friend. Something about her made me want to keep her firmly in the lodger camp. Her inclusion tonight had brought her further into our social circle, which had made me uneasy, but now I was at least relieved she hadn't bought me a gift. That would have tilted things even further.

'Here you go,' said Scott next to me, producing a small cubic gift wrapped in candy pink tissue paper.

'Oh God,' said Orla, and I turned to see her holding her phone, staring at the screen. There had been no ring tone, just like before when her work had called to cancel, but now she stared at the screen, an expression of worry etched into her features.

'Everything OK?' I asked.

'Yes . . . I . . . I just need to take this, I'm so sorry . . .' She flashed me an apologetic wince and hurried out of the room, leaving the kitchen door open as she entered the hallway.

I turned back to the present in my hands and read the tag. *To Jules, all my love, always, Scott xx*

As I smiled at him, Orla's voice came from the hallway. 'Really? No! You're joking?'

All heads turned towards the kitchen door. Orla was pacing up and down in the hallway, her phone clamped to her cheek. 'That's brilliant! Oh my God, thank you *so* much!' Her tone was so emphatic it sounded like she might burst into tears. She ended the call and strode back into the room, all the apologetic concern wiped clean from her face as she stopped dead with a cartoon-like grin.

'Guess what?'

'What!' we all chanted like a Greek chorus.

'I got the part! The one I auditioned for the other day – for the show in Shoreditch!'

'Wow, that's brilliant!' said Scott.

'I know!' She clasped her hand to her chest in that familiar, theatrical gesture. 'I mean, the director is one I've been dying to get on my CV, and the theatre company is just . . . ahhhh, I'm so happy!' She did a little bounce on her feet, her blonde waves bobbing around her shoulders.

'Congratulations!' Maggie was on her feet and hugging Orla, so I stood up too, making my way round the table with Scott's present still clutched in my hand.

I pulled her into a hug, patting her back and saying, 'You clever thing, well done you!'

The room was suddenly buzzing again; the mellow atmosphere of the post-cake present-giving seemed to have evaporated.

'I just . . . I'm sorry I'm going to have to celebrate this!' She swept over to the fridge and flung open the door, pulling out the bottle of pink prosecco I'd bought in Sainsbury's.

'Quite right!' Scott chimed. 'I'll get the glasses!'

I watched them all leaping into action, Orla untwisting the wire from the neck of the bottle, Scott delving into the cupboard over the toaster for the champagne flutes, Nick putting the remains of my birthday cake back in the tin, and Maggie clearing away the bowls to make room on the dining table.

I didn't know what to do, so I just stood there watching, then silently placed my unopened present back on the table. No one seemed to notice I was the only one not helping. They chattered away, firing questions at Orla about the show and who the director was and what size theatre she'd be performing in, and before I knew it a flute of pink fizz was pushed into my hand and we were all standing around the kitchen island, raising our glasses and toasting 'To Orla!' with the prosecco I'd bought for my birthday.

Chapter Eight

The next few weeks were a relief. Orla was in rehearsals for the Shoreditch play, after which she usually went for drinks with cast members or, if she finished early, had shifts booked in at the hotel. This meant she was out until late, and Scott and I hardly saw her.

In the days following my birthday, I'd thought a lot about Orla. As with the keys, and the lost phone, and the dizzy spell in Richmond Park, there were dual feelings battling against each other. Why was I so bothered she'd opened my birthday prosecco? It was because the occasion was supposed to be a celebration of my birthday, and Orla had commandeered it. But had she? Maggie and Nick were there, Scott had cooked a delicious meal, Maggie had made me a cake, I had gifts to open . . . everyone had made such a fuss of me. Was I really that bothered we'd ended the evening toasting Orla's achievement? By my own admission, I didn't like being made a fuss of and wasn't good at being the centre of attention. So shouldn't I have felt relieved when Orla's good news took the heat off me?

I'd opened Scott's present on our bed that night, sitting cross-legged opposite him on top of the duvet. It was a delicate golden chain with a circular pendant upon which was engraved a curly, cresting wave.

Scott had given me a bashful smile. 'I guess Maggie and I both went for the same watery theme . . . great minds and all that.'

'It's so beautiful,' I'd said, running my index finger over the ridges of the engraving. 'Thank you.'

I'd leaned forwards and kissed him. He wasn't always the most romantic gift buyer, so I knew he'd really put some thought into this. As we'd sat on the bed together I'd wondered about asking Scott about Orla's announcement and the prosecco, but then I'd felt that familiar stab of uncertainty. What exactly would my point be? That she shouldn't have told us her fantastic news? That we should all have pretended it hadn't happened just because it was my birthday? That we shouldn't have been excited for her and celebrated with a toast? All of these thoughts were ridiculous, so I put them from my mind and instead focused on what a wonderful evening my lovely husband had planned for me.

And after a week or so of not really seeing Orla, these thoughts faded until they took up no space in my head at all, leaving plenty of room for thoughts of new projects, contracts and art supply orders.

One Sunday morning in early April, I dragged myself sleepily into the kitchen in search of coffee. I flicked on the kettle to make a tea for Scott (who was still in bed), and slotted a shiny turquoise coffee capsule into my machine, choosing my favourite chunky yellow mug. As I yawned and circled my shoulders, my gaze snagged on movement in the garden. It was Orla. She was crouched down in the unruly grass, dew darkening the hem of her pale green skirt. Her back was to the window, her slim frame wrapped in a thick-knit cream cardigan. She straightened and turned slightly to one side, and I saw she was holding a thick, red candle. The flame stuttered in the spring breeze, and she brought her other hand up to shield it. She closed her eyes and tilted her head to the sky, her mouth forming silent words. Was she praying? Was this some kind of ritual we'd never noticed her performing before?

The coffee machine began spluttering as it ran out of water, and I turned and hastily flicked it off. When I looked back up, Orla was staring straight at me. A smile flickered on her lips and I raised my hand in a subdued greeting, somehow sensing this wasn't the moment to shout 'morning!' and wave. She gave me a sad smile and I knew I couldn't just go back to making my coffee. I walked around the kitchen island and slid open the patio doors, stepping out into the chilly air. I hugged my fluffy dressing gown around me.

Orla still stood with the candle. 'Sorry, I didn't think anyone would notice at this time.'

'Don't say sorry. Are you OK?'

She nodded, her eyes flickering towards the candle, then back to me. 'I'm fine. It's . . . it's silly, really.' She placed the candle on the circular wrought-iron table we'd been meaning to get rid of for the past couple of years as the white paint was peeling and the rust had set in. 'It's just today is . . . well.' She took a deep breath. 'Today is the ninth anniversary of my dad's death. It's just a silly thing I do every year.'

'I'm so sorry, Orla.' I felt a swell of tenderness towards her. I knew what it was like to lose a cherished parent.

'The happiest memories I have from my childhood are playing with my dad in the garden of our little terraced house. It was a bit like this, you know? A patch of grass and a small patio. So anyway, every year I go outside wherever I happen to be living, and I light a candle and just . . . have a chat with him, really. Sounds stupid when I explain it.' She wrinkled her nose and gave her head a little shake.

'It doesn't sound stupid at all.' My voice was emphatic, and Orla looked deep into my eyes, the pale blue of hers seeming to intensify the longer she stared. 'My . . . my mum died five years ago, and I still talk to her all the time.'

'Oh, Jules. I'm so sorry – I had no idea.' She strode quickly towards me and wrapped her arms around me, squeezing me ferociously. She smelt of smoke and lavender.

Then she released me, holding me at arm's length for a moment before turning towards the patio chair and opening a wooden box I hadn't noticed sitting there. It was made of dark, chunky wood, and looked like something you'd find in one of those hippy shops that sold incense and crystals. Small motifs were crudely carved around the sides. Elephants, perhaps.

Orla ran her slender fingers over the contents before snatching something up and turning towards me with another candle, this one pine green and smaller than her red one. 'Let's light a candle for your mum too.' Her face was suddenly animated, a look of something akin to glee radiating from her.

I felt something fall inside me. 'Um . . . I'm not sure I need—'

'Please, Jules. Honestly, just try it. I promise it'll make you feel so much better, releasing some of that grief to the sky, bringing you closer to your mum . . .'

There was no way I could say no after her little speech, so I gave a stilted smile and took the candle from her outstretched hand, holding it aloft as she flicked a small silver lighter against the wick.

'Now close your eyes,' she instructed.

Oh God, please don't make me speak, I thought.

'And say, or think – internalise or externalise – any feelings you'd like to share with your lovely mum right now.'

I closed my eyes and bit my bottom lip as an image of my mum pursing her own lips together, trying not to laugh, came to mind. *Mum, don't!* I internalised this celestial warning. *This would be the worst moment to start laughing, please don't make me laugh . . .* In my mind's eye I saw her silently draw her fingers across her lips, as if zipping them closed. I felt a smile creeping onto my face.

'Oh, Jules, that's wonderful! You're smiling! Do you feel connected to your mum by whatever message it was you sent her?' I opened my eyes and looked at Orla's radiant face.

For some reason, and taking me completely by surprise, I felt tears prick my eyes and blinked, panicking they might be about to tumble down my cheeks. I cleared my throat and gave a soft laugh. 'Actually, yes. I do.' I smiled at her and she reached her hand out to squeeze my arm gently. 'Thank you,' I added.

'Thank *you* for joining me in this. This is one anniversary I won't forget. Perhaps your mum and my dad are up there right now laughing at their daughters lighting candles in the garden.'

'Maybe.' I nodded. This had been a strange experience, but not entirely unpleasant.

I watched Orla packing away the candles and the lighter into the wooden box. 'Coffee?' I said.

'Oh God, yes! I'd *kill* for a coffee right now.'

I thought about Orla and her little ritual as I slipped into the frigid water of the Thames a week later. It was my first swim of the year and I'd been experiencing that itch inside me to get back into the wild swimming. The weather was mellowing, but still I gasped as the shock of the water hit me. I left myself no time to dwell on it, forcing my head down and under the surface, pushing my arms through the icy water while my limbs screamed. Surfacing and feeling that rush of dopamine, I thought about how we all have our coping mechanisms when dealing with grief. Perhaps Orla was more of an introspective griever who liked to light candles and send up prayers, whereas I preferred replacing maudlin thoughts with the adrenaline of immersing myself in freezing cold water. It's not that I didn't think about Mum in quieter times or speak to her – of course I did. But I didn't feel compelled to mark the date of her death by lighting candles or any such rituals.

I thought back to the conversation I'd had with Orla in the kitchen after the episode with the candles. I'd shared with her that Mum had died of breast cancer, and that it had been full-on in terms of care as I was an only child and my dad had died when I was four.

Mostly, I felt for my mum, as she was so distraught at me being left on my own. I'd told her I wasn't alone, that I had Scott, and that we were going to have babies and live long, full, busy lives. She'd liked hearing that. I'd sit by the side of her bed at home in those final days, stroking her paper-thin skin and staring into her bloated face that was barely recognisable as that of the woman who'd cared for me my whole life, and I'd talk to her about Scott and our future babies, and sometimes she'd manage a laugh, and I'd think, *There you are, Mum . . . you're still in there.*

Orla had listened to my recounting of this time, occasionally reaching her hand across the table to squeeze mine. Then she'd told me about her dad. About moving back to Ireland to spend more time with him when he became ill, but her younger brother being hostile and possessive over his care. 'But why would he be like that? Why wouldn't he let you help?' I'd asked. What followed had been a heartbreaking story of a childhood with an overbearing sibling and a grieving father who'd never got over the fact his wife, Orla's mother, had left him and the children when Orla was only four.

'It sounds like you had an amazing dad, though.'

She'd sniffed and nodded. 'Oh yes, he was amazing. And whenever Sean wasn't around, we'd have an absolute blast. I just . . . I wish I'd been there when he died. After Sean threw me out of the house, I came back to London. I think I believed everything would be OK in the end. I don't think it had really hit me that it might be the last time I ever saw him. I went to his funeral, of course. But . . . that's the last time I went back.'

I swam over to the low, grassy bank where I'd left my things, hauling myself out of the water, skin burning. I wondered if I should offer to take Orla wild swimming. She'd shared her ritual with me, perhaps I should share mine with her. But as I dried my reddened skin, eyes falling on my puffy dryrobe, the thermos flask Maggie had given me, my stash of cookies I always brought, I felt a pang of possessiveness. I didn't want to share this with her. This was *my* thing. It was something I did alone. It wouldn't be the same with someone else's chatter in my ears. And I also had a niggling fear that if I did bring her along once, she'd expect to be invited every time. I imagined sneaking out of the house with my things, clicking the boot of the car shut quietly so she didn't hear and rush out to join me. No, that would be disastrous.

It's working. Jules seems to be mellowing towards me a bit. It was great that I got to hang out with them on Jules's birthday – that really got my feet under the table. I think we bonded a bit more from that. And the huge bonus there was meeting Maggie. Oh my goodness, what an absolute angel of a woman! The most fun, generous, empathetic person you could ever wish to meet. And that in itself reassured me – because someone like Maggie wouldn't be friends with someone like Jules unless she thought she was a good egg . . . so I'm still confident I'm on the right track. That I've chosen well.

I'm glad Jules and I had that special moment in the garden with the candles, too. It seemed to break down even more of those barriers between us . . . maybe thawed some of her frostiness? Scott and I are already close, obviously – we spark off each other. Kindred spirits. But Jules isn't quite there. At least, she wasn't, before the candles. I could see her scepticism as soon as I explained what I was doing, so I'm glad I stuck to my guns and made her do it – she really seemed to connect to her mother's energy then, and she was grateful to me. It was a lovely moment. And then we had coffee and

I had a chance to explain about my family – however depressing that situation might be.

So yes, all in all I'm happy with how it's going. I sense I'm finally winning her over.

Chapter Nine

The following weekend we went to see Orla's play in Shoreditch. She wasn't a lead character in this one, but the production was good and I found I could follow the Austen-esque storyline more easily than the previous play. Scott and I joked that we'd become theatre aficionados, thanks to Orla.

The three of us had a drink in a nearby pub afterwards. This time there were no lost keys or phones, but Orla was unusually subdued and I felt a knot of anticipation clench inside me as we shrugged on our coats to leave. It sounds silly and overdramatic, but I wanted to pull Scott to one side and whisper, *Something's going to happen on the way home. You wait.* But at the time, saying something felt bitchy and unnecessary. After all, I had no tangible reason to feel this way.

We waited for our train home at Waterloo, sitting on a metal bench facing the departure boards. Orla, who had complained of a headache on the Tube, was now leaning forwards and circling her fingers at her temples, a deep frown creasing her face.

Scott placed a tentative hand on her back. 'Do you need some painkillers? I can go and get—'

'No, really, I'm fine,' she offered weakly.

Scott flashed me a tense smile before getting up and striding over to the sandwich bar between platforms five and six. He returned a minute later with a large bottle of chilled water, which he handed to Orla.

She didn't say anything, but closed her eyes as she took several sips, then replaced the cap and held it to her forehead, her head thrown back and her golden waves falling around her shoulders. I noticed several passers-by casting her glances, which looked either concerned or simply intrigued. Scott's gaze remained on Orla, only breaking it to look at me with the occasional questioning expression, as if I should know what to do or say.

But when they announced our platform, all I could manage was a terse, 'Let's just try and get home, shall we?'

Scott helped Orla to stand and continued to hold on to her elbow as he guided her through the ticket barrier and onto the train. I found myself trailing behind, holding her rucksack and coat, my own handbag slung awkwardly over one shoulder. Despite the cold weather, the carriage was stuffy, the dark windows frosted with condensation. We pushed further inside, my hopes of finding at least one seat free slipping further away with every step. But I needn't have worried on Orla's account; a man in a navy suit hastily folded his laptop and sprang to his feet as soon as his gaze alighted on her hunched form.

We thanked him and settled Orla down. I found myself casting reassuring smiles at fellow passengers who were looking at us enquiringly. Orla remained oblivious to these glances, her eyes still closed, her water bottle still clasped to her forehead. I thought back to the episode in Richmond Park, the taxi ride home, Orla's promise that she'd go and see a GP about her dizzy spells. Although this seemed different. This seemed more like a migraine than a dizzy spell. I wondered if she'd been to see a doctor, but realised this wouldn't be the right moment to ask. The train stopped at Clapham Junction and I saw her eyes flicker open for a moment, taking in the thinning crowd as people pushed to alight onto the drizzly platform. Now there was room to breathe and I felt a slight releasing of pressure inside me as I found the room to inch my heels apart and set Orla's heavy rucksack on the floor.

'Perhaps we should get a taxi from the station,' suggested Scott. 'I don't think she should be walking all that way up Richmond Road if she's feeling like this.'

I nodded, reaching for my phone in my coat pocket. I tapped on the screen to unlock it. 'Yeah, maybe an Uber is best.' I felt the train slow as it pulled into Norbiton station.

As I clicked into the Uber app on my phone and went to select our postcode, I noticed Orla stand. I turned towards her. 'We've still got one more stop—' But my words were cut off as the bottle of water slipped from Orla's grasp and her eyes widened then closed. I watched her sway, then pitch forwards and collapse, landing with a thud, her hair a messy halo of gold against the grubby carriage floor.

A woman screamed, more people gasped, the man with the laptop swore loudly. The air was suddenly filled with a high-pitched whining sound, and I looked up to see a white-haired woman with a Sainsbury's bag for life holding onto the passenger emergency alarm. Scott was already crouched down next to Orla, saying her name over and over, trying to get a response. I felt strangely removed from the situation. Eyes were on me, as if people were expecting me to do something, but I felt paralysed.

Unfreezing, I dumped the bags and coats on an empty seat and crouched down like Scott. 'Let's get her into the recovery position,' I said, my voice sounding bizarrely calm.

'I don't know how to do that!' said Scott, his voice shaky with panic.

'It's OK, I do,' I said, adjusting the position of Orla's legs and pushing her onto her side, raising one arm above her head.

'Yes, ambulance please . . .' I looked at Scott to see him pressing his phone against his face. 'Norbiton station . . . we're on the train that's on . . . oh shit, what platform are we on?'

A tall man in a tracksuit and huge white trainers jumped onto the platform and called back, 'Platform two!'

'. . . Two, platform two . . . yes . . .'

I listened to him giving the details of what had happened while I pushed Orla's hair from her face and repeated her name. Her eyes remained closed and her breathing seemed steady. She looked like she was asleep. I gave her shoulder a shake and said her name more loudly, but she didn't respond.

By the time the paramedics arrived there were fewer people on the train, most having decided the situation was under control and that they needed to find alternative routes home. But a few bystanders remained, clearly hoping to see this particular drama to the end.

'Do you know this lady?' said a male paramedic in a thick south London accent as he leaned over Orla, lifting her eyelids and shining a light into her rolling eyes.

'Yes, she's our friend,' said Scott without a moment's hesitation.

A snide part of my brain I was trying to silence added, *She's our lodger, actually. There's a difference.*

When he'd ascertained her family were back in Ireland, and she had no next of kin here, we were told one of us could travel to the hospital with her in the ambulance.

'You should go,' said Scott in a hushed, urgent tone.

'Why me?'

'Because you're a woman, and it looks weird if I go . . . plus, they might want to test, you know, women's things . . .'

'Women's things?' I said, casting him what I hoped was an appalled look.

'You know what I mean, Jules, don't be obtuse.'

'So you know the word "obtuse", but not the words for "women's things"?'

'OK, now's *not* the time!' His tone was sharp, and I realised with the sting of his reproach that he was right. I was being ridiculous.

'OK, I'll go with her.'

He gave a curt nod, and I turned and followed Orla, strapped into her stretcher with a red blanket over her, still seemingly unconscious.

Orla was wheeled though heavy swing doors, down several white corridors, and eventually through a waiting room where I was told, 'Please wait here', before watching them push the trolley through yet another set of doors. I settled myself on a red plastic chair attached in a row to others by a metal bar that ran under the seats. A mother tried to cradle a writhing toddler a few seats down, but he was too restless, and I felt the rocking and juddering of the seat under me as he fought to free himself. A woman with black straggly hair rested her head in her hands, and I couldn't tell if she was crying, sleeping, or just trying to find a comfortable position.

Doctors and nurses in varying uniform colours walked through and I glanced at the signs on the wall, trying to guess who belonged where. *Orthopaedics. Haematology. Cytology. Chaplaincy. Diagnostic imaging.* I wondered where Orla was and what she was having done to her.

I texted Scott intermittently, then messed around on my phone for a while until it clicked into low battery mode, then I slid it into my handbag, deciding to save it for getting an Uber home. I was contemplating finding a vending machine for a coffee, when one of the double doors opened and I was taken aback to see Orla emerge, her expression grave and one sleeve of her red jumper pushed up above the elbow to reveal a taped-on cotton-wool bud, where they must have taken blood. She hobbled over to me, blinking slowly and offering me a weak smile.

'Hey . . .' I said, taking a step towards her and extending my hand to squeeze her good arm. 'Have . . . have they discharged you?'

She closed her eyes and nodded. 'Yes . . . they've done some tests . . . said I really need to get some answers about what's been happening.' Her nods changed to shakes. 'They're a bit concerned, to be honest, so the lead paramedic said he was going to escalate my case to . . . I don't know, some specialist or something?' She shrugged and winced as if the action caused her physical pain.

I wanted to say, *Well, they're not concerned enough to keep you in longer than an hour*, but what I actually said was, 'The main thing is we can get you home, yeah?'

We walked slowly back along the corridors and I held the heavy doors open for Orla. At the entrance to the hospital I helped her into her coat, then crossed to a black cab, as there was a taxi rank just there. We were silent in the car. In the kitchen Orla repeated what she'd told me about the paramedics being concerned, then saying they'd taken her blood and were going to fast-track it through haematology because they were so worried about her.

I watched Scott's expression as Orla explained. He never took his eyes off her, his expression set in a grim picture of concern.

'You'll tell us the results when they come back, won't you?'

'Scott,' I said, more harshly than I'd intended. 'Orla doesn't have to share her medical results with us.'

'No, I just meant—'

'It's OK,' Orla interjected, holding up a hand. 'I know what Scott means. He just wants to know if there's anything of concern I should share with you. After all, we are living together.' It was the first time I'd seen her smile since we left the pub.

'Yes, that's exactly what I meant,' he said, casting a grateful glance at Orla, then turning back to me with a scowl. 'We're Orla's de facto family here – we've got to look out for her.'

De facto family. I tried not to let my face contort into an incredulous frown. For the second time that night I wanted to shout, 'She's our *lodger*!' at him.

Orla let out a small whimper then, and Scott and I broke eye contact to turn towards her. She held her fingers to her lips, and I was shocked to see her eyes brimming with tears. Her gaze was set on Scott and she gave a little sniff before she spoke. 'That's . . . that's just so lovely, thank you. No one's ever . . . it really does feel like you guys are sort of my guardian angels.'

She lunged forwards and wrapped her arms around Scott, who flinched in surprise before reciprocating her hug with a good-natured laugh. 'Of course,' he said, patting her back rather awkwardly.

When it was my turn to be hugged I found myself inwardly wincing. This was not what maintaining distance between us and our lodger should feel like. Orla's tall frame dwarfed me, her hair enveloping me in its lavender-scented softness as she leaned over me. I felt like a child being hugged against her will by an overemotional aunt. She pulled away, holding me at arm's length and offering me a watery smile.

'Perhaps we should all try and get some sleep,' were the only words I could find.

'Sleep sounds glorious,' she said, and I detected a hint of the familiar, theatrically confident Orla peeping back through. This Orla was a world away from the ghost of a woman we'd ushered onto the train at Waterloo only a few hours ago.

As we all trudged our way up the stairs, whispering goodnights to each other as if there were other sleeping people in the house to be mindful of, I made a decision. I needed to speak to Scott about Orla. I needed to tentatively put forward the idea of finding a different lodger. I couldn't continue to feel like this around her. But I also realised I'd need to explain it better. Scott seemed genuinely fond of Orla, and I'd need to offer him proper reasons for asking her to move out. 'There's something not quite right about her,' wasn't going to wash. Neither was 'I don't completely trust her' or 'she's getting too close to us'. No. I'd have to think of a better way of explaining myself. Because at this point I knew that if she stayed around much longer, things would get worse. Much worse.

Chapter Ten

The moment to bring up the subject came a few days later. Orla was out, and Scott and I spent a blissful evening sitting at the metal table in the garden, sharing a bottle of rosé and savouring the last rays of what felt like a summer sun. We made plans for the garden, which primarily involved us buying a lawnmower that actually worked rather than the rusted box of rattling metal that had belonged to Scott's aunt. I talked about 'climbing plants' and 'herbaceous borders' and 'perennials' as if I knew what those words really meant, and we agreed to visit a garden centre at some point in the next few weeks.

We clinked glasses and Scott grinned at me, both of us drawing breath and pronouncing in unison, 'It *could* look lovely,' which had become our go-to sentence whenever we discussed the garden.

I was feeling so relaxed and happy, it seemed a shame to spoil it by talking about Orla, but I didn't want to put it off any longer.

I took a gulp of wine. 'Can we talk about Orla for a minute?'

Scott looked at me with a puzzled amusement. 'Sure.' He shrugged. 'Sounds serious.'

'No, it's not that . . .' I sighed. 'Look . . . she's a lot of fun, and for the four months she's been here, it's mainly been working out—'

'But?'

'But something about her puts me on edge. I can't articulate it properly, which is really frustrating, but . . . she's always the centre of attention whenever she's around. Haven't you noticed?'

Scott rubbed at his mousey stubble. 'I mean, she's an actress, so I guess maybe she can be a bit . . . OTT?'

'But it's more than that. It's not just that she's flamboyant or eccentric. I mean, she's both those things, and that's fine, but it's just the fact that I'm always waiting for something to happen. Waiting for her to lose her keys or faint or . . . step in front of a bus or something.'

'Jules, that's quite a dramatic thing to say.'

'Well, she's a dramatic person!' I threw the comment back to him like a child arguing with a sibling.

'OK, so what are we saying? That the lodger thing has run its course?'

I shifted uncomfortably. I knew we needed the income. And I hated to admit it, but I longed for the days when it was just Scott and me in the house. When I wasn't creeping in wondering if Orla was going to be in the kitchen making a cup of tea, or wafting around the garden lighting candles and speaking to dead relatives, or gatecrashing one of our get-togethers with Maggie and Nick. We'd tried it for a good four months, and we'd give her a couple of months' notice, longer than was statutory, so she had plenty of time to find somewhere else.

'What are we going to tell her?' asked Scott. 'It feels a bit awkward to say we just want her to leave.' He wrinkled his nose and I felt my insides squirm.

'I don't know.' I sighed then took another sip of wine. 'I'll think of something, just leave it with me.'

This would need careful navigating if we didn't want to offend Orla. I was tempted to think of an outright lie, just to avoid her thinking she'd done anything wrong. Because she hadn't. She was an entertaining person, and people gravitated towards her. I saw the looks in strangers' eyes when she bestowed a smile or a kind word. The blush of the taxi driver, the beam of the waiter, the cluster of people that always seemed to spring from nowhere to assist her when she needed them to retrieve her phone from a locked room or provide her with a bottle of cold water or . . . or ask her if she was OK as she searched frantically for her lost keys. Yes, Scott and I had both fallen under Orla's spell the first time we'd seen her. She was a compelling mixture of charisma and eccentricity, but with a hint of vulnerability. And that mix could be endearing. Something about asking her to leave made me feel awful. And guilty. She hadn't done anything *wrong*, and I couldn't face admitting to her that I simply wanted my house back.

I gave myself a few days to think about what I was going to say to her, a creeping nausea sitting heavily in my stomach. I found it hard to concentrate on work. I kept finding my attention drifting, my gaze rising from the paper on my desk and fixing blindly ahead on the street through my window. One morning I felt so wretched after my coffee I ran to the downstairs bathroom, convinced

I was about to be sick, my diaphragm spasming as I leaned over the toilet bowl. I looked in the small mirror over the basin, my skin pale and grey shadows smudging under my eyes. If worrying about Orla was doing this to me, I really needed to get a move on and speak to her.

The following Saturday I still wasn't feeling better, so I shuffled to the bathroom while Scott was on his morning run. I opened the cabinet, rifling through the shelves for something that might take away this nausea ... Alka-Seltzer or something similar. It was as I was shifting packets and bottles from side to side that my eyes fell on a tattered oblong box I hadn't thought about for three years. I remembered buying it when we were living in New Cross, just before I started taking regular birth control. We'd had a scare when my period had been three days late, and I'd rushed to the pharmacy, getting there only two minutes before it closed on a Friday night. I'd been terrified, then cried so hard with relief when the test had been negative. But since then we'd got married, and we'd started talking about perhaps trying for a baby in a year or so, and as my fingers rested on the thin card of the box, stroking the pink lettering on the side, I suddenly knew, even without taking the test, that I was pregnant. Why had this not occurred to me?

The pill I was on meant I didn't really get periods, and if I did they were unpredictable and didn't last long. Plus I wasn't the most organised person when it came to taking the pills and clearly the idea of becoming pregnant didn't hold the terror it once had ... so, of course, that's what it was.

I was surprised at myself. I'd felt as reluctant about having a baby as I had about getting a lodger. But for some reason, this felt right. I followed the instructions on the box, briefly wondering whether these things expired and if I should get a new one just to make sure. I rested the test on the edge of the bath as I waited for the results to show, my heart beating hard against my ribs as I imagined the look on Scott's face if I showed him a positive test when he came back from his run.

I peeked through my fingers, then lowered my hand, then reached forwards and held the test up to inspect the tiny window. Two red lines. My heart lurched and heat surged up through me, making my cheeks burn hot. I was pregnant. I felt my lips curve into a smile. OK, it wasn't perfectly planned in terms of timing. We'd decided we were going to think about it more, save up some more money . . . but now that it had happened, I realised how much I wanted this. As much as I'd been teasing Scott about his eagerness, and trying to play my own enthusiasm down, now I was going to have to admit I was head over heels in love with the idea. And I knew Scott would be too.

'Jules?' I flinched at my name called through the door. It was Orla.

'Yes?'

'So sorry to bug you. Any chance I could have a bath? I'm feeling really achy this morning. Hope I'm not coming down with something.'

'Ummm . . . yeah, sure.'

'Only if you're not having one?'

'No . . . no, I'm finished in here. I'll be out in a second.'

'No rush!'

I heard her footsteps pad back up to the attic room and stared again at the two dark red lines. Replacing the cap on the test and pushing the empty box down into the wastepaper basket under two empty loo rolls, I stood up and turned on the tap in the bath.

'Bath's running for you,' I called up the stairs on my way to the bedroom.

'You're an angel,' Orla called back down.

I went into our bedroom and closed the door, taking the test out of my dressing-gown pocket, sitting on the bed and staring at it, unable to wipe the grin off my face.

As I heard Orla walking back down the stairs, gently humming under her breath, I realised the timing was perfect. I'd been so stressed at the idea of explaining to Orla why she had to leave. Wondering what possible lie I could think up that would stop her feeling offended. And now I didn't have to. What could be more reasonable than a couple asking a lodger to leave because they were having a baby? We'd need the extra space, we'd probably need to redecorate the attic, or at least spruce it up a bit, and we'd need extra room for the storage of baby things. It made sense. And I was confident Orla would completely understand.

Chapter Eleven

Scott got home ten minutes later, and I felt my heart flutter at his footsteps on the stairs. I was still sitting on the edge of the bed when he pushed the door open, his T-shirt translucent with sweat and his sandy hair darkened with moisture and sticking up at all angles. He grinned and took his AirPods out, dropping them on the bedside table and leaning over to plant a kiss on my lips.

'Hey, lazy bones. You still in your PJs?'

'I got a bit distracted so I haven't had a shower yet.'

'OK,' he said, pulling his T-shirt off over his head. 'Can I jump in before you then? I'll only be five minutes.'

'Actually, Orla's in there having a bath. Says she's achy and might be coming down with something.'

'Oh, OK. I can wait.' He tossed his clothes into the laundry basket and grabbed a bath towel hanging from the back of the bedroom door, wrapping it round his waist before sitting on the bed next to me.

He leaned into me and nuzzled my neck. 'We can kill some time while we wait, can't we?'

I laughed and gently pushed him away, sliding the pregnancy test out of my dressing-gown pocket. 'Actually, I've got something to show you.' I held it up for him to see.

He blinked at the test, puzzled. 'What am I looking at?'

'Do you know what this is?'

'I . . .' His gaze flicked between the test and me and back again, his lips curving into a hesitant smile. 'I think I do . . . but . . .'

'But what?'

'What are you saying? What does this mean?'

I laughed and leaned in to him, kissing him tenderly then whispering, 'It means we're going to have a baby.'

Scott sprang up, hands going to his mouth, then back down, his face glowing with the biggest smile I'd ever seen on him, his cheeks looking like they were about to burst. He sat back down and grabbed my hands in his and I could see tears brimming in his eyes. He pulled me into his arms and I didn't push him away or tell him he was too sweaty. I slid my hands around his back and we held each other for silent seconds as it all sunk in. We were having a baby. We were going to be parents.

'And . . .' he said, pulling away and seeming to struggle to find the words he needed. 'You're . . . you're OK with this? I mean, it wasn't like we planned it right now, we were going to wait a little longer—'

'I thought I wanted to wait. I thought I was unsure about the whole thing, but as soon as I did the test I knew I wanted it to be positive so badly. I know this is right for us. Right now. I . . . I'm so happy!'

'Ah, this is the best day of my life, Jules!' He jumped up again and punched the air like I'd seen him do watching football. 'I mean, don't get me wrong, our wedding day was pretty awesome, but *this*!'

I laughed again, loving every moment watching him. 'I know. I agree, this feels like a pretty perfect moment.'

There was a knock on the door. 'Bathroom's free!' Orla chirped.

'Thanks,' I called back, not wanting this moment to be burst by anything. Wanting to stay floating like this with Scott in our own bubble of euphoria.

'I think the bath helped a bit, actually,' her muffled voice continued through the door. 'I'm feeling less achy now.'

'Great, that's good,' I said, willing her to traipse back up to the attic.

I glanced at Scott who was wandering around the room, still grinning, picking things up and putting them down at random, completely consumed by our news.

'I'm going to get dressed and head to work, but I'll be back this evening,' Orla said.

'OK. See you later.' *Please just go.*

I looked over at Scott who'd stopped pacing and was looking at the bedroom door. He sank back down onto the bed next to me and together we listened to Orla's retreating footsteps. He picked up my hand and moved his thumb gently over my knuckles. 'This is a good time to ask her to find somewhere else to live, I think.'

Relief flooded through me. 'Yes. Exactly what I was thinking.'

'Perhaps we could talk to her this evening when she gets back? Have a proper sit down, tell her our news and explain we need the place to ourselves to prepare for the baby?'

I nodded and rested my head against Scott's shoulder. 'Perfect,' I said.

I had a picture-book deadline fast approaching so had planned to get a good amount of work done that day, even though it was the weekend. But the more I tried to focus, the more my mind played and replayed what I was going to say to Orla that evening. Admittedly, my imaginary conversation with her had become easier since I'd learnt I was pregnant. After all, now I had a solid reason for suggesting she find somewhere else to live. And I had Scott's full support, too. He knew how important it was that we had our own space in the coming months. And it's not like we were asking her to move out as soon as she'd arrived – if we gave her a couple of months' notice, she'd have been with us six months. Of course, things would get tighter with money again, but we reasoned that six months of rental income would still have helped with our loan repayments. And as far as Orla was concerned, she'd described herself as a 'bit of a nomad' when she'd first moved in, so I really couldn't see this being a big problem for her, especially as she seemed to have so many friends who would no doubt be up for house sharing.

I found my hand going to rest on my stomach and stroking it, a ridiculous impulse when I knew the 'baby' was made up of only a few cells at this point. But, I reasoned, he or she was still *there*. Still *real*. By mid-afternoon I'd given up trying to concentrate and downloaded a baby development app onto my phone, before logging onto my GP's booking system and making an appointment – a quick Google search had informed me that was the first thing I needed to do in order to be referred to the hospital for scans etc.

At five o'clock there was a knock on the door and Scott's head peeped around, the grin on his face just as big as it had been that morning when I'd first told him.

'Aren't your cheeks hurting yet?' I laughed.

'Absolutely, but I just can't stop!' He shuffled into the room. 'Please say you can stop work now and we can go to the pub for a celebratory drink?'

I dropped my paintbrush into the cloudy pot of water. 'Lovely idea. Let's do it! Although mine will have to be an orange juice or something equally boring, won't it?'

'Oh God, yeah, forgot about that.' He winced, ruefully. 'Do you mind if I have a pint though?'

'Course I don't. You're drinking for two now,' I said. 'Let's go.'

We walked hand in hand to the pub, the sun warming my skin as my thoughts swam with images of babies and all the details of pregnancy, along with intermittent flashes of Orla's face. I imagined her leaning in to kiss me on both cheeks and squeaking with excitement for us when we broke the news to her. I imagined her expression growing serious and her nods of understanding as we explained we'd need the attic room back. I imagined her saying something like, 'Oh gosh, *please* don't feel bad, I *totally* understand!'

We sat in the pub, on the same sofa I'd occupied the first time we'd met Orla. Scott nursed a pint and I sipped a J2O.

We talked about what it had been like doing the pregnancy test and why I'd chosen that particular moment, and Scott asked me how I'd felt the second I'd seen those two red lines. And I told him the truth – I'd felt a surge of complete elation, which made me realise this was absolutely what I wanted.

We talked about whether we thought it would be a girl or a boy (he thought boy, I thought girl), but neither of us expressed a preference. We talked potential names and we realised for the first time in our relationship that I had a higher tolerance for the unusual than Scott did.

'What's wrong with "River"?' I asked. 'OK, it's not exactly in the same region as "John", but it's unusual . . . and it's a cool word—'

'Just because something's a "cool word" doesn't make it a good candidate for a human name! "Taramasalata" is a cool word – doesn't mean we should name our child that.'

'I don't know,' I said with a mischievous shrug. 'It shortens nicely to "Tara", I suppose?'

He let out a raucous laugh. 'Oh my God, I can see I'm going to have to fight my corner on this!'

Our conversation moved on to talking about Orla, and what we were going to say to her when she got home.

'I think we just need to sit her down and be honest,' I said. 'We can explain that the pregnancy was unplanned, that although we knew we wanted kids, we didn't mean for it to happen so soon. It's not like we'd intended on asking her to move out six months after she'd moved in.'

Scott nodded thoughtfully. 'Yeah, I think that's the best approach. And it's not like six months is a flash in the pan, is it? She's had a good run of it. Plus, like you said before, we will give her two months' notice, which is loads more than the standard notice you have to give lodgers.'

'Yep. Sounds good.'

We finished our drinks and ambled back towards home. It was nearly time for Orla to get back from work, and although a tiny part of me was bubbling with nerves, the overwhelming feeling I had at that time was of euphoria at the pregnancy. That feeling of walking on air obliterated everything else and made me feel that nothing that could happen could dampen down this soaring feeling that floated through me. The only twinge of soreness came when I thought about how much I longed to call my mum and share the news with her. She would have been so happy for me and for Scott.

I pushed open the front door, kicking my shoes off as Scott closed the door behind us.

'Tea?' I said, walking through to the kitchen.

'Actually, I really fancy another beer now,' Scott called after me.

'Show off!' I called back, crossing to the kettle and filling it at the sink.

It was as I turned to rest it back on its cradle that I noticed Orla sitting at the dining table.

'Shit!' I shouted, my hand flying to my chest, heart beating furiously. 'Jesus, you made me jump!'

Scott rushed through the kitchen door. 'What's wrong?'

'Nothing! I just didn't see Orla sitting there and she startled me.' I laughed, but Orla didn't move. Her head was resting in her hands and she appeared to be staring at an empty space on the table in between her elbows.

'Orla?' I said tentatively, taking a couple of steps towards her. 'Are . . . are you OK?'

She sniffed, her hands falling to the table in front of her. She turned her head slowly towards us and I saw her eyes were bloodshot from crying, the skin around them puffy and raw.

'Shit, what's wrong?' said Scott.

She didn't answer. I walked up to the table, pulled out a chair and sat down next to her. 'Orla, you're scaring us now. What the hell has happened? Are you hurt? Has something happened to you?'

She shook her head slowly and sniffed again, but her gaze was vague, as if she couldn't really see anything or anyone in the room. I looked down at the table and noticed a piece of paper lying there, three straight creases in it, as if it had been folded into an envelope not long before. The header at the top read 'Kingston Hospital NHS Foundation Trust.'

The letter was facing Orla, and it felt like too much of an intrusion to pick it up and start reading, but as my eyes scanned the page I could make out certain words and phrases: *results of your most recent scans and blood tests . . . regret to have to inform you . . . serious condition . . . white blood cells . . . operation may be necessary . . .*

I felt the blood leave my face as a coolness tingled down my arms and into my quivering fingers. 'Orla,' I said, reaching out a hand and placing it gently on her forearm. 'Please tell us what's happening. We can help you.'

Her eyes locked on to mine then and her chin quivered. 'It's . . . it's the dizzy spells. I . . . when they took me in the ambulance after I fainted, they did some tests. I'd forgotten about them . . . I mean, I haven't had a dizzy spell for a little while now . . . so I thought . . .' Her voice drifted off but her lips kept on moving. She looked like a macabre marionette, with her large sorrowful eyes and her pale face drained of colour.

'What does the letter say?' I prompted gently, not wanting her to think I'd read it before she'd given me permission.

The kettle boiled furiously in the background and I willed it to click off. Eventually it did, leaving us in a grave silence that was even worse.

She cleared her throat, her eyes flicking from me to Scott, then back to me again. 'It . . . it says I've got a rare blood disease . . . it could be fatal.' Her face crumpled and she began sobbing. I leaned forwards and pulled her towards me, holding her close, rubbing her back and rocking gently while her whole body shook and her sobs filled the air.

Chapter Twelve

We made tea and sat at the dining table, the letter from the hospital sitting between us, untouched, as if no one wanted to acknowledge its existence, and at the same time knowing it was everything. It was the reason Orla was sitting hunched and defeated, head in her hands, letting out sporadic sobs, each one tightening my insides further. I couldn't imagine what receiving such news would be like. My hand went once more to my stomach and stroked the fabric of my jumper. How different our days had been. I'd received the best medical news I could imagine, and Orla had received the worst. Scott and I glanced at each other and I knew there was a silent agreement between us that there would be no talk of pregnancies and of Orla moving out. Not today.

I struggled for something to say, while the letter kept drawing my eyes back to its seemingly harmless form on the table. Something twisted in my gut and I found myself speaking, almost to myself. 'I . . . I can't believe they sent a letter like that . . . that they didn't make an appointment to speak to you and make sure you had someone there with you when you heard the news . . .'

Orla sniffed. 'I called them up when I opened it . . . I just couldn't believe it was real, you know? I thought there might have been a mistake. I mean . . . not that I'd

wish this on anyone else. But I thought the same as you
. . . that they couldn't just send me a bombshell like this
in the post.' She shook her head, fresh tears in her eyes.

Scott extended his hand and rested it on her forearm.
'Is there anyone we can call for you? A friend or relative?
Maybe you should have someone come and stay with
you while you . . . digest this news.'

I felt a surge of tenderness towards Scott. While I'd
been busy feeling indignant at such a callous administration process at the hospital, Scott had been worrying
about Orla, and how she could best be supported at
this time.

Orla shook her head and withdrew, leaning back in
her chair and crossing her arms over her chest, as if to
defend herself. 'No. I don't have anyone I'm afraid. My
father died years ago, I never really knew my mother,
and my brother . . .' She gave a bitter laugh. 'Well . . .
Jules knows about him.'

The brother who'd so heartlessly kept Orla away
from her dying father. The control freak who'd caused
her to want to move away from Ireland and never go
back. 'But . . . don't you think he'd like to at least know
about your diagnosis? Do you think perhaps if you told
him it might—'

'Bridge the gulf between us?' She looked at me
and her expression was one of disgust. 'I know you're
trying to help, Jules, but if you knew my brother . . . if
you'd met him, you'd realise that finding out I had a
life-threatening condition would have no bearing on his
emotions whatsoever. He's not made of normal stuff.
He's . . . he's not got an empathetic bone in his body.'

Her tone grew harder the more she spoke and I felt I'd overstepped. Whatever I wanted to happen, I didn't want to be a source of more stress for Orla in the face of this devastating news.

Luckily Scott came to my rescue. 'And there isn't anyone else? I mean, a best friend? What about your old roommate, the one you lived with before you moved in here?'

Orla shifted in her seat. 'To be honest, we weren't that close. We met doing a show at Edinburgh Fringe, then moved in together, but she's been touring pretty much constantly since then, so we never really became proper friends.'

As much as my heart ached for Orla in that moment, and as devastated as I felt for her, the more I heard her speak about her alienation from everyone in her family and all her friends, the more a creeping sense of dread tingled over my skin and sank into me. Were we really the closest people on earth to Orla? Us? The people who were about to ask her to move out? Were we really the only people she had? The dread began to bubble inside me, churning up the seeds of panic. *Come on, Jules. Calm down. One thought at a time.*

I took a deep breath and formed the question in my mind before I spoke. 'What's the next step, Orla? What's the name of the condition, and what have the hospital said about treatment?'

Her gaze seemed vague and unseeing as she looked at me, as if she didn't quite understand the question. 'It's an autoimmune disease . . . something about a malfunction in the white blood cells?' She reached for the letter and held it in her trembling fingers. 'Apparently, treatment is highly individualised, but they've asked me to go in for my first session on Monday. I think they use chemo drugs . . .' Her voice trailed off and she stifled another sob with her fist. I felt a pang of sympathy so strong it brought tears to my own eyes.

I nodded, hoping my voice would be steady when I spoke. 'Great . . . they're acting swiftly. That . . . that's good, isn't it?'

She gave an uncertain nod back.

Orla didn't have a car, and Scott would be at work all day on Monday. 'I'll take you to the hospital and stay with you while you have your treatment.'

'No,' she said, her eyes widening. 'You've both been so kind to me, I can't ask you to take hours out of your day to drive me to appointments and hold my hand . . .'

'Orla.' I sounded stern now. 'I'm not letting you go off to your first treatment session on your own on a bus now, am I?'

'I could get an Uber . . .' she said, but her voice was weak.

'I'm taking you in our car and I'm staying with you. You don't know how you're going to feel afterwards. You can't be wandering around Kingston on your own. Also, it might be emotionally difficult as well as physically . . . you might need someone.'

She squeezed her eyes shut, her face crumpling for a moment before she seemed to rally and collect herself with a sharp intake of breath. When she opened her eyes, she looked at me levelly. 'I would really appreciate a lift to the hospital, and a lift back home afterwards.

But please, I'd like to undergo the treatment on my own. I . . . it's personal, you know?'

'Oh God, of course! It's your treatment . . . I'm not going to force my way into the room,' I said, attempting a reassuring laugh. Orla gave a twitch of a smile. 'I'll take you, and then you can call me when it's over and I'll come and get you. OK?'

She nodded, a little subdued, like an obedient child.

Orla stayed in her room for the rest of the day. Our bubble of euphoria had burst, and now the house was cast in a sombre cloud.

'What are we going to do, Scott?' As I asked the question that evening over dinner, I knew there was an element of it that was completely selfish. I didn't just mean *how are we going to support Orla through the most difficult time in her life?* What I also meant was *how can we move on as we approach a new life as a family of three, with a seriously ill woman in the house who's relying on us to support her both logistically and emotionally?*

Scott shook his head and took another sip of his beer. 'The timing could not be worse, I have to say.'

I prodded at my pasta. 'I mean, it's awful, but . . . I can't believe she doesn't have anyone. I mean, she's so much fun. Everyone seems to love Orla, and she talks about her acting friends all the time. It seems crazy she doesn't have close friends, or at least some family who'd be of help to her. I just don't see how we can support her in the way she . . .' My voice trailed off.

'What?' said Scott. 'What have you just thought of?'

'I think I know who we need to talk to.'

'Who?'

'Maggie. This has got Maggie written all over it. Her charity is all about people who don't have the support they need in times of medical crisis. Whether that's financial or emotional . . . I'm sure Maggie will be able to think of some practical ways we can help Orla.'

'That's a bloody great idea,' said Scott.

I grabbed my phone and texted Maggie, asking if she was free for a coffee the following day. Two minutes later she replied. *Absolutely! xx* We arranged to meet at a little Italian place in Kingston called Giuseppe's, at three o'clock. Maggie would be thinking it was just a casual meet-up. She would have no idea how much news I had to tell her.

The cafe was bustling in a way I hadn't imagined for a Sunday. I'd settled in a corner facing the door so I'd see when Maggie arrived, and I already had two lattes (one decaf) sitting in front of me when she walked in.

As ever, Maggie looked chic in a way that seemed effortless and uncontrived. She wore a Breton-striped top teamed with boyfriend jeans and a chunky gold necklace. Her sleeves were pulled up to reveal layered leather bracelets on one wrist and a large-faced watch with a white leather strap on the other. It would never have occurred to me to buy any of these items on their own, but Maggie was the sort of person who randomly threw clothes, jewellery and accessories onto herself and managed to make the combination look uniquely stunning. Her dark, cropped hair was tousled as usual, the blonde streak in her fringe swept sideways out of her eyes. My oversized mauve jumper and skinny jeans seemed so pedestrian now.

When it came to telling Maggie I was pregnant, I was grateful for the hubbub in the cafe. She slammed her cup down, the contents sloshing into the blue saucer, before exclaiming 'Fucking hell!' loudly enough to elicit amused smiles from two middle-aged women at the next table.

She reached for my shoulders and pulled me into a fierce hug. 'This is AMAZING! I mean . . . I didn't think you guys were on the brink of getting pregnant, but it's planned, right?'

I explained that although it wasn't exactly planned, it had kind of been on the cards for a while, and was definitely a good thing. We talked about next steps, doctors' appointments, whether we'd find out the sex of the baby, our disagreements about names, etc. Then I explained about how we both really felt it was time for Orla to move out.

'Oh God, absolutely. I'm sure she'll completely understand about that. I mean, it was never going to be forever, was it?' Maggie said with a cheerful shrug before finishing the last of her coffee.

I sighed. 'Yeah. That's where things get a bit complicated.'

She frowned. 'What do you mean?'

I told her about coming home last night and finding Orla at the kitchen table with the letter from the hospital. Maggie watched me tell the story with a burgeoning expression of horror on her face, her hand going to her mouth as I explained Orla's predicament . . . and therefore ours.

'Shit,' she said softly when I'd finished, her gaze falling to the table and flickering around, as if she could somehow work out the answer to this conundrum by reading the grain of the polished wood. 'Well, in terms of support for Orla, I'm sure she meets some of the criteria for us to offer her help.' Maggie's tone had changed from her friendly, chatty one to her authoritative work voice. She looked up at me. 'She has no family who can help her, and being self-employed and relatively low-paid I'm sure we'll be able to assist her in some way. It's . . . it's just so sad. Poor Orla.'

Chapter Thirteen

When the text reminder from the GP surgery pinged onto my phone on Monday morning, my stomach gave an excited flip before a realisation squashed it. I'd promised Orla I'd take her to hospital for her appointment. I called the surgery and rearranged my appointment for Friday before heading upstairs and knocking on Orla's door. I'd imagined cajoling her out of her room, a pasty, nerve-ridden shadow of her former self as she embarked upon this horrific journey. I was surprised then when her chirpy voice called 'Coming!' through the bedroom door.

She hurried out, her hair loose and newly washed falling in damp waves over her shoulders. She had applied subtle make-up and wore a pale blue summer dress with capped sleeves.

I smiled. 'How are you feeling? You look great.'

'Aw, thank you so much. I'm actually feeling grand today. Can't believe what I'm off to do. Doesn't seem real, you know?'

I nodded. It really didn't. 'I just want to say, I'm still completely happy to come in with you and wait. You must be nervous . . . and if you need someone to chat to while you're having the treatment, then—'

She placed a hand on the bare skin of my arm, my skin tingling under the coldness of her fingers. 'You are so sweet. But honestly, I'd really rather do this by myself.' She tapped a straw bag that was slung across her body. 'I've got books, *Marie Claire*, chocolate, and my phone, so I'm not going to be bored!'

'OK. But promise me you'll call when you're done and I'll come and pick you up?'

'That would be amazing. Thank you.'

We barely spoke in the car, but in my peripheral vision I saw her take the letter out of her bag, fold it and put it back, then take it out again and reread it. She seemed completely preoccupied with it, flattening it out in her lap, folding, opening and refolding it on repeat for the whole journey. It was now creased and tired-looking, and I wondered how many times she'd read it, processing those awful words. I wondered if she'd balled it up in her fist and thrown it across the room, only to retrieve it and scan it again and again.

We turned into the car park and Orla fiddled with her fingers, looking down, shaking her head ever so slightly. It took a while to find a parking space and eventually she said, 'Actually, there's no point in you parking. I can just hop out here.'

'But shouldn't I at least come in with you while you find the right department?'

'It says in the letter I should go to Outpatients and ask for the Haematology department. Honestly, the main entrance is just there.'

I slowed as we approached the entrance and I pulled into a loading bay while Orla shoved the letter back in her bag again, flashed me an uncertain smile and opened the car door.

'Good luck,' I called after her.

'Thanks,' she said, slamming the door and walking towards the main entrance. I watched her in my rear-view mirror, opening up her bag again and bringing out the letter as she walked through the sliding doors and out of sight.

I drove home and tried to concentrate on some character sketches I'd been mulling over for a new author. I took out some paper and sharpened a fresh HB pencil, but once I started I couldn't help glancing at my phone every couple of minutes, wondering if Orla was about to call. After an hour or so I made myself a cup of tea and settled back at my desk, picking up my phone and idly tapping into Facebook as I sipped. There was a notification on the little bell symbol at the bottom and I tapped on it, surprised to see I'd been tagged in a post. I didn't often go on Facebook, preferring Instagram where I could post photos of my doodles and sketches, and thus promote my work more visually. Facebook was the preserve of old school friends and uni mates.

I read the notification. 'Orla Sullivan has tagged you in a post.' I tapped on it, and my screen filled with a photograph of Orla. She was in a hospital room, it was clear to see. She wore a hospital gown with pale blue motifs printed on it, and next to the bed was a red chair, and an array of wires and leads, as well as some sort of monitor on a trolley with a lit-up screen and various dials and buttons. She'd scraped her hair back and she looked pale as she smiled weakly into the camera. The caption said: 'First round of treatment today. I'm still reeling from the shock of the diagnosis of this rare and potentially fatal blood condition, but I know that today is the first step on my journey to recovery. I can't tell you how grateful I am to the gorgeous @JulesBurton and @ScottBurton for supporting me through this. #recovery #KingstonHospital.'

She'd only posted the picture about fifteen minutes ago, but already there were seventy-two 'likes', and a string of comments, all offering sympathy and kind-hearted emojis. My finger hovered over the 'like' button but somehow I couldn't bring myself to tap it. It seemed a trivial and meaningless action set against what Orla was going through. And it also didn't feel like something to 'like'. If I was honest, I was also taken aback by the fact she'd shared this moment on social media, espe-cially as she'd asked me not to come with her because she wanted to keep it private. But then, I reasoned, shar-ing on social media was different to having someone in the room with you. And perhaps this was her way of letting family know what was going on without having to directly contact them.

I set my mug down and clicked into Orla's friend list. There were just over three hundred names, and we had two mutuals – Scott and Maggie. I scrolled through the list of friends, looking for anyone with the surname 'Sullivan', but found no one. I remembered her saying her brother was called Sean, but there was no one of that name on the list, nor anyone with the alternative spelling of 'Shaun'. I clicked into a few profiles at ran-dom and discovered they were mostly acting friends, their cover photos and posts pertaining to shows they were in, auditions they'd just had, or part-time work they were struggling with. There were a couple of Irish-looking names, a Roisin and a Patrick, but when I clicked on them they were also actors, Roisin having been in *Kilcroom High* with Orla. She was the oldest friend I could find from my sporadic detective work.

My phone began buzzing in my hand and Orla's number flashed up. I jumped, as if I'd been caught snooping around her Facebook account before I realised that was ridiculous and there was no way she could know I was on her profile page at that very moment.

I answered. 'Hello?'

'Hi, Jules?' Her voice sounded quiet and sleepy.

'Yes, I'm here, are you OK?'

'I'm fine. Can you come and pick me up?'

'Of course, I'll come right now.'

She didn't say goodbye, but I heard the beep of her ending the call. I remembered how Mum had felt after her first round of chemo. Of course, Orla didn't have cancer, but if she was being given similar drugs, the effect would probably be the same. The sickness and fatigue. The aching muscles and the dizziness. I suddenly felt guilty for not having prepared anything for Orla's return from hospital. Perhaps I should have bought some flowers, or some scented candles for her room. Mum always liked those things – but then, Orla wasn't Mum. Perhaps she'd see those things as succumbing to her illness, when she was trying to be strong and stay positive.

Orla was waiting on a bench in the sunshine just outside the main entrance when I arrived. She walked falteringly towards the car and slid into the passenger seat. 'Thank you,' she said, almost in a whisper.

'How did it go?' I asked as I pulled out onto the road.

She sighed. 'It was . . . as you'd expect, I suppose. It's taken it out of me.'

'I remember how poorly my mum felt after her chemo. You should get some rest.'

Orla turned to look at me and there was a short pause before she said, 'I'd forgotten your mum had chemo. That must have been tough.'

I swallowed, suddenly wondering whether reminding Orla about Mum had been a good idea. After all, there wasn't a happy ending to Mum's story. 'Yeah, it was tough. But Mum had cancer, and she was a lot older than you are . . . not as fit and healthy,' I said, turning to look at her as we waited at traffic lights. 'You're going to boss this,' I added with a smile.

She smiled back, then looked down into her lap, adjusting her handbag which made a rattling sound. 'They've given me more medication than I've ever had in my entire life.'

'Well, they know what they're doing.'

'I suppose so,' she said, sounding resigned again. It wasn't like Orla to sound defeated, and I worried that if she was already feeling this way, then she needed something to lift her up and give her some hope.

'You know, I hope you don't mind, but I was speaking to Maggie about you,' I said, turning onto the Richmond Road.

'Maggie?' she said, sounding a bit confused.

'Yes . . . you know, because of the charity she works for. Not that you need charity or anything,' I said hastily, wondering if I'd made another faux pas. 'It's just that

Kind UK are experts in working out what people in your position need, and I'm sure they'd be able to at least help you fill in any relevant paperwork, or apply for any grants you're eligible for. You know, if you have to miss work or anything.'

'Right, yes. I suppose that's a good idea.' She sounded distracted. 'Thanks, Jules.'

We pulled up outside the house and Orla hauled herself out of the car as if her limbs were made of lead. I offered to make her some tea but she said she just wanted to have a lie down, so I left her to drag herself laboriously up the stairs, listening to her feet scuff on the carpet as she rounded the corner to make her way up to the attic.

I made myself a coffee and headed to my studio to try and catch up with some work. I managed to email off some preliminary sketches to my publisher, but the deadline was looming for the character sketches. I'd have to crack on with those and send them off so we could discuss them in a Zoom meeting next week once the publisher and author had had a chance to go over them. I set up some clean paper, clipping it to my board. Then I logged into my computer and clicked into the picture-book text I was working with, splitting the screen with some character notes I'd made off the top of my head when I'd first read it. I was about to put pencil to paper when my phone lit up, displaying another Facebook notification.

I picked up the phone and tapped on the screen, which instantly took me to Orla's profile again. Except this time it wasn't her actual profile, but a Facebook page that seemed to have been newly set up, entitled 'Orla's Battle'. The blue button invited me to 'Join Group', so I tapped on it.

The page that came up held the title of the group, and the cover photo at the top was the photo she'd posted earlier on her private page: the one of her in the hospital bed, wearing the gown and surrounded by medical equipment. There were only five members of this group so far, and I imagined she'd sent the invitation to all her Facebook friends at the same time. The first post was an exact replica of the one she'd put on her profile, but just above it was a new photo. This one showed Orla in her bed upstairs, her head laid back on the white pillowcase, her blonde hair falling in waves around her shoulders. The camera was held far enough away for us to be able to see the cottonwool bud held in place by white tape in the crook of her arm, presumably where they'd administered the drugs. Her face was pale and she offered the camera a wan smile. I read the caption: *First treatment session today and my God it's taken its toll on me. I want to sleep forever! But I know that's not an option – because I'm not going to take this lying down. Think you can beat me? Think again! #BSH #histiocytosis #survivor #fighter #KindUK*

The last hashtag surprised me. I'd only just suggested Orla speak to Maggie about her diagnosis, and yet she'd already tagged Maggie's charity in her post. I supposed that was to attract Maggie's attention. Perhaps she felt less vulnerable doing it this way rather than calling her directly or relying on me to put them in touch with each other. Even as I reread the caption and thought about this, the number of members of the group was increasing. Messages began popping up in the comments, renewals of the sympathies the first post had received, along with motivational words, hearts and strong arms. *You got this! You're a fighter, Orla!*

I googled #BSH and found it referenced the British Society of Haematology. Then I googled 'histiocytosis' and discovered that, rather than being a specific illness, this term was used to describe a group of blood disorders that affected the immune system. Depending on what sort you had, it could damage tissue in the bones, skin, lungs, liver, lymph nodes, bone marrow . . . the list went on. Some versions were more common in children, some affected adults, but they were all rare – and they were all very serious. Single courses of treatment were sometimes successful, but equally they could fail or a patient could relapse.

I scrolled down the list of comments and noticed a new message had popped up at the bottom. It was from the official Kind UK Facebook account and it said: *Fighting right by your side, Orla. Will be in touch soon. Xxx*

Chapter Fourteen

The week sped on, and my sense of dread and anxiety linked to Orla's diagnosis became intermingled with the excitement of my GP appointment on Friday. This was ridiculous, as there would be no scan – it was far too early for that. There would only be a simple conversation to get me 'in the system' and referred to the hospital for my antenatal appointments. But still, the prospect brought a smile to my face every time I thought about it.

In the end, the appointment lasted no longer than ten minutes, during which time my height, weight and blood pressure was taken, all deemed to be normal, and my contact details confirmed so the hospital could get in touch to arrange my twelve-week scan. Twelve weeks. That seemed like an age to wait – six whole weeks. But as I walked home another thought loomed large. The time was ticking, however slowly, towards the moment we'd be forced to address this situation with Orla. I couldn't hide the pregnancy from her much longer, and I was sure she wouldn't want me to. She already felt that Scott and I were doing so much for her and being inconvenienced. She'd feel terrible if she thought her illness was the reason we hadn't told her about me being pregnant.

The following Monday I gave Orla a lift to the hospital for another treatment session. I'd assumed they'd be treating her several times a week, but apparently that wasn't the case. They were tailoring the plan to Orla's specific test results and had decided to start off with a month of weekly sessions instead.

Once again she insisted I didn't wait for her, so I came home to get some work done, then collected her when she called a few hours later. Once again she'd been radiant when I'd taken her to the hospital, wearing a summery pink, knee-length dress, and her face tinted with a rosy blush. But just like the week before, she emerged from the hospital looking like a broken woman, dragging her feet. A nurse in lilac scrubs called after her and I watched through the windscreen as Orla twisted around, accepting something in a white paper bag. She offered the nurse a small smile and the nurse squeezed Orla's upper arm sympathetically before heading back inside. Orla crossed the car park and slumped with a heavy sigh into the passenger seat, casting me a weary glance.

'Forgot my new pills,' she said, holding the paper bag aloft before stashing it in her handbag at her feet. She sounded so defeated, I wanted to say something to cheer her up.

'Maggie's coming over tomorrow so we can have a chat about how Kind UK can help,' I said, hoping this news would lift her spirits.

She nodded. 'Thanks for arranging that, Jules.'

'Of course,' I said. We drove home in silence.

Maggie rang the doorbell at five thirty the following day and bustled in holding a pile of files and books, which she set on the dining table. Orla was cradling a mug of steaming tea. She didn't get up to offer Maggie her usual effusive greeting, but Maggie bent down to squeeze her shoulder and kiss her cheek, in a professional way which somehow seemed to convey both sympathy and affection, but neither too much nor too little of either.

I pottered in the kitchen making coffee for Maggie and listening to what she was telling Orla. She asked her about her diagnosis and pored over three letters from the hospital that Orla provided her with. I watched Maggie writing in her little notebook and nodding as she transferred the key information across.

'I've got emails too,' Orla said tentatively. 'Shall I print them out for you?'

'If you're comfortable then you can just forward them to me if you like, but honestly,' Maggie gestured towards the letters Orla had supplied, 'there's more than enough info here for us to make a really good start with working out how to help you.'

Orla explained that she'd put her temping placement on hold for a month while she had the first round of treatment. Maggie said that was very wise, and that there were several funds they could apply for to help her make ends meet while she wasn't working, especially as her work was freelance, or tied to a contract that included very little statutory sick pay.

The term 'make ends meet' sent a shiver through me. Why had this not occurred to me before? Obviously the rent Orla paid was coming out of her earnings, either from acting work or from her temp job at the hotel. Of course she wouldn't be able to pay that rent if she was hardly earning anything. I felt my heart beat in my chest like a frightened bird. Perhaps Scott and I should have a chat about reducing her rent, or even letting her off rent for a month or two? Surely that was the right thing to do? I felt a stab of resentment, then immediately berated myself. Orla was going through the most horrific time of her life – how could I feel bitterness at the fact I wouldn't be able to decorate her room as a nursery right this minute? Or move Scott and me up to the attic so we could redo our room for the baby? Perhaps I could move my studio downstairs so the baby could have the box room. No, that room was my studio and I loved it. This was not the plan. I felt my pregnancy elation breaking apart and slipping through my fingers like shards of broken china.

'Are you OK, Jules?' Maggie's voice interrupted my thoughts and I glanced over to her, then looked down at the cooling coffee mugs on the counter in front of me.

'Um . . . yes, I'm fine. Sorry, were you talking to me?' I carried the mugs over and set one in front of Maggie.

'I was just saying that I'll fill in the relevant paperwork for Orla and get her to sign, then we can apply for financial support – it sounds like her treatment plan is going to be quite gruelling, and we're not quite sure how she's going to react to it, so committing to regular work is going be problematic.'

Orla nodded solemnly and chewed her bottom lip.

'But,' Maggie tried for a brighter tone, 'I was also going through some other things we can do, if Orla's up for it.'

I lowered myself onto a chair. 'Right, and what are those other things?'

Orla leaned forwards, a surprising sparkle in her eyes. 'Maggie's been telling me about some of the incredible fundraising events Kind UK have organised recently.' She glanced at Maggie, who nodded as if to encourage her to continue. 'There are local church groups who link to Kind UK to run events for people with life-threatening diagnoses, and bake sales, and celebrity endorsements—'

Maggie chimed in. 'I was explaining that the mum I was telling her about last week managed to get some traction with Mean Feat—'

'The boy band?' I said.

'Yep,' Maggie continued. 'Apparently the lead singer's mother had the same diagnosis several years ago, and he retweeted a couple of this mum's tweets encouraging their fans to donate to her crowdfunding, and *boom* – instant financial relief for her and her family. The band donated too and even sold T-shirts at one of their gigs with her hashtag across the front.' Maggie smiled at Orla and Orla beamed back, before reaching out a hand and squeezing Maggie's forearm.

'Wow,' I said, feeling suddenly overwhelmed, not only by Orla's diagnosis but by the enormity of this under-taking. But then I looked at Orla, and she didn't seem overwhelmed. She seemed euphoric. I supposed this was what hope looked like.

Scott arrived home from work about twenty minutes later and joined us at the table, looking over all the pam-phlets and folders Maggie had brought and listening to Maggie and Orla getting him up to speed on what the 'plan of action' was. It felt bizarrely like a work conversa-tion and reminded me of meetings I'd had with publishers and agents where a new project or picture book was in the offing and everyone was excited and bright-eyed, full of ideas and brimming with enthusiasm.

That night, in bed, I logged into Facebook and saw Orla had posted an update on her Orla's Battle page. 'Brilliant meeting with @MaggieVarma from @KindUK today! I'm feeling positive. I can do this! #nevergiveup #bloodcondition #KindUK #FightForOrla.' There was a photo of her and Maggie. I hadn't noticed when, but it had clearly been taken around our kitchen table earlier that evening. Their faces filled the photo, beaming, cheeks pressed together.

I scrolled down and saw a photo I'd not noticed, one that had been taken the day before. It showed Orla in a hospital gown, next to another woman wearing green scrubs. The woman was Black, with her hair braided back in thick plaits, one of them dyed royal blue. Both women grinned into the camera as the nurse dabbed a swab at Orla's arm, her stethoscope dangling from her neck. Orla had taken the selfie, her other arm was stretched high. The caption said, 'I could not have been in better hands for my treatment session today. Ngozi, you are an absolute star. #nevergiveup #BSH #KindUK.'

I noticed that #FightForOrla wasn't included in yesterday's post, and realised she must have come up with it after Maggie had told her the story about the band who latched on to the mum's hashtag and had it emblazoned on T-shirts at their gig. Perhaps she was hoping something like that would happen to her. Or perhaps Maggie had advised her to think of a catchy hashtag that would make her journey easier to follow. This post had about one hundred and seventy likes and loves, and fifty-two comments underneath, more of the same outpourings of sympathy and solidarity. Today's post had even more: five hundred and eleven reactions, and almost three hundred comments. Several comments were from strangers – people who weren't even friends with Orla. They said things like *My son was diagnosed with a brain tumour last year. May God bless you and keep you safe . . . Kind UK helped us so much when my mother had leukaemia. You're in good hands!*

The group now had nine hundred and twenty-five members. That was a huge leap. It just showed, I thought, how emotive a diagnosis like this was, and how it galvanised people. When my mother was diagnosed with cancer, it had never crossed my mind to involve social media at all. In fact, I knew Mum would have outright rejected the very idea. *Why the hell would I want to advertise my illness on the internet?* I could hear her say in my mind. *It's not a spectator sport.*

But I supposed that, for some people, maybe it *was*.

The fact that so many people would be invested in a journey like this, who wanted to see if there was a happy ending, could really be harnessed in terms of fundraising and awareness. I felt a swell of hope for Orla. She was exactly the right person to get the most out of this. She was beautiful and didn't shy away from attention – she was used to it, being an actor. She was comfortable putting herself out there, having people looking at her, scrutinising her. I could understand how strangers scrolling social media might be taken by the photo of the beautiful woman with the golden hair who'd just had such a devastating diagnosis shatter her life. She was precisely the right person to be a charismatic fighter . . . someone who could raise awareness of this rare and potentially life-threatening illness.

The next treatment session seemed to wipe Orla out completely. My mother's chemo had been daily, with short gaps between sessions, and I know she'd suffered terribly with nausea and muscle pain. Orla's treatment, although only once a week, seemed to be causing her increasing tiredness. I collected her from the hospital after her third session and had to jump out of the car to support her as she hobbled towards where I'd hastily parked. Her face looked almost yellow in the sunlight and she held the back of one hand to her mouth as if she might be sick.

At home I helped her up the stairs, asking if I could bring her anything. She asked for some iced water and a cold flannel which I quickly ran downstairs to prepare. I wondered how quickly the stairs would become a problem for her if she had to have another course of treatment – if this course didn't work. I felt the walls closing in and shook my head fiercely to dislodge this thought. No, that wouldn't happen. Of course it would work. Of course she'd get better.

It's so cruel that the treatment feels worse than the disease itself. But I suppose anything that involves chemo or radiation therapy is going to zap you. The nausea, the exhaustion, the thumping headaches, the fuzziness, the dry skin. It's brutal. And I don't think most people quite appreciate that. I suppose that's why I thought it might be a good idea to set up the Facebook page – to give people a glimpse into the life of someone suffering from a serious blood disorder. And the response has been insane – people are really engaging and reacting, and that, in itself, is giving me such a lift.

Maggie (bless the universe for creating Maggie!) has been trying to convince me to go down the crowdfunding route, but I've been thinking really carefully, and I don't want that. This isn't about money – it's about making connections with real people. It's about being an inspiration. And as long as I can work part-time (when I'm not holed up in the attic after hospital visits), I think I can just about make enough to pay my rent. That should keep Jules happy.

Jules . . . this whole journey has shown me there's more to her than the steely-eyed cynic I'd first pegged her for. She can be caring and nurturing. She can be kind. I think this situation is helping to bring out another side to her – a more empathetic side. I feel grateful Jules has taken a leaf out of Scott's book and decided kindness wins out in the end. After all, I've experienced my fair share of cynics in my time. Doubters. Questioners. People who say they love you, then turn around and cast you out, as if you were no more than a used tissue. And I've made a promise to myself that it won't happen again because I don't think my heart could take it. The betrayal. If it did happen again, I don't know what I'd do.

Chapter Fifteen

Orla's last treatment session was at the beginning of June. I drove her there as usual, and came home to fit in some work before she'd need picking up. I was about to push open the door to my studio when I heard a flapping sound from the attic room above. I wondered if Orla had left the window open and perhaps a bird had flown in and become trapped. So I walked up the stairs and tentatively pushed open the door to her bedroom.

Sure enough, the tall windows were open, the curtains fluttering in the breeze. But it wasn't a bird that was making the flapping sound, but a hardback book that sat on the coffee table, the pages fluttering frantically. I closed the book and turned it so the spine faced the open window. I didn't want to close the windows, as perhaps Orla had left them open to get some fresh air into the place – something that might help ease her nausea when she got back.

I should have left immediately, but I couldn't help casting my gaze around the room. I hadn't been in there since that time after the walk in Richmond Park, when I'd come up to persuade her to make a GP appointment about her dizzy spells. The room had been a bit messy back then. Now it was in complete disarray. Clothes were strewn across the floor, books scattered sporadically on top and peeping from underneath. I spotted an empty crisp packet by the bathroom door, and what looked like a discarded mascara tube next to it. More coffee rings patterned the surface of the table, and a teaspoon was stuck to a dried patch of something orange. The bed wasn't made: the duvet was lying next to it and the pillows were still in place, but one with the cover half off. I tiptoed over to the bookcase, which now only housed a handful of titles, the rest having been dispersed about the room. Two empty triangular sandwich packets were stacked inside each other on one shelf, beside a KitKat wrapper. A large tub of Greek yoghurt perched on a lower shelf, the smeared remnants dotted with pale green patches of mould, which were being enjoyed by a bluebottle as it crawled around the rim.

I felt queasy. This was not a nice environment for anyone to be living in, let alone someone who was trying to deal with the symptoms of a serious illness. I wondered if Orla was just a messy person, or if this squalor was the result of her not being physically fit enough to tidy her room. I felt an urgent need to run downstairs and fetch a bin liner, scoop the detritus into it before bundling all her clothes and bedding into the washing machine, hoovering the floor, wiping down the sticky surfaces. If I did all that now, I could have her room fresh and clean by the time she got back home. I could have the bathroom sparkling, the bed made, the sheets crisp and smelling like a summer afternoon. I could even light a couple of fragranced candles. How much lovelier would a room like that be to come home to and recover in? But no, I couldn't do that, because it would be a horrible breach

135

of privacy, a huge overstepping of my role, and something that could embarrass Orla far more than it would make her feel better. So, leaving everything but the hardback book untouched, I walked back through the door, closing it on the chaotic scene I'd just uncovered.

As I descended the stairs to my studio, I wondered about the conspicuous lack of any photographs in Orla's room. I knew she didn't know her mother, that her father had died, and her brother was an impossible character, but I still wondered at the absence of any photos of friends or special events. If her family history was too painful, wouldn't there at least be photos of more recent times? Shows she'd been part of, nights in the pub with her actor friends, birthday celebrations with her old housemate, or with her friend Matt?

It had never occurred to me when I'd been reluctant to agree to a lodger that we should be thinking of anything other than the person being agreeable, with their habits and routine complementing ours. It had never crossed my mind that we might end up feeling responsible for someone who was, essentially, completely unconnected to us. That we would start to feel beholden to someone who was suffering a potentially terminal illness when we knew almost nothing about them, and had only known them for a matter of months. Once again that creeping feeling came over me, that racing of my heart and tingling in my fingers. Our spacious house began to feel smaller, the air thicker and more stifling.

After Orla's final session, the waiting began. She told us the hospital would be in touch with the results, to let her know if the treatment had been partially or completely successful, and what the next steps would be. Her white blood cells, spleen and bone marrow had been monitored as well as her liver and kidney function tested. I had expected Orla to be wracked with nervous energy during this time, or to be so distracted with the waiting that she would find it difficult to focus. But it seemed that along with her feeling physically better after the treatment was over, she experienced a newfound vitality.

One morning she swept into the kitchen with a bunch of wildflowers she'd picked (I didn't know from where, as they looked shop-perfect from the cool pink tulips to the giant daisy wheels), announcing, 'For you and Scott for just being the best support I could ever have hoped for at this God-awful time!'

She met with Maggie on a regular basis, frequently without me. I knew they had a 'plan of action' and that this involved various local groups and fundraisers. Orla went to meet the local vicar who included her in his sermon the following Sunday. The local beauty salon got in touch to offer Orla a free facial and manicure. The Wych Elm (where we'd met Orla for the first time) sent her vouchers for a meal for two, which she gleefully held aloft to the camera in a Facebook post where she tagged Maggie, along with #girlsnightout #FightForOrla.

The whole #FightForOrla thing now seemed to be really gaining momentum, and I was happy for her. There was never any mention of a crowdfunder or any other formal fundraiser for her specifically. That wasn't to say she wasn't fundraising – but when she did, it seemed to be for local causes like Kind UK, rather than for herself.

Orla didn't seem to be motivated by money in the slightest. She was a jobbing actor, after all – hardly the most well-paid career. She was in her thirties, but never seemed to talk about material things she wanted, future houses or holidays. The only thing that seemed to excite Orla was other people's reactions, whether that was an audience watching her on stage or a fundraiser she'd organised with Maggie for the local cancer community. Other people's praise and adulation seemed to be all she needed. Even when she was seriously ill.

This newer version of Orla (with her illness) was all about interactions. She was all about sharing her story. But more than that, her connection to local charities really seemed to have put a spring in her step. The treatment had taken her sparkle away, but her growing online following and the part she played in the local fundraising community had put it back. I wondered, therefore, what would happen if the doctors gave her the best news possible – that her condition had been cured. That the first round of treatment had worked and she was now better and could reclaim her life and her health. I wasn't a religious person, but I prayed for Orla that this would be the case. That all this would be a small, temporary blip in the theatrical, free-wheeling life of Orla Sullivan, that she would soon be well again and we could all go back to life as we knew it.

Then, I supposed, things would simply fizzle out. Well-wishers would send effusive messages of congratulations, love-heart and champagne-popping emojis. Orla would thank her followers for their words of kindness that had helped her through her darkest hours, and then she would delete the Facebook group and go back to being Orla Sullivan the actor, temping at the hotel and auditioning for theatre work. Every day I hoped for this for her and for all of us. Whenever Orla's phone rang, I felt a spike of anticipation that it could be the hospital calling with news. When I checked the doormat for post in the morning, I flicked through the envelopes, scanning them for an NHS letter that might bear news from the Haematology department.

One Friday morning I asked Orla when she was expecting to hear back.

'About what?' she said as she looked up from her coffee.

I was taken aback. 'From the hospital – your results . . .'

'Oh, God, silly me! I was just thinking about that show I did in Shoreditch and my mind completely slipped into another universe where I was waiting for audition news . . . God, wouldn't that be fabulous? Waiting to hear back from an audition rather than from the bloody hospital?' She sighed. 'Anyway, sorry, you were asking about that . . . I think they said it could take a few weeks. They needed to check scans and also do all the blood work. They took so much blood from me, I'm not sure how I've even got any left!'

I gave a weak laugh. 'Right. So it could be any time now. Hopefully they don't keep you hanging on too long.'

'Oh, I should expect it'll be any day now. But I'm feeling positive.' She set her mug down on the table and beamed up at me.

'That's good.' I nodded, unsure what else to say.

'I mean, no news is good news, right? I'm sure if there was anything terrible to report they'd have got in touch by now, wouldn't they?'

I felt a quiver of uncertainty. I didn't know how to answer such a huge question, nor what to base it on. I shook my head. 'Honestly, I have no idea.'

She blinked and bit her lip and I realised that hadn't been the most positive thing I could have said. I scrambled for something else to add. 'But you're right . . . no news is good news!' I felt a fake smile curve my lips and I held my coffee mug aloft in a pathetic attempt at a 'cheers'. I made a promise to myself I wouldn't broach the subject again unless Orla brought it up.

The second half of June brought with it sweltering weather. The air was humid in the house, and the sun blistering when I ventured outside. I often found myself gravitating towards the river, where the trees offered shade and the breeze swept down the Thames, stirring the scorched grass and sending ripples across the water.

My nausea had not yet receded, and I always travelled with a packet of biscuits in my handbag, along with a large bottle of water. I never actually vomited, which in a way felt worse, as there was never anything I could do to properly ease the waves of sickness. I'd find myself with a sudden, desperate need to sit down, anywhere, close my eyes, sip my water, cram a biscuit into my mouth. It seemed counterintuitive to eat when feeling like this, but it was the only thing that seemed to help.

But beneath my queasiness was a bubbling excitement about the pregnancy. My bump wasn't showing yet by any stretch of the imagination, but there was a hardness underneath I could feel when I pushed my hand down on my soft stomach, or when I tried to suck my tummy in. At that stage it could easily have been my imagination, but I felt there was definitely something 'there' and that something made all the nausea worth it.

Our twelve-week scan was at nine thirty one Friday morning, and I could hardly contain my excitement. I couldn't drink coffee since the nausea had become so bad, but I felt like I'd had three double espressos as I jiggled on the bar stool in the kitchen waiting for Scott to be ready to leave.

He drove us to the hospital, taking his hand off the wheel to squeeze my knee every time we stopped at a red light, turning to me with one of his cheesy grins. The car park was crowded as usual, and even though we'd left plenty of time, I felt myself getting stressed and sweaty as the panic set in. *What if we missed our appointment time and they couldn't fit us in?* At last we found a space and headed into the Outpatients department, from which we were given directions to the maternity unit.

As our shoes squeaked along the shiny white corridors and the smell of antiseptic washed over me, I remembered racing after the paramedics when Orla had been rushed in by ambulance. I felt the usual twinge of guilt. How different our experiences of this hospital were.

Despite my worries, the appointments were running fifteen minutes late, so we settled ourselves on the red plastic chairs, Scott fetching me some water in a cone-shaped cup from the water cooler. They'd told us the image would be clearer if my bladder was full so I'd been resisting the urge to go to the toilet for the past hour.

At last we were called in by a curvy young woman, her black hair slicked into a low ponytail. She told me to lie back and make myself comfortable, smearing the cold gel onto my stomach and pressing with surprising force with the ultrasound device. Scott squeezed my hand and I felt my pulse accelerate. *Please let everything be OK, please, please, please.* I found myself scrunching my eyes closed as the silence stretched on, Scott's thumb gently stroking my hand. Then a dull, blurry beat met my ears and my eyes sprang open as I twisted towards the monitor. There was a grainy, moving picture on the screen, an undulating shape, and at the centre, a tiny, flickering heartbeat.

The image blurred further and I realised it wasn't the screen, but my eyes filling with tears.

'There you go,' said the sonographer. 'There's baby, and they're looking good!'

'Oh my God!' I found myself saying. 'That's amazing! There's . . . there's their heartbeat, that's . . . that's just so . . . clever!' It was such a stupid thing to say, but I didn't care at that moment.

Scott laughed and planted a kiss on my forehead, his own eyes glistening with tears. 'Proud mum already.'

'Quite right!' said the sonographer. 'Never too early to show some parental pride. And you'll probably be pleased to hear there's only one foetus, so no twins for you this time round.'

'Oh God, I hadn't even thought of that,' said Scott. 'Wow – that would have been a shock!'

We continued to make silly jokes and laugh ridiculously as the sonographer did all her checks and measurements, the relief and wonder of the moment making us both chatty and delirious.

We left the maternity unit about twenty minutes later, four ultrasound printouts stashed in my handbag, and daft, happy grins on our faces. We'd decided this was the moment we were going to tell Orla the news. After all, the twelve-week scan was usually when couples announced pregnancies.

It was exactly as I was imagining the moment of telling Orla that I saw her.

Orla was a distinctive figure, being so tall and willowy with those beautiful blonde waves that floated down her back. I could only see her from behind, and within a second she'd disappeared around a corner.

'Did you see Orla?'

'What?' said Scott, glancing around.

'I just saw Orla – wait there . . .' I left Scott's side and rushed to where I'd seen her disappear moments before. Sure enough, when I looked around the corner she was there. She was wearing a long, floaty maxi dress in greens and blues, and a lightweight cream cardigan. She held a door open for an elderly couple before passing through herself, into a section of the hospital signposted 'Haematology'.

I wondered about calling after her, but something stopped me. She hadn't told me she had an appointment today, so she clearly didn't want me to know. Perhaps she was meeting with a consultant who'd give her the results of her tests. A knot of discomfort tightened inside me. I wondered if telling Orla about the pregnancy this evening was going to go to plan.

Chapter Sixteen

Maggie, Nick, Scott and I sat around the dining table that evening, Maggie cooing over the black-and-white image of our little 'Wotsit' – a nickname Scott had come up with after commenting on how curled up the baby looked.

'I've got to be careful though,' said Scott. 'Jules does go for crazy names so there's a risk she's actually going to want to use "Wotsit".'

I gave his arm a playful slap and took a sip of my non-alcoholic fizz that Maggie had been sweet enough to bring over. I'd explained we were going to tell Orla about the pregnancy this evening when she got home from work, and Maggie had said she'd happily be there in case Orla wanted to talk about potential next steps if she immediately felt she should be moving out. We decided we wouldn't broach the subject of her moving out this evening . . . we'd just let the pregnancy news sink in, and then see if she brought the subject up herself. If not, then we'd speak to her in a few days' time when she was more used to the idea and would perhaps be more likely to have thought through the implications of a newborn's arrival.

It was six thirty when we heard the front door open, and I felt a small flutter of my heart as I waited for Orla to appear at the kitchen door. She breezed in, her smile widening as she caught sight of Maggie and Nick, and she crossed the room to hug them.

'Lovely to see you both! What's the occasion?' She gestured towards the two open bottles of fizz on the table.

There was a beat of silence then, which thankfully Nick decided to obliterate. 'Sit yourself down.' He waved his hand towards an empty chair and reached to pour her a glass. Orla sat.

'So, we have some exciting news,' said Scott, squeezing my thigh and glancing at me. I could tell he was letting me do the next bit.

I took a deep breath and slid the scan photo across the table towards Orla. Her eyes flicked down to it and she blinked before extending her hand and picking it up delicately at the corner. She looked up at me, her eyes widening as she glanced at Scott then back to me. She put her champagne flute down and her hand went to her mouth as she gazed once again at the image.

'Oh my God!' she said at last, taking her hand away from her face, her wide mouth spreading into a huge, dazzling smile. 'Guys! This is . . . this is INSANE!' She put the photo down on the table and leapt to her feet, coming around the table and throwing her arms around Scott and me simultaneously.

She straightened up and wiped the back of her index finger under each of her eyes as if trying to stop tears falling. 'I'm SO bloody ecstatic for you! This is AMAZING!'

I felt the tension ebbing away from me, and the smile spreading across my face. 'Thanks, Orla.'

She bustled back round to her side of the table, sitting back down and placing her palms flat on the table.

'So, tell me everything! Like, when did you find out, and what did they say at the scan, and . . . Oh my God, have you been having morning sickness and not told me about it?' She clutched her chest dramatically.

'Um, I've had a bit of queasiness, but seriously . . . nothing I needed to worry you about.'

'Well, I don't know, Jules,' said Nick, folding his arms across his wide chest, face creased in a mocking frown. 'I think Orla's had it far too easy these past few weeks – the least you could have done is make her run around after you a bit.'

Nick can be a bit much sometimes, but it's moments like these when you can always count on him to dispel tension and come up with the right jokes at the right time. Orla obliged with her glittering laugh, throwing her head back and wiping her eyes again. 'Absolutely! God, I've been resting up in my luxury penthouse accommodation, the least I could have been doing is bringing you water and ginger biscuits. Actually – have you tried ginger biscuits? They really do help with nausea.'

I laughed. 'I've been getting through about a packet a day, actually.'

Orla smiled, but it was a different smile now. There was something forlorn about it. She reached her hand across the table and squeezed mine. 'I guess we've been feeling sick at the same time these past few weeks.' She stared into my eyes and I felt an intense surge of guilt. Just like at the hospital when I thought about Orla going there for life-saving treatment, and me going there to look at scans of my baby.

I nodded and squeezed her hand back, before with-drawing it and taking a sip of my fizz, wishing suddenly that it wasn't non-alcoholic.

'Well,' she said, sniffing and taking up her glass. 'I'd like to propose a toast to Jules and Scott, and their gor-geous little baby-to-be. Congratulations, guys!'

'Hear, hear!' said Nick, and we all clinked our glasses and sipped.

'And . . . as we're all together, I have an announce-ment too.'

We all looked at her, my eyes flicking briefly to Mag-gie, who flashed me a questioning look back. My stom-ach lurched as my mind replayed the image of Orla walking through those double doors into Haematology.

'As of today . . .' Her eyes glittered as she took in and released a deep breath. 'As of today, my tests are clear!'

'What? Oh my God!' Maggie launched herself on Orla, and Scott and I leapt to our feet, crossing around to Orla and wrapping our arms around her.

'That's amazing!' I said.

'Too bloody right!' boomed Nick. 'Course they are. No stupid blood disease is going to take down Orla Sul-livan!' He laid a bear-like arm across her shoulder and gave her a squeeze.

'Thanks, Nick. Thanks, everyone.'

So we toasted again, this time to Orla. And on this occasion, I couldn't have been happier that our news was being usurped by hers, or our prosecco being used to toast her instead of me. I felt light and floaty, like I was about to leave my seat and levitate up to the ceiling. I'd been so nervous about giving Orla our news, especially after spotting her at the hospital earlier. But not only had she been ecstatically happy for us, but she had her own brilliant news to share too. And it was the best outcome any of us could have hoped for.

'And, before you guys have to say anything . . .' Orla said, resettling in her chair. 'I think, given both sets of news this evening, it's probably about the right time for me to think about moving on.'

Silence. I didn't know what to say. I hadn't expected for a moment that Orla would come to this conclusion so quickly, and by herself.

She laughed. 'Don't look so surprised! This was never going to be a permanent arrangement, was it? And with me being well again, and you guys needing to "nest" or whatever the term is, you really need your space back.'

Scott and I glanced at each other. It was Scott who spoke. 'I mean, at some point, before the baby's born . . . I suppose, yes, that would be ideal. I mean . . . for everyone involved, not just us.'

'Absolutely!' Orla chirped. 'I mean, I love babies as much as the next girl, but I have to say that, when looking for rental accommodation, "living with a howling newborn" isn't first on my list of things I search for.'

We all laughed, and I felt a bit silly at how big a deal I'd made of the prospect of suggesting Orla should move out. Yes, she was a little outlandish, and yes, she'd been through hell recently, but she was a decent human being. And she was also an actor in her prime with no partner or children who, as she'd explained so perfectly herself, had no intention of living with a newborn and two frazzled parents.

I felt the weight of all my worries drifting away from me, making me as light-headed as if I'd been drinking the real fizz. The baby was fine, Orla was fine, and Orla was gladly moving out. I had absolutely nothing to worry about.

Orla posted a photo of herself with a glass of prosecco on her Facebook group, with the caption: 'Today I got the best news anyone could ever get. My treatment has been successful! I've been given the ALL-CLEAR!!' There followed a slew of emojis – hearts, champagne bottles, streamers. At the end there were the usual hashtags. #FightForOrla #BSH #KindUK #survivor. The messages began pouring in at once. *Over the moon for you, Orla! . . . Go girl! I knew you'd do it! . . . You're an inspiration, Orla! Just waiting for my own good news. Cross everything for me! . . . You got the ending my little boy should have had, but I'm so, so happy for you!*

I scrolled back to look at the first post Orla had made when she'd set up this group, and was surprised to note it hadn't even been seven weeks ago. That seemed impossible. I thought back to that day we'd come home from the pub and found her reeling at the kitchen table, the life-changing letter from the hospital lying in front of her. The words that had sprung from the page and seared themselves into my brain . . .

Regret to have to inform you . . . serious condition.

It had seemed there was no coming back from this. The condition sounded brutal. And yet, not seven weeks later, it was all over.

Over the coming days Orla continued to post on the Facebook page, this time with shout-outs to all the people who had supported her through her journey (including Scott and me, Maggie and Kind UK), and the people who'd been generous enough to send her special treats when she'd been at her lowest: the beauty salon and the pub. There was, as yet, no sign of her stepping out of the online spotlight she'd created for herself.

Chapter Seventeen

One Saturday morning in July, I was sitting in the kitchen, having a coffee with Maggie. We chatted about her work, my pregnancy, vague holiday plans.

I was putting our mugs in the dishwasher when Orla swept in, immediately noticing Maggie and wrapping her arms around her. 'Hey, Mags, so good to see you. How are you?'

I was the only person who ever called Maggie 'Mags'. It was strange hearing Orla say it.

'I'm good! Just have a few errands to run this afternoon, but are we still on for later?'

I straightened up and turned towards them.

'Absolutely! Meet you there about six?' said Orla.

'Fab.' Maggie slung her handbag over her shoulder as if to leave, and I realised no one was going to explain unless I asked.

'What's going on later?' I tried not to sound put out. After all, they were allowed to have plans that didn't involve me. They'd become close.

'Oh, there's a special service at All Saints that Kara's going to,' said Orla, her face radiant with a smile that insinuated I'd know who she was talking about. I must have looked blank. 'She's the mum Maggie's been working

152

with. She had the cancer diagnosis and Kind UK are helping her with some fundraising, you know?'

'Oh, OK,' I said, with what I hoped was an encouraging nod.

Maggie frowned. 'I hope you don't mind we didn't invite you. It's just it's at the church, and I didn't really think it was your thing . . .'

I laughed, but it came out as a derisive snort. 'Because I'm a heathen and might turn to dust as I cross the threshold?'

'Oh, you're so *funny*, Jules!' said Orla, putting her hand to her chest in her theatrical way.

'It's not that at all,' said Maggie, and I could tell she knew me well enough to detect I was feeling a bit left out. 'It's just a charity awareness thing – a work event for me. Orla met Kara a couple of weeks ago and they really hit it off, so . . .'

'Absolutely.' Orla had been nodding the whole time Maggie was speaking and continued to do so as she gave her own little speech. 'It's about being supportive of fellow sufferers, you know? Giving back now I've been lucky enough to have survived. Prayers and blessings, that sort of thing.'

Maggie turned back to me. 'I didn't think it was your vibe.'

It really wasn't my vibe, and I'd probably have said no even if I had been invited. 'You're right – I think I'll leave you guys to it. I have an important evening planned with Netflix and a tub of Ben and Jerry's.'

'Sounds divine!' chirped Orla.

When Maggie left, throwing a 'See you later!' to Orla, I felt strangely deflated. It was odd to feel left out when you were an adult, not a child in a playground. And these immature emotions – namely that someone was getting on too well with *my* best friend – brought back those nagging thoughts about Orla. Uncharitable thoughts. Thoughts I could never articulate to anyone, not even Maggie. Especially not Maggie. Because now, as I thought about Orla skipping off to church to spend her evening in the bosom of this charitable community, I couldn't help but marvel. I marvelled at how recent Orla's devastating diagnosis had been. At how quick and effective her course of treatment had been. At how she'd rallied, bounced back, reinvented herself as a survivor. And how, after such a short space of time, she seemed to have her feet so firmly under the table with her new tribe.

As I pushed the button on the dishwasher and closed the door, hearing the whoosh of the machine starting up, I realised I'd already made my decision without really thinking about it. I took out my phone and texted Maggie.

> Hey, do you mind if I actually do come to the church tonight? I'd like to be there to support Orla. And to see you in action too of course! Xx

Her reply came a couple of minutes later.

> Oh my God, of course you can come! We'd love to have you there! Xxx

I only felt fractionally guilty that I wasn't being entirely honest. I mean, of course I felt huge sympathy for anyone who'd received a life-changing diagnosis, and for their loved ones too. It wasn't so long ago that Mum and I had been those people. But, in this case, support wasn't really the reason I was going. I was going because I wanted to watch Orla. I wanted to see what she was like among people who were still being treated for devastating illnesses when she'd not long been given the all-clear. I wanted to see what Orla looked like in 'support' mode, putting the fight of others ahead of herself, stepping back while others took the limelight. At this point I had to admit to myself I wasn't going to the church out of loyalty and compassion, but out of a twisted – and growing – fascination.

Chapter Eighteen

I'd knocked on Orla's door to let her know I'd be coming and been greeted by rapturous exclamations. 'Oh my God, thank you *so* much, Jules' and 'This means *so* much to me.'

We walked together, All Saints being only a fifteen-minute saunter from the house, and all the while Orla chattered about Kind UK, the amazing work Maggie did, Kara and her diagnosis. I nodded and made sympathetic noises, but if I was honest, Orla's intense exuberance at the prospect of the event made me edgy. I felt like I was walking an overexcited puppy and I longed to get there so I could let her off her lead. I was desperate to hook up with Maggie, or at least mill about with other people who might dilute some of Orla's energy.

I was grateful, then, when the church came into view. All Saints was set back from the road at the end of a leafy row of Victorian terraced houses. There was a bricked courtyard at the front, bordered by shrubs and rose bushes, and in this space a considerable crowd of people had congregated. The evening was balmy and the fading heat of the sun still radiated from the stone around us, despite the church casting the space in shadow.

We spotted Maggie immediately and Orla bounded over, clasping her shoulders and planting kisses on her cheeks, despite them having seen each other only a couple of hours before. I followed, joining them and a group of women who were now taking turns to embrace Orla.

I was introduced to Kara, who sat in a wheelchair with a child of about ten standing uncertainly by her side. Kara kept one arm around the girl's waist as she chatted animatedly to Orla and Maggie about the week's news in terms of her ongoing treatment, hospital appointments, scheduled tests. An older woman stood on the other side of Kara, chipping in occasionally. I realised she must be Kara's mum. I nodded and asked the odd question, but felt ill-equipped to delve too deeply into what seemed to be such a personal subject. Orla, however, seemed to hold no such reservations, I supposed from feeling not too far removed from Kara's situation.

'So you took the plunge, then, with your hair?' Orla said.

I felt a surge of embarrassment at the subject of Kara's hair being brought up with such enthusiasm, and in front of *me*, a stranger. I plastered a smile on my face but could feel its tautness in the muscles of my jaw.

But Kara just beamed at Orla, her ice-blue eyes twinkling as she laughed. 'Well, it was falling out in clumps so I didn't have much choice!' She made the buzzing sound of electric clippers and mimed shaving her head. She squeezed the girl, who turned and gave her mum a shy smile. 'Eva helped me, didn't you, sweetheart?'

The girl nodded. I felt a sudden, unexpected sting of tears behind my eyes. I remembered helping my own mum shave her head. We laughed a lot while we did it, in that morbid sort of way you laugh at truly awful moments in your life. But looking at this fragile, shy girl in front of me, I could not imagine the horror of having had to do something like that at such a young age. I wasn't for a moment judging Kara's choice to involve her daughter – Eva was obviously old enough to need to know the truth about what was happening to her mum, and I'd no doubt that involving her in the process was a way of helping her deal with the inevitable changes that were happening. But the idea of going through something like that when still a child, or of being a mother having to watch your own daughter observing your cancer journey . . .

'Well, you've done an amazing job, Eva!' Orla leaned in to Eva and slid her arm around her shoulder. Eva responded, wrapping both her arms around Orla's waist and smiling softly. 'My God, clippers terrify me ever since my brother asked me to give his hair a trim when I was eight and I ended up shearing a bald patch into the back of his head.'

Everyone laughed and I realised any tension in the air around us was projected purely by me. I was so intent on not embarrassing myself or saying anything that could be construed as remotely insensitive, I was tying myself in social knots for no reason. And here was Orla, the life and soul of the gathering as always, taking centre stage and putting people at ease and making people laugh. For all my complaints about her attention-seeking, she really was a breath of fresh air in a situation like this. And that was reflected in the faces of Kara and her daughter and her mum. I didn't know how many times they'd met each other (it can't have been many in such a short space of time), but they clearly adored Orla.

Gradually people began drifting into the church, settling in the chairs either side of the aisle. It was a beautiful, cavernous old church, which had been modernised extensively. There were no wooden pews, but upholstered chairs set in rows on red carpet. The vaulted ceiling was made of pale stone which ran down to arched windows of stained glass. At the front was a carpeted dais with a draped altar, overlooked by a giant backlit cross.

Orla ushered us into a row, taking the aisle seat herself and leaning across to say something to a woman who sat opposite. They extended their arms and squeezed hands like old friends. *When had she met these people? How had she got so close to them in a matter of weeks?*

The vicar stepped onto the dais and crossed to the lectern, and a hush settled on the congregation. He looked no older than twenty-five, with a gangly frame and glasses that were too big for his narrow face. But his voice was deep and sonorous, and I realised he was probably older than he seemed.

'Thank you, everyone!' He spoke into a small microphone that was clipped to the lectern. 'For those of you who might not know me, I'm Reverend Paul. And I want to say how heartening it is to see so many of the community here today, at this wonderful event. Most of us here today have been touched by illness at one time or another – whether that's our own illness or that of a loved one. Many people here have lost beloved friends and relatives. I could go on and tell you my own stories on this subject, but it's not Sunday, so this is not my gig.' A smattering of laughter rippled across the room. 'Therefore, I think this is a good moment to hand over to our first speaker, Maggie Varma, Communications Director of Kind UK.'

There was enthusiastic applause as Maggie made her way up to the front, a wide smile on her face as she approached the lectern. She looked comfortable and contented – something I would never have been if I'd had to speak in front of this many people. She delivered a concise, informative speech about Kind UK and the work they do, to plentiful nods and murmurs of approval from the audience. At the end there were whoops and cheers, none louder than from Orla next to me who stuck a thumb and finger in her mouth and gave such a shrill whistle I had to resist the urge to cover my ears.

Next, Kara took to the stage. Her mother pushed her wheelchair up to the front, and Reverend Paul brought her a handheld mic. From there she delivered a devastating speech detailing her diagnosis and the implications for her husband and two children, as well as for her mother who had moved down from Liverpool to live with them and help with childcare. Despite the desperate circumstances, Kara spoke with optimism and strength, the smile rarely slipping from her face, and I found myself clenching my fists, hoping with everything I had inside me that she would recover. That she'd get better and see her children grow up, that her mum wouldn't have to take her grandchildren to their mother's funeral. I found my eyes trained on the cross on the wall above Kara's head, thinking, *I know I don't usually pray, but please God, if you're there and you're listening, do something amazing for Kara and her family.*

After Kara, a stocky man in a bright pink shirt introduced himself as Craig Lowe, a trustee of a local charity he'd set up three years ago when he'd lost his wife to breast cancer.

'Creating and running Stardust Foundation has kept me going over the last few years . . .' He sniffed and cleared his throat. 'And yes, yes, I know it sounds like some sort of intergalactic space travel programme—' appreciative laughter '—but that's exactly what Lorna would have wanted it to sound like, because she was crazy about space and planets and all that . . . I can't count the number of times we've been to the Science Museum, but I guarantee it's more than anyone else in this room!' More laughter. It struck me then how much laughter there had been this evening. Among these stories of devastated lives, there was so much humour and joy. I bit my lip, a memory of my mother's face flashing across my mind. She would have enjoyed the humour. The camaraderie. It wasn't self-centred or indulgent – it was what kept hope alive for everyone in this room. It was connecting and uplifting.

'Kind UK did amazing things for Lorna and me when she was ill, and the things they do are galaxies away from what a little operation like Stardust can do. We can't even compete. But what we are all about is the little experiences. We're about interconnectivity, and we're about seizing moments. And it's with this ethos in mind that it's about time I came clean about a little side project we've planned for this evening . . .' Craig left a cheesy silence as he surveyed the audience, some of whom were murmuring gently. 'Amy, come up here . . .' He flapped his hand at the front row and a young, auburn-haired woman stood and walked uncertainly towards Craig, a playful scowl on her puzzled face. 'Now, Amy's used to talking to big crowds as part of her job so I know she doesn't mind me dragging her up here, and don't worry, Amy, I'm not going to make you do a speech!'

Amy leaned towards his microphone. 'You better not!' she said, to more titters.

'But in all seriousness, Amy lost her wonderful dad, Keith, last year to cancer, and she's been one of the most amazing community members throughout his illness, and since his death.' Amy smiled at Craig and looked down at the floor. Craig put a hand around Amy's shoulder and gave her a squeeze. 'And I'm not here to put Amy on the spot and talk about her dad's illness or anything like that, but I do want to talk about Keith and what a brilliant guitarist he was. Or perhaps, *thought* he was, might be more accurate?'

Amy laughed, then leaned forwards again. 'As his loving daughter I couldn't possibly say—'

'It's OK!' Craig held a surrendering hand to the audience. 'Keith and I were best mates for years, so I'm allowed to take the mickey out of his guitar playing – I did it when he was alive so there's nothing new there!'

I took a moment to glance around at the warm smiles on the faces of everyone I could see. It was as if I could physically feel the comfort this was providing Amy and everyone else who was suffering. It was like some sort of invisible balm radiating from every person in the congregation. As if their smiles and laughter and sympathy had somehow become a tangible thing that could be absorbed through the skin, into the heart. This was not simply banal banter. This was important. This was special.

'So . . .' Another cheesy pause. 'You told me last time we met up that your dad's guitar was just lying around the house, and that it kind of made you sad.'

Amy nodded and sniffed again.

'Well, I hope you don't mind, but I got your aunt Charlie to smuggle it out of the house this evening . . .' He extended an arm and a white-haired woman bustled forwards holding a pale Spanish guitar by the neck. She handed it to Craig, squeezed Amy's shoulder and retreated to the front row.

'Now, as anyone who knows me will tell you – I'm an even worse guitarist than your dad, and I know you don't play, so how would you feel if we got someone who actually *can* play to come up and bring this instrument to life again? For your dad?'

Amy beamed at Craig then turned her searching gaze to the crowd, applause trickling through the rows.

'Orla!' Craig boomed, holding the guitar aloft like a summons. 'Come up here!'

Adrenaline surged through me as I turned towards Orla. Her face was alight, her smile almost too big to be contained as she rose from her seat as the applause grew louder and was intermingled with cheers and exclamations of 'Amazing!' and 'Go, Orla!'

I turned to Maggie who had an expression of rapturous astonishment on her face. 'Didn't you know about this?'

'I had no idea! Craig must have arranged it with her!' Maggie continued to clap manically as Orla made her way to the front, hugged Amy and took the guitar from Craig.

163

A chair had appeared on the dais, seemingly from nowhere, and Orla ascended the steps, her floaty skirt flaring and settling around her in long, Renaissance-like folds as she sat. Craig and Amy settled into their seats on the front row, hopeful gazes trained on Orla. The vicar ran on from the side with a microphone stand to which he attached the mic before checking with Orla it was at the right height. She smiled and nodded as an awed silence settled upon the church.

Then she began to play. The mellow sound of the nylon strings melted into the air around us, reverberating against the stone, blending and rising towards the rafters. I watched her elegant fingers pluck the instrument, her body arched over it like it was a sleeping child, the gentle waves of her hair falling forwards, gilded by a shaft of muted evening sunlight. Everyone was transfixed.

Then she began to sing. *You'll remember me, when the nights grow long and dark, when you cannot hear my heart, you'll remember me . . .*

I felt the melody tingle down my spine as goosebumps rose on my bare arms. Her voice was pure and clear like a bell. I felt the congregation around me become still as if holding a collective breath, no one wanting to move in case they broke the spell. I looked towards the end of the front row and watched someone's arm slide around Amy's shoulder. I wondered if she was crying.

When the last notes of the song died away there were several moments of complete silence. From outside came the faint swoosh of a bus driving past. Orla looked up, resting her palms on the strings and offering a humble smile to the audience.

Then the whole place erupted. It seemed everyone was on their feet at once, clapping and cheering and wiping their eyes. Maggie blew her nose next to me and when I looked at her I could see her mascara was smudged.

A man in the row behind me was muttering, 'What a thing . . . what a thing . . .' I found myself rising from my seat, my hands clapping along with everyone else, even though I wasn't really thinking about what I was doing. I watched Amy walk towards Orla, who now stood on the platform next to her chair, and launch herself at her. Orla clamped her arms around Amy, still holding the guitar by its neck. I watched Amy's body shudder as she sobbed into Orla's shoulder, turning her head to say something into her ear. Orla nodded and rubbed Amy's back.

After a few moments, Orla gently gave the guitar back to Amy, and the vicar reappeared. Gradually the applause died down.

'Well,' said the vicar. 'I wish I had a reaction like that to my Sunday sermon!' There was a ripple of laughter and more sniffing. 'What a beautiful thing to witness. Orla . . . what is there to say? You've given Amy and everyone here today an unforgettable gift. Thank you so, so much.'

Orla gave a self-deprecating little bow, which prompted more applause, then she hugged Amy once again and they both made their way back to their separate seats. Orla sat next to me and Maggie reached over to squeeze her arm and whispered, 'You are *incredible*!'

The woman in front turned around to say 'well done', and the man behind leaned forwards to squeeze Orla's arm.

165

She turned her full-beam smile on both of them. 'Thank you so much, it was really nothing,' she said with a little shake of her head.

'No,' said Maggie. 'It was *everything*.'

I sat between them, with Maggie's arm stretched across my lap as she pawed at Orla, and I felt so awkward. I turned to Orla, but all I could offer was, 'Yeah, it really was great . . . you have a beautiful voice.'

'You guys,' she whispered, batting away our compliments with a flap of her hand.

Soon the event was over and we found ourselves milling outside again. But this time we weren't clustered around Kara in her wheelchair, and people weren't asking Maggie about Kind UK or Craig about Stardust Foundation or Amy about her dad and his guitar. This time, it was all about Orla.

166

Chapter Nineteen

I didn't see much of Orla in the following weeks. She'd secured some work at Hampton Court Palace, dressing up in Tudor clothes and showing school kids around, plus she was doing evening shifts at the hotel. Scott was working late as they had an audit coming up and his boss was asking for all sorts of extra work to be delivered.

One evening I found myself sitting alone on the sofa, shovelling in mouthfuls of pasta (with butter, as pesto had started to make me feel queasy), my laptop perched on my knees as I tried to catch up with work emails. When I'd made some headway, I found myself opening up Google. Without thinking, but as if I'd been meaning to do this all evening, I typed in 'Orla Sullivan' and pressed return.

Several articles and photos of *Kilcroom High* popped up, publicity shots, Irish newspaper stories, all from years ago. Orla's most recent headshot was at the top of the images section, along with a review of the show she'd done in Shoreditch.

I scrolled down until I found her Facebook pages, but I didn't click on them. I scrolled further. I didn't know what I was looking for, only that I wanted a little bit more than what I already knew. Everything we knew about Orla came from her, and I wondered if I could find anything out for myself. Usually, when you knew someone well, you also knew other people from their life. Relatives, friends, perhaps a partner or a work colleague. But with Orla, we'd never known anyone else. Even the acting friends we'd met at her shows had been transient – people who were close to her for the duration of the show, but then seemed to fade away. Orla would frequently go for 'cast drinks' after rehearsals or performances, but she never mentioned those people again after the show had closed. It was as if they ceased to exist the moment they walked off stage together for the last time.

She'd become so entrenched in our lives from the moment we'd met her, I wondered why she hadn't clung to anyone else quite so strongly. I supposed there was Maggie. But Maggie was different – Maggie belonged to us and Orla was only close to her because of her diagnosis. But where were Orla's people? Her best friends? The ones she'd go to when she was feeling sad or lonely or fancied a night out?

I remembered about Matt – the friend whose flat she'd left her keys at the first time we met. Then I remembered her housemate, the one she'd been living with and had moved away from to move in with us. She never mentioned these people any more. How close had they actually been to Orla? Close enough to move in with her. Close enough to buy her a cherished keyring. But not close enough to keep in touch with?

At the bottom of the first Google page I saw Orla's name on a cancer discussion group. Puzzled, I clicked into it. My misgivings, however, soon vanished as I realised her contributions to the page made perfect sense, given the treatment she was undergoing, and its similarity to cancer treatment. She'd responded to a few people's posts, mainly offering support and kind words. One woman was complaining about the queasiness after chemo sessions and Orla sympathised, mentioning the ginger biscuit remedy she'd told me about at the kitchen table. The woman had responded with hearts and kisses.

On another page she'd started a thread herself:

Is anyone else really struggling with side effects from IV Vincristine? I feel so sick and completely wiped out 24/7. And what's with the tingling hands? I can barely hold my phone to type this – think I need to ask my consultant to try me on a different drug.

The post was flooded with sympathetic responses, suggested remedies for the symptoms, and ideas of how to broach this subject with her specialist. She responded to each comment with effusive thanks and praying-hands emojis. I thought back to when Orla was having her sessions. I knew she'd felt a bit sick, but I couldn't remember her having complained of tingling hands, or of having trouble holding things. But then she was holed up in her bedroom for much of the time, so perhaps I just hadn't noticed how much she was struggling, I thought with a pang of guilt.

I clicked back out of the discussion board, then tapped into the next page of Google results, expecting the useful links to peter out as they became more and more tenuously linked to Orla. But a few searches down, I noticed another discussion board with Orla's name attached to it. But this one wasn't a cancer board. I clicked into it, my pulse spiking as I read the title – *Support Group: Bereavement by Suicide.*

Something told me I should shut my laptop. I should look away. There was doing a general Google search of someone, and then there was this. I had no right to read personal posts written by Orla from ten years ago. But then, this wasn't personal. It was in a public forum and she hadn't disguised her name. Perhaps there was another Orla Sullivan? Yes, there must be, but no, as I clicked into her profile I saw the username was the same one registered to the cancer support discussion group. This Orla Sullivan was definitely her.

Without making a decision, I found my gaze sweeping the words on the screen, taking in the post Orla had made all those years ago, a post I was sure she would never dream I would be reading now.

> I just can't believe he's gone. I know that sounds like a cliché, and I don't mean it like that, I mean, I literally can't believe it. I need to speak to him. How am I supposed to process this without him? It's just so sick that I have to go through the shittest time of my life without him. Liam's the one person that could make me feel better, but he's gone.

Someone called CherryBlossom74 had replied:

> I'm so sorry for your loss. This is the denial phase. I was where you are about three years ago and it's the

toughest time. There's nothing I can say, but to let you know you're not alone. We're all here with you.

Orla had responded with praying hands and a pink heart emoji, before adding.

And is it normal to feel angry? I mean, actually angry with him for doing this to me? That sounds terrible. That's such a fucked-up thing to say, I'm sorry, it's just I'm livid with him for leaving me like this. Jesus, I'm sorry. It's late and I'm drunk and I'm just in bits. We were going to start a life together. Why did he do this?

My heart felt like it was trying to hammer its way out of my chest. I sat up and placed the laptop on the coffee table. Orla's fiancé had killed himself. This was horrific. My mind tried to grapple with the potential psychological consequences of something like that happening. I wondered at my earlier thoughts about Orla's friendship circle, and how she didn't seem to have any close friends. I could see how that might happen if you'd suffered such a devastating loss and in such a painful way. Maybe you stopped letting people in, because you realised how much you had to lose.

I felt nauseated. What a thing to have had to go through. For all Orla's attention-seeking, she'd never once mentioned this part of her life. Perhaps it was too painful. She'd shared with me the details of her father's death, but this was something different. This was a young person taking their own life, a life that Orla thought she'd be sharing. I felt a hard lump forming in my throat and swallowed it down as my eyes began to sting.

I picked the laptop back up and clicked into Facebook, heading to Orla's personal page rather than her treatment journey page. The last time she posted on here was just at the beginning of her treatment, before she set up the dedicated page, and as I scrolled I realised she was hardly ever active here. The posts were dated months apart, and a lot of them were shares of other people's posts, like a theatre promoting a show she was in, or a photographer offering acting headshots at a discounted price.

It didn't take me long to whizz back through the years. There were a couple of photo posts in 2015, views of the sea from high up, craggy rocks and seagulls and a gunmetal sky. One of the posts was captioned, 'God, I miss this place. I wish I didn't have to leave. I'm going to miss this view, and I'm going to miss you too, Dad. Get well soon! xxx.'

Then I remembered – Orla told me back in April it was the ninth anniversary of her Dad's death. These photos must have been taken when she went back to Ireland to see him, just before he died. My insides twist again. She lost her fiancé ten years ago, and then a year later, her father. She must have been so torn up. What a dark time that would have been for her. And to imagine her brother being so heartless when she went back to Ireland, after everything she'd been through . . .

The comments section was full of sympathy, just like on Orla's treatment journey page. I noticed there was nothing from anyone with the surname Sullivan, or any-one named Sean.

I went back to her timeline and scrolled back further, nerves fluttering. And there it was.

A photo filled the screen, Orla's rosy-cheeked face on one side, and a pale, chiselled man on the other, their beaming faces pressed together. The wind was buffeting his unruly black curls around his face, just as it was catching the feathery strands of Orla's blonde waves. Behind them there was only sea and sky, an amber sun sinking towards the horizon. Orla wore an orange woollen hat, and the man a houndstooth scarf around his neck. Orla's left hand was placed against her chest in a pose that looked strikingly familiar to me. It looked like the 'oh my goodness, thank you *so* much' pose she adopted when she was being theatrically grateful for something. But this time the pose wasn't a gesture of thanks – it was to showcase the delicate diamond ring that sparkled on her third finger. The photo was captioned: 'Today my dreams came true. Can't wait to be Mrs Carroll!'

There were a hundred and twenty-four likes, and fifty-seven comments. I scrolled through the thread, my thumb halting as a name jumped out at me: Sean Sullivan. So she had been Facebook friends with her brother once. His comment somehow made me feel sad. It simply said, 'Happy for you, sis. Xx'. How could everything have gone so wrong between them? Clearly there'd been a time when they were, if not close, then amicable.

I clicked out of Facebook and into Google, typing in 'Liam Carroll death'. I wasn't expecting anything to come up. After all, deaths by suicide aren't habitually reported in the press. They're quiet, private events that families deal with alone. But the articles that sprang onto my screen made me realise that sometimes these cases are reported more widely – on occasions when the police have been involved.

The first article I clicked on was from the *Kilridge Herald*, and it bore the clunky headline: 'Man in Carrick Healy Death Bridge Plummet Named'. The article went on to say a man who had fallen to his death from the bridge the previous week had now been named as local nurse, Liam Carroll. But from this point onwards the article seemed mainly focused on the ongoing safety concerns about the bridge, and how a new local petition had been set up to prohibit crossing until new safety measures had been put in place. Police still had the area cordoned off.

I clicked on the next article. This one was from the *Irish Times* and read 'Family Questioned in Carrick Healy Death'. The headline was misleading (no doubt deliberately), as it went on to describe how family and friends of Liam Carroll had been contacted by police to try and ascertain his state of mind leading up to the tragic incident. The last line stated, 'Mr Carroll's fiancée is being looked after by friends, and asks for privacy at this difficult time.'

'Jules?'

My whole body jolted, my laptop bouncing from my lap, glancing off the table before landing on the floor as I twisted on the sofa towards Orla standing in the doorway. Her face was set in an amused frown and her eyes flickered towards the laptop. My gaze followed hers and I reached for it, slamming it shut and praying she hadn't had time to read the words.

'God, I'm so sorry, I scared the absolute bejesus out of you!'

I placed the closed laptop on the coffee table and gave an awkward laugh. 'Don't apologise.' I pressed a hand to my chest, feeling my heart thudding beneath my palm and in my head.

She came and sat next to me, a concerned frown knitted on her face. 'Are you sure you're OK? Jeez, I feel awful scaring you . . . you know, in your condition.'

I took a calming breath. 'I'm absolutely fine, honestly. Anyway, you're back from work a bit early, aren't you?'

She nodded, sliding a hand around the back of her neck and rubbing the base of her skull. 'Yeah, I had a bit of a migraine coming on, so they let me go early.'

'Oh no . . . are you OK? I mean, do you need anything?'

'No, I'm all good, don't worry! Think it's just been a long afternoon staring at a screen so my eyes have seized up.'

I nodded, hoping she'd want to head up to the attic and leave me to myself again. Part of me wanted to ask her about everything I'd found online, but I knew that would be a massive overstep. And a greater part of me wanted to be alone so I could carry on googling.

As if reading my mind, Orla gave a big sigh and stood up. 'Well, I think I'll head up. Busy day being Catherine of Aragon tomorrow, so need some rest.'

I gave another feeble laugh. 'I hope you feel better. Do you have painkillers?'

'Ha, don't you worry about that. I've got a whole stash of them upstairs from when I was having treatment, so I'll be pain-free and fast asleep before you know it.'

I nodded and gave a hopeful smile.

'Actually, there was just one thing I was wondering today . . . it's your scan in a couple of weeks, isn't it? The one where you find out the sex of the baby?'

'Um . . . yes?' I said, wondering why the odd segue, and where this was going.

'Well, I wondered if you'd thought about a baby shower? I mean, if you did it on the same day it would be brilliant! We could invite Maggie and Nick over, and whoever else you want, and you could do one of those gender-reveal cakes or something?' Her eyes glittered as she said this, clearly warming to her topic. 'If you got the sonographer to write the sex on a piece of paper and seal it in an envelope, then Maggie could make you a cake with either blue or pink sponge . . . Oh my God, that would be epic!' She clasped her hands together and gave a little jump on the spot, headache seemingly forgotten for the moment.

I felt my mouth moving but couldn't quite get any words out. That's because the words I wanted to say were: 'That sounds completely horrific, and not at all like something I would ever want to do.' The idea of making such a fuss about announcing the sex of the baby, then asking Maggie to make a cake, then getting a load of people over specifically to make them watch us cut into it while showering us with gifts, made me feel awkward in the extreme. Why couldn't she understand that? But then, of course, making a fuss was what Orla did best.

I opened my mouth to gently dissuade her from the idea, but she held out her hands and spoke first. 'OK, I know what you're going to say – you hate the idea. You don't want anyone making a fuss of you because that's just not your style.'

I was taken aback. She had it perfectly. 'Um . . . yes, that's right, actually.'

'So how about we frame this differently?'

'What do you mean?'

'Well, we spoke about me moving out, didn't we?'

My heart gave a flutter of hope. 'Yes, we did.'

'And I think the time has come for me to put that plan into action. I've been looking for somewhere, you know, asking round, and I think I might have found something.'

'Really?' I tried to keep the unbridled hope from my voice.

'You remember my friend Matt? The one whose flat I left the keys at? Well, he can't afford his place alone any more, so he's looking for someone to share the rent. It's a tiny place but the location is fabulous. And it's got the most fantastic views over the docks at Greenwich.'

'Sounds brilliant.'

'And it just so happens he's looking for someone from the end of August. Which coincides beautifully with your scan, according to Scott?'

Wow, she really has thought this through. 'Yes, that's right.'

'So never mind the gender reveal and the cake and everything. Let's get a couple of people round – even if it's just Maggie and Nick – and you can tell us if you're having a boy or a girl, we can pop some champagne and I can say my goodbyes? We can toast to "new beginnings".'

I had to admit my initial resistance had completely dissolved. Orla had managed to tweak this concept to make it much more attractive. Of course, she'd now placed herself at the centre of the celebrations, but at this stage her manoeuvre simply made me smile: that was, after all, Orla's way. And I really did like the idea of popping some bubbles and telling Maggie about the baby. I also (however uncharitably) liked the idea of celebrating Orla moving out. We were all in agreement: the time had come, she was moving on to a place she was obviously excited about, and this was about to become a family home. Surely all those things warranted a small get-together and a toast or two? Yes, I would agree to this. Because I couldn't fathom how it could be anything other than harmless fun.

I can't remember being this happy in years. Or maybe ever? Watching their expressions when I told them my results were all clear was more than I could ever have wished for. They were elated! The love they feel for me was written across every inch of their faces . . . the way they beamed and shouted and leapt up to hug me . . . I've never had such validation before, from anyone. It just goes to show how, when you find the special people, you really have to hang on to them. Because not everyone is special like that. Not everyone accepts you.

Then I said I'd be moving out. And of course they respected my decision . . . but they weren't fooling me! I saw the way Scott tensed, how Jules held her breath. In a way, that was even more gratifying than the moment I told them my results. Because that was the moment I realised they didn't want me to leave. As fabulous as the baby news is, and as ecstatic as they are about my all-clear, it still means the end of an era . . . and it was their obvious disappointment at the idea of losing me that made me realise how deeply they care.

But there's more to this now. I can't only think about Scott and Jules – because there's a whole community of people out there who need me. And the thrilling thing about my results is that now I'm getting so many people posting on my Facebook and sending me private messages, telling me what an inspiration I am. Telling me that my story has helped them keep the hope alive ... hope that one day they'll receive good news themselves. And when Craig told me about Amy's dad and his guitar ... he practically bit my hand off when I offered to perform in the church as a surprise for her! What a gorgeous, warm-hearted community I've found myself at the centre of. I never dreamed I'd get to a place where just being myself would inspire and invigorate so many people. It's like it's my calling. As if the universe has placed me here for a reason.

Chapter Twenty

It was a Friday morning and blisteringly hot. I woke up with a sticky sheen of sweat all over me. My hardening belly was slick to the touch and the bedsheets were damp and ruckled underneath me. I felt enormous, despite still only being in the second trimester, and I knew the lethargy this heat had brought was the main reason. Scott had already left for work, and I pushed myself up to sitting, running fingers through my sweat-tangled hair. I grabbed last night's water and downed the rest of it. I had two hard deadlines fast approaching, but as I placed the glass back down and felt the oppressive stillness of the bedroom air, I knew exactly what I was going to do that morning. And it wasn't sitting in a sweltering box room scanning sketches.

I pulled on my swimming costume and a sundress, quickly brushed my teeth, grabbed my ready-prepped tote bag, shoving in a litre bottle of water and a packet of cookies, then I headed to the car.

There was a wild-swimming group that met in Thames Ditton in a Friday morning. I'd joined them for a while, before realising I really didn't want to swim in a group – it wasn't a social activity for me. I prized the quiet thinking time (and, in the early days, grieving time) too much. But since I'd slipped into my second trimester, Scott had made me promise I'd not go wild swimming alone. To be honest, there was usually traffic of some kind on the Thames – whether that was other swimmers, or kayakers, or people walking dogs on the towpath. The places I usually chose were not remote. But I'd promised Scott I'd only swim where there were 'a good number of people', just in case I got into difficulty. So, although I had no intention of joining the group, I decided I could swim near them and that way be keeping my promise to Scott.

I walked from the station car park and down the dust track towards the water. Hampton Court Palace stood on the bank opposite, its redbrick chimney stacks peeping through the trees. When Scott's aunt left us the house and we started talking about moving here, I was worried I wouldn't be able to find a local swimming spot. We'd come from Cambridge, and I'd been spoilt by the idyllic flood plains of Grantchester Meadows with its grassy banks and weeping willows. I'd worried everything I'd heard about the Thames was true – that it was disgustingly polluted and dangerous for swimmers. And in some places it *is* true – it would be ill-advised to swim east of Teddington, where the river becomes tidal and flows through central London. But here, it's almost like a different river. The flow is gentle and the water clear. Sometimes I can imagine I'm back in Cambridge when it's a quiet day and I'm swimming along the green curve of the water with its overhanging trees. Then I catch sight of Hampton Court Palace, or hear the swoosh of the traffic over the ancient bridge, and it brings me back. But over the past year I've grown to love this place, where nature meets history, and the bustle of the town meets the calm of the water.

I set my towel out to warm in the sun, just downstream from where the official Thames Ditton Swimmers were gathering. Slipping silently into the river, the bliss of the cold water sent a surge of euphoria through me. I pushed away from the bank, dipping my head under the surface and feeling the icy tingle on my scalp, washing away the clammy, sticky feeling I'd woken up with and making my whole body feel fresh and clean. My limbs sliced through the water and I felt the fizzing of the happy chemicals in my brain sending electricity through my veins.

I surfaced and changed to breaststroke, telling myself I'd get to the bridge then turn around and come back. Most of the swimming group were now in the water, a couple of them descending a concrete slope, the water lapping at the thighs of their wetsuits. I couldn't imagine being zipped into a thick, sodden wetsuit in this weather. Yes, the water was freezing, but with the temperatures we'd been getting this month, it was difficult to resist the urge to strip naked and jump in.

As I approached the bridge and the water was cast in the shadow of the cool stone above, I felt a sharp twinge down low in my abdomen. My hand went automatically to the fabric of my swimming costume. But the pain was gone. I continued my gentle strokes through the water, telling myself I'd be getting all sorts of strange pregnancy aches and pains in the next few months, and that it was completely normal.

Then it came again, this time so strong it made me catch my breath. As I did, I inhaled a mouthful of water, which caused me to start coughing and gasping. I doggy-paddled, bringing my legs down to see if I could find purchase on the riverbank, but it was too deep.

The sharp pain was gone now, replaced by a tight, cramping sensation that stretched right across my belly, like someone pulling a belt around me. Frantic, I twisted towards the bank, towards the concrete slope, all thoughts of swimming technique abandoned as I flailed in the freezing water, gagging on more mouthfuls of water as I tried to call for help.

Two men from the swimming group were chatting on the bank, adjusting their goggles and zipping belongings into waterproof bags. They were the nearest people I could see and, as another cramp swelled across my abdomen, I swallowed down another mouthful of water then shouted, 'Help!'

It came out shrill, more like a squeal, but it cut through the noise of the traffic on the bridge above and bounced off the stone around us. Both their heads snapped towards me and with only a split-second pause, they leapt onto the slope, waded a couple of steps before launching themselves into the river. I watched the white water of their splashing limbs approaching and a voice in my head kept repeating *just stay afloat, just stay afloat.*

I felt their arms on mine, one of them twisting me onto my back, hands under my armpits. I reached my hands towards my stomach, holding my palms against the tautness of my bump, willing the cramps to stop.

I kept my gaze on the brick of the bridge above, until my heels made contact with concrete and I pushed my legs down to stand.

The hands were still there, more hands now, holding me, guiding me. A towel was thrown over my shoulders. *Can you stand? Can you walk? What happened?*

I heard my own voice, small and hoarse. 'I had cramps . . . in my stomach . . . I'm . . . I'm pregnant.'

A woman's voice cut through. 'Sit her down over here.' She sounded older. Authoritative.

Suddenly I was in the sunshine, being guided down onto a rug. A bottle of water was brought to my lips and I drank thirstily, desperate to wash away the tang of the river water.

At last everything seemed to still. I breathed. I stroked my bump, grateful there were no more cramps for the moment. But then the thoughts crowded in. What had I done? What had happened to the baby? Was the cold water too much? Why hadn't I done more research on this, rather than a cursory Google search about wild swimming during pregnancy? How could I have been so selfish? Perhaps it was bad the cramps had stopped; perhaps that meant something worse.

My mind was reeling. I could hear people talking around me but I couldn't work out what was being said, just words here and there. *Shock . . . swallowed some water . . . get her checked over . . .*

Someone put two biscuits in my hand and I realised they were my cookies – someone had brought my bag and all my stuff over from where I'd left it. The bottle of water was mine too. Someone held a phone up to my face and I realised it was my screensaver, a photo of Scott and me on holiday in Spain two years ago. Then the phone was gone and someone was handing me another cookie. I ate on autopilot, aware only of my swirling thoughts and the buzz of voices around me.

'It's OK, she'll be here soon,' the older woman said. I didn't know who she meant – perhaps a friend of hers who was a medic or a midwife or something? But how long until she arrived?

'I . . . actually, I think I should probably go . . . I can call . . . try and make an emergency appointment—'

'You can't leave on your own! You're not in your right mind – you've had a shock.'

I looked at the woman for the first time and saw she was grey-haired and had small blue eyes like tiny sapphires set in folds of brown skin. Her expression was kind but her mouth was set in a hard line – she wasn't going to let me go anywhere.

So I sipped my water and stroked my stomach, wishing I was at the stage where I could feel the baby kick and know everything was all right. I felt like I was in a strange, riverside hospital room, waiting for an unknown doctor to come and discharge me. Parents and a toddler walked along the opposite bank, the child insisting on holding an overloaded ice-cream cone by themselves, swatting away any offer of help from their parents. My hand slid further around my stomach, and my resolve hardened. I tucked my legs underneath me and pushed myself up to standing.

'Steady on!' said the woman, standing with me and laying a firm hand on my arm.

'I really appreciate your help, and thank you for calling your friend and everything, but I'm feeling so much better now and I really think I need to get to—'

'Oh, that'll be her now!' said the woman, waving to someone.

I followed her gaze and watched a tall figure approaching along the towpath, a floaty orange maxi dress flicking up at her sandalled feet. Her hair was loose and strands of gold floated around her head in smoke-like tendrils as the breeze from the river swept over her.

Orla.

'I . . .' My voice caught in my throat. 'What? How is . . . how is she here?' My voice sounded harsher than I meant it to, but I couldn't gather my thoughts.

The grey-haired woman smiled at me. 'I called the last person in your WhatsApp messages. You know, when someone doesn't put an emergency number in their phone, that's really the best you can do!' She beamed at me, obviously thrilled with her own presence of mind and detective skills.

I fought down the rising agitation inside me and tried to harness something that felt remotely like gratitude towards this stranger who'd gone to such lengths to make sure I had a friend come to my rescue. But all I could think was 'why wasn't Scott the last person to message me?' and 'why the hell don't I have an emergency contact programmed into my phone?'

'Jules!' Orla ran up to me, arms wide, enveloping me in a hug that smelt of lavender and sun cream. 'Oh my God, are you OK? What happened?'

'I'm fine, honestly, I just had some cramps while I was swimming, but they're gone now—'

'She probably needs checking over at the maternity unit.' The woman spoke to Orla as if I wasn't there and Orla nodded her head vigorously in response.

'Absolutely, I'll drive her there now.'

'But you don't have a car . . .' I said.

'I'll drive yours.'

'But you're not insured on my—'

'Jules.' Orla held me by the shoulders and looked into my eyes with such intensity I couldn't look away. 'The most important thing is that we get you to the hospital for a check-up. It's a ten-minute drive from here; the insurance doesn't matter. OK?'

'But I can drive . . .' My voice petered out as both women shook their heads at me. This was the first time I'd noticed all the men had melted away, either back into the river or towards their beach towels and water bottles.

'You're not driving anywhere. Scott would never forgive me if I let you drive after what's happened.' She crouched down and started throwing my belongings into my tote bag. She picked up my sundress and bunched it up and I, without being instructed, held my arms up to allow her to pull it down over my head. I felt like a naughty child being hurried up by a busy parent.

She slung the bag over her shoulder and placed a hand on my back, turning towards the grey-haired woman. 'Thank you so much for all your help.'

'Yes, thank you . . .' I added, weakly. 'And please thank them . . . the . . . the men who came and got me . . . I don't know their names . . .'

She nodded. 'I will. You just feel better, OK? And maybe no more wild swimming until after the baby's born?'

I felt the heat flush my face as I gave a mute nod. Embarrassment surged through me as I waddled next to Orla, who strode lithely along the riverbank, so much taller and more graceful than me. All the while she rested a parental hand on my back, and it took every drop of willpower I possessed not to shrug it off. And the worst part was that she really had gone out of her way to come and rescue me. I had no choice but to feel grateful, beholden even. I hated that.

Chapter Twenty-one

I gave my name at reception and was asked to wait in the same area I'd waited for my twelve-week scan. On a table next to me were leaflets detailing the symptoms of an ectopic pregnancy, and another with information about the recurrent miscarriage unit. A couple opposite clutched black-and-white printouts of their scans, and I watched the man take out his phone and take a photo of them. A woman next to the water cooler sat hunched over, her head in her hands, while her partner rubbed her back, a frown creasing his brow. A little boy of about three ran up to him, and he forced a smile, gesturing towards a stack of toys in the corner, encouraging him to go and play.

Not for the first time I considered the brutality of this place. Here, you could have someone living the best moment of their life alongside someone who was living the worst. Someone who'd just had a miscarriage confirmed, sitting next to someone cooing over scans of their perfectly healthy baby. Someone who'd rushed in with unexpected bleeding, next to someone who was in the early stages of labour. It was so heartbreakingly strange.

As I mulled this over, I realised I didn't yet know which side of the fence I was going to fall myself. Would I be walking out of here elated at being told nothing was wrong? Or would I be calling Scott, tears streaming down my face, begging him to come and get me? *Don't be stupid, Jules . . . you just had a few twinges, there's nothing wrong with the baby.*

'Shall I call Scott?' Orla's voice cut through my thoughts.

'What? Um . . . no, don't do that.'

'But it's probably lunchtime now – he might check his phone if you at least send him a message?'

I gritted my teeth. Orla was right, I should let Scott know what was going on. He'd be furious if he knew I'd gone through all this and not even tried to get hold of him. So I sent him a message:

Hey sweetheart, don't want to worry you but just getting checked out at the hospital cos I had a few cramps. Sure nothing to worry about. Call me when you get this. Xxx

'Juliet Burton?' The voice startled me and I glanced up at a severe-looking woman in her fifties with wiry, sand-coloured hair and black-rimmed glasses. Orla and I stood up in unison, and I felt the need to raise my hand, as if to confirm it was me, not Orla, who was the patient. The woman's face conceded a professional smile and she held her door open for me. Orla stepped forwards too and I turned to her.

'Really, Orla, you don't need to come in—'

'Nonsense!' She smiled. 'It's no trouble at all.'

I thought back to Orla refusing my company when she was going through treatment and wondered why she couldn't see I now wanted the same privacy she'd requested back then. But perhaps she didn't see this as the same thing. Perhaps it *wasn't* the same thing.

Just like in the car park, I felt a helpless sense of surrender. Of not wanting to drag anything out for longer than it needed to be. So we both ended up in the obstetrician's room, Orla watching me intently as I relayed to Dr Grant exactly what had happened. The doctor fired intermittent questions at me as she scribbled on her notepad. *How many weeks are you? Are you a frequent cold-water swimmer? Have you had these pregnancy cramps before? Have you had any bleeding? What does it feel like now?*

Eventually she stood up and ushered me to a large, padded chair in the corner of the room. She placed a wide length of paper-towelling over my lap and asked me to lift my sundress to expose my swimming costume. Then she wrapped a black strap around my body, under which she placed three plastic discs with wires which ran to a machine. She tapped some buttons, before attaching a cuff to my upper arm and taking my blood pressure. Orla watched every movement the doctor made with stern concentration, as if she was an examiner, assessing the doctor's every decision.

Dr Grant wasn't a great talker, and I could tell she was intent and focused on getting to the bottom of the medical puzzle, rather than being one of those doctors who delighted in making patients feel at ease and untroubled. I reminded myself that getting answers was more important than being placated by a fuzzy bedside manner, but at that moment I really could have done with some inane chat about the weather.

I tried to distract myself by looking around the room, trying to read the tiny words on the computer screen, seeing how many birds I could count in the branches of the tree outside the window, watching two planes streaking lines across the sky, counting the seconds until their vapour trails crossed. I turned my head to one side and spotted a teddy bear on the shelf above the machine I was hooked up to, next to some medical tomes. It was small and purple, and wore a T-shirt bearing the name 'Pam' in swirly pink writing. I wanted to ask if that belonged to a patient, or whether Dr Grant's name was Pam and a patient had gifted it to her, but before I could decide whether or not to speak, Dr Grant did.

'Right,' she said, stabbing at more buttons on the machine before unstrapping me. 'You can pull your dress down now.'

I did as I was told and came back to sit in the chair next to Orla.

'There's nothing to indicate any problems with baby – heart rate is completely normal, which is a good indication that baby's happy.'

I felt a swell of relief washing over me, making me light-headed. I found myself nodding as if to emphasise her good news, making it more real, more true. 'So, what were the cramps then?'

'Well, the monitor picked up on some slight Braxton Hicks – these are sort of practice cramps our bodies produce during pregnancy to prepare for labour. Now, it's a bit early for you to be experiencing these, but they might have been triggered by the cold water.'

I nodded again. I'd read about these cramps. They were nothing, everything was fine. 'And what about the sharp pain I had . . .' I glanced over at Orla, wishing again she wasn't here. 'The pain I had low down that was like a stabbing . . .'

'Ah yes, this sounds like classic round ligament pain; again, it's very common in pregnancy – it's just your ligaments stretching and preparing themselves. These can be quite sudden and severe – people sometimes get them when they cough or sneeze – but, again, they might have been triggered by the cold water.'

My disappointment at the realisation I probably shouldn't be wild swimming again during my pregnancy was muted by the pure euphoria of knowing the baby was OK. This was fine. I could stop the swimming for my baby. As long as the baby was OK, this was a small price to pay.

There was a rap on the door and a man with horn-rimmed glasses poked his head around the door. 'Sorry, do you have a moment to go over those bloods with Dr Rashid?'

'Yes, tell her I'm on my way.' Dr Grant picked up a folder from her desk and gave me her warmest smile yet. 'Do you have any more questions?'

'No, thank you so much.'

'Pleasure,' she said, standing and waiting for Orla and me to gather our belongings and head to the door. 'Any more cramps, any bleeding, or anything else you're worried about, you know where we are.'

I nodded as we all walked out into the waiting room, and I thanked her again, watching her head down the corridor. I turned to Orla, who I realised hadn't said a single word since we'd been called into Dr Grant's room. 'I just need to call Scott,' I said, pulling out my phone.

'Of course! Take your time.'

I walked further down the bustling corridor, pressing the phone to one ear and my finger to the other to hear myself better. But Scott still didn't pick up. He was probably in a meeting. But whatever he was doing, I knew he'd be anxious after receiving my first text with no follow-up, so I typed out another message:

Everything's fine! Just seen obstetrician and she gave me and Wotsit a complete once over, just some normal cramping, nothing to worry about. See you later. Xxx

Orla and I walked back towards the entrance, out through the stream of cool air by the sliding doors and into the raw heat of the midday sun. Orla was still being unusually quiet as if her mind was elsewhere. It was rather disconcerting.

As we rounded the corner towards the car park, a nurse in lilac scrubs nearly barrelled straight into us. 'God, I'm so sorry!' she said as we manoeuvred round each other. Then she stopped and took a step back. 'Orla?'

'Oh . . . Kayleigh, hi,' Orla said, taking a step back herself, her mouth moving silently as if unable to decide what words it should form.

'I thought . . . you're not . . .' Kayleigh's smile dipped into a frown.

'No!' Orla cut in, shaking her head. 'No . . . I'm just here with my friend, Jules.' She gestured towards me and I smiled.

'We should probably get going,' Orla said, moving away, clearly reluctant to make conversation with Kayleigh. 'Have a good rest of your day!' she called as I scuttled after her.

'You too!' called Kayleigh, raising her hand to wave as Orla half ran across the zebra crossing towards the car.

Once we were inside and the air-con was on, I turned to Orla. 'Was that one of the nurses who did your treatment?'

She nodded but didn't say anything.

I sighed. 'Orla, I'm so sorry about today.'

'What do you mean?' She faced me, eyes wide with confusion.

'I mean dragging you all the way to the river to chauffeur me to the hospital, making you wait around, then not realising how traumatic that would be . . . bringing back memories of your treatment.'

'Oh, honestly, it's fine!' she said, shaking her head and flapping her hand to dismiss my comments. 'It's . . . it's been no trouble at all.' She paused and looked down at her hands. 'I . . . I guess, I just hadn't really thought about what being back here would feel like. It's not just the hospital corridors and seeing the staff . . . it's everything . . . the smell, you know? It was just more overwhelming than I'd considered it might be. That's all.'

'Well, you didn't need to show up, and you certainly didn't need to stay with me, so I really appreciate it. Thank you.'

'You're welcome.' She beamed then, showing all her beautiful white teeth. 'Now, let's get you home.'

Scott was flustered and stammering when he called me back half an hour later as I sat at the kitchen table with a mug of tea Orla had made me.

'I'm so sorry I didn't pick up, I just—'

'It's fine . . .'

'No, but this has made me realise I should put your number on the safe callers list so it comes through at all times – if you go into labour and I don't—'

'Whoa, we're a bit far off from that just yet!'

'I know, but still – if anything happens while I'm at work . . .' His voice trailed off and I could picture his worried frown, eyes darting across the floor as he imagined all sorts of scenarios playing out.

'OK, that's a good idea about my number coming through. But don't go getting worked up about today, OK? Everything is absolutely fine.'

'But you're not going wild swimming again . . . are you?' I heard the pause and realised he'd added the 'are you?' because he didn't want it to sound like he was telling me what to do.

I sighed. 'No. No, I'm not. At least, not until the baby's born.'

'OK . . .' I could practically hear him thinking how best to voice his relief. 'That's . . . that's probably a good idea.'

We said our goodbyes and I laid my phone back on the kitchen table.

'That's so lovely, isn't it?'

I'd been so absorbed with my conversation with Scott I'd forgotten Orla was there. 'Sorry?'

'It's so lovely,' she continued, 'you know, to have someone who's that worried about you, isn't it? Someone persuading you to stay safe, and making you promise to take care of yourself. It's . . . it's romantic, isn't it?'

I nodded slowly. I hadn't really thought of it in terms of romance, but I supposed it was sort of romantic. I had a sudden impulse to ask Orla about Liam. About the fiancé she'd so tragically lost ten years ago. About whether or not there'd been anyone since then. Anyone to worry about her, or to make sure she stayed safe. *I suppose that's what we are to her now.*

She looked down into her mug. Her long fingers picked something from the surface of her tea, inspecting it before rubbing it away on her thumb. 'I should go and get changed for my shift at the hotel.'

'Oh God, I'm sorry you had to leave work this morning to come and get me.'

'It's fine, honestly, I was just finishing up at Hampton Court when I got the call, so it was perfect – I was just around the corner from you.'

'Well, I . . . I'm really grateful for everything you did today. Thank you.'

'Seriously, Jules, don't mention it. You and Scott have done more for me since I moved in here than anyone else in my whole life. You supported me when I thought I was dying.' I looked at her and saw the watery sparkle of tears. 'I can never repay you both for being there for me. Today was nothing.'

She gave me a sad smile, then stood and walked from the room. And once again I felt a weight pressing down on me. An intensity in our relationship I didn't want. I felt suffocated by it. Suffocated by the knowledge that she felt such gratitude towards us, and such closeness to us. I wished she had never been diagnosed with this disease – of course I did. But I felt sickened that a huge part of that wish came not from concern for Orla, but from a desperation to disentangle her from our lives. I didn't want to have been her saviour, any more than I wanted her to have been mine today. I didn't want our lives to be linked by such heavy chains. I wanted her to be the fun woman we met in the pub, who simply became our lodger. Who lived upstairs, went about her own business and paid us rent every month. But no matter how time passed, and how much closer it got to the day when she would move out, it seemed every interaction between us pulled us closer together, knotted us more firmly, like wet rope.

I tried to keep my mind fixed on the leaving party, as I'd now come to think of it. Because that little get-together Orla was planning would be the end. The moment the knot was finally teased open, the threads untangled just enough for us to break free, and for me to be able to breathe again.

Chapter Twenty-two

The following week felt settled and calm. I occasionally experienced the sharp, round ligament pains the obstetrician had explained to me, but the fact she'd reassured me they were normal meant they didn't worry me. The Braxton Hicks contractions hadn't happened since, which made me think it must have been the cold water that had caused them so early in the pregnancy. My nausea was ebbing away each day, and I found myself able to eat and drink things I'd been finding it difficult to stomach only a couple of weeks previously ... green pesto, peanut butter, bananas.

Work was busy, with several deadlines happening to fall within the same month, and a couple of new projects I hadn't wanted to turn down taking up a lot of time in terms of initial sketches and proposals. But I was good-busy and had a real spring in my step. I loved all the projects I was working on, the doctor at the hospital had reassured me my baby was doing well, and I had the twenty-week scan where we'd find out the sex of the baby to look forward to. I was also excited Orla was moving out and Scott and I would finally have the house back to ourselves again. I could start nesting, storing baby equipment in the attic and deciding which room we were going to call the nursery. I might order some paint samples, I thought.

Orla had several auditions in quick succession, one for a touring musical, one for a fringe theatre production in east London and one for a yoghurt commercial. The first commercial audition had led to a recall three days later, and the theatre auditions had required quite a lot of prep in the form of songs to learn and lines to memorise. On several mornings we could hear Orla practising a song (something from *Chicago* I think) in the shower upstairs, and one evening I'd listened at the bottom of the attic stairs, thinking she was having an argument on the phone, only to realise she was rehearsing lines from the play. So between her regular shifts at work, her auditions, and my heavy workload, we didn't see much of each other. I was, however, buoyed on the couple of occasions we did bump into each other in the kitchen, as she threw me comments like 'I really need to chuck some things away before I move out next week' or 'Do you have any spare cardboard boxes? Just packing some stuff up for the move.' These left me in no doubt she was as keen to move out as I was to say goodbye to her.

I felt a glow of contentedness when I imagined Scott and I curled up on the sofa together, chatting baby names, knowing we were the only people in the house. I'd even mellowed to the idea of us keeping in touch with Orla. I wondered if she'd occasionally text us the details of a new play she was in, and we'd rock up to watch, meeting her in the pub for a drink afterwards, knowing she was no longer in any way our responsibility, and that we'd be getting separate trains home.

Our twenty-week scan came round, and there had been no let-up in the hot weather. The air outside was humid and sticky and smelt of hot tarmac as we got into the car on the driveway. Despite my positive feelings about the pregnancy, it was hard not to become anxious on scan days. What if the scan revealed anomalies that hadn't been picked up previously? What if the strong heartbeat from two weeks ago was no longer strong? What if the baby wasn't growing properly?

We sat in the same waiting room I'd sat in with Orla only a week before, with the same leaflets on ectopic pregnancies and recurrent miscarriages. Dr Grant emerged from her room and called in an eager-looking young couple, her gaze flicking towards me momentarily but showing no signs of recognition, and I wondered how many hundreds of patients she'd dealt with since my impromptu visit.

Eventually, a sonographer with a name badge that read 'Emmy' called us through. My heartbeat was insistent in my ears as she slicked the cold gel onto my stomach, imploring me to 'relax'. I kept my eyes trained on the grainy image on the monitor, as swirls of grey morphed across the screen, like a murmuration of swallows.

And there it was, the flickering bean of a heartbeat. 'There's baby,' Emmy said, smiling. 'And all is looking good . . .' She drew her words out as if not wanting to leave too much silence. Perhaps she'd learnt that silence spurned anxiety. Perhaps she'd had scans herself and knew how it felt. She went on to reassure us that all limbs were present and correct, then set about clicking on the screen with a mouse as she took the required measurements.

Eventually she asked, 'So, are we finding out the sex of the baby today?'

We both nodded vigorously. 'Yes,' I said. 'If . . . if you can tell us then we'd like to know.' My voice sounded small and childlike, and Scott squeezed my hand and gave me a smile I knew he reserved for when he was finding me sweet.

'OK, well, if you're sure, I can already tell you . . .' She looked at us, one final questioning glance before the cat was out of the bag.

'OK,' we said in unison.

She smiled. 'It's a baby girl!'

I felt myself draw in a quick breath as tears welled up. Scott wrapped his arms around me and I found myself quietly sobbing into his neck. I don't know why – we'd have been thrilled whether she'd said boy or girl. It was just that somehow the confirmation made the baby seem so much more real. This was a real baby. Our baby. Our little baby girl.

I felt like a helium balloon floating out of the hospital, lighter than air and only tethered by Scott's hand holding mine. Everything was all right, the baby was healthy, and we were going to have a little girl.

'Are you going to be able keep this a secret until Maggie and Nick get here later and the celebrations are under way?'

'Of course I am!' I said, grinning up at Scott as we climbed back into the car.

'And Orla? You're not going to blurt it out as soon as you see her when we get home?'

'My lips are sealed until the appropriate moment when we're all together this evening,' I promised.

As we approached the house and Scott put his key in the lock, I couldn't help but experience a flashback to the time we'd arrived back at the house together, euphoric from our trip to the pub to celebrate my positive pregnancy test. The time we'd discovered Orla, distraught at the kitchen table having just received her devastating diagnosis.

As we kicked our shoes off by the door I gave a tentative call. 'Hello?'

There was a flash of movement by the kitchen door and Orla appeared, a look of panic on her face. 'No, you're not supposed to be back yet! Don't come in!'

'What? Why?' I asked, a surge of adrenaline bringing heat to my face.

Then came another voice from the kitchen. It was Maggie. 'Because we're not finished in here and you're not allowed to see yet!'

I felt the panic dilute. 'OK, I'll head straight upstairs and finish off some work . . . is that OK?'

'Yes, perfect,' said Orla, clasping her hands together with glee. 'And don't come down for two hours – that's when Nick's arriving and when we can get the party started.'

'Can I help with anything?' asked Scott with a helpless shrug.

'Nope – women only planning this one.'

'Oh right, charming. I know when I'm not wanted. Might as well go for a run then.'

So we retreated; Scott to get changed for his run, and me to my studio. I told myself I'd finish some sketches and send some emails, but really I spent the time gazing at the scan photos, googling baby names and eagerly anticipating this evening's 'party' and the celebration that would herald the beginning of the next stage of our lives.

At six thirty I tentatively knocked on the kitchen door and was granted entry. Maggie and Orla had gone all out on the decorations. Pink and blue balloons were strung in rows around the room, and along the patio windows hung bunting emblazoned with the words, 'Boy or Girl?' The dining table was laden with food – ring doughnuts with blue and pink frosting, a platter of delicate white triangular sandwiches, a huge glass bowl of strawberries, a glistening chocolate fudge cake. Orla thrust a flute of pink fizz into my hand, assuring me it was non-alcoholic, and I nodded mutely, still trying to process what had been done to transform the room.

'Wow! You girls have gone to town!' said Scott as he walked through the door, hair still wet from his post-run shower.

'Well, we wanted to make sure Jules had the best ever gender-reveal party!' said Orla, offering Scott a glass of bubbles that was faintly tinged blue. Orla saw him eyeing it suspiciously and giggled. 'We got a bit carried away with the whole boy–girl theme so I added food colouring to the prosecco.'

'That was all Orla's idea!' Maggie laughed and grimaced at me.

Scott took a sip. 'Well, if anything I think it's improved the taste.'

Orla beamed. 'I can add more if you like?' she said, teasingly.

'You know what? I think I'm OK . . . but thanks.'

I sipped my drink, which tasted like Appletiser without the apples, and looked around the room. I remembered my reluctance to have a 'gender-reveal' party, and how Orla had reassured me we could do something that wasn't really about the baby. That's how she'd got me to agree to this. She'd described a simple get-together where we invited Maggie and Nick, told them if we were having a boy or a girl, then toasted Orla's new place and 'new beginnings'. But this wasn't that. This was exactly what I didn't want. A huge fuss made out of announcing the sex of the baby: everything pink and blue and screaming 'gender-reveal' party.

But then I gave myself a talking-to. What did it actually matter? It was still going to be the same people here – me, Scott, Maggie, Nick and Orla. Why was it important whether there were pink and blue balloons strung up around the room? Or gender-reveal doughnuts? Or dubiously coloured fizzy drinks?

Nick arrived ten minutes later holding a large pink gift bag which he proffered after an inquisitive glance at Maggie, clearly to check he'd brought the right thing and was handing it over at the right moment. Inside, wrapped in blue tissue paper, was a gorgeous set of newborn onesies, with tiny little red-and-blue boat motifs.

'Mags, they're gorgeous, thank you . . . you didn't have to get a present for the baby.'

'Well, isn't that the whole point of a baby shower or a gender reveal or whatever you're calling this?'

I glanced at Orla, trying to telepathically convey our agreement about the party. 'Actually, it's not—' But my words were cut off by the doorbell. I put my glass down to go and answer it but Orla was too quick. She gave a little squeak of excitement and bounded into the hallway. I followed, and was taken aback when she threw open the door to reveal Kara, sitting in her wheelchair, and another woman with red hair whom I half-recognised.

Orla embraced them both, exclaiming, 'Amy! So glad you could make it!' as she hugged the mystery woman. Then I remembered – Amy was at the church service. Her father had died of cancer, and it was his guitar Orla had played when she sang that evening.

I stood by the kitchen door and could feel myself gawping at them. I willed myself to smile, unsure what exactly they were doing here. Orla kicked the shoes in the hallway towards the shoe rack to give Kara space to manoeuvre her wheelchair into the house. She wore a yellow sundress, the straps resting lightly on her protruding collar bone. Her arms were also painfully thin, and a green and yellow scarf was wrapped around her head. She looked up and noticed me.

'Jules, lovely to see you again.'

'You too, Kara,' I said, feeling awkward and unprepared. 'How are you?' I cursed myself for asking such a stupid question when she was clearly so ill.

But Kara just smiled. 'I'm all right, actually. Between chemo rounds, so not feeling too bad at the moment.'

I nodded. 'That's . . . that's great. And, Amy, I don't think we met at the church – I'm Jules.'

Amy held out a hand and I shook it. Orla laughed. 'Look at you, Amy, all businesslike with your handshakes.'

Amy laughed. 'Oh God, sorry. Old habits and all that. Anyway, it's lovely to meet you, Jules. Thanks so much for having us.'

'Oh gosh, it's no problem at all. I mean, I haven't planned any of this, it's all Orla and Maggie's work.'

'And we've loved every minute of it!' Orla beamed. 'Anyway, let's take you girls into the kitchen and get you some drinks!'

Orla made the introductions, then bustled about preparing drinks for the new guests. She encouraged us all to help ourselves to the buffet, explaining what everything was and asking if anyone had any allergies. It was a strange feeling, watching her play the hostess in my own home. But then, this was all her idea, so it sort of made sense.

Orla threw open the patio doors. 'It's just so stifling, isn't it? I mean, I don't think opening the doors has helped, the air's so muggy out there.' She started up our large electric fan on the breakfast bar, muttering about 'getting some air moving'. Then she began fiddling with her phone and the Bluetooth speaker, and some summery, Cuban-style music started up. She turned down the volume so it was just bubbling away in the background, then picked up her own glass of fizz and looked about the room, giving a contented sigh.

'What do you reckon? Happy with how it's turned out?' she said, turning to me.

'Absolutely, it's . . . it's great. Thank you.' I watched Maggie chatting to Kara, and Amy laughing with Nick and Scott, and thought yes, this is a nice bunch of people. And I felt a sudden lightening of my mood as I realised it made total sense Orla would invite Kara and Amy – they were her friends, after all. And this party was supposed to be a celebration of Orla moving out and on to new pastures. So of course she'd want to invite people too. I had Maggie and Nick; she had Kara and Amy. I suddenly couldn't think why I'd found it so strange to see them at the door. Perhaps it was just because I hadn't expected it – like the blue and pink balloons.

A new thought suddenly struck me. 'Is Matt coming?'

'What?' Orla gave me a puzzled frown.

'Matt . . . I wondered if you'd invited him along?'

'I . . .' Her mouth curved downwards as if I'd said something truly perplexing. 'Why would I invite Matt?'

'Well – this was supposed to be a sort of leaving party for you, wasn't it? As well as a gender-reveal, of course. And as you're moving in with him, I thought maybe he'd be making an appearance too?'

Her eyebrows lifted and she nodded slowly. 'Oh! Yes, of course. Sorry, I'm so slow on the uptake! I actually did mention it to him, back when I first had the idea, but unfortunately he's in a show at the moment so he couldn't make it.'

'Oh, OK.' I sipped my drink, that familiar tightening sensation turning in my stomach. The feeling that had nothing to do with the pregnancy, but everything to do with Orla. Why, I wondered, if she'd invited Matt to begin with, had she reacted with such confusion when I'd asked the question? And, as always with Orla, I couldn't pinpoint exactly what my suspicions were. I couldn't articulate the problem, even to myself. This was a small thing. A forgotten invitation. A misheard question. This didn't mean anything. It was inconsequential. But, as I was learning, nothing was inconsequential when it came to Orla.

Chapter Twenty-three

Minutes later there was a chiming of metal on glass, and I looked towards the buffet. Orla stood there, beaming.

'OK, you chatterboxes! Time to pipe down while I say a few words!'

There were titters from Kara and Amy, and a booming 'bloody actresses!' from Nick, which made Kara and Amy laugh louder.

'I'm not here to steal the limelight,' Orla continued with a pointed glare at Nick. 'But I just wanted to say a huge thank you to Jules and Scott. You opened your home and your hearts to me back in January when I was merely a damsel in distress—'

'—in the pub,' added Nick.

'Ha! Yes, a damsel in distress in the pub, thank you, Nick! And you truly got more than you bargained for over the coming months. But, without getting all saccharine, you guys are the best. You looked after me in my hour of need because you're just such bloody special people. Not everyone would have done that – but you did. And I'll never forget it. And tomorrow I'm moving out. And as sad as I'll be to leave, I'm so excited for you guys and everything that's to come . . . I just hope you'll remember me, and perhaps come and watch me in my god-awful plays from time to time.' She raised her glass in the air. 'To Jules and Scott!'

I sipped my drink as everyone smiled at us, Scott putting his arm over my shoulder and giving me a squeeze. As everyone's eyes remained on us, I felt a mounting pressure to say something myself. Unsure how to launch into an improvised speech, Orla came to my rescue.

'Now, let's get to the main event – Jules, tell us whether your gorgeous little bubba is going to be a girl or a boy!'

Everyone cheered, and Nick put his glass down so he could hammer out a drum roll on the table.

'OK . . .' I began tentatively, aware I needed to eke this out a bit, as was the custom. 'Firstly, I'd like to thank Maggie and Orla for arranging this lovely do for us all. You've both outdone yourselves, and Scott and I really appreciate it. Secondly, Orla . . .' I swallowed, finding my words suddenly claggy in my throat. 'It's been wonderful living with you. You really are the life and soul of the party, and you've coped with a difficult few months with incredible spirit and gumption, which is . . . truly admirable.' The words felt somehow false; my tone unconvincing to my own ears. But looking around I could see the earnest smiles on everyone's faces, and I knew they were buying it. They were convinced, which made me wonder why I wasn't. 'So I just wanted to say, yes, absolutely we'll be coming to watch you in future plays – you can't get rid of us that easily!' More laughs. 'And let's drink a toast to your new home, and to new beginnings.'

'To new beginnings!' Everyone clinked and sipped.

'And now, the moment you've all been waiting for . . . the gender reveal . . .' I gave what I hoped was a dramatic pause, making eye contact with everyone in the room before I continued. 'Scott and I can now reveal that we are having a . . . girl!'

Cheers and gasps erupted around the room, and I couldn't help but give a little laugh, thinking about how they would have been identical cheers and gasps had I said 'boy'. But still, even the bah-humbug party-pooper in me had enjoyed that moment and its celebration of our baby.

A sharp bang caught me off guard. I jumped, stepping back from a hug with Nick. I looked across at Orla but she'd disappeared in a shower of sparkling pink confetti.

'Oh God, sorry, everyone! I didn't realise it'd be as loud as that!' she said, flapping her hand to disperse the shimmering cloud of pink.

I breathed, waiting for my heart rate to return to normal as everyone laughed at the obliteration of the buffet by the tiny plastic discs.

'Pink plastic fudge cake anyone?' Nick said.

'Oh crap! I'm so sorry!' Orla giggled again as Kara and Amy swept forwards to try to salvage the ganache and the strawberries. I joined them, placing my glass down to pick the confetti off the top of the sandwiches, and attempt to unstick it from the doughnut frosting.

Amy and Kara chattered next to me, and I picked up snippets of their conversation – Kara talking about where her daughter wanted to go to secondary school versus where she and her husband thought was more suitable. I smiled, imagining Scott and me having a similar conversation in years to come. Then I glanced at Kara and felt my heart contract. Would she survive to see her daughter start secondary school? Did speaking about normal stuff like this make her forget for a moment, or were her illness and its dreadful possibilities weighing down on her every second of the day?

I looked up, wondering if Orla would contribute to their conversation in her usual carefree manner, putting people at ease and knowing exactly what to joke about and when. But she was nowhere to be seen. I glanced around the kitchen but there was only Scott and Nick chatting to Maggie by the breakfast bar. Moving towards the patio doors I cast my gaze around the garden, but she wasn't there.

I don't know why this unnerved me. She could have been in the bathroom, up in her room, taking a phone call or just having five minutes to herself. I tried to quell the first flutters of anxiety that were winging their way up from the pit of my stomach into my chest. I looked around the room. Amy and Kara had finished gathering up the confetti and were in animated conversation by the buffet table, and Scott, Nick and Maggie were laughing at something in the kitchen. Maggie caught my eye and mouthed the words 'You OK?' I nodded and forced a smile, and she turned back to Scott.

I felt like I was on the outside looking in. Everyone else was enjoying themselves, completely oblivious to the change in the air. I felt like a barometer, attuned to this slight pressure fluctuation that had set my needle quivering. But I was being stupid. This was just about my past frustrations at Orla's sometimes dramatic behaviour. This was because the last time we all had a party in this room together, she'd put my nose out of joint with her acting-role announcement on my birthday, when she'd opened my prosecco and interrupted the moment at which I was meant to open Scott's gift. Nothing like that was going to happen today. And if she did waltz in here with news of a potential acting job, I'd be thrilled for her. I didn't want the limelight today – I was happy for Orla to take it. Yes, I reasoned. More prosecco-popping and more toasts to Orla would be just fine. This thought calmed me and I felt the tide of my anxiety ebbing away.

This newfound peace made it all the more startling when the scream came.

Every head turned towards the hallway, all eyes watching as Orla threw open the kitchen door, her phone clutched to her ear and her face contorted into an anguished grimace. Her eyes flickered around the room, then she slowly brought the phone down, staring at it as if it was an object she'd never seen before – something alien and terrifying.

Maggie and Amy rushed to her side, taking her arms and guiding her towards a bar stool. There, she slumped forwards, her head in her hands and her hair falling across her face. My stomach roiled, sending waves of nausea pulsing through me. I was the only one who hadn't moved. I felt paralysed. I stood by the patio doors watching everyone fuss and fawn over Orla, pushing her hair back from her face, stroking her arm, laying a hand on her shoulder, gently asking her questions. But I knew before she even brought her head up to face her audience what she was going to say. I don't know how, but I just knew.

And eventually it came. She waited for the voices to quieten, then she let her hands drop to the table and brought her gaze up, eyeing each of us in turn before delivering the line I knew she would, as surely as if I'd been a prompter in the wings, holding the script: 'I've just had my test results . . . I've relapsed. It's back.'

Everyone gasped or exclaimed or swore. The three other women reached for her, the two men stepped back, looking at each other with devastation etched on their faces.

I laughed. It was terrible.

I felt it like a convulsion spasming through me, and I clamped my palm across my face, terrified it would come again, desperate to keep it down, muffled inside me. Thank God the others were too preoccupied with Orla to look my way, and too engaged with their own words and questions to hear the awful sound I'd made . . . the scoffing, disbelieving snort that had escaped my lips. And now, with my hand pressed to my mouth, I felt my head begin to shake. I didn't decide to do it, and I couldn't stop. It was as if the same impulse that had caused me to laugh had now taken over my nerve-endings and was moving my head back and forth. Maggie looked up, then came towards me, arms outstretched, pulling me into a hard embrace and whispering into my ear, 'I know, I know . . . it's OK . . . we'll get through this . . .'

I couldn't bring myself to hug her back, or take my hand away from my face. I just stood, rigid, staring at Orla over Maggie's shoulder, watching her tear-streaked face as she relayed her phone call with the hospital. 'They said the blood tests and the CT scan I just had have come back positive . . . I need to start treatment again on Monday, this time combined with radiation therapy. And they might need to operate. I just . . . I can't believe it, I . . . everything was so perfect . . . I thought it had gone.'

As Maggie released her hold on me, I felt my hand drop to my side and I found my voice. 'They called you at seven thirty on a Friday night to break that news to you? Over the phone?' There was a beat of silence and all eyes turned to me. I'd said those words more harshly than I'd meant to, but I couldn't control it. I felt like I'd lost control of certain elements of my body, and all the while my heart pounded in my chest.

'I know!' Orla said, shaking her head. 'Isn't that brutal?'

Everyone shook their heads sympathetically, having taken my outraged tone as a criticism of the hospital.

'I just . . .' Orla continued. 'I've got so much to do . . . I'm moving in with Matt tomorrow . . . he lives in Greenwich at the top of this huge apartment block and—'

'Orla, your doctors are here in Kingston,' Kara said. 'I mean, of course they can transfer you, but from experience, if you're happy with your consultant at this hospital, it's really best for continuity's sake that you stay under their care – they know you personally and how you responded to your last course of treatment.'

'Also, you don't know how you're going to feel after treatment,' Maggie said. 'Especially if your sessions are daily this time round – you don't really want to be struggling up to a top-floor apartment, I mean . . . what if the lift breaks or something?'

I watched Orla's pitiful face, upturned as she drank in every word Maggie said. 'Yes, I hadn't thought of that . . . of course, you're right . . .'

Oh God, this cannot be happening.

The next few minutes were blurry. Maggie went back to Orla's side, while Scott came over to me, lowering me onto a chair and stroking my hand with his thumb, pulling me towards him and kissing my hair.

'What are we going to do?' I whispered, closing my eyes.

I felt the rush of his sigh in my ear. 'What *can* we do? We just have to do our best, like we did before. Take her to her appointments, hope it works this time round.' He took my shoulders and held me. I opened my eyes and looked into his sorrowful face. He attempted a smile. 'She's got our support, and she's got Maggie and the whole of Kind UK behind her . . . not to mention her friends in the charitable community. I'm sure she'll beat this.'

And I realised then that Scott hadn't understood my question. I hadn't meant: *How are we going to cope with the devastation of Orla's illness?* I'd meant: *What are we going to do now we can't ask her to move out?*

And maybe that made me a horrible person. I looked at Scott, then I turned and looked over at Maggie and the others still huddled around Orla. Someone had placed a mug of steaming tea in front of her, and a box of tissues. Amy rubbed her back and Kara held her hand. Nick and Maggie leaned in, listening intently to whatever Orla was murmuring to them between sobs. And here I was, the only person in the room trying to work out how the hell we were going to get Orla out of our lives now.

It's the most heartbreaking thing in the world when the elation that comes from being told the disease is gone is wiped clean away by the word 'relapse'. And the thing about this disorder is you never know when, or even if, it's going to happen. It could be the next week, month, year, decade . . . or never. So your joy is always tempered with worry. Or at least it should be, if you want to play it safe with your emotions.

But in reality there are no emotional tricks you can play on yourself to blunt the sharp stab of horror you feel at those words . . . 'It's back. We have to start treatment again.'

It was the best moment for it to happen, though. Not only did I have Scott and Jules with me, but Maggie, Nick, plus Amy and Kara. It was, for all its awfulness, a beautiful moment in that sense. Having all those loved ones surge towards me, all that support flowing around the room, washing over me and lifting me up. The reassurance that of course I wouldn't have to move out . . . of course I could stay just where I was. In the place I was loved the most. In my home.

Chapter Twenty-four

I'd been looking forward to the following week. My work that was due was nearly done, and I'd been planning on powering through so I could take some time off at the end of the week to go shopping. Now we'd had the twenty-week scan and knew all was well, I'd felt a sudden urge to buy things for the baby. I wanted to look at some buggies (or 'travel systems' as I'd learnt they were called). I wasn't much of a shopper when it came to buying things for myself as I tired easily and found I procrastinated far too much. But thinking about choosing things for our baby was different. I wanted to peruse the shelves of dummies and bottles, the rows of Babygros and sleepsuits. I wanted to start thinking about cots and bedding and paint colours and cuddly toys. I supposed this was what 'nesting' was all about. My clothes were also getting tight and uncomfortable, and I wanted to visit a maternity shop in Richmond I'd heard good things about. I'd also envisaged Orla would have moved out by now, so I'd have more headspace for the baby.

But this wasn't how it played out. I took Orla to the hospital every day and, just like before, she said she didn't want me to wait for her. So every day I ended up coming home, attempting to focus on work, failing miserably, then going to pick her up. I didn't finish any of the work I'd intended to complete, and had to beg an extension on some preliminary sketches I was doing for my new author. She and her agent were understanding, but I was angry with myself – I'd never missed a deadline in my career so far, and I prided myself on submitting my work punctually. When Friday came around there was still so much to do, so I had no chance of making a shopping trip or even thinking about baby paraphernalia.

Orla became more and more tired and withdrawn as the week went on. She informed me on one of our drives to the hospital that she'd be having treatment every day for five days, followed by a two-week break, then repeat, for four cycles. It sounded gruelling, and thinking about how her first round of treatment had wiped her out, I wondered how she'd cope with this more aggressive schedule.

But I have to admit, worrying about how Orla was going to deal with her treatment wasn't my main cause of concern. When she told me her schedule, my mind selfishly slid towards the maths: four rounds of three-week cycles. That was twelve weeks. Orla would finish her treatment when I was in my final weeks of pregnancy, and then have to wait for the results to see if it had been successful. Last time, that wait was at least three weeks. This would take us right up to the wire in terms of when the baby was expected to be born. Would Orla still be living with us when I went into labour? When we brought the baby home from the hospital? I couldn't quieten my racing heart when these thoughts ran through my mind.

But apart from Orla's terrible fatigue and her shrinking into her bedroom to convalesce, there was a strangely contrasting occurrence online. Orla was back. The same evening she'd found out that her condition had returned, she'd updated her Facebook page with the news and received an outpouring of sympathy.

Throughout the following week she posted photos of her receiving her treatment, and at home in bed afterwards. Photos of her face, sallow-skinned and shadow-eyed, peering into the camera. Photos of her holding up pill bottles, captioned 'Never been a fan of antibiotics but they've told me I have to' with a crying-face emoji, or 'Painkillers, nausea-killers, infection-killers – so many pills I rattle when I walk! Hope they work!' with a fingers-crossed emoji.

But this time it wasn't just the Facebook group. Orla set up similar accounts on Instagram, X and TikTok. I watched videos of her explaining how her treatment was going, how she was feeling, even what music she was listening to in order to cheer herself up. Some of these videos were posted from the hospital while she was hooked up to her IV line or in the waiting room or walking the corridors, and others were taken up in her attic room.

It felt strange to see my own home featured in these videos. She never showed other parts of the house, and the videos usually only showed her face as she spoke to the camera, but I still felt a faint sense of invasion as I watched the likes and reactions and comments piling up, knowing these videos had been filmed in the room just above my head, a room we'd decorated ourselves and opened up to Orla when she had nowhere else to go. A room that was possibly going to be our baby's nursery . . . if we ever got it back.

Over this week of treatment, Orla's persona itself was contrasting. Whenever we spoke, she seemed barely able to stay awake. Either that or she was so nauseated she clamped her arms around her torso, taking frequent sips from a plastic water bottle. Her conversation diminished as the week wore on until by Friday we hardly spoke on the journey to and from the hospital. But the videos she posted online were always wordy and eloquent. They weren't long, but in them she was animated and articulate.

After the first week of therapy was done, Orla improved. She'd skip down the stairs in the morning and we wouldn't see her until the evening. Her social-media following increased daily, and I couldn't help checking in regularly to see how many new people were engaging with #FightForOrla. It was in the hundreds and counting.

One afternoon, I saw that her Instagram bio had been edited to include a link to a website. Clicking on it I was taken to a site called 'Orla's Fight', and found myself gawping at a circular headshot of Orla, with the website name emblazoned across the top of the screen in sloping, midnight-blue letters. Another photo underneath showed a grey-skinned Orla seemingly asleep in a hospital bed, tubes winding under her gown and an oxygen mask pressed to her face. When had this been taken? Who would have taken a photo of her during her treatment with her eyes closed? Not for the first time I found my head shaking as I struggled to form the questions I wanted to ask myself, the questions I wanted to ask Orla, but couldn't. There was one question I could ask her, though. And I asked it one Saturday morning in our kitchen.

'Your website's great – how did you do that?'

She put her coffee down on the breakfast bar and beamed at me. 'Oh! Maggie introduced me to this wonderful guy called Gary who does all this whizzy website stuff – we went out for dinner last week with Mags, and he said I should send him some stuff and he'd see what he could do. So I sent him some photos and a bio and . . . hey presto!'

'Wow, I mean – it looks incredible. I spent weeks trying to cobble together my website and it looks nowhere near as good as yours.' I remembered watching endless YouTube videos about WordPress and hosting and domain names and getting so frustrated I wanted to throw my laptop out of the window.

Orla took a sip of her coffee. 'I'm so lucky – Kind UK footed the bill. They did one for Kara last year too. And Gary's such a poppet, he does them for half price or something. Anyway, I'm blessed with the support.'

Later that day, I should have been in Adobe Photoshop editing final drafts. But I wasn't – I was back on Orla's website. In the 'About me' section, she explained all about her diagnosis and how her condition affected her white blood cells and therefore her immune system. She explained it caused dizzy spells and could ultimately attack internal organs, including the liver, spleen and bone marrow. She then explained she was a freelance actor and went on to give details about *Kilcroom High,* explaining she'd been in the hit TV series in the early 2000s, and that this had been her 'springboard into the acting world'. It was a bizarre addition to the medical information, but I supposed it might help with engagement if people recognised her from the series. Perhaps they'd feel closer to her, knowing they'd watched her on TV all those years ago.

Orla's page now had over three thousand followers, and the comments rolled in as I watched, presumably from people who'd seen the notification the moment it had been posted, as I had. *Oh my God I used to LOVE that show! You were amazing. You got this! #FightForOrla.* I had a sudden thought. Should *I* be posting on her social media and website pages? Should I be commenting and 'liking'? No, don't be silly, said a voice in my head. You're supporting Orla in other ways. You know everything that's happening with her illness. These pages are for people who don't know, who are removed, and who want to show their support through an online community. I decided then that I would never interact with any of these pages. If I started, it could become awkward; I could start to feel guilty I hadn't commented for a while, so would feel I should, or maybe that I hadn't 'liked' anything for a few days or I wasn't being supportive enough. No, I would stick to giving Orla lifts to the hospital and making her sandwiches. Those were my roles. She wouldn't want us to do any more than we were already doing.

The blog section of the website had taken all the Facebook posts and collated them into dated entries with titles like 'Diagnosis' and 'The Journey Begins' and 'Fighting For Orla'. I found myself clicking on the 'Subscribe' button to make sure I was notified the next time she posted.

In this break between treatment sessions, Orla was barely at home. It was fantastic that she felt well enough to resume her temping when she wasn't undergoing treatment, but I knew it wasn't just her work keeping her out. She had catch-ups with Maggie, coffee mornings with Kara, Amy and their support group that met at the local bakery, posters she dropped off at libraries and cafes detailing the local groups and charities, like Stardust Foundation, and meetings at the church where she was trying to set up some more events to raise awareness of rare blood disorders. She was like a one-woman marketing machine, and I wondered whether Maggie had ever considered giving her a job at Kind UK.

I used the weeks Orla wasn't undergoing treatment to knuckle down and complete the work I'd neglected when I was ferrying her to and from hospital. I also held in my mind that I'd be on hospital taxi duty again when her next round started, so I tried to get ahead with the work I already had booked in. But even as I did this work, the lure of social media was a constant hum in my mind, and my phone was only ever an arm's length away, ready for me to grab when the screen lit up with a new notification from one of Orla's pages.

It was a strange sort of obsession. Most people are preoccupied with their own social media – how many likes or interactions or comments people have left on their *own* posts. Those short, rapid-fire doses of dopamine that we, as a society, had come to crave. The bizarre need we all seemed to have developed for the approval of strangers. But this was different, this wasn't about me. I was an invisible participant in these groups and on these pages, only ever observing, never interacting. When I saw Orla had posted a new photo or a new blog post, my rush came from sporadic surges of something else, not the dopamine lift of a 'like' but something darker. A solitary, unshared feeling. Incredulity. Disbelief.

I watched her follower numbers tick up and up every day, until they were in the thousands across all social-media platforms. Her website now featured videos of her talking us through her medication, her treatment sessions, her skincare routine (because the drugs had dried out her skin and she needed special products to combat this). Comments flooded her posts: *you're a hero, Orla . . . you're my treatment guru! . . . God bless you* and endless cries of #*FightForOrla*.

The night before her treatment resumed for the second round, she posted a new blog on her website and across all socials. It said:

This week has been a tough one. I'm restarting treatment tomorrow, and I know the ride will be rough. Like so many others fighting a similar battle alongside me, I'm dreading the onslaught of symptoms, but at the same time I'm eager to get started as I know this will take me one step closer to beating this thing once and for all!

At the beginning of the week I had to go into hospital for tests – these were to make sure my kidneys and liver are functioning correctly, and to check my platelet count before treatment can resume. I also had to undergo some extra tests because of breathing difficulties I experienced last time. I'm happy to report that all tests came back clear, which means I've been approved to begin my second round of treatment tomorrow morning.

A massive thank you to my dear friend @arty_jules who will, once again, be giving up so much of her week to taxi me to and from hospital. Her support means the world to me, and I can't begin to explain how desperate I'd be right now without her and @scottie.burton90.

I read the entry in my studio, my shoulders tensing at the 'dear friend' section. We weren't supposed to be dear friends. We were supposed to be people renting a room out to her. She was supposed to be our lodger. How had this happened?

Then my eye caught on the photo that accompanied the post.

It was a selfie and showed a mournful-looking Orla sitting in a hospital chair, staring directly into the camera. Only her head and shoulders were showing, but there was enough distance for us to see the large machine beside the chair, wires snaking from it towards Orla. The caption read: *Extra monitoring of oxygen levels.*

Something in this photo was bothering me, and it took me a moment to realise what it was. It wasn't the caption or Orla herself or the monitor . . . it was the shelf above the monitor. Because on this shelf was a teddy bear. It was small and purple, and emblazoned across its T-shirt, in curly pink words, was the name 'Pam'.

Chapter Twenty-five

I recognised that bear. And it only took me a few seconds to remember where from – the day I'd suffered cramps when I'd been swimming, and Orla had come to my rescue. She'd driven me to the hospital maternity unit and we'd seen Dr Grant, the obstetrician. And in that room, where I'd been hooked up to the monitor, was that small, purple bear.

My mind spiralled into several different thoughts and questions while I stared at my phone screen, bringing it closer to my face. Could there be several such bears throughout the hospital? Could 'Pam' be an acronym for something medical? But no, surely the most likely thing was that 'Pam' was Dr Grant's name, and this was *her* bear.

I brought up Google and went to the Kingston Hospital website, navigating to the maternity unit and searching 'staff'. And there it was – a list of all the staff who worked on the unit. And there *she* was: Dr Pamela Grant. This was her bear. Given to her by a colleague or family member, perhaps.

I clicked back into Orla's page and looked at the photo again. Now the machine caught my eye. I hadn't been paying much attention to it, but I realised the monitor she was sitting next to looked just like the one I'd been hooked up to in Dr Grant's room to measure my contractions.

And then there was Orla's dress. Only the top of it was visible, around the neckline, but it was unmistakably the orange maxi dress she'd been wearing that day. It had stayed in my memory because I'd watched her approach us along the towpath after the stranger had used my phone to call her. At first she'd simply been a tall figure in a floaty dress, then I'd realised it was Orla and felt it like bolt of electricity . . . like the flash from a camera, imprinting the memory of her image in my mind like a photograph.

I went on to remember the end of my hospital appointment. Dr Grant had been called away by another doctor, and I'd gone into the corridor to call Scott . . . I'd left Orla by Dr Grant's office. The room had been empty. *Had she . . . could she really have . . . ?*

When Scott arrived home that evening, I was ready with my phone. I ushered him into the living room and shut the door. Orla was upstairs, and I knew from Instagram and X she was busy responding to messages of support from her followers and posting updates on her state of mind ahead of her treatment resuming tomorrow morning. But still, she could come down any minute, and I didn't want her to overhear what we were saying.

I explained everything to Scott, the fact that Orla had posted that blog earlier with the photo of her in the hospital room at the top. I explained something had stopped me in my tracks, and then went on to tell him about the bear. He listened with intense concentration, his brow furrowed and his eyes trained on the phone screen, which I held up to his face. My heart hammered as I spoke, and I felt as I imagined a witness giving evidence in court might feel, desperately willing a jury to believe what they were saying.

When I'd finished, he took the phone from me and brought it closer to his face, blinking at the screen and chewing his lip. 'Are you sure? I mean, could this perhaps be a different bear? Does "PAM" stand for something, I mean . . . in medical terms?'

I swallowed. 'Well, actually, that did occur to me when I first saw the photo, but then I looked up Dr Grant's name and it's "Pamela", so obviously it's her bear.'

Scott winced. 'I mean . . . that's not really conclusive evidence, is it?'

I felt a surge of heat through me at his patronising tone and swallowed down my annoyance as he handed my phone back to me and reached into his back pocket to bring out his own phone.

Swiping and tapping at the screen, his face suddenly brightened and he read out what he'd found: 'The NHS PAM (or "Patient Activation Measure") is a means for providers to ensure they "have robust assurance arrangements in place to provide and maintain high standards of safety, security and suitability for their premises and equipment at all times".' He looked at me, a note of near triumph behind his expression as he slid his phone back into his pocket. 'If this is an NHS-wide initiative, then maybe those bears are everywhere? Could be a fun way management decided to remind staff about it?'

I gave a derisory laugh. 'Scott, the NHS are haemorrhaging money – I hardly think they're going to pay for purple teddy bears to display in every hospital room across the country!'

'Well, I don't know!' He sounded irritated now. 'Maybe it's not in every room, maybe just in a couple of departments. Or maybe the bear gets moved around . . .'

I felt my eyes grow round and my mouth fall open. 'Did you miss the bit about Dr Grant's first name being Pamela? It's *her* bear, OK?'

'OK, I just . . .' He tousled his hair and frowned at me, then attempted a half-hearted smile. 'I can't believe we're arguing about a teddy bear.'

'It's not the teddy bear we're arguing about – it's your inability to admit to yourself, and to me, that this is weird. Not just the bear, but the fact that the machine Orla's next to is the contraction-monitoring one from the obstetrics department, *not* an oxygen-monitoring one. And that she's wearing the same dress she was wearing the day I saw Dr Grant in that very same room.'

He sighed. 'Firstly, we don't know it's the same room – I hardly think you're an expert on specialised hospital equipment, who would know the difference between a contraction monitor and an oxygen monitor – and secondly, how do you know Orla hasn't worn that dress since that day? It's perfectly feasible she went to a separate hospital appointment wearing the same thing. I mean, it's been bloody hot, and that's a summer dress – which doesn't strike me as grounds for . . . for whatever it is you're accusing her of.'

I stared at him, my hand going to the firm curve of my belly. My voice came out as a whisper. 'I can't believe you don't think this is weird . . .'

He sighed. 'Look, Jules – I know the fact Orla is still living with us is not ideal. I know you were looking forward to "nesting" or whatever you call it, and getting the baby's room ready, and beginning our new life . . . and God, I'd love that too! But sometimes you have to look at the bigger picture. We're *so* lucky. We have each other, and we have a beautiful house and a gorgeous little baby girl on the way. Orla has none of those things. Plus, she has an illness that could be terminal. I just think, for now, we have to do the right thing. We have to support her, the way Maggie's supporting her, and the rest of the community is supporting her—'

'But they're not supporting her like *we're* supporting her! The support Maggie's giving Orla is part of her *job*. And everyone else is just throwing "likes" and emojis and comments at her. They're not providing her with a *roof* over her head! They're not driving her to the hospital and making her meals and sharing their *home* with her. They're not giving up their child's *bedroom* for her!'

'OK, now you're sounding dramatic—'

'Don't you—' I stopped myself, bringing my hand to my mouth and trying to quell the surge of tears.

'Hey . . .' Scott stepped forward and wrapped his arms around me. 'I'm sorry, I didn't mean to upset you, I just don't know what to say . . . there's not really a way round this at the moment. And is it really that terrible? Orla keeps to herself most of the time, and she's managing to pay her rent in full every month. Is it so awful having her here?'

I felt myself stiffen against Scott's embrace, unable to reciprocate, such was the burning indignation inside me. Scott had made me feel ridiculous and callous and – what had he called me? – *dramatic.* And from the chaste kiss he planted on the top of my head, before smiling as he headed though the double doors into the kitchen, I could tell he thought he'd calmed his unreasonable wife in an admirably measured way. I could also tell he thought the subject was now closed.

Well, I thought, a rising determination swelling inside me. The subject was *not* closed.

Resentment grew in me as the days ticked by. Scott swanned off to work every morning, pecking me on the cheek and heading out of the front door before Orla even woke up. It was me who was left at home, offering her coffee or toast to 'settle her stomach' before driving her to the hospital, trying and failing to get enough work done, then collecting her again, making her lunch and leaving it outside her room, knocking on the door when I collected her empty plate and calling 'Do you need anything?' softly, in case she was asleep. I found myself playing pretend conversations with Scott over and over in my head, ones in which I explained this to him. Explained that it was easy for him to say, 'Is it really so bad living with Orla?' when I was the only one who really had any contact with her. I was stuck at home with her, I was looking after her. I was also the one who held suspicions about her, however vague those might be. Scott had no idea what it was like – he simply left for work in the morning, then returned home to me – Orla being either up in her room or out somewhere at a support group or a Kind UK meeting or seeing Kara and Amy. His only acknowledgement that I was the one shouldering the burden of care was the occasional comment along the lines of 'You're being so amazing with Orla' or 'You're such a trooper, doing all your work and still caring for her'. But my bitterness interpreted these comments as sticking plasters. They were placatory, intended to calm my annoyance. And when faced with my workload, my carer's duties and my personal feelings about Orla, they were meaningless.

I'd noticed our car journeys to the hospital had become almost silent. When I did speak I sounded wooden; so desperate was I to dampen down the irritation in my voice, I had stripped it of any emotion. *How was today? Do you need water? Shall I get you some lunch?*

As always, Orla seemed to become weaker and frailer as the days went on. But on Friday when I picked her up, she kept glancing at me as I drove back to Seymour Avenue.

Eventually she spoke. 'Are you OK, Jules?'

'Me?' I was thrown. 'Yes, of course. Why do you ask?'

She sighed. 'You just seem ... quiet, that's all. Is everything OK with you and Scott?'

A stab of annoyance flared inside me. Here I was ferrying her to and from the hospital every day when I was twenty-four weeks pregnant, and she was supposed to have moved out, and she was assuming it was Scott and I who had the problem? Also, how dare she think I'd confide in her about our relationship anyway – we were

235

not *friends*. She was our *lodger*. But even as this refrain entered my head for the thousandth time, I knew it was becoming weaker – she had become so much more than our lodger. And all entirely against my will.

'Scott and I are just fine, thanks,' I said, keeping my voice a dull monotone.

She turned to look out of the passenger window, and I could see her in my peripheral vision, twirling her fair hair into a thick rope before raking her fingers through it and starting again. 'I really appreciate everything you and Scott are doing for me, you know. I hope you realise how grateful I am . . .' Her voice was soft and almost dreamlike.

'You don't have to keep saying that, Orla. We know you're grateful.' This time I couldn't keep the hint of irritation at bay.

'I don't know what I'd do without you,' she said, turning to look at me.

We'd stopped at a red light, but I kept my head resolutely facing forwards; the only response I could manage was a taut smile that wouldn't reach my eyes.

Saturday morning, I pulled the covers over my head against the sound of Scott coming back from his run and rummaging about the room for a clean towel. I must have drifted back off to sleep because then he was next to me, fresh from the shower, in clean clothes, and placing a steaming mug of tea on my bedside table.

'Morning, sleepyhead,' he said, kissing me tenderly on the lips. 'How are you feeling?'

'Fine. Tired. Thanks for the tea.' I hitched up to sitting, feeling a tightening across my bump and placing my hands there as the contraction passed. It had terrified me in the river, but now I knew these contractions were just my body practising for labour, I found them sort of comforting.

Scott grimaced and lowered himself onto the edge of the bed next to me. 'Are you OK? Is it painful?'

I smiled. 'Nope, not at all. Just like someone tightening a band across my middle.'

'I wish I knew what it all felt like,' he said.

'You won't be saying that when I'm in labour,' I said, winking at him as I picked up my mug and took a sip.

'Ha, you're right there! Much better to leave that level of pain to you ladies,' he said with a teasing frown.

'Well, with the fuss you made when you stubbed your toe last week, I think you might be right.'

'Oh my God, agony! That pain was probably at least twice as bad as childbirth! If not three times!'

'Yeah it sounded like it—'

Our laughter was cut off by a sudden cry from above. We fell silent and waited, staring at each other over the wisps of steam that rose from my tea. Then came the sobbing. It was desperate and raw, and interspersed with low moans.

Scott stood and I set my tea back down on the table, swinging my legs out of the bed. We both made our way up the attic stairs, the sobs and moans growing louder as we approached Orla's bedroom door.

Scott knocked softly and there was a sniffing sound and a quavering 'come in'.

We cast each other a wary glance before Scott pushed the door open and we entered. My first thought upon seeing the room was how different it looked from the last time I'd been in there. That time, the floor had been strewn with discarded clothes, books, makeup and empty chocolate bar wrappers. Used mugs had been dotted about, and splodges of food stuck to the surfaces of the table and shelves. I remembered the almost empty carton of Greek yoghurt, spotted with mould.

But now the room was like another space entirely. The floor was clear, and the bed made, the white duvet pristine and without a single crease. All the books had been replaced onto the shelves, and the glass of the coffee table sparkled in the sun that poured in through the open French windows. There was one book on the coffee table, a hardback that was emblazoned with large capital letters: *Bad Blood: Surviving Against All Odds*. On the bed were about twenty bottles of pills of various sizes and colours, laid out in an arc, all the lids facing towards the top of the bed. I felt a sudden jolt of panic. Had Orla taken something? Had she overdosed?

Orla was nowhere to be seen, but the door to the bathroom was ajar and I could see the light was on in there. Scott hung back and I stepped forwards, knocking lightly on the bathroom door then pushing it gently.

The door swung open to reveal Orla sitting on the closed lid of the toilet, one hand clamped over her mouth and the other holding something black and cylindrical. It took me a moment to process what I was looking at, because Orla didn't look like Orla. Her head was completely shaved, only small blonde tufts sticking up in patches from her scalp. And the white bathroom tiles were almost completely obscured by a carpet of thick, golden hair.

Chapter Twenty-six

'Oh my God.' It was Scott who spoke, pushing past me to kneel on the bathroom floor next to Orla and put his arms around her.

I stood in the doorway, watching, feeling a blank numbness creeping over me. My words felt like they were calcifying inside me, even the blandest platitudes unable to make their way from my lips. *Oh, Orla, I'm so sorry. You should have told us and we could have been here for you. How can we help? What do you need?* I knew all of these were probably appropriate things to say right now. But I couldn't bring myself to say any of them.

Orla leaned in to Scott and he pulled her closer, rubbing her arm and making soft shushing noises as you would to soothe a baby. My hand went to my stomach, my thumb stroking my bump. *It's all right. Everything will be OK.*

'I just . . . I knew it was time, you know?' Orla sniffed and brought her gaze up to meet Scott's. Then she turned to me. 'I couldn't put it off any longer . . . I couldn't stand to watch my hair falling out in clumps every time I touched it.'

'Of course, of course,' soothed Scott. But all I could do was think back to the car journey yesterday, and seeing

Orla twisting her thick hair into a spiral and combing her fingers through it. *No . . . don't go there. That's a poisonous thought.*

I knew I needed to say something, so I knelt on the floor in front of her, taking the clippers from her hand and looking into her tear-stained face. 'Would you like me to help you?'

She sniffed, her eyes round and red-rimmed as she gave me a watery smile. 'That . . . that would be good. Thank you.'

Scott stood up, squeezing Orla's shoulder and murmuring something about making tea before heading downstairs. I gently went over her scalp, taking off the sorry little tufts she hadn't been able to reach. When I was done, I turned the clippers off and placed them on the edge of the sink. Orla had a bin bag ready and began gathering up her hair. I hesitated, not knowing if she'd want me to help, or would rather be left alone for this moment. I crouched down and she didn't say anything, so I helped her, heaping handfuls of soft, caramel waves into the bag.

Children's books never being far from my mind, this action made me think of the fairytale Rumpelstiltskin . . . the man who lies about his daughter being able to spin straw into gleaming strands of gold . . . and the devil-like character who appears and makes the daughter promise to give him her firstborn child.

It was at that moment Scott reappeared at the door, snapping me from my daydream.

'Knock, knock,' he said, handing Orla a mug of tea which she reached up for with trembling hands.

'Thank you . . .' Then she was sobbing again, placing the mug down by the sink to prevent the contents sloshing over the side. 'Thank you both so, so much.'

Scott crouched down and took her hands. 'You don't need to thank us.'

'No but I *do*!' Her voice was firm, emphatic. 'You . . . you both have no idea how much you mean to me . . . everything you've done and are doing. I . . . I couldn't wish for better friends.'

Scott glanced at me, his eyebrows raised as if to say, *See? She needs us. How could you be so suspicious of her?* Perhaps I was reading rather too much into one fleeting expression, but that's how it felt at the time. It felt accusatory. And once again, Orla's words squirmed inside me, the impulse to correct her so overpowering . . . *We are not supposed to be your friends. We are not supposed to mean this much to you.*

In bed that night, I turned off the light and hunkered down with my mobile phone. There were several notifications across my social-media apps, and they were all to do with Orla. She'd clearly spent the afternoon writing a lengthy blog post which she'd put up on her website, before linking it to her Facebook, X and Instagram. There were also photos – her newly shaven head, her sore eyes staring into the camera, the bottles of pills, the book on the coffee table . . . both of which I now realised had been so artfully laid out so they could be presented like this on social media. There were shots of her hair strewn across the bathroom floor, photos she must have taken before she burst into tears, causing Scott and me to appear, alarmed, at her bathroom door.

The response was overwhelming. I mean, *I* felt overwhelmed, and the posts weren't even mine. Orla now had tens of thousands of followers, and her posts were regularly being shared, often by big accounts. Someone called MrsHealthLifeLove, who had over three hundred thousand followers on Instagram, reposted Orla's photos, along with the link to her website. This influencer was all about making the most of life with her picture-perfect meals, healthy walks and beautiful home. She mentioned in her repost that her sister had died from leukaemia, which for her meant that anyone in a similarly horrifying situation was her 'spirit sister' and should be supported to 'triumph over one of nature's biggest cruelties'.

It was like she'd attached a lit firework to Orla's online presence. The comments, reactions and followers shot up as I watched, the numbers ticking ever higher every time I refreshed the page, something I couldn't stop myself doing, almost compulsively, as I sat in the dark, staring at my glowing phone screen clutched in my hands.

On Sunday, Maggie came over. Not to see me, but to see Orla. She'd seen Orla's posts from the day before and wanted to comfort her, so she brought cakes and pastries and fresh coffee in paper cups from the cafe at the end of our road. Orla was nowhere to be seen, so Maggie gave me a quick hug, placed my decaf latte down on the breakfast bar, then headed upstairs, the paper bag clamped under one arm, and the two coffees held in each hand.

I tried to get some work done in the studio, to catch up with the hundred things I'd neglected the past few weeks since I'd been swept up in the turmoil that was Orla's life. But I couldn't concentrate. I left the door open so I might be able to hear what was going on up in Orla's room, but I heard nothing but the occasional bubble of laughter, intermingled with the odd sniff, and what could have been sobs but were too muffled to discern.

Three hours later, Maggie descended the stairs, briefly popping her head into the studio to say goodbye and to apologise for dashing off – she and Nick had an afternoon planned with some of his old uni mates who were only in town for one night. I watched her cross the red-brick driveway and open her car door, then turn, look up and wave at the house. I waved back, but I wasn't sure if she was waving at me, or at Orla in the room above.

I was determined to take the following week by the scruff of the neck. I'd spent so much time ferrying Orla to and from the hospital, then when I'd had the chance to catch up with my own work, I'd spent my time distractedly scrolling through her social-media feeds, counting her followers and reading all the hundreds of comments on each of her posts. This week would be different. I had to knuckle down, meet my deadlines (especially the extended ones), and absolutely stop getting distracted by all things Orla.

One morning I walked into Kingston for ten o'clock, knowing that was when my favourite local art supplies shop was open. It was sunny, but not too hot at this time in the morning. Wispy clouds scudded across the cornflower sky like strokes of acrylic painted with a wide brush. That reminded me I needed some new wash brushes. This shop stocked Winsor & Newton (a classic, and my favourite brand), so it would be a good opportunity to buy a new set. I reached into my pocket to add brushes to my list.

As I pulled my phone out I noticed a woman emerge from the station coffee shop. She was holding a bright pink smoothie with a domed plastic lid, and she'd stopped to tear open a packet, removing a long straw and slotting it into the hole in the top. She crumped up the packet and walked to a bin, throwing it in and turning back towards the station. I felt myself staring, trying to place her. She was tall, Black, and her hair was braided in thick plaits that fell almost to her waist. But what had prodded something in my memory was the fact that one of the plaits was a vibrant, royal blue colour, and I couldn't help feeling I'd noticed it somewhere before. She stopped once again and began single-handedly rummaging in her bag while trying to hold her drink steady, and I found myself manoeuvring around so I could see her face better.

When she looked up, our eyes met. I had it. I'd seen this woman in a photo with Orla. It was weeks ago, one of the first photos Orla had put up on social media, and it showed this woman, a nurse, swabbing Orla's arm just before her treatment session. Orla had mentioned her in the caption – I just couldn't remember her name.

I felt an overwhelming urge to speak to her. To ask her about Orla. My feet seemed to move of their own volition, and I watched the woman coming closer and closer until I was almost in her personal space. She looked up again from her bag-rummaging.

'Hi,' I said, unable to think where to start. 'This is . . . this is really weird, I'm sorry, but . . . I think we both know someone . . .'

Her eyes narrowed. 'Right . . .'

I sighed. 'I'm sorry, that's so vague. What I mean is, I think you know Orla . . . Orla Sullivan?'

Her face fell.

I felt panicked, as I suddenly realised my mistake. 'Oh God, I'm sorry, I know you're not allowed to talk about patients. Confidentiality and everything, I just—'

'Patients? What do you mean?' Her expression was one of of utter confusion.

'Orla posted a photo of you online when she was at the hospital. She said you were an amazing nurse . . .'

The woman threw her head back and laughed, making me take a step back it was so sudden and unexpected. 'Do you know what?' she said, the laughter subsiding as she shook her head. 'That shouldn't surprise me. Nothing about Orla should surprise me any more.' She had a south London accent, and she continued to shake her head as she delved into her handbag once more, retrieving her purse and slinging her bag back on her shoulder. 'She your friend?'

'Yes . . . no . . . I mean, she's our lodger.'

'Oh wow!' The laughter was back, but this time it was darker, almost incredulous.

'Why . . . why would it surprise you that she'd called you a good nurse?'

She blinked at me and smiled, a flicker of something that could have been pity flashing across her face. 'Because I'm not a nurse at all. I'm an actor, just like her.' A trickle of ice slid down my spine. I stared at the woman, waiting for her to continue. She sighed. 'I was her roommate until about eight months ago when she did a runner. So when you see her back at yours, you tell her she still owes me a month's rent, cos she's completely ignoring my calls and has blocked me on socials.'

She turned towards the station as I felt the blood draining from my face. I couldn't believe what I'd just heard. And I still couldn't let go of what I'd seen online.

'But . . . but the photo of you . . . she said you were a nurse . . .'

As she turned back towards me I started tapping on my phone screen, desperate to show her the post.

'I promise you, I'm not,' she said, her tone mocking. 'I do know my own profession, you know.'

'No, of course, I'm just saying . . . why?' I looked back and forth between her face and my home screen, my fingers fumbling to scroll through Orla's social media, wondering where exactly I'd seen that photo.

'I've got to catch my train or I'm going to miss my audition,' she said, backing away from me towards the station barriers.

'But can I contact you? I . . . perhaps I can get you your money, from Orla?' I said, desperate to know more.

She swiped through the barrier, but then stopped and looked back at me, as if weighing up what I'd said. 'Abi Obasi,' she said. 'I'm in a show at the Arcola at the moment – google it and you can find me.'

The last words were overlaid by the echoing Tannoy system announcing the next train to arrive at platform three. She turned and disappeared around the corner, and I was left standing on the concourse, reeling from this new information. Reeling, and yet somehow elated.

Chapter Twenty-seven

I sat in my studio, a tote bag full of new, untouched art supplies on the desk in front of me, mobile phone clutched in my hands. I stared at the photo that lit up my screen, reading the words that captioned it: 'I could not have been in better hands for my session today. Ngozi, you are an absolute star. #nevergiveup #BSH #KindUK.'

Her name wasn't Ngozi. And now it made sense that Orla hadn't actually tagged the name, just typed it out – because it wasn't her name. And even if she'd used her real name, she wasn't a nurse. Orla had blocked her on social media. Did this mean Abi would never have discovered this photo? I suppose not if her account was private. But what about the public Facebook group . . . the 'Orla's Battle' page? Orla's website? Her Instagram and X accounts? I clicked into each of them in turn, and I felt my outrage solidify as I realised this photo didn't appear on any of those. It was as if Orla had used Abi's photo as an initial starting point, but then realised she might be found out if she went public with it, so left it off her posts that were starting to reach a larger audience.

When I scrolled right back to the beginning of her website blog, my heart lurched as I saw an almost identical photo, except it had been cropped. Orla's face and shoulders filled the screen, and you could see Abi's hand

swabbing the crook of her arm, and the end of her stethoscope dangling down, but not her face. This photo was
captioned: 'I could not have been in better hands for my
treatment session today. The nurses at Kingston Hospital are absolute stars! #nevergiveup #cancerjourney
#KindUK.'

I felt a cynical laugh erupt from my lips. I could not
believe what I was seeing. I swiped out of Orla's website and tapped into my contacts, thumb hovering over
Scott's number. But no. Not yet. This needed more
thought, more investigation. I knew from Scott's previous reactions to my doubts about Orla that he would
have a string of justifications ready to defend Orla and
make my questions sound mean and unnecessary.

So instead, I googled 'Abi Obasi Arcola theatre'.
Her black-and-white headshot sprang up, alongside the
rest of the cast of *Buried Child* by Sam Shepard, which
appeared to be running for three more weeks. I clicked
on her biography and read the string of acting credits:
touring Shakespeare, Edinburgh Fringe, two West End
musicals, *Death in Paradise*. At the end were links to
her social media. I clicked on the Instagram icon, then
composed her a private message:

Hi Abi, I'm sorry for accosting you earlier at Kingston station. I'm just really confused about what's
going on with Orla. She's been lodging with us since
January, and had told us she'd left her old place on
good terms as her roommate's boyfriend wanted to
move in, and the landlord was happy to swap the
contract over. Since then she's been diagnosed with

a serious illness and has been undergoing treatment at Kingston Hospital – she posted this photo
on her Facebook back in May, and you can see the
caption underneath . . .

I sent the message, followed by a screenshot of the photo
with the caption showing at the bottom. Then I followed
it up with:

What do you think's going on?? Any ideas welcome
because I feel like I'm going crazy. Thanks. Jules.

I didn't say any more. I didn't mention how Orla's behaviour had set my senses quivering since she first moved
in, how she seemed driven by a need for attention, how
she disrupted when the focus was on someone else, how
there were things about her diagnosis that didn't add up.
I didn't want to influence Abi in any way. I just wanted
her interpretation, clean and untainted by any of my
experiences or opinions.

By the time I'd made a cup of tea and returned to my
desk, I had a reply:

Are you actually kidding me? Is this real? That's a
photo of me and Orla at Edinburgh Fringe last summer. That's where we met – we were both in this
play called *Critical* which was on at the Pleasance
Courtyard. Orla was having such a shit time cos
her long-distance boyfriend was being a dickhead.
Every night it was Liam this, Liam that. Anyway,
he was back in Ireland and calling her every night,

and she was in tears all the time, so I'd stay up late and listen to her talk about him, and I'd cook for us and anyway – we bonded. And the show was fab – it was based in a hospital, and this photo was us just messing about during rehearsals. I can't believe she would use that photo to pretend I was her nurse, and the NAME – that's my sister's name! Orla met Ngozi once when she came to visit just before Christmas. I cannot believe this!

A photo from a rehearsal for a play? Abi's sister's name? What the hell was she playing at? Also, pretending Liam was still alive all those years after he died . . . why? To gain sympathy? As stunned as I was by these revelations, Abi's message hadn't given away much about Orla herself, and I needed to know more. I typed back:

I'm as shocked as you. But I have to ask – was there anything strange about Orla's behaviour when you lived together? I mean, did she lie about anything? Or did anything really dramatic happen? I don't know where I'm going with this, I just feel like I'm not getting the whole story with her. Did she mention the boyfriend again?

I didn't want to say I suspected Orla of using her dead boyfriend's name to elicit sympathy. Abi replied a few minutes later.

I'm sorry, Jules, I can't tell you much else. We met last summer, did the show in Edinburgh and then moved in together cos we both needed a new place in London. I guess I didn't realise I'd be touring so much when I agreed to move in with her, cos then I went on tour until December, and she moved out in January just before I left to go touring again. If I'm honest, I hardly know her. And the way she just left one day without paying her rent was bang out of order. She definitely didn't leave on 'good terms' like she told you, and I don't have a boyfriend who conveniently took over her half of the rent – just a couple of pissed-off parents who had to help me out until I found someone else to move in! I'm sorry about her diagnosis, that's rough. But yeah, if you could get her to pay that month's rent she owes then I'd be really grateful. Thx.

Abi had left her phone number at the end of the message, but I felt suddenly deflated. I was pleased I'd got to the bottom of the photo, and that I now knew for a fact that Orla had lied about it, but I was disappointed at how little Abi seemed to know about Orla herself. I'd been hoping for tales of deception and drama. Shared outrage at Orla's narcissistic behaviour. Instances where Abi had discovered Orla lying or cheating or overacting. But, although Abi was disgusted at the photo, it seemed she knew little about Orla, other than that she was 'fun'. And her main concern, rather than solving the complexities of Orla's character, seemed to be the missing month's rent. But I supposed that was understandable – after all, Abi didn't live with Orla. She didn't have anything to do with her any more. She wasn't involved in her diagnosis or her living arrangements, so after being perplexed as to why Orla would have lied about the photo, I can see why the money would be the thing that annoyed her the most.

I replied saying I'd do my best, and shared my own phone number, and that was it. It didn't exactly feel like a dead end, but it wasn't the grand denouement I'd been hoping for.

But meeting Abi had given me a lift of sorts. It made me realise that being proactive about my niggling feelings concerning Orla was the best way to deal with this. I needed to do something – not sit in my studio poring over her social-media updates with these questions and doubts simmering inside me. Especially when those doubts had proven to be unshareable – Scott wasn't interested in hearing them, and Maggie seemed to be Orla's new best friend, so I couldn't say anything to her.

I felt a flutter of hurt when I thought about Maggie and Orla. Maggie was supposed to be my best friend. We'd known each other for eight years – ever since Kind UK had approached me to judge an art competition for a community fundraising project. Maggie had been their representative that day, and we'd hit it off immediately, heading straight for the Pimm's tent after the competition was over, then giggling our way through the rest of that sweltering day before sharing phone numbers and promising to keep in touch. And we had. We'd even ended up living in neighbouring suburbs all these years later. And now Orla was here and she was the one Maggie came over to see and went for coffee with, and called to check up on. I felt like such a child even having these thoughts . . . of course Maggie was allowed to have other friends. I didn't feel possessive of her. It was just a return of that feeling I'd first had all those months ago when Orla had lost her phone in the pub . . . it was complete incredulity that the people I love, that I understand, that I 'get', could look at Orla and see someone so completely at odds with the person I saw. What sort of spell had she cast, and why was I the only person who seemed immune to it?

But was I the only one?

I clicked into Facebook and onto Orla's page. I scrolled and scrolled back through the years, knowing I had to get to that post announcing her engagement to Liam. At last I found it, Orla and Liam's faces smiling out at me, the wind buffeting her hair and a diamond ring glinting on her finger. I tapped into the comments section and scrolled down until I found the comment I was looking for: *Happy for you, sis. Xx*

I tapped on Sean's name and his sparse profile filled the screen. He looked like Orla in the photo – high cheekbones, sapphire eyes. His jaw was more angular and his nose wider, but you could definitely see the sibling resemblance, even down to the honey-coloured hair. In his photo he wore a red, thick-knit jumper, and was flanked by two chestnut-haired girls of about six. Twins, perhaps. He smiled amiably at the camera as if mid-laugh, and I tried to reconcile this affectionate, fatherly image with the type of man who would eject his sister from their childhood home and prevent her from saying goodbye to their dying father. I couldn't. But then, as I knew, photos could be deceiving.

I tapped on the message icon, but the button was unresponsive – his account was set to private. He could only accept messages from people he'd added as friends. This meant there was only one thing for it. With trembling fingers, and a prickle of dread on the surface of my skin, I tapped on the blue button: 'Add Friend'.

255

Chapter Twenty-eight

Days went by with me distractedly checking Facebook for a reply to my friend request from Sean. Once again I found my mind consumed by Orla and whatever it was she was up to. I tried to focus on work but frequently found myself gazing, unseeing, out of the window, paintbrush poised above paper, imagining what secrets Sean might help me uncover.

One evening, Scott and I were settled on the sofa watching a true-crime documentary while Orla was at a church support group with Maggie when the words 'friend request accepted' flashed up on my phone screen. My pulse spiked and I grabbed my phone, tapping on the notification. I was somewhat stunned Sean had accepted my friend request when he had no idea who I was. This seemed at odds with someone who would have their entire account set to private. But then my phone pinged with a Facebook message:

> Just accepted your friend request. Where do I know you from please?

So this is how he played it. He accepted the request, made you explain yourself then, if he didn't like what you said or decided you were a scammer or a bot, he blocked you.

I'd have to tread carefully here. I typed slowly, considering each word.

> Hi Sean, I hope you don't mind me getting in touch. Your sister, Orla, is our lodger at the moment, and I just had a few questions. She doesn't know I'm messaging you – she explained you don't really speak any more. But there have been some strange things happening, and I suppose I wondered if you could shed any light on her state of mind . . . I'm just trying to understand her a bit better. Best wishes, Jules.

I read it three times before pressing send.

'You watching this or shall I put something else on?' Scott said, causing me to flinch.

'No, it's fine . . . I'm keeping half an eye on it, I just . . . I'm just sending a couple of work emails I forgot to send earlier.'

He nodded and looked back at the screen, taking a large gulp from his mug of tea.

The minutes slipped by, and I kept unlocking my screen to look at the message. I knew it had been read, as Sean's profile photo was showing in the bottom right-hand corner. I waited as I chewed my lip, wondering if I should have been more careful with my phrasing. Wondering if shouldn't have alluded to the fact they were no longer speaking. If he blocked me now, that was the end of it. I didn't know how else to get in touch with anyone who might know Orla to any meaningful degree.

Ping! I looked down at the screen and was surprised at how long the message was. This was no curt 'I can't help you' reply – this was a proper response.

'Actually,' I said, looking over at Scott. 'I'm really tired. Do you mind if I go to bed?'

'Are you feeling OK?' His brow furrowed as he asked the question.

'I'm fine, promise. Just really want to read a chapter of my book and call it a day I think.'

I leaned over and kissed him, trying to keep my movements slow and tired, and not reveal my eagerness to scurry up to the bedroom so I could concentrate on what Sean had written.

I shut the bedroom door, sat on the bed and unlocked my phone.

Hi Jules. I'm sorry you're having to deal with Orlaith. As far as commenting on her 'state of mind' is concerned, I'm afraid many years of trying to analyse that has yielded little in terms of my understanding. I'm glad to know she's at least alive and well, as I've had no contact with her for several years now. I don't really know how I can help you. All best, Sean.

The message was vague. I noticed the Irish spelling of Orla's name, and wondered about that. I had so many questions. I clicked into the reply box and typed:

Thank you so much for getting back to me, Sean. I'd really like to explain further and get your opinion.

258

Please, if it's not too much of an imposition, could I
speak to you?

I typed in my phone number and pressed send. Two minutes later my phone began to ring. I quickly slipped into
the studio and closed the door, knowing Scott would
likely leave me alone in there if he came up to bed.

'Hello?' I kept my voice down and cast an anxious
glance towards the door.

'Jules? It's Sean.' His voice was much softer than
I'd expected, and his Irish accent much stronger than
Orla's.

'Hi Sean. Thank you so much for agreeing to chat to
me. I know this is completely out of the blue.'

'It's fine. I understand why you'd have questions. So
go on . . . what's she been doing?'

A wave of relief washed over me. Sean knew. He
knew what Orla was like. I didn't know where to start.
I also felt uncomfortable sharing her diagnosis with
him, when Orla had told me they'd parted on bad
terms and that she wouldn't be sharing the news with
him herself.

Instinctively, I grabbed a notebook and pen. I began,
tentatively. 'Maybe I'll just go from the beginning . . .' I
told Sean about meeting Orla in the pub when she'd lost
her keys, and about her moving in.

When I told him about her fainting on the train, he
gave a scornful laugh. 'Yep, that sounds like Orla.'

'What do you mean?'

'The fainting. That's been a theme since she was a
child. Did she tell you that?'

'No . . . I got the impression it was a recent thing due to . . . well, some health problems she's been having.' I scrawled *fainting since childhood* in the notebook.

He sighed. 'Orla's been fainting for as long as I can remember. I don't know whether it was an attention-seeking thing after our mother abandoned us, or maybe . . . well, there may have been some jealousy surrounding my situation too, I suppose. Some rivalry for attention.'

I nodded as I scribbled, remembering what Orla had said about her mother leaving when she was four. That, combined with having to share her father with a younger sibling could well have resulted in severe sibling rivalry.

'Anyway,' Sean continued, 'Dad used to have to collect her from school all the time cos she'd fainted. She had blood tests and all that but they never showed anything. Then she started going to acting classes at the weekend . . . Centre Stage I think they were called. And that's where she got called to audition for *Kilcroom High* . . . I'm guessing she's told you all about that?'

'Yes, she has.'

'Course she has. Never goes five minutes without mentioning that.' His tone was derisory. I remembered how quickly Orla had shared her stint on *Kilcroom High* with us when we'd first met her in the pub. We'd only just sat down with our drinks and she was telling us about it. 'Anyway,' he said. 'The fainting stopped for a while when she started acting. Almost as if the fainting had been replaced by the acting and singing and all that. Any opportunity to perform in front of family or at school or anything and she was there – acting her socks off, singing her heart out. Just generally making sure everyone was looking at her. So when she auditioned for the TV show and actually got it, oh my God, it was unbearable.'

'What do you mean?'

'It was all she talked about. Morning, noon and night. It was all about her audition, everything they'd said about her and why she was so wonderful. I mean, of course we were happy for her – it was an amazing achievement, and she'd beaten loads of girls to the role. But it was the way she went *on* about it, you know? Then it got worse. She started filming, and any time we were together as a family it was just relentless . . . what filming was like, what the director had said, all the in-jokes she shared with the other actors. Obviously, Dad didn't help matters cos he was as thrilled as she was. At the start, that is.'

'Just at the start?'

'Well, things got really intense when the producers asked her to change the spelling of her name. So, she'd always been Orlaith spelt the Irish way . . . you know, with i, t, h on the end? Well, the producers knew this programme was massive across the UK and that most viewers weren't actually from Ireland, so they asked if she'd be up for changing the spelling so all the "fans" would know how to say it. Jesus Christ, that set her off. She made the school change her name on their records, and even messaged family members about it when they sent Christmas cards.' He gave a humourless chuckle. 'I told her, it doesn't matter how the school or family spell your name – it's just for the TV show you need to change it. But she wasn't having any of it. I think she liked having to explain to everyone . . . you know, *why* she'd changed it. That gave her an excuse to talk about the show, and her "fans". I think honestly, if she wasn't mad before, then when the show ended for her, that sent her over the edge.'

'You mean, when she stopped filming?'

'Yeah – because that wasn't her choice, you know?'

'No, I don't. What happened?'

The phone line distorted as Sean breathed out heavily. 'Orlaith thought that now she was a huge TV superstar, her course was set. She was headed for the stars. London, the West End, Hollywood, all that. Dad tried to manage her expectations, reminding her the contract was only for a bit part on one season of the show. But Orlaith was convinced they loved her so much they'd write her in to the subsequent seasons, that she'd become a constant fixture.'

'But that didn't happen?'

'Nope. Just like Dad had explained to her – she was contracted for the one season, and they'd already written the script for the next one. There was no place for her in those storylines. Her character was someone's cousin who'd visited for the summer, they had a few adventures, then the cousin went home and that was that. Orlaith was completely stunned when it got to the end of filming and they threw her a little "goodbye" party. She kept expecting them to say, "Only joking! Please stay for the next three seasons, we all love you so much!" But they didn't.'

'So what happened when the show ended?'

'She went back to stage school; again, acting the big "I am". Obviously with her new attitude it was difficult for her to make friends. She moved schools because she was so unhappy. And that's when the fainting started again. It was almost as if she realised the acting thing wasn't going to work out, so she reverted back to fainting.'

'So you think she was faking it?'

There was a pause. 'I hate to say it, but yes. In fact, with everything that came afterwards, I'd almost guarantee it.'

'What came afterwards?' My voice was an urgent whisper. It was terrible, but I felt like a child being read a ghost story around a campfire. Scared, yet desperate for more.

'She got engaged to a guy. Liam was his name, and he was actually a really good mate of mine. I introduced them, more fool me.' He cleared his throat. 'Everything seemed great – Orlaith seemed happy, and I knew she was in good hands with Liam. He was steady, you know? A decent, steady guy.'

It felt wrong not to acknowledge what I knew about Liam. I couldn't let Sean go on to tell me about the death of his friend and act as if I was shocked at the news. It didn't seem right. 'I . . . I read online about what happened to Liam. I'm so sorry.'

Sean cleared his throat again, and when he spoke his voice seemed thicker. 'It was just so out of the blue. I mean, I knew his family and everything . . . they were devastated. But it's almost as if I wasn't allowed to deal with his death because it all became so quickly about Orlaith.'

'In what way?'

263

'Look, I know no one really knows what's going on in someone else's mind or in their relationships, but I knew Liam like a brother. There was no way he was depressed enough to throw himself off that bridge. It was clear to anyone who knew Liam that it was a terrible, tragic accident. That bridge was dangerous and everyone knew it. There'd been several near-deaths in previous years, and parents all over the Carrick Healey area warned their kids about playing on it. So yeah, it was weird he was even there at all . . . but it wasn't suicide.'

'But . . . isn't that what the police decided had happened? Suicide?'

'No. They ruled accidental death. It was Orlaith who kept on about the suicide – telling her friends and the church group, anyone and everyone. It was bizarre. It was almost as if an accident wasn't enough for her. She needed to make the situation so much worse . . . so much more about *her*. She kept on and on about how she couldn't forgive Liam for not telling her how he'd been suffering. How it made losing him so much worse because she knew he'd kept this part of himself a secret . . . it was exhausting. We all kept saying to her that the police investigation showed no such thing, but she just wouldn't stop singing from the same song sheet.'

I realised Sean was right – none of the newspaper articles I'd found had mentioned suicide explicitly. One of them had said police were trying to ascertain Liam's state of mind at the time, but then there was no follow-up implying they'd discovered anything. The only reason I'd attributed Liam's death to suicide was because of Orla's online entry on that suicide bereavement forum.

Now I knew how their stories differed, there was another point I wanted to clear up. 'Orla said that when your father was dying, you threw her out of the house.'

Sean gave another derisory snort. 'I'm sure she did. You want to know the truth? Dad had been ill for a long time with heart disease. I'd begged Orla to come back and see him. When she finally did, she sat in the kitchen most of the time, unwilling to engage with him at all. She watched the doctors coming and going, lurking around in the bedroom doorway, but then scuttling back downstairs as soon as they were done. Then after a few days it started again – the fainting. Honestly, I couldn't cope. My wife and I were Dad's full-time carers, cooking for him, washing him, reading to him . . . and then Orla shows up, and instead of helping, she just sits there, another mouth to feed, another person to clean up after . . . and then she starts fainting, and I . . . I just lost it. So yeah, I suppose she's right, I did throw her out. Or, well, I said it might be better if she stayed in the B&B in the village instead as there was a lot going on at the house and we were struggling. But, you know Orla. That obviously blew up and became a big drama. So she didn't go to the B&B, she stomped off back to London and . . . and I suppose in her retelling, we became the bad guys.'

I nodded. I could see it all. As Sean had been speaking I'd found myself recognising patterns of behaviour in Orla I'd seen so many times myself. It was almost as if life, as it stood, was not enough for her. Things needed to be accentuated or emphasised or shaken up. She seemed overwhelmingly driven by a narcissistic need for attention. A need to 'put on a show'. And now I'd finished listening to Orla's family history from her brother, I had a new question: how far would Orla go to keep her audience captivated?

Chapter Twenty-nine

It was a Wednesday evening between Orla's rounds of treatment, and I was cooking spaghetti Bolognese when she came into the kitchen. She'd been wearing a thin headscarf since she'd shaved her head. Today it was sea-green with turquoise swirls in a paisley pattern. It reminded me of something Kara would wear.

She offered me a vague smile and shuffled up onto a bar stool, resting her chin on her hands.

'How are you feeling?' I said, swatting away an intrusive thought which said, *What would Orla do now if you told her you'd had a long conversation with Sean?*

'Not as good as I should be really,' she said, blinking slowly at me. 'This blasted migraine's back. The last round of treatment really knocked me for six. I just can't shift this bloody pain.' She squeezed her eyes shut.

'Are you hungry? There's loads of Bolognese. You can eat with us or take it up to your room . . . whatever you'd prefer.'

Her smile widened and her chin quivered. 'That's so lovely of you, Jules.' Her hand went to her chest in her usual gesture of thanks, and I felt my jaw clench.

I turned back to stirring the pan and laughed. 'It's just Bolognese.'

'If you don't mind, that would be fantastic.'

'Of course,' I said, trying to sound offhand and casual and not provoke any speeches from Orla about how she wouldn't know what to do without me, and how Scott and I were the most precious friends she could ever wish for. 'Scott's just having a shower after his run, but he'll be down in a sec—'

'Speak of the devil!' Scott's voice cut in, and I turned towards the kitchen door.

I felt my stomach drop and my mouth fell open. 'What . . .?' I couldn't form the question.

Scott stood in the doorway, his arms spread wide as if to say, *what do you think?* But all I could do is stare at his head. Gone was his tousled, mousey hair. His head was completely clean-shaven, the skin reflecting the circular downlights from the kitchen ceiling.

'Oh my God,' Orla whispered, perfectly verbalising my own sentiments.

'What have you done?' I managed.

'I'm so glad you're here, Orla – I wanted you to be the first to see it. I . . .' He crinkled his nose and rubbed a palm over his head, suddenly looking doubtful. 'I saw a video online of someone who shaved their head in solidarity with a friend who had cancer, and I thought . . . well, you were so upset when we found you in the bathroom. I just . . .' His eyes were trained on Orla, and he grimaced, as if suddenly worried about her reaction.

I watched her eyes widen and her hands go to her mouth. Then she flew off the bar stool, across the kitchen, and flung herself into Scott's arms so violently he staggered back against the doorframe.

'Oh, thank God,' he said, wrapping his arms around her and beaming at me over her shoulder. 'I thought I'd made a horrific faux pas for a moment!'

Orla sobbed into Scott's neck. 'I . . . I can't believe you did that . . . f-for me . . .'

He rubbed her back. 'Hey . . . we're in this together, aren't we?'

I stood staring at them, the wooden spatula raised in one hand, my other hand resting on my bump. The thing that brought me back into the moment was the smell of burning.

'Shit!' I said, turning back to the hob and twisting the dials off. I faffed about with the pans, scraping the bottom of the Bolognese to mix in the burnt bits, then placing the colander in the sink to strain the pasta. My mind swirled, a sickening sensation worse than any I'd felt so far writhing coldly in my stomach.

I was finding it impossible to comprehend that Scott felt so invested in Orla that he would do this. This was surely something you'd do for your child or your parent, perhaps your sibling; I hadn't even done this for my mother. *Should I have? No, she wouldn't have wanted that. Does Orla want this? Of course she does. She wants every possible scrap of attention she can get. This act of Scott's will have blown her mind – she will feed off this like a succubus.*

I wanted to run. I didn't want to watch Orla fawning and pawing over Scott. I didn't want to sit through dinner with them, her casting earnest glances at us both and professing how much she loved us, and Scott telling her how we were *there for her* on her *journey.* I wanted to scream.

But instead I served up dinner onto three plates, and I sat and ate my spaghetti Bolognese. I smiled at Scott and told him he'd done a wonderful thing, and I listened to Orla telling us we were her saviours and that she couldn't wish for better friends.

'I'm glad I've caught both of you this evening, actually,' she said, taking a sip from her wine glass. It seemed Scott's gesture of solidarity had rid her of her migraine, and she'd enthusiastically accepted his offer of a glass of Malbec. 'I'm going away for a few days.'

I felt an uncharitable flush of pleasure at this news. 'Really? Where?'

'Oh, just to visit a friend I haven't seen in a while. She lives in Norfolk. We used to go to school together and we've just reconnected on Facebook.'

I found myself nodding, a desperate flicker of hope tickling my insides. Could this friend be someone who was once close to Orla? Someone who understands her? Someone who lives alone and needs a roommate? I was running away with myself in the most absurd way, but my mind could not resist it.

'I'll probably be back on Sunday,' she said.

My bubble burst.

Of course she'd be back.

Something relaxed in me over the next couple of days. Just the fact that Orla wasn't in the house during the day, and wouldn't be back in the evenings, was enough for the tension to ebb away. I focused on my work, flying through the watercolours I'd been putting off for the past two weeks. I caught up with my emails and made sure I checked in with my new author. I felt I'd regained control of my work situation.

On Friday, I had an antenatal appointment. Scott took the morning off work and we both went together. There was no scan this time, but the midwife took measurements of my belly and assured us the bump was growing at a healthy rate. She asked me lots of questions about how I was feeling, went over our potential 'birth plan', and Scott and I were thrilled to hear the baby's heartbeat on the monitor. It felt so good to have this moment of complete focus on our baby, and we strolled out of the clinic holding hands. We chatted more about girls' names, and also discussed what would happen when I went into labour. The hospital had birthing pools in the maternity unit, and as I was low risk I'd said I'd like to try that as pain relief, while keeping my options open in terms of an epidural. Talking about these things in such detail made the pregnancy feel so much more real. And as we walked and talked I realised how much all this stuff with Orla had been eclipsing my focus on the baby. In that moment with Scott, I felt so free, and so elated. All that was important was us, and our baby. But that realisation meant another one followed close behind – the realisation of how much I was dreading Orla's return.

October had been wet and cool, and I had to admit I was glad the stifling mugginess of summer was long gone. I worked in the studio on Sunday while Scott cooked a chilli. Maggie and Nick arrived at three bearing wine and homemade cupcakes.

'So tell me about your appointment, how did it go?' Maggie said as we settled at the table

'All good . . . the midwife is happy with growth and everything—'

'And did they confirm your due date?'

'Yep that's not changed – sixth of January.'

Maggie nodded and asked more questions, occasionally leaning forwards to squeeze my knee and give a little squeal of excitement. We ate at the dining table, and Nick teased Scott mercilessly about his shaved head, while Maggie fiercely defended him for his selfless act of heroism and allyship. I smiled and stayed quiet, unable to find the right thing to say.

I was therefore relieved when Nick launched into a hilarious story about overtaking an ice-cream van in Richmond Park on his Vespa the day before, and we all laughed and told him he was a wannabe *Quadrophenia* idiot, which he loved. I sipped my soft drink and leaned back in my chair, a warm contentment swirling inside me as I gazed about the group. It had been ages since it was just the four of us, and I hadn't realised how much I'd missed it.

Maggie got up to fetch her handbag from the living room, and as she disappeared through the double doors we heard her shout, 'Oh, God!' Her voice sounded panicked and unlike Maggie, and the three of us leapt up and rushed in to her.

Orla was sitting hunched on the sofa, her face pale and her eyes closed. She had a bandage wrapped around her head, only the crown of her head exposed and showing the spiky regrowth of her hair. Maggie approached her with a tentative reach of her arm, laying it on Orla's shoulder.

'Orla? Are you OK?'

The rest of us just stood there watching. Slowly Orla opened her eyes, her gaze flicking towards Maggie, then us. There were dark shadows under her eyes, in stark contrast to her pale skin. I'd never seen her look so ill. I had a sudden flashback to a children's version of *Macbeth* I'd illustrated last year, and the way I'd depicted Banquo, the spectre at the feast.

Her lips parted and she spoke as if she found it painful. 'I'm all right. I . . . I was on my way in to see you all, but I . . . I just needed a minute.'

Scott and I glanced at each other and the silence felt heavy. I felt compelled to say something. 'Have you just got back? From seeing your friend?'

She squeezed her eyes closed again, and when she opened them and looked up at me, her expression was apologetic. 'I'm so sorry, Jules. I lied about that.'

I felt that familiar sliver of ice down my spine. 'What do you mean?'

'I didn't go and stay with a friend. I . . .' She looked around the group then, slowly making eye contact with all of us before continuing. 'I've been at the hospital since Thursday. They operated. I didn't want you all worrying about me, so I made up the visit to a friend.'

It felt like we all took a breath at the same time. Maggie was the first to speak. 'What do you mean, operated?'

She gave us all a glassy-eyed stare. 'It's OK,' she said. 'It was just a small procedure . . . a lesion on my skull. It's not a big deal.'

Maggie crouched down in front of Orla and took her hands. 'Oh my God, Orla, you should have *told* us. What were you thinking going through this on your own?' Maggie sounded like she was about to cry, her voice distraught with emotion.

Nick and Scott sat either side of her; Scott lay a hand on her back.

Orla sniffed and shook her head, a feeble smile playing on her lips as if she was trying to be brave. 'You're all so wonderful, and that's why I knew I couldn't tell you. You'd all have insisted on coming to the hospital and bringing me things, and collecting me afterwards, and . . . and I've already been such an imposition on you all, I couldn't bear the thought of being so much trouble.'

'So how did you get home?' asked Maggie.

'In a taxi.'

'For God's sake, Orla.' Scott sounded genuinely cross. 'You've just had an operation on your *skull*. You are not an "imposition". For the last time, we're your friends. We want to be there for you, and you should have at least called us to collect you!'

'Hear, hear,' said Nick.

Once again I couldn't find the right thing to say. Or rather, the things I wanted to say weren't appropriate. And the worst, most unspeakable thing was that I wanted to ask if I could take the bandage off her head and see the incision.

Chapter Thirty

The mood had shifted and the party was over. Maggie and Nick said their goodbyes, Maggie making Orla promise to call her the following day so they could arrange to meet up. Maggie wanted to know all about the operation and Orla's treatment plan, and chat through how Kind UK could help her more.

Scott made Orla a cup of tea while I collected up the half-finished plates of chilli. Eventually, Orla decided to retire to her room, and I managed to make an offer of help without the words sticking in my throat.

'Can I bring you up anything? Something to eat, or . . . or some painkillers or anything?'

'That's so kind, Jules, but no. I have everything I need upstairs, and I don't think I could force anything down now even if I wanted to. I'll see you both tomorrow.'

She shuffled from the kitchen and I heard her laboured steps on the carpeted stairs, then the creak of a landing floorboard. Scott set about tidying the kitchen with an energy I'd never seen him use for any domestic task before. He swiped rubbish from the counter into the bin, used a dust pan and brush for the floor, wiped the surfaces, and even scrubbed the pan he'd cooked the chilli in – something we usually left to soak overnight. And all the while he wittered, almost to himself, about poor

275

Orla and the terrible things she was going through. How could the hospital discharge her without a friend or relative there? How was she supposed to continue to work? Why weren't her family in Ireland checking in on her?

Of course, I had my own responses to these questions but I couldn't say them. I felt a fresh barrier had been created between me and the others. A new pane of unbreakable glass. On one side was Orla, with Scott, Maggie and Nick. And on the other side was me. Alone. And things were different on their side. Orla was different. I felt that with every interaction we had with her, our views of her grew further apart. The closer she grew into an angel on their side of the glass, the closer she grew into the devil on mine. And no matter how loudly I shouted and hammered on the glass, there was no way any of them would be able to hear me. In fact, I worried that the louder I shouted, the bigger and stronger the barrier would become. I'd seen the look in Scott's eyes when I'd shown him the photo of the purple bear – he was aghast. What was I doing questioning the actions of a dying woman? A dying woman who was one of our closest friends?

I couldn't take Scott's frantic indignation on Orla's behalf any more, so I made excuses about having work to finish off and left him in the kitchen. He barely seemed to notice when I walked out, leaving him shaking his head and reaching into the fridge for a beer.

I shut myself in my studio, the only room in the house I felt any sort of freedom or peace these days. It was a space that was completely mine.

But still, I could not escape Orla. Because the moment I sat down, I felt my usual compulsion to take out my phone and search social media for what I knew I would find: the posts. And there they were. New ones from this very afternoon. Photos of Orla lying on a hospital bed, sitting in a chair with lines snaking into her arms, resting her head on a pillow with an oxygen mask covering her mouth and nose, and now, upstairs in our attic room, her pale face and dark-circled eyes peering mournfully into the camera.

There was even a lengthy blog post on her website detailing her admission to hospital on Thursday and the updates the doctors had given her along the way, including the many new prescription drugs she was now expected to take alongside her existing ones: 'just to stay alive'. I wondered when she'd written it.

I remembered that blissful feeling I'd had on Friday walking hand in hand with Scott after hearing our baby's heartbeat. I remembered laughing in the kitchen with him earlier today while he cooked the chilli. I tried to recall that soft, warm contentedness that had flowed through my veins as I sat laughing with the people I loved around the dining table. I remembered all these things but I couldn't revive the feelings inside myself because, once again, Orla had come in and obliterated them. I wondered how long she'd be here, chasing those moments away. Would she be weeping at the kitchen table when we brought our baby home for the first time? Would our child's first smile be captured on video alongside an announcement from Orla that she needed more surgery? Would our daughter's first steps be celebrated alongside an announcement from Orla that she'd relapsed? These thoughts swirled inside my brain, gathering an oppressive darkness like rainclouds before a storm. I'm not sure how long I stayed in the studio, thinking these things and scrolling through Orla's posts, but I lost track of time, and was only startled from my internal world by the sound of Scott swearing in our bedroom next door.

When I went in he was staring angrily at his phone in his hand, the other hand resting on top of his shaven head.

'What's wrong?' I asked, worried he'd hurt himself somehow and relieved to see he hadn't.

He looked up, his face a concerned scowl. 'You'd better shut the door,' he whispered.

I did as he said, then turned back to him. 'You're scaring me, Scott. What's wrong?'

'It's . . .' He didn't seem to be able to tear his eyes away from his phone screen, so I approached and hovered at his side, trying to see what he was looking at. 'Look,' he continued, tilting the screen so I could see. 'It's . . . someone's just commented on one of Orla's posts. I don't know if she's seen it yet, but . . . it's horrible.'

I stared at the phone screen. He was showing me a post I'd been looking at myself only about twenty minutes ago in my studio. It was on Instagram and showed a series of photos of Orla at the hospital, along with a caption: *The doctors are happy with how surgery went on Thursday to remove the lesion on my skull. We'll know how successful removal was when test results come back. Keep everything crossed for me! #FightForOrla #KingstonHospital #NHS #KindUK*

There were hundreds of likes and comments, most of which I'd read earlier. But at the bottom of Scott's screen was a new comment from a user called TruthBomb365, and it read: *Come on now, Orla. Isn't it time you told the truth? You might have all these people fooled, but you don't fool me.*

My heart hammered in my chest and I looked up at Scott. 'What do you think it means?'

He breathed out through gritted teeth. 'I was worried this was going to happen.'

'What?'

'Well . . . Orla putting herself out there on social media. It's full of spiteful people who pick on anyone . . . I mean, it's sick, but if you've had something horrific happen to you then you can bet that at some point the trolls will find you and twist the knife.' He stared at his phone, shaking his head.

'You don't . . .' I didn't know how to phrase my thoughts without getting Scott even more riled up. 'I mean . . . do you think it could be from someone who knows Orla? Someone from her past, maybe?'

Scott frowned at me as if I'd just started speaking Danish. 'No, Jules. This is an internet troll who's decided to victimise and bully a seriously ill woman.'

I felt a flash of annoyance. The fact I'd come to Scott with concerns about Orla's behaviour, and now someone *else* was also raising questions should at least give him pause, shouldn't it? I had a sudden urge to tell Scott about meeting Abi at the train station – to show him the photo Abi had told me was completely fake because she wasn't a nurse at all. I wanted to tell him about speaking to Orla's brother, Sean, and the picture he'd painted of an emotionally unstable attention-seeker. But from the horrified look on Scott's face, I knew how that would play out. He'd see me as 'siding' with this spiteful stranger, and it would push him even further away from me. I imagined laying out my 'findings' as they stood, and him looking at me as if I was mad. Because all I had was a feeling inside me, that and the word of two total strangers. I was hardly about to march up the attic stairs and rip the bandage from Orla's skull. And at this point, even if I did, I wasn't entirely convinced of what I would see . . . or not see. I felt like I was going mad.

I needed to bide my time. Gather my evidence and present it clearly, so there was no doubt in his mind I was telling the truth. First, I needed to work out exactly what the truth was.

'I just hope Orla hasn't seen this comment. She'll be so upset.'

'Well, if it's a troll like you say, then she doesn't have anything to worry about, does she?' Scott didn't appear to have heard me, occupied as he was stabbing away at his phone. 'What are you doing?'

'I'm replying to the idiot. Telling him to leave her alone.'

'Do you think it's a good idea to engage? Shouldn't you let trolls do their thing and not feed their egos?'

He ignored me and continued prodding the screen. 'There,' he said at last, throwing his phone on to the bed. 'I just think that if Orla spots it, it'll make her feel better to see we're defending her at least.'

I nodded, tapping into Instagram on my phone and navigating to the post to see what Scott had said.

Trolling a seriously ill woman who has thousands of supporters is pretty pathetic, mate.

We got ready for bed in silence but I couldn't help checking my phone every few seconds. Scott's comment gained hundreds of likes, and the post itself countless more comments in the same vein as Scott's. *Fucking troll, get a life . . . Absolutely despicable . . . Ignore the twats, Orla. #FightForOrla.*

I turned my phone off and put it in the bedside drawer, hoping that would stop me checking on it throughout the night. But I couldn't sleep for hours. My mind kept churning, wondering what Orla's reaction would be. Because if she hadn't discovered the post yet, then she would tomorrow morning.

I needn't have worried about broaching the subject of the troll with Orla. At 9 a.m., before I'd even reached the bottom step, I could hear her wails of anguish from the kitchen. I entered to find Scott crouching with his arm around her, and Orla herself in her usual pose: eyes cast down, head in hands, body wracked with sobs.

I crossed and sat next to her, extending my arm and resting my hand on hers. I didn't need to say anything.

She looked up at me, her face a tear-streaked mess under her bandaged head. 'It's all lies, Jules! Complete and utter lies!'

My gaze flickered towards Scott. 'There's been another comment by the troll.'

I felt a single pulse of my heart and a burst of adrenaline as I reached into my back pocket and pulled out my phone. Navigating to Orla's Instagram I scrolled to the post in question and searched for the comment. And there it was: *I'm not a troll. Just someone who knows Orla a lot better than any of you. Perhaps ask her about her fainting fits. Don't believe everything you see and hear from this woman.*

'It's so vicious,' she sobbed. 'I don't know who would do this . . . it . . . I suppose it could be Sean. I mean, he was always out to get me . . .'

I thought about the softly spoken man on the phone, and the sad, measured way he'd told me about his life with Orla and her constant dramatics. But with the mention of the fainting, I could see how she might think it would be him.

I felt I needed to contribute somehow. 'What about someone you used to live with? Or someone you did a show with?' I was thinking about Abi, although I didn't think she fitted in with the fainting fits. Still, we seemed to be brainstorming and it was something to say.

Orla shook her head while Scott continued to stroke her back, an action that made me feel simultaneously queasy and furious. 'No, I . . . I haven't lived with anyone who would spread such vicious lies about me. All my housemates have been so lovely and we've always parted on good terms.'

Apart from when you've left them with no notice, owing a month's rent, of course.

'What about someone from back in Ireland?' Scott said, his voice insufferably gentle. I noticed how, when I'd suggested it was someone who actually knew Orla, he'd scoffed at the idea. But now Orla was listing possible culprits, he was fully invested. 'I mean – maybe it could be someone who was jealous of you starring in *Kilcroom High*?'

Orla sniffed and looked at Scott. 'Maybe,' she said, weakly. 'There were a lot of girls who went for the part . . . I mean, hundreds, you know? There would have been a lot of jealousy.'

I gritted my teeth, wondering why I was surprised she'd use this moment to brag about how many competitors she'd fought off for her TV role.

I couldn't resist it. 'But *Kilcroom High* was twenty years ago, Orla. I think they've probably got over it by now.' *Unlike you*, I didn't add. 'So maybe someone else from Ireland?' I wasn't proud of it, but it gave me a sort of twisted satisfaction, listing pockets of people who would have disliked her throughout her life for the same reasons I disliked her now. People who would have started off like Scott and Maggie, thinking she was the most fun person they'd ever met, only to discover she was an attention-seeking liar.

She nodded again, then seemed to go into a sort of trance-like state. 'Yes . . . maybe . . . maybe one of Liam's friends . . . they weren't always very friendly with me . . . Bobbie . . . or Kieran . . .' Her voice was little more than a whisper at that point, but I'd heard the names and filed them away in my head for later.

Losing your hair is brutal. It's a reminder that you're not invincible, and that this is really happening. It's not just something that happens to 'other people'. So the way Scott reacted, shaving his own head in solidarity with me, in that moment I felt a rush of love so strong and so pure, I thought it would knock me off my feet. He did that for me.

Then to come home and tell them about the operation to remove the lesion on my skull . . . the avalanche of love and concern from them all . . . you should have told us! . . . how did you get home? . . . you are not an 'imposition' . . . we're your friends! *I felt like I was glowing inside at that moment.*

But to have this crack appear. This troll. I mean, of course Scott is beside himself with outrage on my behalf, and I love him for that. But it doesn't change the fact that I don't know who they are or why they're doing this. Maybe Scott's right . . . maybe it is just a random crackpot. Most trolls are. But I can't shake the idea it's one of Liam's awful friends. I didn't know Bobbie very well, but I could tell she was a bitch. The way she looked down on me. I even caught her rolling her eyes once. And then there was Kieran . . . smug, self-satisfied, nasty little man. Yes, Kieran's got 'troll' written all over him.

He always was a stirrer. That's what I tried to tell Liam, not that he believed me.

But it's not significant who the troll actually is, as long as Scott and Jules don't pay him – or her – any heed. I've not come this far, and created this life, and this home, to have it all taken away.

Chapter Thirty-one

The contrast with how I'd felt when Orla had been away could not have been starker. Gone was the relaxed, productive, positive Jules who met her deadlines, communicated well with her collaborators, and had time spare to daydream about her unborn child. No. Orla was back with a bang, and as always, life was now all about her.

I spent hours online researching the two friends of Liam's she'd mentioned at the end of our conversation in the kitchen – Bobbie and Kieran. I started with Facebook. Orla wasn't friends with either of them. And although Liam's account was still live, and seemingly curated by friends and family, I felt awkward trying to befriend a dead man in order to mine his contacts for information about the woman who was once his fiancée.

However, I did manage to find a comment on their engagement post, simply saying 'Congratulations', which was made by a Bobbie Chapple. The circular avatar showed a chocolate brown cockapoo. Clicking on it took me to the profile page, and I could see enough of the private profile to work out that Bobbie was female, and now worked in finance in the US. Her messages, however, were open, which meant I could send her a message without having to befriend her first.

I started simply, like I had with Sean:

Hi Bobbie, you don't know me, but I'm currently living with someone called Orla Sullivan. I think you used to know her back when she lived in Ireland? I just wanted to ask some questions if you've got a minute. Thanks, Jules.

Kieran was harder to find. There were no comments or 'likes' from him on any of the posts I'd seen so far, so I had to start scrolling back further. This was time-consuming. I worked on the assumption that if Kieran didn't get along with Orla, he'd be unlikely to 'like' her posts. So I focused only on the ones that involved Liam. At last I found one she'd posted a year before the engagement, a photo of Liam standing in front of a pub sign emblazoned with the gilded words 'The Pickled Pig'. The caption said, *Dinner tonight with this gorgeous man at my favourite Kerry pub.* There were twenty-two 'likes' and one of them was by someone called Kieran Douglas.

I clicked into his profile, surprised to see it wasn't private, but then disappointed to realise that, even so, he hardly ever posted anything. What infrequent posts there were, were of him refurbishing old motorbikes. The last post was from five years ago. Nevertheless, I clicked into messenger and sent him the same message I'd sent Bobbie, hoping he at least still checked his messages. But I felt deflated. Bobbie seemed like my most promising lead at the moment, but there was no guarantee she'd get back to me, or even that she was the right Bobbie.

Once again, I found myself sitting at my desk, paints and brushes and half-finished sketches in front of me, trying to focus on what I should be doing, but my thoughts were on Orla, and my eyes flickered to my phone with the flash of every notification.

Orla had retreated to her room after the appearance of the troll, and I didn't see her for days. Scott was regularly in a bad mood when he came home from work, moaning about contracts and extra workloads, but I suspected he was still upset about what had happened to Orla, because he kept looking at his phone, and on the few occasions I glimpsed the screen, I could see he was on Instagram. It seemed Orla and her online world were consuming him as much as me, albeit in different ways.

The troll's comments weren't now only confined to Instagram, though. They also appeared on X, and were gaining the same attention, and the same defensive responses from Orla's allies, who I noted included the official Kind UK account as well as Maggie's personal account, Kara and Amy, the Stardust Foundation, the local church, the restaurant and the beauty salon who'd both helped raise money and provide vouchers for Orla early on, and even MrsHealthLifeLove. The influencer who'd first raised Orla's profile waded into the comments, calling out the troll for being a 'spiteful human', and reassuring Orla that she'd had her own fair share of 'internet loonies' and that ignoring them was the best way to proceed and thus 'protect her beautiful energy'.

Orla, while offering profuse thanks to all her faithful defenders, didn't actually address the troll themselves. I wondered if she was too scared to provoke them, too scared of what else they might say. But I was desperate for more, and couldn't help checking and re-checking Facebook messenger every few minutes in case a message had come through from Bobbie or Kieran that I hadn't noticed.

Then, one came through from Bobbie as I was about to turn out the bedside lamp one night. I gave a sharp intake of breath when I saw her name, but thankfully Scott was already snoring next to me. I opened the message with a racing heart, hoping it would be filled with information, the way my phone call with Sean had been. But it was disappointing.

Hi Jules, thanks for getting in touch. Can't tell you much about Orla, I'm afraid. I moved to California not long after she got together with my friend Liam. What questions do you have? If you're planning a surprise or something for her then I'm not your girl – think I met her about 3 times max. Sorry! Bobbie x

I typed a quick reply, thanking her for taking the time to answer. But then, before I sent it I couldn't resist adding:

Not planning a surprise for her. It's more of a character reference I'm after. Did you like her? Jules x

Her response came about a minute later.

No problem. To answer your question, and to be completely honest – not really. Thought she was a bit of a princess. Sorry if that's not what you want to hear. Hope she's grown up a bit now and is the perfect roommate for you. B x

The perfect roommate. That she definitely was not. I drifted off to sleep with Bobbie's messages floating through my head, wondering what it must be like to have known Orla so briefly – to have met her three times, disliked her, then never laid eyes on her again. How blissful that sounded. And it was the fact it sounded so blissful that made me realise how helpless I felt. How trapped. I was trapped here, in this house, with Orla. I was trapped because I was pregnant but unable to focus on my family and my baby. I was trapped because my husband, the person I trusted the most in the world, was completely beguiled by this woman whom we could not get rid of.

The following morning, while I was drinking a cup of tea at the breakfast bar, a message pinged onto my phone which, when I look back, was the catalyst for everything that followed. The message was from Kieran. Kieran, who was completely disengaged with Facebook and who hadn't posted for five years. Kieran, who only posted photos of rusty motorbikes. Kieran, who I was sure would not see, let alone acknowledge my message. But he had seen it, and he did respond. And this is what he said:

Well, that's a name I haven't heard in a good few years. Hoped I never would again, to be honest. I'm assuming you want to 'ask a few questions' because Orla's up to her old tricks again? Ask away. Don't expect me to hold back though.

I felt an electric pulse of anticipation tingle through me. If Scott could see what I was doing now he'd be appalled.

But it was worth it. Or it *would* be worth it in the end, when he finally believed me and Orla was out of our lives. I typed back.

> Thank you so much for replying, Kieran. I wasn't sure you would. My husband and I have been living with Orla for months now, and her behaviour is getting more and more strange. There's something about her . . . I don't know how to explain it, but I wanted to have the opinion of someone who knew her way back. I've already spoken to her brother Sean, but I thought you might have a different insight, as you were Liam's friend and not connected to Orla. Perhaps he told you things he didn't tell Sean? I'd be grateful for anything you have.

I sipped my cooling tea as I waited for him to reply. Desperate for it to be soon so I could be put out of my misery and not have to navigate another day trying to function while waiting for notifications on my phone. The minutes ticked by. Then it came. *Ping!*

> I don't know where to begin with Orla. So I'll lay it out simply, as I saw it, and as I heard it from Liam. They dated for about a year before he proposed. Me and Liam's other mates didn't like her much – thought she was a bit up herself. But Liam obviously liked her, and to be fair to her, she could be a laugh sometimes. But then she started acting weird. Liam worked at the hospital and he said she kept turning up all the time. She said she was just surprising

him, but she wasn't – he'd find her wandering the corridors, and one time he even caught her in one of the store cupboards. That's when alarm bells rang and he thought maybe she had an addiction and was looking for drugs? She swore blind she wasn't. Anyway, then they had a massive row. Liam was beside himself. Next thing, he says he's found something online that seriously made him have doubts about her. Obviously, we all thought he'd found her on one of those webcam sites, you know. But he wouldn't say. It's horrible cos we even joked about it down the pub when he wasn't there. Then he died, and we never saw her again. And I've felt shit about it ever since, to be honest. He was going through something awful with that woman, and then he was dead, and we never found out what it was.

I read the message twice, drinking in every word. I imagined Orla skulking around the hospital where Liam worked, using him as an excuse to wander the corridors. Simultaneously, my mind conjured up the photo of Orla sitting in the hospital chair, the purple teddy bear perched on the shelf behind her.

I found myself slipping off the bar stool, leaving my now cold cup of tea on the table, and heading towards the stairs. Orla had gone out early this morning, keen to meet up with Maggie in town and go over her upcoming events and fundraising opportunities. Her demeanour as she'd skipped off had jarred. She'd been perky, full of energy. It was almost impossible to believe she'd been under the knife so recently. But it seemed the prospect of meeting Maggie and chatting everything through had put a spring in her step. Maggie had texted me about it last night, along with a long rant about the 'scum troll' who'd had Orla in floods of tears on the phone to her. I'd given all the right responses, I thought, but tried to end the text conversation as quickly as possible. Pandering to Orla and her superfans was becoming tiring. I longed to be on the other side of this.

I walked up the stairs, my footsteps light as a strange instinct told me to be as quiet as possible despite the fact I was alone in the house. Turning the corner to ascend the staircase to the attic felt particularly wrong. Yes, this was my house, but this was Orla's domain, and I had no business being in her room without her knowledge. This was the type of thing landlords got in trouble for. But this wasn't a normal situation, I reminded myself. *And this is my house.*

I pushed open the bedroom door and was met with the squalor I'd witnessed before. It struck me then, the only time I'd seen Orla's bedroom neat and tidy was on an occasion when she'd known Scott and I would come up here, the time she'd started sobbing after shaving her head. I crossed to the bathroom and peered inside. Shower gel and shampoo bottles littered the shower cubicle; empty toilet rolls were scattered across the floor. The sink was toothpaste-smeared and the mirror had a diagonal streak of what looked like lipstick across its surface.

I turned back to the room and walked to the bedside, careful not to disturb the clothes that were strewn across the floor. There was a dusty glass of water and a paperback thriller on the bedside table. The drawer underneath was empty. In a crinkled plastic bag in the corner I found a huge selection of medicine bottles, all containing pills. I took one out and read the label: multi-vitamins. Another contained a drug called Mebeverine. I googled it on my phone and discovered it was used to treat irritable bowel syndrome. The next bottle contained paracetamol, and the next Cardicor which I learnt was a beta-blocker to lower blood pressure.

I threw the bottle back in with the others and dropped the bag back where I'd found it, then crossed to the squat wardrobe in the corner, the door of which stood ajar. And when I opened it fully, I could see why. Underneath where the clothes hung, was a jumble of items I found hard to process at first. There was an oxygen mask, linked to a long plastic tube. On its side was an oxygen tank, and on top of this a tangled mass of wires and tubes. I reached in and pulled on them, realising they were attached to three separate IV bags, like water pouches, one labelled 'sterile saline solution' and the other two 'omnia 0.9% saline solution'. They were full. There was a stack of bandages and a piece of patterned fabric, which, when I picked it up, I realised was a hospital gown. As I crouched down and rifled through these items I saw that the other reason the wardrobe door wouldn't close was because there was a metal stand, its five coastered feet too bulky to fit in the cupboard. It was a collapsible IV stand with four little hooks at the top to hang IV bags from.

There was a bang behind me and I spun around, heart pounding. But it was just one of the French windows swinging open in the breeze and clanging against the radiator. I turned back to Orla's medical hoard, reeling, wondering what it must all mean. Was she treating herself at home with all these things? Did people hook themselves up to IVs at home? That didn't sound right. Surely you needed to be a trained medical professional to insert a needle into a vein. And I hadn't even found any needles – just the bags and tubes. Also, why the hospital gown?

I closed the wardrobe door and sat on Orla's bed, taking my phone from my back pocket and tapping into Orla's Instagram and scrolling through the photos. There it was. A photo of her during her last treatment week, wearing the same hospital gown (or an identical one) as the one in the wardrobe. The photo showed her lying down, an IV stand next to her from which hung a fluid bag, the tube snaking down and ending in a bandage at her arm. But as I looked more closely I realised there was nothing distinguishing about the surroundings. The pillow on the bed was white, and the wall behind the IV stand was white. This photo could have been taken in the hospital – or in this room. The caption said, *Another exhausting round of treatment today at Kingston Hospital. I don't know how my body can handle this much longer. #FightForOrla #nevergiveup #KindUK.*

I was about to begin scrolling again, but something stopped me. What was I doing? What would more photos show me? More of the same. More generic hospital gowns and white beds and IV tubes and oxygen masks. I was getting nowhere.

I clicked back into Kieran's message and reread it, wondering if I should write to him again and try to find out more. But this time, one sentence jumped out at me: *Next thing, he says he's found something online that made him have serious doubts about her.* What could Liam have found?

Chapter Thirty-two

I left the room with a sudden, overwhelming urge to be out of there in case Orla came home and caught me. I scurried down the stairs from the attic and slipped into my studio, closing the door behind me and sitting at the desk, phone still clutched in my hand. Then, for the second time, I googled Orla Sullivan. I scrolled back and back through her show appearances and newspaper reviews, back to any entries I could find that happened just before Liam died. I knew from the articles I'd found previously that he'd died in August 2014, so I scrolled until I found an entry from that July. As I clicked on the link I realised I'd read this result before. But no, that didn't make sense, the date couldn't be right. Because this link took me to the cancer forum . . .

> Is anyone else really struggling with side effects from IV Vincristine? I feel so sick and completely wiped out 24/7. And what's with the tingling hands? I can barely hold my phone to type this – think I need to ask my consultant to try me on a different drug.

I stared at the words, reading them for the second time in my life, but this time with my gaze flicking back and forth between them and the date at the top of the page – 20 July 2014. Why hadn't I noticed last time? This wasn't a post from her recent round of treatment, as I'd thought when I first read it. This post was ten years old. I felt an icy prickle of goosebumps on my arms.

She'd done this before.

This was what Liam had discovered. He'd found her pilfering medical equipment from the hospital where he worked, then he'd found this post online and realised what she was doing; that's why they argued, and that's why he had doubts about her. I wished more than anything that I could reach back through time and speak to Liam. To ask him what he went through with Orla and what I should do now. But he was gone.

I took a screenshot of the forum entry and the date, then I made a decision. It was time to speak to Scott. I'd gathered enough evidence to make a clear case against Orla. Our baby's due date was getting closer and I couldn't bear this any longer. I needed him onside. I needed him to believe me. What more evidence could I get? No doctors were going to share confidential information with me, but with the messages from Kieran and Abi, the phone call I'd had with Sean, as well as the staged photos and the medical equipment stashed in her wardrobe – *surely* he'd agree that the stories Orla was telling us just weren't adding up.

Buzzing as I was from my discoveries, I made myself take my time. I decided I would present my evidence as a professional would – by laying it all out, physically, on the table for Scott to see. This would not be rushed, this would be done properly, so there was no way he could continue to defend Orla. I printed off the Facebook conversations I'd had with Kieran and Bobbie, and the Instagram messages I'd exchanged with Abi, along with the accompanying photo of Abi and Orla in the Edinburgh Fringe production. I also printed off Orla's original post where she claimed this photo was from her first treatment session, and that the woman in it was a nurse called Ngozi. As I collated these messages, posts and photos, I often found myself shaking my head in disbelief. How could she think she'd get away with this?

I printed Orla's 2014 cancer forum post and slipped that into a folder next to Kieran's message explaining how Liam had found something online that had made him doubt Orla. Yes, those two pieces of evidence belonged together. As I worked, the picture became clearer in my own mind: all the links were there to see, every lie with an accompanying photo, post or comment. I had to stop myself pinning these exhibits to the wall of my study and winding lengths of red string around drawing pins . . . making a proper incident room of it. I knew that would be ridiculous, but I honestly felt I had a live investigation on my hands, and that anyone would be able to see we had grounds for an arrest . . . or at least for a confrontation, for a discussion about Orla moving out.

I was going to lay all this in front of Scott on Thursday, but he came home in a foul mood, saying Truth-Bomb365 had been 'at it again'. We were in the kitchen, and I clicked into my Instagram and read the comment.

Factitious disorder is a serious psychological syndrome where someone deceives others by appearing sick.

Underneath was a link to an NHS article about the disorder, and its historical name: 'Munchausen syndrome'.
As I read the comments underneath defending Orla, a
new one from Scott popped up:

> You're the only one round here 'appearing sick',
> mate. Stop harassing innocent people and get a life.

Scott threw his phone down on the counter with a clat-
ter. 'You know what pisses me off too? They've not even
got the courage to open their DMs, or the comments on
their own account. So I can't even message them pri-
vately to tell them to fuck off.'

I sighed. 'You know, this isn't your responsibility?
You know, it's not for you to tell them to fuck off?'

But Scott wasn't listening to me. He stomped around
the kitchen, clattering pots and pans as he cooked us
dinner, and I knew I couldn't make this moment worse
by presenting him with my damning evidence. He was
in 'defending Orla' mode, and me adding fuel to the
fire would not help matters. It would have to be done
another day.

Orla was out on Friday evening with Kara and Amy. I
decided this was my moment with Scott. He came home
from work a little earlier than usual, as sometimes happened on a Friday. He also seemed more relaxed as he
brought a beer out of the fridge and a non-alcoholic one
for me. We sat opposite each other on the breakfast bar
and sipped from our bottles, making small talk about
our days and discussing who was going to cook. As we

covered these mundane subjects, I felt my insides twisting into a tangle of knots. The blue folder with all my findings was on the counter next to me and I felt as if it was looking at me like a third person in the room, its gaze on my face, trying to attract my attention, calling me to action.

'You OK?' said Scott, taking another swig then placing the bottle down. 'You're a bit quiet.'

I nodded. 'Actually, I want to talk to you again about Orla.'

I felt him stiffen. There was a beat of silence, then he began twirling the base of his beer bottle. 'OK. Go on then.' There was a false brightness to his tone, and I felt a wave of nausea. I really didn't want to do this. But I had to.

I reached over and pulled the file in front of me. Scott gave a soft laugh. 'What's this?'

I cast him a glance that seemed to wipe the smile off his face. I'd decided I would start with Abi – I needed to begin with a clear, outright lie that was backed up by someone else. So I told him about recognising Abi from her photo and asking her about Orla, but about her denying she was a nurse. I explained about the photo – taking the printout from my file and sliding it across the table so he could see.

'This photo is from a play they did in Edinburgh and is nothing to do with Kingston Hospital, or her histiocytosis treatment. This woman is called Abi, not Ngozi as it claims in this caption . . .' I tapped the page again, then slid the printout of Abi's message towards him. '. . . as you can see explained by Abi herself on Instagram.'

My heart pounded against my ribs and my mouth felt dry. I took a swig from my bottle before continuing. I explained about contacting Sean, and our phone conversation. Scott took his eyes from the papers in front of him and stared at me with a grim expression that made my face burn. This was the part I was most worried about – the secret messages and phone calls. How would he react to those? What would he say? But he didn't say anything as my story unfolded.

Next I explained I'd gone up to Orla's room. Here I'd decided to tell a white lie. I didn't want him to know I'd gone up there with the clear intention of snooping around, so I said I'd stored some art supplies in the wardrobe last year and wanted to retrieve them. I told him what I'd found: the IV stand, the saline bags, the bandages, the hospital gown, the oxygen mask.

Scott's expression hardened and he leaned back on his chair, arms folded. I ploughed on, not wanting to lose momentum now I had almost covered everything. Finally, I laid out my Google search which had revealed the cancer forum on which she'd discussed the chemo-drug side effects. I placed that printout in front of him on top of the others, the date highlighted in pink at the top.

I stabbed at the date and, for extra effect, said it out loud. 'Twentieth of July 2014.' Then I leaned back, mirroring Scott with my arms crossed, trying to arrange my features into a strong, resolute expression.

I'd expected the whole thing to be more of a discussion – maybe even an argument. I hadn't envisaged Scott allowing me to complete what felt like a presentation.

And now it was over and Scott was staring at me, I didn't know what to say.

'Well?' I ventured. 'Aren't you going to launch into Operation Worship Orla?' I hadn't meant to say anything so petulant, but I couldn't bear his angry eyes boring into mine. I couldn't bear his silence. I couldn't bear any of this for a moment longer.

He took a breath, and seemed to consider his words. 'So, do you know who this troll is, then? Is it one of your new mates? Someone from Orla's past who's spoken to you and had all their ancient grudges stirred back up again?'

'What?' I stared at him, aghast. 'I'm not stirring anything up! And they're not "ancient grudges" – these are *real* people who have had *real* experiences with Orla. Don't you think it's strange how many there are who have grievances with her? Isn't *that* what you should be focusing on?'

He stared down at the table, at the pieces of paper fanned out in front of him. Then he reached into his back pocket and took out his phone.

'What are you doing?' I asked, my voice quivering.

'I'm calling Maggie.'

Chapter Thirty-three

He went into the hallway. He actually stepped into the hallway and shut the kitchen door to have a private phone conversation with *my* best friend.

I sat at the breakfast bar, staring at my half-finished beer, listening to the rumble of his voice on the other side of the glass door. Eventually he came back in.

'She's on her way over,' he said, his voice deadpan.

'Maggie? Why?' I was shocked.

'Because we need to talk this through once and for all and I can't do it by myself because you won't listen to me. Maybe you'll listen to Maggie.'

'*I* won't listen to *you*? What are you talking about, Scott? I'm the one who's not being listened to! I've been banging on about Orla since the beginning, and now I've finally got all this evidence together to back up my suspicions and you're still looking at me like . . . like I'm crazy! And now you're calling Maggie over . . . for what? For some sort of *intervention*? So she can reason with me and help me see sense?'

'Well, you've kind of forced my hand with this, Jules.' There was a flash of pity in his eyes as he said this. Something sorrowful. And it was so much worse than the anger that had been there before.

When the doorbell rang, Scott went to let Maggie in. She entered the room with a worried frown, shrugging off her handbag and crossing to me, enveloping me in a hug I didn't want to let go of. I needed my friend, and I wanted her to believe me so desperately. But as she pulled away and looked into my eyes I could see the concern etched on her features, and I wondered what the hell Scott had said to her on the phone.

'So go on then,' she said, nodding towards the papers on the table. 'Tell me what's going on.'

So I went through everything again and, unlike Scott, Maggie's body language remained open and receptive. She picked up the papers I handed her and looked at them carefully, nodding as I explained what each of them showed before placing them carefully back down. When I'd finished, I felt a flickering ember of hope. Maggie would see this the way I did, and together we'd help Scott understand.

She placed the final piece of paper down on the table, the one with the cancer forum entry from 2014, and placed her palm gently on top of it before raising her eyes to mine. 'OK. We've heard and seen everything here, and there's a lot of stuff, and we can see you're extremely upset.' Her tone, like Scott's pitying look, was insufferable. 'So now, do you mind if I show you some documents I've brought along?'

I felt my spine straighten. I hadn't predicted her saying that. I shrugged. 'Of course.'

She cast a quick glance at Scott before delving into her handbag and bringing out a yellow A4 folder made of thin card upon which was a sticker printed with

Orla's name, mobile number and our address. It was several times thicker than my blue folder, and from it Maggie produced a sheaf of papers that seemed about the thickness of an average paperback novel. She pushed my printouts aside and spread her papers out, handing them to me at random, waiting for me to peruse them individually before silently passing me the next.

There were NHS-headed letters from consultants at the hospital, all addressed to Orla, detailing tests and treatment plans. There were blood test results with her name and NHS number and blood type. There were clinical documents written from one consultant to another that Orla had been copied in on, that were unintelligible to someone non-medical. They talked of medicines and post-op care and test results and blood platelet counts and oxygen levels and histiocytes. Nothing was blanked out, all the consultants' names were used in full, as were their PAs', along with their phone numbers. Some of the documents were printed-out emails that clearly showed doctors' email addresses alongside Orla's in the sender and recipient fields. Lastly, there were scans. Full, cross-sectional images of Orla's body, others of her skull, her personal details clearly showing at the top, the lesion on her skull highlighted red in some images, but in others grey and illuminated like the warped corona of a solar eclipse.

After what felt like an eternity of silence, Maggie spoke, her voice soft. 'Jules – these are Orla's medical documents. She's been sharing them with me from the beginning. At first, I asked for them so I could help her apply for funding. Then she decided she didn't want that. She said that there were others who needed the financial help more than she did. But I've been keeping everything anyway, in case she got to a point where she changed her mind.'

'Did . . . did you ask her for all of this?' I said, the question somehow feeling weak and silly.

'No.' Maggie gave a soft laugh. 'Actually, I only needed a fraction of this for our Kind UK paperwork – most of it is just stuff Orla's volunteered in case it's useful, and so I can be a better friend to her on her journey.'

I looked up at Maggie and Scott, and into their hopeful faces, something curdling inside me.

'Maybe . . .' I willed my voice not to quiver. 'Maybe she faked all those.'

'For God's sake, Jules.' Scott sounded angry. 'Are you saying you think she faked *all this*?' His arm swept over the mountain of paper in front of us.

'I'm saying it's possible, if not highly likely!' Oh God, I sounded deranged. I needed to claw this back. 'What about the photo? She faked *that*. What about Abi Obasi?'

'OK, that is a definite lie Orla told,' said Maggie with a conceding nod. 'But you have to remember, Jules, that doesn't mean she's lied about her diagnosis.'

'What?' I felt the conviction leaving me, my voice weakening even though my pulse still thundered in my chest.

Scott latched onto what Maggie was saying. 'That's right – I mean, you've said yourself a million times, Orla is a drama queen. I think we can all agree on that!' He made an attempt at a placatory laugh. 'She's an actor and she's eccentric. OK, she might have told a fib about a photo that she thought would look good on social media and represent the reality of her treatment well, but that doesn't mean she's lying about her illness.'

'Lots of patients feel self-conscious about how they look during treatment,' continued Maggie. 'Perhaps she wanted to commemorate the moment, but with a photo that showed her looking better than she did at the time?'

'But she lied about Abi's name and said she was a nurse!'

'That is strange behaviour,' continued Maggie. 'No one is denying that. But it doesn't mean that all *this*,' she gestured to the papers again, 'is a lie.'

'And the hoarding of medical equipment in her wardrobe?'

'We don't know how much of that she actually uses at home,' said Maggie. 'Supplementary home treatments are very common in treating all sorts of illnesses.'

'The fainting she faked as a child?'

'Well, that's Sean's word against hers,' said Maggie. 'And quite frankly, from everything she's told me about Sean I wouldn't take anything he said too seriously. He sounds like a nasty piece of work. As do these old "friends" of Liam's. She's told me all about them, Jules, especially Kieran. He stirred up some of the last arguments she had with Liam before he died. She can never forgive him for that. And in fact, she's pretty convinced he's the person behind the TruthBomb365 account that's been trolling her.'

I felt something slipping away from me. I'd been so hopeful this would be the end of it. So scrupulous in my evidence-finding. I'd been prepared for some disbelief and shock, but I'd been completely blindsided by being shut down on every point I'd made. Was I mad? Had my need to reclaim my house and my space resulted in my brain concocting this far-fetched scenario where Orla would pretend to be suffering from a possibly terminal illness? I couldn't process that as an explanation for the deeply uncomfortable situation I was now in.

'But . . . what about the fact she's on a forum ten years ago looking for sympathy because she's undergoing treatment? Doesn't that ring alarm bells?'

Scott sighed. 'Orla is under no obligation to tell us her entire medical history. This can be a recurring condition, as we all know – why is it so unbelievable she might have also suffered from it ten years ago?' He gave a shrug. 'She might just not want to talk about it with us. And why should she? She's our lodger, Jules.'

'Oh fucking hell!' They both flinched. I couldn't blame them – I'd even surprised myself at the force of my words. But now I couldn't stop. 'Now she's our *lodger*, is she?' A crazed laugh escaped my lips. 'I thought she was our *best friend*. I thought we were her *guardian angels*. Oh my God!' My voice was rising and becoming almost hysterical. 'All this time I've been saying she's *just our lodger* and everyone's been making out she's *so much more* than that, and now it suits you . . . hey presto! She's our *lodger* again? Someone who's above questioning? Above suspicion? Even while she's living under our roof and taking up every inch of our emotional space with her *constant bloody need for attention*?'

'Jules . . .' Scott looked frightened now. He stood and crossed around to my side of the table. 'Calm down, this stress is not good for you—'

'I know it's not! That's the whole bloody point!'

He raised his arms slowly as if he wanted to hug me but was scared to attempt it. I scrambled inelegantly off the bar stool and stalked away from him. I couldn't bear his patronising touch. I paced the room like a caged bear. Tears stung my eyes and when I looked up at Scott and Maggie I was embarrassed when those tears slid down my cheeks.

'Jules . . .' Maggie whispered softly, her expression tragic. But she didn't approach. Neither of them dared to move or say any more. They seemed paralysed by their concern for me. They honestly thought I had completely lost all sense of reality. Had I?

'I can't do it any more . . .' I said. 'I can't live with her any more.' My head was shaking as if of its own accord, and I knew I was acting every bit the crazed lunatic they thought I was.

Scott nodded, then held his hands out in a gesture of surrender. 'OK, OK . . . we can talk about this. We can work it out. You were wary of taking a lodger in the first place, and I didn't listen. And then early on, before Orla was even ill, you said you weren't sure about the arrangement – I should have listened to you back then. I shouldn't have let it get to this point.' He cast a glance at Maggie as he said this last bit and I bit back my irritation. Scott was attributing all of this to my not wanting a lodger in the first place. He clearly believed I'd level such a horrific accusation at someone, just because I didn't want to live with them any more. Or did he think my hormone-saturated brain had made me believe my own outrageous theories? Yes, that was probably it . . . Scott thought I was suffering from some sort of pregnancy psychosis and that I needed humouring.

Maggie obviously agreed. 'Perhaps . . . perhaps we need to look for alternative arrangements for Orla. Would that help?' She was speaking as if I was a child who needed placating because they'd been told they couldn't go to the park. It made me feel sick. But at that moment, it was the best offer on the table.

I nodded, fresh tears spilling down my cheeks. 'I think that would be for the best. Can Kind UK sort something out for her?' My voice was weak and quivery.

'I'll speak to some colleagues and see what we can do. Perhaps . . . I mean, maybe she could even come and stay with Nick and me?'

Christ, I didn't want that. I didn't want to lumber Maggie and Nick with Orla. But in that moment I couldn't see past my urgent need to detach her from us. I nodded. 'Whatever you can do to get her out of this house, I would be grateful.'

Neither of them spoke. I didn't think there was anything else to say, so I scooped up all my papers, slid them back into the folder and went up to bed, feeling like my insides had been hollowed out. I didn't care how they did it – I'd leave the logistics up to Maggie and Scott. They could work it all out downstairs without me. Of course I desperately wanted them to believe me. But if they wouldn't entertain my theories for even a second, then the next best thing was that Orla simply disappeared from our lives. I would have to content myself with that.

Chapter Thirty-four

The appearance of November's twinkling lights and the festive music that wafted from shops usually made me feel a warm, childlike excitement. But this year was different. The Christmas paraphernalia reminded me that almost a whole year had passed since we'd met Orla – a whole year of this creeping unease. This discomfort in my own home. And now it also reminded me that time was passing in my pregnancy. We'd been having conversations about Orla moving out since the very beginning – conversations that had come to nothing. Scott and Maggie had agreed to find Orla somewhere else to live. But we'd been here before, hadn't we? Somehow she always managed to do something that ensured we couldn't ask her to leave. And now, with my due date only a few weeks away, it terrified me that she might be able to do it again.

If my presentation of evidence to Scott and Maggie hadn't made me feel deranged, then the following weeks certainly would have. It was as if nothing had happened. Scott brought me tea in bed in the morning before he left for work, pecked me on the cheek, and told me to have a lovely day. He usually cooked when he came home from work, and would call me from my studio when dinner was ready. We sat at the dining table now, as the bar stools were becoming uncomfortable for me to perch on with my ever-growing bump, and we chatted baby names and birth plans.

But there was something off between us. There was no denying it. Our words were polite and careful, as if we were treading on cracked ice that could splinter at any moment, plunging us both into icy waters.

My only contact with Maggie, and indeed the only acknowledgement the whole episode hadn't been a bad dream, was a text from her:

> Hey, my lovely, hope you're OK. I know you're under a lot of stress with work etc, not to mention the baby's imminent arrival! We don't want you worrying about Orla – please leave all that to me and Scott. Xxx

So I was right. They'd both decided I'd kicked off about Orla because I was 'pregnancy crazy', and they wanted to make sure I didn't approach Orla myself – God forbid I upset the patient and damage their sacred friendships. Well, that was fine. I'd happily leave it to Scott and Maggie. Perhaps I'd leave it to them to ferry her to and from the hospital for her next appointments too. If they were the ones taking her, collecting her, making her food, then spending the afternoon watching her gleefully posting her medical updates from her bedroom, maybe they'd start asking the same questions I had.

Posts from TruthBomb365 became more frequent – *Orla is a liar . . . she's a narcissistic attention-seeker* – and I watched Scott and Maggie bravely defending Orla in the comments sections, wondering if Orla found me conspicuous in my online absence, wondering if she was waiting for me to join in with their defence of her.

I also wondered if Maggie and Scott were cursing me for digging into Orla's past and awakening this troll from their bitter hiding place. It still amazed me that, with all the accusations I'd levelled at Orla, the fact there was someone else online saying the same thing (it was Kieran, according to Maggie) hadn't given them pause . . . it hadn't made them think, *Hang on, maybe there's some truth to this*. Was my theory really so outlandish?

One morning I woke up to an unexpected Instagram message from Abi:

> Hi Jules, not sure what you said to Orla but she's just paid me two months' rent, so thank you so much for that! Look at the message she sent:

Underneath was a screenshot of Orla's email to Abi.

> Hi Abi, hope you're well. I'm so sorry about what happened in January – I had a family medical emergency and just upped and left, and then I knew you were going on tour so I didn't get in touch, and I realise now I completely left you in the lurch. Please accept my apologies, and two months' rent to make up for it. I've transferred the money directly into your account. O xx

The audacity of Orla was something else. As if her flit could be explained away by a 'family medical emergency'. What about how she'd ignored Abi's calls and messages and then blocked her on social media? Did a 'family medical emergency' explain that? But then perhaps she was desperate – maybe she suspected Abi of being TruthBomb365 and thought this message and two months' rent would placate the troll and stop their online exposés. But whatever the reason for Orla coughing up, I was glad Abi had her money and some sort of closure as far as Orla was concerned. Something, I had to admit, I was a little jealous of.

Scott had a networking event in London Bridge one Wednesday evening and would be home late, so I headed up to my studio. Orla was out with Maggie, which made me uneasy: I now hated Maggie spending time with Orla more than ever. I also wondered if Maggie had been tasked with broaching the subject of Orla finding alternative accommodation. I pondered how Scott and Maggie had decided to frame it – I was sure my pregnancy would be front and centre of the conversation and they'd make it sound as if it was simply a case of us wanting more room for the baby. Maybe tonight would be the night Maggie asked Orla to move in with her and Nick. Maybe a coffee would turn into celebratory drinks. I pictured them both in the Grey Horse (one of our favourite haunts), Orla ordering a bottle of prosecco in a silver ice bucket and her and Maggie giggling and hugging and toasting to being roommates. I pushed the thought away. It made me feel sick. I felt so alone.

In a desperate moment I sent a message to Kieran with a link to Orla's website, asking what he thought of it. I needed to have *someone* on side. Someone who felt the same way I did about Orla, someone who would back me up. But was it that? Or was I just smarting from the fact my theory about Orla's condition had gone up in smoke? Was I still desperately clinging to my hunch because I couldn't bear to have been proven wrong?

I reached across my desk and opened the notebook I'd scribbled in when I was speaking to Sean on the phone. I wasn't looking for anything specific, just hoping to find comfort among the words I'd scrawled while talking to someone who knew how difficult Orla could be. Someone else who got it. I turned over the first page and my gaze caught on a phrase I'd noted down, before sketching a box around it. The words were: *some jealousy surrounding my situation.* I'd forgotten Sean saying that. I'd assumed at the time he'd been talking about the jealousy Orla would have felt at having to share her parents with a new sibling. But there was something about the phrasing that jarred . . . and it had obviously stood out enough at the time for me to scribble it here.

I picked up my phone and fired off a short Facebook message to Sean, asking what he'd meant by his 'situation'. Was he referring to simple sibling rivalry, or was there something else? Then I put my phone on silent and placed it on a shelf by the door so I wouldn't be constantly checking it, and I went back to sit at my desk.

By 9.15 p.m. I'd scanned in some new pencil sketches, and was focused on placing them in my storyboard template on the computer, when I heard the front door open. It was too early for Scott, and I felt a flash of irritation as I realised Orla must be back earlier than I'd predicted. I really didn't want to get into a discussion about living arrangements at that particular moment so I kept still, hoping she'd scurry up to her bedroom without knocking on my door.

I listened to her laboured steps on the stairs, then their approach along the landing, willing them to continue up to the attic. But they paused outside my door. Then came a tentative knock. My heart dropped.

'Come in,' I said, swivelling round in my chair

She opened the door and stepped in, a small smile playing at the corners of her mouth. She wore a pale pink scarf wound neatly around her head and a button-down denim dress. A waft of floral perfume pervaded the room.

'Hello, Jules,' she said, blinking at me in a strange, distracted sort of way.

'Hi.' I felt an intensity settling upon us. A knowledge that something had shifted, and that a conversation was about to happen, whether I liked it or not. 'How was Maggie?'

Orla crossed her arms and nodded thoughtfully. 'You know something – she's the best. Everything that woman does is incredible. She's an absolute trojan for that charity – works her socks off for our community and all with a smile on her face. Honestly, she's an inspiration.' Her last words were slurred, and I realised they had been drinking after all.

I smiled. 'I couldn't agree more.'

'And she's done nothing but support and validate me since the first day I met her.'

317

I thought *validate* was an interesting choice of word. But of course . . . that's what Orla had always wanted. Validation.

Orla pressed one hand to her chest and closed her eyes, swaying slightly where she stood. She'd definitely been drinking. She opened her eyes and fixed her gaze on me. 'So, two things happened this evening . . . shall I tell you what they were?'

A shiver of dread. 'Sure,' I said, trying to keep my voice light.

'Firstly, Maggie took me for a drink and explained perhaps it was time you and Scott were left alone to feather your nest before the baby arrives . . . I mean, she took ages to say it, and broached the subject in a typically "Maggie" way, you know – subtle and diplomatic and beautifully low key. You know, for a moment she almost had me thinking it had been my idea in the first place! She went on about newborns and the racket they make and all the stuff they need and how much room they take up . . . obviously, all things I already know, but still, she laid it all out in front of me. Then she said she and Nick were thinking of getting a lodger . . . and BAM!' She clapped her hands together and I flinched. 'There it was! Fab idea, don't you think? I mean, Maggie and I get along so well. Sometimes I feel like we're sisters, rather than friends. That's how close we are.' She gave me an unwavering stare as she said this and I felt that familiar nausea writhe in my stomach.

'But anyway!' She shook her head as if to get herself back on track. 'That all sounded hunky dory – I mean,

I'd love to move in with Maggie, of course. So I was thinking FAB, everyone gets what they want: you get space for your baby, Maggie and I get to be roomies!'

'OK,' I said, tentatively. 'Sounds like it's decision made, then.'

'It does, rather, doesn't it?' As I'd noticed on previous occasions, the more emphatic Orla got (and perhaps the more alcohol she drank), the stronger her Irish accent became. 'But then, do you know what happened?' She cocked her head with mock puzzlement.

I bit my lip, adrenaline beginning to simmer inside me. 'No,' I said, like a naughty pupil answering a teacher.

'I went to the toilet!' She cackled and pressed her palm to her chest again, wiping the fingers of her other hand under her eyes as if to remove tears of hilarity. 'No, but seriously,' she continued. 'I did go to the toilet, and while I was in there I checked my email, and you'll *never* guess who I had a message from.'

'Who?'

'It was my old friend Abi. She was replying to an email I'd sent her the other day. And do you know what she was saying? She was— well, actually, I'll tell you exactly what she was saying, hang on—' She stumbled as she reached into her handbag to retrieve her phone, then squinted at the screen as she stabbed at it. At last she cleared her throat. '*Orla, it's a surprise to hear from you after all these months. I couldn't believe it when you did a runner on me like that – that put me in a really shitty position . . .* Blah blah blah . . . Oh! Here's the bit . . .' She cleared her throat. '*I don't know what Jules said to you, but I'm glad she made*

319

you realise you needed to do the right thing. Thank you for the rent payment. I was really sorry to hear about your health issues, but please don't put any more fake photos . . . et cetera, et cetera . . . *Wishing you all the best. Abi.'*

Orla cocked her head again, as if she was waiting for an explanation. And the bizarre thing is, I almost felt like I owed her one. This was the most ridiculous impulse I could have had. Orla herself had as good as admitted she'd run out on her last roommate without paying the rent, then posted a 'fake' photo of said roommate on social media without her knowledge. And yet, I was the one who supposedly owed Orla an explanation. I gave myself a mental slap. *Fight fire with fire, Jules.*

I frowned, presenting Orla with a parody of her own questioning expression. 'Yeah . . . I'm glad you brought that up. Care to explain?'

Her eyebrows shot up. 'Do *I* care to explain?'

I laughed. 'Yes, Orla. That's exactly what I'm asking. I mean, I recognised Abi from your post and wanted to thank her for taking such good care of you, so I trotted up and asked her about you – only to be told Abi wasn't a nurse and that the only reason she knew you was because you'd lived together and you owed her money. So . . . can you see why I, perhaps, might think it was *you* who owed *me* an explanation, rather than the other way round?' I hadn't meant my voice to turn facetious, but I took an unexpected and dark delight in challenging Orla in this way after all these months of holding my tongue. At this point I wasn't even thinking about her illness any more . . . there were so many other things that just weren't *right*.

Orla swallowed and blinked, and I watched her chest rise and fall faster, as if she was trying to contain something. 'Do you know what that message from Abi made me realise?' she said, as if I hadn't just called her a liar and a thief. 'It made me realise the reason Maggie was asking me to move in with her must be because you'd told her about meeting Abi. That was the moment I knew there was more to this little drinks invitation of Maggie's. So I decided to come clean.'

My pulse throbbed in my chest. 'Come clean about what?'

Orla shrugged and smiled. 'About Abi. I told Maggie about leaving the flat we'd shared, explaining how it had been a terrible time for me. I had a close friend who called in the middle of the night in crisis and I ran to be by her side . . . that was just before I moved in with you and Scott . . . then I was in such a state I completely forgot about the rent money—'

'*Sorry?*' I felt myself grimacing in disbelief. 'You left your rental with no notice to rush to your friend's side, and you took *all* your belongings with you, then blocked your roommate from contacting you?' Orla blinked but didn't say anything, so I continued. 'Also, you just said it was a "friend in crisis", but you told Abi it was a "family medical emergency", so which was it, Orla?'

Orla stared at me, arms crossed, statue still but for one finger that tapped her upper arm. 'See, this is what I mean, Jules. This is what I mean about Maggie being the most wonderful and understanding person . . . she doesn't challenge me or ask a million questions; she just listens and—'

'And believes every single lie that comes out of your mouth?'

The silence that engulfed my words was pierced by the *ping!* of my mobile phone, which, unfortunately, wasn't on the desk behind me, but still perched on the bookshelf by the door. I watched Orla's eyes instinctively flicker towards the screen and stay there. She turned her head, face scrunching up as she lurched towards the phone, grabbing it before I had to time to get to it myself.

'What the hell? Orla! That's my phone!' I hauled myself up to standing and stepped towards her.

Orla backed away, clutching my phone in her white-knuckled grip and scowling at the screen. 'Sean?' She looked at me in disgust.

Shit.

'You've got a Facebook message from *Sean* on your phone, Jules! Have you been talking to my bastard of a brother? Have you *both* been talking about me behind my back?'

I reached for my phone, but she twisted out of my reach, then walked out onto the landing.

'Orla! Give me my bloody phone back!' I said, following her and trying to reach round and grab it from her. But she writhed away again, stabbing and swiping at my phone screen, trying in vain to unlock it.

'What have you been saying to him? What have you been *fucking* talking about?' Her voice was shrill, her expression manic. The joking, mischievous tone had disappeared and she looked livid and terrified all at the same time.

I tripped on the corner of the landing rug, clutching at the banister as I stumbled, my other arm instinctively cradling my bump. Just as I was about to straighten up, a contraction like none I'd felt before took my breath away. I winced, willing it to subside.

Orla spun round, ignoring the fact I was hunched over, my face twisted in pain. 'No fucking wonder I'm being trolled . . . Sean will have spoken to Kieran, and all Liam's other shitty friends . . . did you tell him about Abi too? Who else have you spoken to . . . Kieran? Bobbie? What the hell have you been playing at, Jules?'

I felt a surge of rage and pulled myself up to standing, wrapping both arms around my bump, ignoring the wave of tightness that came again, pulling at the muscles in my abdomen, sides and back, drawing me in and squeezing me like I was in a vice. 'What have *I* been playing at? What have *you* been playing at, Orla?' I spat the words, all the venom finally pouring out of me.

'I can't believe this is happening again . . . do you know what it feels like to be constantly challenged by the people who are supposed to love you?'

We're not supposed to love you. You are our lodger.

'It's like Dad and Sean all over again. It's like Liam.' She stopped at the top of the stairs, her gaze darting about the landing as she spoke, wild and unpredictable.

I took two steps towards her. 'And why do you think they didn't believe you? Why do you think Liam heard alarm bells when he found you skulking round his hospital?' I swallowed before throwing down my trump card.

'Why do you think he might have had questions when he found you posting on cancer forums . . .' I took a breath before I risked my next words, '. . . when you were perfectly healthy?'

She stared at me, the colour draining from her face. There was a moment of terrible silence. 'Oh my God, you're just like him . . . you've taken everything I've built up and decided to destroy it.' Her voice was menacingly quiet now. 'You're going to do what he said he'd do . . . you're going to persuade everyone I'm a liar.' Something came into focus in her eyes then, a hardness. 'I couldn't let him do that, Jules. I couldn't let him call me a liar.'

Her last sentence sent a spasm of frozen terror down my spine. What did she mean by that? Now an icy wave of panic sluiced through me as I realised how powerless I felt, even in my own home, because Orla was holding onto my phone – my only means of communication with the outside world.

I took another deep breath and tried to keep my voice calm and steady. 'Orla. Please, just give me my phone.' I stared into her ice-blue eyes, which were rounded now as they stared back. But her expression was anything but vacant. Something was happening behind those eyes, some sort of calculation I couldn't fathom. Her lower lids twitched and I watched the muscles tighten in her face. With calculated slowness, she brought up her hand, proffering my phone.

I reached for it like someone would reach for a loaded gun, fingertips skimming her clammy palm as I took it from her. She still stared at me as if working something out. A sudden need to call Scott rushed up on me, and I glanced down the stairs towards the front door, another part of me wanting to be out of the house as far away from Orla as possible. She'd always made me feel uneasy. But now she was scaring me.

I twisted away from her and swiped into my phone. 'I'm calling Scott,' I said. She tracked me with her eyes as I paced the landing, but she still didn't move.

I looked at my phone and was about to click into contacts when I couldn't help but read the first few words of the notification from Sean.

Hi Jules. By my 'situation' I meant my Langerhans cell histiocytosis. Orla must have told you about that?

My breath froze in my lungs. I tapped on the message and read the rest.

I was diagnosed at two, and was in and out of hospital for years. Thankfully, tests showed Orla didn't have the condition too but she had to watch me get a lot of medical attention for a long time. Dad and I always wondered if that might have triggered her 'fainting'.

I looked up at Orla who still stared at me, her gaze unwavering. I opened my mouth to speak, but before I could find the words, I felt a hot gush of liquid between my legs, soaking my trousers and spreading over my bare feet and into the carpet. My brain refocused.

No, this cannot be happening. Not now. It's too early.

Orla took a step back, her gaze sweeping over me, her face set in a horrified expression. I looked down at my phone, swiped out of Sean's message and brought up Scott's number, pushing past Orla at the top of the stairs. My hand reached for the banister as my other went to click on Scott's number.

Then I felt it. Something hard slammed into my shoulders. I lost my footing on the step below, my knees buckling as I watched the banister come flying towards my face, knowing there was nothing I could do to stop the full force of it, which cracked hard against my forehead. It's strange, but I remember the sound of it more clearly than the feeling.

Histiocytosis, in any of its forms, can be devastating. But what people don't seem to understand, is that it's not just the person with the diagnosis who suffers; the damage can be just as severe, if not worse, for close family members. For example, the psychological effects of having a younger sibling with a life-threatening illness are beyond most people's comprehension.

I'm not talking about the fear of the sibling dying, although maybe in some cases that might be the main concern. No, I'm talking about the horror of watching a mother who's always doted on you, their only child, suddenly become obsessed with a new child. And then for that new child not only to take up every waking moment of that parent's day, but for him to be diagnosed with a condition that requires endless hospital stays, tests, scans, operations, check-ups, readmissions, home treatments. And for the mother to be psychologically unfit to cope with such an overwhelming situation, and to simply leave . . . leave the first child, the original child, the much-loved daughter, because of the all-consuming attention needed by this tiny, sickly shadow of a human.

I spent my whole childhood willing Sean to get better. Praying the universe would see fit to allow just a *shred of parental attention to be awarded to me. I knew it was too late for my mother – she was long gone. But perhaps, if Sean got better, then it would be my turn. My opportunity to be centre stage. My chance to stand in the spotlight.*

Then my prayers were answered: Sean was cured. And my God did I try to claim my stage.

I tried in every possible way I could think of. The acting was quite predictable – everyone knew I had talent there and it didn't surprise anyone when I got the part in Kilcroom High. *But that didn't seem to impress people as much as I'd hoped it would. No . . . my brother had shown me that the only way to get true, undiluted, unconditional love and attention was to be someone who needed help.*

So I became that person. The person they clearly wanted me to be.

And what happened? They still barely tolerated me. Dad and Sean had always been exasperated by me, so when I met Liam . . . sweet, empathetic Liam with his nursing qualifications and his endless patience . . . it was like a sign from the universe that I was on the right track. I'd found my person.

But then he changed. He showed me that his love wasn't unconditional after all. Oh, he made out he was being all understanding . . . said he'd 'stick by me' while I got the psychological help I 'so clearly needed'. He just didn't get it. There's nothing wrong with seeking out empathetic people. I mean, what could be more natural than wanting unconditional love? Surely, that's what everyone wants?

And that's what I thought I'd found here, in Seymour Avenue with Scott and Jules. But this time, I didn't just have one person. This time I had everything. I had the gorgeous home. I had the perfect couple as housemates. I had Maggie and Nick. But the love didn't stop there . . . it just kept growing, and expanding. I had my online followers, and the church and the local charities. The events and the fundraisers. This was huge. This was everything I'd ever wanted.

And then Jules did what Liam did. She threatened to take it all away.

Chapter Thirty-five

The darkness was invaded by sensations I couldn't understand. Waves of pain flooded through me but I couldn't move or register what they were. I just wanted them to stop. Was this a nightmare? Was I asleep? Eventually there was something new. A voice. A voice was shouting my name. I was being moved and jostled and lifted. There was a stab of pain in my arm, then something pushed over my face. I felt myself flail in response, trying to push it off as a sudden surge of adrenaline pulsed through me, causing my eyes to spring open.

Bright lights, moving figures in green, Scott's stricken face looking down at me, a siren wailing.

'Oh my God, she's awake!' he shouted, twisting to look at the figures. I watched one of them lay a hand on his shoulder, while another leaned over me, shushing quietly under her breath, pressing something over my face again. My eyelids were unbearably heavy. I wanted to ask Scott what was happening, but I couldn't stay awake. I surrendered again to the blackness.

I woke up to beeping and more bright lights. Scott's face hovered over me. 'Jules?' His voice was desperate and sent a sharp spike of panic through me.

Everything swooped into focus. 'The baby!' I cried, as a wave of pain washed over me. I grasped at my stomach, but it felt strange – my bump was covered in a tangle of wires and pads.

'It's OK,' said Scott. 'It's just to monitor the baby. She's OK.' I'd never heard him sound like that – panic and relief all mixed together, his voice quivering as if he was about to cry.

I looked at the mass of wires and tubes that snaked from my bump, and both my arms, to machines and IV stands, and for the first time I noticed the other people in the room. A woman came forwards and shone a light in my eyes, a strained smile on her face.

'Do you know where you are, Jules?'

'I . . . I'm in hospital?'

'Do you remember what happened?'

I glanced at Scott whose face was set in a grimace, as if he didn't want to hear about it.

Memories blinked through my brain in a frantic montage. *Reaching for my phone. Orla's face. My hand on the banister. My foot slipping. My head hitting wood.* I felt a throb of pain in my skull and lifted my hand to my forehead where I felt the softness of some sort of dressing. Even through the padding it was painful to touch.

'Did . . . did I fall down the stairs?'

The woman nodded. She seemed pleased with this response, unlike Scott whose expression crumpled as he brought his hands to his face.

Then he looked at me. 'That bloody painting, Jules. I'm so sorry.'

'What do you mean?'

'That painting of the woman walking into the sea . . . at the top of the stairs. It fell off as you were walking down. Maybe it tripped you up? It was on top of you when I . . . when I found you.' He grimaced again, as if the memory was causing him physical pain. 'I should have fixed it to the wall properly, like you said.'

'But . . .' I was about to tell him I had no memory of the painting, and ask him what Orla had said happened, but another contraction flooded through me, leaving me speechless with its intensity.

When it passed, so had the moment to talk about Orla. I turned to the closest midwife. 'Will my baby be OK?'

Over the next few hours I must have asked this question at least twenty times, each time receiving an answer I either couldn't process because of my brain being so fuzzy, or an answer that was so non-committal it was meaningless. *You're in the best place now . . . we're doing everything we can for you and your baby . . .*

Time was impossible to measure . . . I had no frame of reference, and my mind was too pain-addled to comprehend the hands on the clock, or process the changing shifts of the staff who came into the room. I was given a mouthpiece to breathe in gas and air, finally something that seemed to blur the edges of the pain. I held onto the contraption with desperate fingers as the midwives told me to slow my breathing . . . *calm* . . . *calm* . . .

At 6.57 a.m. the following day, as the first pinkish rays of sun dusted the paper blinds at the window, our daughter was born. I sobbed as she was taken from us and put immediately on a ventilator, her purple body like a fallen baby bird, frail and limp. I reached out but I couldn't touch her. We'd read all about the importance of skin-to-skin contact within moments of birth, but there were greater things at play now. This was a matter of life and death. She needed oxygen more than she needed her mother's touch, and that broke my heart.

Scott and I clung to each other as we studied the faces of the staff who worked on her, all bent over her tiny form, rubbing, prodding, administering. At last she was brought over to us and placed on my chest. I watched her tiny, wrinkled fingers curl and uncurl against my skin and felt a fresh wave of sobs overcome me. Scott kissed my forehead, then our baby's. I leaned down and smelt the damp sweetness of her little head, and then she was taken from me again.

More checks were done on her, and I heard staff murmuring about respiratory distress.

'What's happening?' I said, desperate to know what they were talking about.

A woman with a wide face and large brown eyes came over to my bedside. She wore a badge that told me she was a Consultant Obstetrician.

She smiled kindly and I willed her to speak as quickly as possible. 'Your baby has been born rather earlier than we'd like, and that, alongside the trauma you experienced during labour, means we're going to need to run extra checks on her to make sure she's OK.'

'But she's OK right now?' My voice sounded desperate.

She nodded. 'Initial signs are good, but we're going to have to keep an eye on her over the next few days. But don't worry – as soon as we are done with this set of tests we can give her right back to you. OK?'

Scott and I both nodded emphatically, as if that would somehow help.

The next two days were like coming up for air after a long time underwater. The world came slowly into focus, and it was a different world to the one I'd lived in before. Here, Ellie was the centre of everything. She felt new, but at the same time it was unimaginable that she hadn't always been here with us. We had the relief of watching her learn to breathe on her own without constant intervention from doctors. The staff reassured us that my fall didn't seem to have affected her, and that she was clearly a 'tough cookie' – something I couldn't hear enough. I watched for the midwives' smiles as they checked the way she breastfed, and noted the longer gaps between staff visits to our room.

Ellie slept in a little Perspex box next to my bed, and when she slept I turned on to my side and watched her tiny chest move up and down, feeling a strange mixture of warmth and terror swirling inside me. She was so tiny, and so vulnerable.

Scott went home to get some things for us – baby clothes, pyjamas for me, nappies, wipes – all the things we would have eventually packed in our hospital bag, if we'd had the time to prepare for this. When he got back I asked what Orla had said about my fall, and if she'd been the one to call him and the ambulance.

He looked at me strangely, then squeezed my hand. 'She wasn't at home so I haven't spoken to her, but Orla wasn't there when you fell, sweetheart.'

My heart gave a violent thud. 'Yes she *was*. We had an argument at the top of the stairs, she . . .' I faltered, my mind going to a dark place. *No, that can't be right.* My brain was so hazy . . . I couldn't think straight.

'But . . .' Scott frowned at me, then fished out his phone and showed me a message from Orla from the night I'd fallen. She explained she was going straight from drinks with Maggie to stay at a friend's house for the night and wouldn't be going back home.

I couldn't believe it. She was distancing herself from the accident. Why would she do that? She knew I'd contradict her and say she was there when I fell. Unless . . . unless she didn't think I'd be around to contradict her.

I felt Scott scrutinising my face, and when I looked back up at him his expression was dark and serious. 'You're not saying . . . you don't mean Orla was there when you *actually* fell?'

I nodded. 'That's *exactly* what I'm saying! We had an argument – then my waters broke. She saw it happen. She'd been trying to get into my phone or something . . . I can't remember, anyway, I took my phone back off her, then . . . then I fell. I thought . . . I mean, I just assumed she'd called you or at least called the ambulance?'

'No – I opened the front door and you were just lying at the bottom of the stairs. You were hardly breathing. Jesus Christ, that was the worst moment of my life.' He buried his face in his hands. When he looked up at me again, something had hardened behind his eyes. He stood and grabbed his coat from the back of a chair.

'Where are you going?'

'I'm going to find her. Ask her what the *fuck* she was doing. You . . . you could have died! She . . .' His voice caught and his words faded to a hoarse whisper. 'She left you for dead. You and our baby. Why? Because you had an *argument*?'

Once again, I was assaulted by a barrage of emotions. Rage at Orla, but also relief that Scott believed me for what felt like the first time in months. But I was also scared of him confronting her. Because now, the words she'd spoken that night came back to me. *I couldn't let him call me a liar.* Then there was Sean's message . . . I remembered now. I had so much I needed to tell Scott. But right now I was overwhelmed with exhaustion. I just wanted this over. I didn't want to think about Orla. I wanted to think about our baby.

'Please don't leave,' I said. 'Just . . . please just stay with Ellie and me.' I held out my hand and Scott paused before stepping towards me and squeezing it, his shoulders slumping.

Eventually he spoke. 'Of course I will. Can I get you anything?'

I tried to smile but it didn't feel real. 'Could you bring me some tea?'

He nodded, then drew in a breath, as if it was taking all his control not to march out of the hospital and straight home to confront Orla. Then he draped his coat back over the chair, flashed me a distracted smile, and left the room.

I reached for my phone on the side table, taking a moment to watch Ellie's little chest rising and falling with her sleeping breaths, feeling a surge of love for her that brought on the increasingly familiar sting of milk in my breasts. For months I'd wanted Orla gone and had felt paralysed to do anything about it. But watching Ellie sleep I knew I would not return to a house with Orla in it. I would not share my home with the woman who had left us for dead. And I hoped it would be as simple as a WhatsApp message:

> Hi Orla. Thought you'd like to know that me and the baby are fine. We'll be home in a couple of days. Jules. P.S. Scott knows the truth. And soon everyone else will know too.

It was as Scott returned carrying two paper cups that the grey ticks in the message turned blue. She'd read it. I put my phone back on the table and felt a twinge of satisfaction as I took my tea from Scott.

The following day, Scott went back to the house to pick up a few more things, no doubt hoping he'd also bump into Orla. But when he returned I knew what he was going to say before he said it – there was no sign of her. All her things were gone. Her room was completely empty.

Of course it was.

She knew I was alive. She knew I was coming home and would tell everyone what she'd done, and so she'd disappeared. I knew I should have been full of anger. And it's true that underneath the myriad other emotions I was feeling, there was rage. But the strange thing was, the overwhelming emotion I felt at that time was relief. It amazed me, but I couldn't help the swell of happiness

I'd experienced when Scott had spoken those words: *Her room's completely empty. She's gone.*

It was at that moment a woman in lilac scrubs bustled into the room.

'Oh no, I'm so sorry to wake Sleeping Beauty, but we need to do another heel prick.' She leaned over Ellie's cot then cast me an apologetic smile.

'It's OK,' I said. 'She's so used to them now she probably won't even wake up.'

The nurse gently coaxed Ellie's tiny foot out of her onesie and took out the pin and the test card she used to collect the blood.

As she leaned over, I caught sight of her badge, which was printed with the word: *Haematology*. A memory stirred, and I thought back to the time I'd watched Orla disappear into that department when we were here for my scan. Then I remembered all those medical papers and emails Maggie had shown me, the ones Orla had given her from the same department. The test results and the emails from consultants. I remembered the nurse at the entrance handing Orla the white paper bag of medication after her treatment session. It didn't make any sense. Sean said *he* was the one with the blood disorder. Perhaps she was being treated for something else.

I don't know what I was expecting, but I couldn't help asking the question. 'You work in Haematology?'

She straightened and smiled, fiddling with the card in her hands. 'Yes, that's right.'

'Do you know Orla Sullivan?'

'Orla? Yes! Everyone knows Orla.' Her response surprised me. Whatever the reason for Orla's appointments,

I would have thought patient confidentiality would apply here.

Scott shifted in his seat, a frown settling on his face. 'Well, next time she comes in, tell her we're looking for her.'

The woman chuckled, taking a pen from her pocket and marking something on the piece of card. 'Actually, I'm not sure when her next shift is, but I'll tell her you were asking after her. Does she know about the baby?'

She looked up and beamed at us both in turn.

'Shift?' Scott said. 'What do you mean?'

'Well – she's part-time so she's not here every day. I think Friday's her most regular day.'

I felt the blood draining from my face as Scott cast me a wide-eyed glance before turning back to the nurse. 'She . . . she's not a patient?'

'A patient?' The nurse laughed, but her smile quickly disappeared as she looked at our faces and seemed to retreat into herself. She shook her head. 'No, she's . . . she works in administration for Haematology. You know . . . between acting jobs. She's on the secretarial bank.'

My mouth fell open and I looked at Scott, whose face had turned ashen. We made eye contact, but neither of us knew what to say. Everything clicked into place.

Chapter Thirty-six

Three months later

It took time to get my head around what had happened with Orla. Partly because the events of that evening – the argument, Sean's message, the moment I fell – were all so fractured and blurry in my mind. But it wasn't just that; there was also Ellie. Every waking moment seemed taken up with our daughter. Parenthood was the most exhausting, anxiety-ridden, beautiful thing either of us had ever done, and because it had arrived at the very moment Orla had disappeared, it felt as if Orla belonged to a different lifetime. It was only weeks later, as we were emerging from the newborn fug, that we began talking about her again, and I began thinking.

It's a chilly afternoon in March, and I'm sitting in the cosy alcove of a tiny, steamed-up cafe in Chichester. I sit facing the corner, my back to the draught that wafts through the door every time a customer enters, and the tinkle of the bell that accompanies them. My aunt Celia had been thrilled when I'd asked if Ellie and I could come and visit. Scott was snowed under at work, so I said I was happy to make the trip without him as it was a pretty straightforward drive. I hadn't seen my aunt in far too long, so catching up with her, and introducing her to her great-niece, was special. It made me feel close to Mum, too. We'd been busy about town most of the morning, so this afternoon I told Aunt Celia she should rest, and that I'd take Ellie out for a few hours and leave her in peace. I explained Ellie didn't nap well in a cot during the day – she preferred being bundled against me in the sling.

I only felt a small twinge of guilt that my aunt wasn't the only reason I'd wanted to come to Chichester. Nor was she the only reason I was sitting here in this cafe.

Now, Ellie is asleep against my chest, and I sit stroking her back, nursing a cappuccino and staring out at the passers-by, wrapped up against the chill of early spring. My eyes find a corkboard attached to the wall, upon which are tacked an array of curling posters advertising everything from dog-walkers to Pilates classes to church toddler groups. A page about an author talk at the local library hangs next to a hand-written note advertising a room to rent above the cafe.

'Lemon drizzle?' The lady who runs the place appears at my shoulder, proffering a royal blue plate dominated by a fat slice of yellow cake.

'Oh, lovely, thank you. Looks delicious.' I smile up at her.

Her green eyes crinkle with pleasure. 'No problem, babes. Hope you enjoy!' She bustles off.

I break off a piece and savour the sweet tang of it on my tongue and think about the events that led me to be sitting here.

About two weeks ago I'd received the reply from Matt – Orla's friend whose flat she'd left her keys at the night we met her. The man she'd been going to move in with in Greenwich. Orla wasn't in our lives any more, but I'd still felt compelled to tie up loose strands of thought . . . things that had niggled at me, that had never been resolved because of her hasty departure. Matt seemed a good place to start.

Hi Jules, sorry for the delay in replying. I do indeed know Orla, and yes, I did give her a theatre mask keyring! I don't remember her leaving it at my flat and getting locked out though – I haven't seen her for at least eighteen months I reckon.

And it's really strange the way you met her, because that's exactly how I met her too! I was having drinks with mates in Soho, and she marches in, plonks her bag down on our table and announces she's lost her keys. Anyway, we were all a bit tipsy and someone bought her a drink and before you know it she's sleeping on our sofa, then completely bonded with my housemate Jess, who persuaded us we needed to sublet the spare room to Orla cos she was such a laugh! It was a real shame, because it was great for a while, but then Jess moved out, and I said I was going to get a place with my boyfriend, and she properly kicked off. We didn't mean to upset her, we were just coming to the end of our rental agreement and wanted to move on. But I guess she didn't feel the same. She was also having some tests at the time – said she was suffering from some sort of bone disease or something? Anyway, it was really horrible cos she felt like we were deserting her in her hour of need. To be honest, I was glad to move out and lose touch with her then, as harsh as that sounds. She just got a bit much, you know?

And I've been living with my boyfriend in Kent ever since, so I can promise you I never had any plans to move into a flat in Greenwich with her! Maybe she meant someone else!? Anyway, she's a real character, as you've obviously discovered. Hope she hasn't stressed you out too much! Best of luck. Matt xx

It didn't shock me to hear more of her lies. I should have trusted my instincts. The moment I'd pulled that keyring from her bag after the first night she stayed at our house, my senses had started tingling. But now, if my intention was to find out more about the way Orla thought, then Matt and Sean's messages had been invaluable. They'd shown me a little of what motivated Orla, and (more usefully) a pattern of behaviour. Orla had secured housemates in each case via the same methods . . . by testing people's empathy. By measuring the kindness of strangers. With us and Matt, she'd done this by pretending she'd lost her keys. And with Abi, by pretending she had a horrible long-distance boyfriend. I remembered Abi's message explaining how distraught Orla had been when they'd first met. Orla told Abi she was having boyfriend troubles, and Abi cooked for her, then stayed up late into the night comforting her. I realised now the things these three scenarios had in common: they all cast Orla as the damsel in distress, and the onlookers as her saviours. The lost keys and the awful boyfriend – these were tools by which to gather empathetic people around. They

were ways of measuring how much sympathy someone was willing to dole out. The people who were the
most empathetic or gave the most attention or fussed the
most – they were the ones towards whom she gravitated.
It had been that way since she was a child. That's why
she was so furious when Matt and Jess simply moved
out, casting her aside. That's why she abandoned Abi –
there was no point staying in a house alone, while Abi
was constantly away touring. Who would listen to her
tales of woe?

Then she found us. And we were perfect.

We went along with every crisis she threw at us – until
I didn't believe her any more. But more than that – I followed up my suspicions with research, and didn't stop
until I found out the truth. I imagine that's what Liam
had done too.

The bell above the cafe door jingles, spiking my pulse
as I resist the impulse to turn and look.

A man's voice. 'Hey, Sasha, three lattes to go please,
love.'

'Course, babes! How are you?'

Ellie stirs against me, letting out a short mewing
sound, and I jiggle her and whisper shushing noises next
to her hot little ear. She quietens and becomes still again.
Pulse calming, I settle back in my chair and sip my coffee,
placing it down on the table and picking up the pen and
scribbling, 'Liam – ask Kieran more?' I scan the previous notes I've made (all scrawled in the thick notebook,
which is now almost full), and a memory flickers.

When Ellie and I had arrived home after being discharged from hospital, the painting that had been on top

of me when Scott found me at the bottom of the stairs was propped up against the hallway wall. A week or so later I asked him if he'd done anything to it . . . to mend it or replace any parts. He said he hadn't touched it, or the wall it fell from, not since that night. He couldn't even bring himself to look at it.

But I could.

One evening before bed I sat on the bottom step, placing the baby monitor on the hallway table ready to take upstairs. I took the painting in both hands, running my fingers over the perfect surface of the glass – not so much as a hairline crack. I inspected the back . . . the twisted wire was still intact, as was the backing. The small tacks had not come away from the board into which they'd been screwed, securing the wire in place. I tugged at the wire, but it didn't budge. Placing the painting back, I picked up the monitor and climbed the stairs, inspecting the screw that protruded from the plaster, set snugly in its red wall plug. I know I'd told Scott we should put another screw in the wall as the painting was so heavy, but how many times had we walked past it, up and down the stairs, without it ever having budged? With the backing and the screw completely intact, how could it have fallen?

I don't believe it did.

Scott and Maggie were outraged enough at the fact Orla had left me unconscious at the bottom of the stairs, so I hadn't felt the need to go into any more detail or to talk about Liam. I mean, what would be the point? There wasn't anything we could do about my suspicions – and the police would certainly turn their noses up at my conclusions. But at least I had Scott and Maggie on side now, not just because of Orla leaving me (and my unborn child) that night, but because Maggie took all Orla's medical paperwork into the hospital for one of her Kind UK contacts to look into – and they confirmed it was all fake. Every letter, email, scan, result; it was all pilfered from someone else's medical file, with Orla's details inserted.

'I don't know what to say,' Maggie had whispered when she'd come straight over after finding out.

Scott had shaken his head. 'I'm so sorry, Jules.'

I reassured them I didn't need their apologies. What's done was done, and the main thing was that Orla was out of our lives. I told them I didn't want to spend another second of my life talking or thinking about Orla.

Except that wasn't strictly true. I just didn't want them to know that.

I let Kieran, Sean and Abi know about the medical deception, and the fact that Orla had left me, heavily pregnant, there at the bottom of the stairs. I thought they should know just in case any future roommates of hers ever contacted them for character references. Shortly after that, TruthBomb365 resurfaced, making sure all Orla's followers knew the truth about her.

The fallout was spectacular – because this time the troll's comments were backed up with corroborating comments from Scott and me, Maggie, and Kind UK's official accounts, as well as Maggie's contact in the Haematology department at Kingston Hospital. 'Shocked' was not the right word. Orla's followers had been appalled. Devastated. And I'd had the satisfaction of watching Orla's social-media accounts disappear one by one, as well as her website, and knowing how much that would have hurt her. But, unfortunately, as Orla had never fundraised for herself, she hadn't actually done anything illegal, at least, nothing that could be proven. So this 'story' really only affected the people in the local and online communities who'd taken her under their wing and fed her obsession with the sympathy she'd come to crave. I realised it was heartbreaking, but the depth of betrayal felt by Orla's friends – people like Maggie, Kara and Amy – would not be recognised by the law.

And something else I realised: someone like Orla can't keep their compulsions at bay for long. And the quiet reappearing of Orla on social media, the private accounts that only let in a select group of fellow thespians (people who knew nothing of 'Orla's Fight'), was the first sign that, perhaps, she was ready to re-emerge.

She'd been only too happy to accept a follower named KilcroomHighFan06. I'd had a lot of fun populating my account with screenshots of *Kilcroom High*, and of Ireland in the early 2000s. And I made sure to 'like' every acting post Orla shared too. Especially the ones about an upcoming musical she was about to appear in at the Chichester Festival Theatre, and the 'darling little cafe' she'd discovered in town that was 'the perfect between-show pitstop on a Saturday'.

I take another sip of coffee, my eyes flicking back towards the handwritten note on the cork board. *Room above cafe to rent. Single occupancy. References needed. Ask Sasha (behind the counter) for details!*

The bell above the door jingles and I feel a whoosh of cold air, this time accompanied by a sickly trace of floral perfume. Once again, I don't turn.

It's Sasha's voice I hear first. 'Hey! It must be Saturday again! How was it?'

'Well, you know matinees – they can fall a bit flat sometimes.' The voice sends a chill through me, before the heat rises up my neck and into my face. 'But it's OK, I've got two hours to re-energise and this evening will be amazing!'

'I don't know how you do it, babes. I'd never have the energy.'

'You know what they say – there's no business like showbusiness!'

Sasha laughs. 'Rather you than me, my love. Anyway, what can I get you? The usual?'

'That would be fab, thanks so much, Sash.'

I hear the scraping of a chair against the tiled floor, and the choking of the coffee machine.

The sound dies away, and then, 'Shit!'

'What?' I hear the panic in Sasha's voice, but keep my eyes trained on my coffee cup.

'My keys . . . I . . . Oh my God, I'm such an *idiot*!'

'Why, what have you done?'

'I stayed with my friend last night and I must have left my house keys at his flat. Crap! He left to see family this morning, and I know he's going to be gone at least three days. What am I going to do?'

I chew my bottom lip, fighting the quivering rage inside me.

'What about your housemate?' says Sasha, her voice laced with concern.

'She's away on tour until next month. Wow, I've really screwed up here!'

I want to turn around. I want to turn around and wring her neck.

'Hey, don't worry,' Sasha says. 'I've got the room upstairs. You can stay there until you get your keys back.'

'But . . . you're trying to rent it out . . . I can't do that!'

'Don't be silly, babes – it's just going empty at the moment.'

'Oh my God, Sasha. I can't believe you'd do that for me!'

I squeeze my eyes shut and can see Orla pressing her hand to her chest in that infuriating way and I feel my teeth grind together.

Then I take a breath and open my eyes. I pick up my phone, tap into Instagram, find the profile @Sashas-CafChichester, and click 'follow'. Then I create a post, inserting a screenshot of a statement I'd typed up earlier:

Please read all other posts and comments made by this account before offering a home to Orla Sullivan. Feel free to DM me for more information.

I tag Sasha, and Orla, then post it. But I don't post from my personal account, or from KilcroomHighFan06. I switch to an anonymous profile I created months ago: TruthBomb365. This account had started as an experiment, a way for me to vent my suspicions while keeping an eye on Orla's reactions. I'd had no idea when I set it up where it would lead. Without the 'troll' scaring Orla, she wouldn't have given me Bobbie and Kieran's names.

And without them, I wouldn't have found Orla's stash of medical equipment or made the connection with Liam. I also believed my online comments had scared Orla into paying Abi the missing rent, which had led to Orla confronting me the night I went into labour. I hadn't realised at the time that this profile would lead to me lying unconscious at the bottom of our staircase, or that it would prove to be the catalyst for Orla's downfall. Who knows how long my niggling doubts would have continued if I hadn't created TruthBomb365? And now it would give me so much more. It would give me the satisfaction of making sure Orla never did this to anyone else.

Behind me I hear the ping of a phone. My pulse spikes. I tell myself not to get too excited – it could be another customer's phone. Just a text message. Still, I can't help turning my head minutely to one side and flicking my gaze towards the counter. Sasha is next to the coffee machine, using tongs to place a croissant in a paper bag, but she's not really looking at what she's doing. She's distracted. She's frowning at something on the worktop next to the till.

I'm aware of Orla's voice from across the room. 'Of course it was different when I was filming *Kilcroom High*, but then live theatre is a completely different skill set . . . Sasha?'

Sasha hands the bagged croissant to a customer and holds out the card machine, waiting for the 'beep' before beaming and offering them a 'Thanks, babes'. But when the customer has gone, she doesn't answer Orla. She picks up her phone and stabs at the screen, a puzzled frown on her face.

'Sash, are you OK?'

I hear the scrape of a chair and imagine Orla standing and crossing to the counter. Turning back towards the corner, I try to keep my breaths slow and calm, hoping my thundering heart won't wake Ellie.

'Have you seen this?' Sasha says, her voice containing a trace of coldness I'd not heard before. I imagine her holding the phone out for Orla to see, and I fight the urge to turn and watch.

Whatever happens next is drowned out by the jingle of the bell above the door as another customer comes in. But that's OK – I've heard enough. I drain my coffee, stand up and, with one arm clasped around my daughter, I pull open the door and we emerge together into the fresh, spring air.

Acknowledgements

Writing a book is a solitary pursuit, but it takes a village to get it published. And because of that, I have many people to thank.

Thank you to my brilliant agent, Jo Williamson, who is the most knowledgeable and encouraging agent I could ever wish for. You have my back, and you cheer me on, and I feel so lucky to be in such safe hands. Thank you to Sam Humphreys for your insights early on, and for giving me the confidence to believe in the ending I wanted to write, but hadn't trusted myself to pull off!

Thank you to Justine Taylor for being a wonderful editor, and a font (or fount?) of grammatical knowledge. Thank you to Melissa Cox and Blake Brooks, and the whole Zaffre team, who have been so positive and welcoming to me.

Thank you to Sophie Campbell for telling us a compelling story of your own, which made me realise this subject was one worth basing a novel on. We really need to meet up more often. And not just so you can provide me with inspiration for new books!

Thank you, Jo Beasley, for all the wonderful details about your day as a picture book illustrator that went into creating the character of Jules. If I've made any silly mistakes then that's on me!

Thank you to Jo Van Der Borgh for all the author-chat coffee walks, where we try to make sense this crazy industry, and work out what the hell we're doing. It's fun to be on this roller-coaster with you!

Thank you to Ollie for still being as excited about my writing today as you were when I landed my agent. Your unstinting love and support mean the world to me.

Thank you, Heidi, for being proud of me, like I am of you. You have such a brilliant, creative mind, and I can't wait for the years to come when you tell me what you think of my books . . . go easy on me! Thank you, Maeve, for being such a hilarious little champion of mine. And I'm sorry to disappoint you by not having published a children's book, despite your insistence that I should 'just *try*, Mummy.'

Thank you to all my friends and family, who never seem to tire of asking me about my writing and listening to me droning on and on about it. Hardly a day passes without one of you lovely people saying you've read my book or listened to it or downloaded it or recommended it to a friend, and I could not be more thrilled with each and every message. You're a wonderful bunch, and I'm so lucky to have you!